BLACK HEART

DI JAMIE JOHANSSON BOOK 7

MORGAN GREENE

ALSO BY MORGAN GREENE

DS Jamie Johansson Prequels
Bare Skin
Fresh Meat
Idle Hands

The DS Johansson Prequel Trilogy Boxset

———

DI Jamie Johansson
Angel Maker
Rising Tide
Old Blood
Death Chorus
Quiet Wolf
Ice Queen
Black Heart

The Jamie Johansson Files
The Last Light Of Day

BLACK HEART

1

Annika Olsen

IT WAS sixty-seven feet from the roof of the Gotland University administration building to the concrete pavement below.

And Annika Olsen was standing no more than five feet from the spot where Juni Pedersen landed.

It happened so quickly that Annika missed the flash out of the corner of her eye. It was the sound that registered first. Like when an oar hits the water, paddle flat. A dull slap.

She blinked, eyes stinging, something warm on the side of her face. As she lifted her hand to her cheek to touch the wetness there, not understanding, the faces of the people standing in front of her told the story. The boy was nineteen, studying maths. His eyes widened in shock, lips trembling. He began stumbling backwards before Annika even turned her attention to the girl on his left.

She just started shuddering, her hands flying up to cover her open mouth. Annika saw her uvula quiver at the back of her throat before she let out a scream so piercing it caused Annika's whole body to break out in gooseflesh.

The girl turned and scrambled after the boy, and Annika drew her fingers from her wet cheek and saw them red with blood.

My blood?

She began to turn, slowly, holding her hand before her face, and saw the body.

At first, Annika didn't recognise her. Blonde, petite, with curled hair that was now matted to her face, blood running from her nose, her mouth, her ears, her eyes. They stared vacantly across the ground as her blood leaked out, running into the drain at the side of the road twelve inches beyond her head.

She was on her front, head twisted to one side, arms crooked, legs splayed, facing in odd directions.

It came to her then. Annika recognised her. Juni. Her friend, Juni.

Panic erupted around her, people yelling and shoving, trying to run this way and that. But all the noise had now disappeared, faded beyond the veil of ringing that had fallen in Annika's head.

She just stared down at the girl on the pavement, not quite grasping what she was seeing, what had happened.

Her eyes moved across the body as though she were looking at some strange animal she'd never seen before, taking in her shape, her colour, her features. Her clothing. The books spilling from her bag. Novels, books of essays. English literature. Annika's eyes fell upon the girl's left forearm, the mark there. At first, she didn't know what it was. But then it came into focus, raw and turbulent on the girl's pale, soft skin.

A black heart, etched into the flesh.

And then it was gone.

Arms enveloped Annika, large and strong, and swept her away.

She looked up, seeing the face of a lecturer she thought taught Computer Science. Another was shielding the girl's body, ordering people away.

The lecturer dragged Annika from the scene, his mouth moving. She felt the vibrations of his words against her cheek, her head pressed to his chest, hands pinned at her sides, heels half walking half dragging under her. But what he was saying, she didn't know.

All she could hear was a sharp, high-pitched ringing. And all she could taste was the distinct, metallic tang of blood.

Blood she knew wasn't hers.

———

'Annika?'

She looked up from her position on the sofa. It was leather, brown, faded. Overly soft. The kind you can't get up from easily. She was being forced to sit side-saddle so that her knees didn't rise up in front of her. In her lap, she could see she'd shredded the tissue she'd been given. She'd not needed it for her tears. There hadn't been any, despite the woman in front of her telling her it was okay to cry … five, no, six times. Yeah. That was it.

'Are you with me?' the woman asked.

What a bloody condescending question.

'What you're experiencing is perfectly normal.'

'It's normal to be standing five feet from someone as they hit the ground after leaping from a rooftop?' Annika asked cuttingly.

'We don't know what happened, yet,' the counsellor said slowly. 'She might have slipped, or—'

Annika snorted. 'Bullshit. She jumped. She killed herself. Like the others.'

'We shouldn't—'

'She had the black heart, too.'

The counsellor fell silent.

'I was close enough to see. Trust me.' Annika sat forward now. 'Juni killed herself. Number twenty-three.' She shook her head.

'I know this is scary—'

'Scary?' Annika interrupted again. 'I'm not scared. I just don't understand.'

'And you want to?'

'Of course, don't you?' She searched the woman's face. She was in her fifties, kindly looking, wearing a knitted blouse, oversized fake pearls.

'It's natural to feel a need for closure.'

'I don't need closure,' Annika spat. 'I need to know *why.*'

The woman smiled softly, though Annika could tell by her unfocused eyes that her primary concern was running out the clock. 'That is closure.'

'Juni wouldn't have killed herself,' she replied coolly, 'not like that, at least. Not without … without saying something, or without me noticing. I would have noticed if something was wrong.'

'It's natural to blame yourself for—'

'I don't blame myself,' Annika interrupted. 'I blame … whatever's doing this. I blame the … the hearts. I need to know why.'

'Wanting to understand why Juni decided—'

'I don't need to know why Juni did it. Not specifically.'

The woman's brow creased.

'I need to understand why they *all* did it. There's something that links them. The hearts. They all had them.'

'Of course, we all look for answers in the unknown. It's human to search for patterns, it's how we understand things, how we group things, how we—'

'Actually,' Annika said, standing up from the couch with some effort, 'I just remembered I have to go somewhere.' She didn't, but she didn't feel like this recycled crap was doing her any good. This was her second session with this counsellor. She worked at the university, saw dozens of kids a week, probably, and did nothing except feed them the same regurgitated lines. She'd done it the first session, and now, Annika was sure that it would just be the same thing on repeat. Hey, maybe she was searching for patterns after all.

'Annika,' the woman said, voice firm but sympathetic, 'I won't stop you. But I just want you to know, my door is always open.' She offered a smile.

Annika smiled back. Yeah, so long as it's between 10am and 12pm Mondays and Tuesdays, she thought, or between 1pm and 3pm Wednesdays and Thursdays. Because those are your office hours. And it's actually locked the rest of the time, and you're not even here. But instead of saying any of that, Annika just left, saving her energy.

For Juni Pedersen.

Annika had known Juni since her first year. Their Introduction to English classes had overlapped. Juni had gone down the literature track, Annika had opted for journalism. They still had some classes together, some seminars. They'd stayed in touch, had been roommates in a shared house in their second year and had grown close. This year, Juni had moved in with some friends on her soccer team. Annika had opted to take a room in a shared apartment — quieter, less partying. Juni had always been more social — the life of the party. Always smiling, laughing. Everyone liked her. Girls. Boys. She couldn't imagine what would have driven her to … Annika shook her head in disbelief. Sure, they'd grown apart, who didn't? But they were still friends, still close. They'd pass each other on campus, stop, hug, say they should go for coffee, catch up, spend more time together. They always said that, but never did … But that had been right up until … what, three, four days ago she'd seen her last? She was fine! Laughing, rushing to … somewhere or other. Wearing a dress, pinky orange with sunflowers, or daisies, or butterflies on it. Hair loose, legs tanned, arms clear of any fucking tattoos, or … carvings. Annika shuddered a little. Those fucking black hearts! Every kid, all twenty-three of them who'd killed themselves had one. But why? What did they mean?

Annika pushed out of the building and into the campus. It was after three and the last classes of the day were due to let out soon. But for now, the place was empty. Gotland University was the only one on the island, and by all accounts it was small. Most students lived in the town of Visby itself. And even that wasn't very big, despite being the biggest on the island. It was the sort of place where you couldn't avoid people, where everyone ran into everyone, where everyone drank in the same bars, ate at the same restaurants. There were only a few haunts in town that got busy, mostly with students.

Annika slowed, thinking about it. Juni was sociable, she had friends, lots of friends. She was always out.

She looked up at the administration building, at the roof, and then down at the spot where Juni had landed. Where she'd been standing herself. Five feet to the right and Juni would have crushed her. But maybe the girl would have lived then, and she could have been questioned, asked what drove her to do it?

The black heart.

The black heart.

It's all Annika could think about.

Was it responsible, somehow? Or just a mark of death?

There was just a pale square on the pavement where she'd been. The tent the police had erected had already been removed, the concrete scrubbed of blood. Now it just looked cleaner than everything else.

Annika drew a slow breath. Juni was the fourth student to kill herself in less than a year. The first had brought turmoil to the school, days of mourning, vigils. The police hadn't been that involved. A boy cutting his wrists in one of the communal shower blocks on campus was devastating, but it didn't constitute a crime. When the second body cropped up – intentional overdose, painkillers — they began to take notice. Both came without warning, both were stable, healthy kids with good groups of friends, none of whom saw it coming. People were questioned, interviewed. And once the police discovered both bore the black heart on their arm, things got strained. People got scared. Police officers began patrolling campus.

When the third body was found, just under eight weeks ago, hanged in the local park, the same black heart on his arm, everything exploded. Things had been kept under wraps until then, but word got out, someone let slip that the pattern wasn't confined to the school at all. People were dying all over Gotland. Kids, between the ages of thirteen and nineteen. Twenty-two in as many months. An epidemic of suicides.

The university had been shut down for days. The whole town shut down. Everyone on campus was ordered to stay in their houses, mandated to come to the admin building for DNA swabs and fingerprinting. Mass evidence collecting. Annika had never heard of it, but a quick Google search told her police only did that when they had no other leads. Nothing linked the kids who'd ended their lives. They didn't know each other, they didn't hang out, didn't frequent the same places ... the counsellor was right, people did look for patterns, the police especially, but they'd found none. Nothing except the black hearts.

All classes had been cancelled. All the bars and clubs that were student hangouts were closed. The police locked the whole campus down. But then ... everything just went back to normal. Like the snap of a finger.

The curfew lifted, the bars opened, people went on with their lives. And the police just ... left. Four, five days of disruption, of fear and panic, and then life just went right back to normal.

The strangest thing was that the media weren't reporting on any of it. When the students had found out that this spate of suicides went beyond the campus boundary, that had been a leak, a slip — someone telling someone who told someone else. It hadn't been reported on the news, it hadn't been dropped in a press release by the chief of Visby police.

And now with Juni Pedersen, number twenty-three, Annika thought that the police would be back, everyone would be re-questioned, the curfews, the lockdowns ... that they'd all return. And yet ... there was nothing. The police did nothing. They arrived, set up a tent, took their photos, then removed the body, cleaned the scene, and disappeared. All inside twelve hours. And now all that remained of Juni Pedersen was a clean spot on the pavement.

Annika swallowed. The police had nothing. They didn't

know what was going on. And that meant they didn't know how to stop it.

She felt her hands flex at her sides. Were they even investigating anymore? Twenty-three kids was a lot to look at. Did they even have the resources to look at Juni? While the trail was fresh?

Gotland was Annika's home. She'd grown up in Åminne, a tiny town on the east coast of the island. Juni was from here, too. Not the same town, but somewhere close. Gotland wasn't big. It was a community. One that loved its home, and the people that lived here.

And now one of their own was dead, and no one was doing anything about it.

As the bell rang to signal the end of last period and students began streaming out, laughing, grinning, jostling and talking of the impending weekend, walking right over the spot where Juni had died without even looking down, without even realising, or caring, Annika decided.

If no one else was going to do anything about it, she would. Even if it just meant digging into Juni's life, finding out who she was, and why she'd do this … and she could then pass that information along to the police, so they could finally stop all this. Yeah, that's what she'd do.

Her throat ached; her vision blurry. Annika ran her knuckles across her cheeks to wipe away the forming tears, took one last look at the pale patch of concrete beneath the feet of her peers, and then turned away, allowing herself to be swept along by the crowd.

Juni Pedersen's death would mean something. Annika was going to make sure of that.

2

Lucas Adell

Summer at Sudersand was all that Lucas and Marie Adell ever dreamed of.

The waves rolling onto the white sand, the rustling of the grass on the dunes in the early morning breeze. The sun creeping yellow and warm over the sea to the east. Their bedroom faced the water. A small home, but one that was full of love and joy. Glass doors let out onto their wooden deck, steps leading down to the sand itself. No more than a slow stroll from the shore.

They'd wake often as first light broke the sky, painting it all the colours of the world all at once. They would lie there, her in his arms, his lips pressed gently to the nape of her neck, watching the sunrise through her hair. It always smelled of wild flowers. Gentle and sweet. He'd feel her pulse against his cheek, the rise and fall of her ribs against his arm as he held her.

When she'd wake, he never knew. They'd just lie there, entwined, watching the sun come up, knowing that leaving the sprawling, chugging cities of the mainland behind and moving here was the right choice. For them, for their daughter. Away from the pains and the struggles of the modern world. This was everything they wanted and more.

But this morning, the light was dull and grey.

Lucas Adell opened his eyes, his naked body exposed to the cold air of their bedroom. He shuddered, the covers crumpled at his hip, laid across his leg. His arm swept the mattress slowly. It was damp, cool. Marie was not there.

The waves. He could hear them breaking.

His eyes gained focus, finding the window in front of him. He could smell the salt of the sea, taste it in the emptiness of their bedroom.

He filled his lungs, sitting up suddenly, looking around. 'Marie?' he asked into the gloom.

There was no response.

His gaze turned back to the door. It was open. It shouldn't be.

Lucas swung his legs from the bed and stood, the cool air coating the hardwood floor of the bedroom making his toes tingle. His breathing was fast, heart beating harder.

He stepped from their bedroom onto the deck, looking left and right, hoping to see her leaning on the rail, looking out over the water. 'Marie?' he asked again, voice choked, panic rising in his chest. He let his eyes drift back to the steps down to the sand. To the visible welts there, the footsteps stretching into the distance.

'No, no, no,' he began saying, taking the first, stiffened strides. He broke into a run, hurdling down off the deck onto the beach, following her steps. This far towards the peninsula things were quiet. People rarely walked here. They couldn't be anyone else's footsteps.

Lucas ran hard, heels sinking into the soft sand, causing

him to stumble and lope. His chest burned, heart hammering, breath tight and hot in his throat. He tried to call her name, but he couldn't muster it.

He kept following the tracks, closer, closer, closer to the waves …

He couldn't see her.

'No, no,' he kept muttering, unsure if the words were aloud or just in his head.

The waves grew louder, washing in from the Baltic Sea, dark and choppy as the water deepened quickly off the shore.

'Marie!' he called out. 'Marie?'

The surface grew damp beneath his feet. He followed the tracks, eyes fixed on them.

The sand hardened with the water. The footprints grew shallower.

And then they stopped.

Lucas staggered to a halt and collapsed forward onto his knees, her final step right in front of him.

A wave broke and rolled up onto the shore, splitting around his thighs.

When it pulled back, it took her final footprint with it, leaving smooth sand behind.

He couldn't speak, couldn't do anything.

His eyes slowly lifted to the sea, stretching endlessly into the approaching dawn, dark and vast.

He didn't know where Marie was out there.

But he knew that she was gone.

———

The sun was high in the sky by the time Linus Lundström arrived. He was the polisintendent at Fårösund, the closest town. Though despite it being no more than several kilometres away, it required a ferry ride from the main island of Gotland to Fårö. A single road stretched to Ringside, and then on to Sudersand itself. Lucas and Marie Adell lived further up the coast, right near Avaeken.

When the call had come in, he'd not realised the gravity of it. He'd been asleep, in all honesty. And when his konstapel had called and said that they'd had a complaint from a holiday-goer walking along Sudersand beach that there was a naked man at the water's edge on his knees, Lundström thought nothing of it. Told his konstapel to deal with it.

Then, he'd rolled over and gone back to sleep. It was a Saturday after all, and this wasn't the first time someone had skinny dipped off Sudersand. What was the harm, really?

But when the second call had come, this time, he rose.

'It's Lucas Adell,' his konstapel had said, the waves crashing in the background.

Lundström didn't know Lucas Adell that well, but when a family moved to the island of Fårö, it meant one of two things – either they were looking to get away … or run away.

With so few people living this far north on Gotland, there wasn't much that went on that the local polisintendent didn't hear about. Whether he wanted to or not. A new family moving to the area was newsworthy and he must have been told fifty times that they'd arrived.

For two years, there was no problem. Nothing to even report on. Lucas Adell would bring his daughter to Fårösund every morning for school. She was thirteen then, would be fifteen now. They'd crossed paths a few times. The man seemed nice enough. Though not exactly Lundström's cup of tea. He worked in banking software and stocks, or something, Lundström thought as he killed the engine of his Volvo estate patrol car and stepped onto the grassy verge at the side of the small road that led to the Adell house.

Rebecca Adell — his daughter — she'd seemed reasonably pleasant, too. Stroppy at first, at being forced to move away from Stockholm to come here. Hardly a trendy place for a teenager to find themselves. But Lucas and Marie, his wife, agreed it was best for them all. Get away from the turbulence of the city, embrace the peace and safety of Gotland. Lundström couldn't blame them. He never much liked the big cities either. Too loud, funny smells. He grimaced at the thought, shaking his head as he walked around his konstapel's car, around Lucas Adell's house, and towards the beach access. Beautiful spot, Lundström thought, as he stepped through the grasses and down onto the sand. Lucky family, to get this place. And considering what they paid, a steal. That banking money had served the Adell's well.

Which made it even more shocking that Rebecca had gone missing as she had.

It seemed like a long time ago now. A distant, terrible memory. Though it wasn't all that long ago at all.

Lundström's white hair blew in the sea breeze. He was tall, his long strides carrying him down through the soft sand. His hips complained, as did his left knee. Though he couldn't really recall a time when they didn't now.

He remembered the case. Rebecca went out to meet some friends one night, but never came home. When questioned, the friends said she hadn't arranged to meet them. Her phone had been turned off about ten minutes after she left the house on her bike.

It was as though she'd just dropped off the face of the earth.

.   .   .

The only security camera within twenty kilometres was at the ferry crossing, and no cars crossed that night. It was the only way off the island. A mystery, Lundström thought then, as he thought now.

Police had been called up from Visby to assist, to search Fårö. But to no avail. They scoured the entire island, south to north, west to east. But there was no sign of the girl.

The truth of what happened still remained a mystery. Considering the girl had gone out of the house voluntarily, lied to her parents about where she was going … Lundström thought she probably escaped back to the mainland, somehow. To 'civilisation'. Though no one asked his opinion. Adell had been pretty dismissive of his attempts to help, if anything. Said that he wasn't equipped to lead the investigation. Good luck finding her yourself, Lundström thought. I've been intendent here for seventeen years! I think I know what I'm doing.

As he neared the water's edge, Lucas Adell there in front of him, naked, as promised, he slowed. His konstapel had draped his jacket around the man's shoulders, but seemingly made no attempt to move him. Despite the tourists just down the beach. They looked on curiously. Didn't Adell know that this was a family beach? That Sudersand was a big tourism draw for this part of the island? That if it became known for … for … naked men showing themselves off for the whole world to see, that it could well cost people their livelihoods? He'd always been odd, Lundström decided. Not from here. He didn't understand how things were done. It wasn't the city.

'Lundström,' the konstapel said, turning from his position next to Adell and walking towards his senior. Blom was a short man, with a balding head and a round, button nose that made his face childlike despite the wrinkles around his eyes.

'Blom,' Lundström replied tiredly. 'Why is Adell still on the beach?' He made no effort to keep the bite from his voice. 'This is a *family* area. Children. Nice people. Do I have to explain to you why—'

'It's his wife, sir,' Blom said quickly, reluctant to cut Lundström off.

'His wife?' Lundström said. 'Yes, where is she?' He looked down at Lucas Adell, unmoving, round shouldered, head hung, knees splayed. A collapsed visage of a man. Drunk, Lundström thought, sniffing the air to see if he could detect the aroma.

'That's just it,' Blom went on, dropping his voice, presumably so Adell couldn't hear. 'She's …'

'Spit it out.'

'She's gone.'

'Gone? Gone where?' Left Adell, probably, Lundström thought. Not surprising.

Blom swallowed, looked down, and then turned to face the sea.

For a moment Lundström didn't understand. But then he seemed to, his eyes slowly falling on Adell. 'Jesus,' he muttered. 'Are we … are you sure?' His voice was a whisper.

'Her footprints,' Blom said, pointing to them.

Lundström hadn't even noticed as he'd sloshed right through them. He knew that they'd been under strain since Rebecca went missing, but … this? To …

He looked at their house in the distance, the door still wide open, and then at Adell once more, on his knees in the sand. Broken.

Lundström swallowed and then cleared his throat, looking around at the spectators down the beach. 'Get him up,' he said to Blom, gesturing at Adell, his hand shaking. 'This is a family beach.'

———

Inside the house, Lundström sat across the kitchen table from Lucas Adell. The man was damn near catatonic.

'Right then, Adell,' Lundström began, hands laced in front of him. The day would be warm, but the house was still cool from the morning air. A clock ticked over Adell's shoulder, showing the time draining away. Before he called this in, Lundström needed to know what he was dealing with.

The kitchen and living room were open concept, with a vaulted and pitched ceiling, lots of exposed wood and high-end furnishings. Lundström tried vaguely to hide his envy as he glanced around, not that this fancy shit was his style. A waste of money in his eyes.

Blom put a cup of coffee down in front of Lundström. He'd helped himself to it while Adell sat there, a towel across his lap to hide his exposed genitals. He could guess again if he thought Lundström was about to dress him like a child. The man had his hands limp at his sides, his eyes staring at the surface between them.

Lundström regarded him over the rim of his coffee cup while he took a slip. Jesus, even the coffee tasted expensive.

The man cleared his throat but Adell didn't look up. 'Before we go any further, we need to assess the situation here, but to do that, you're going to need to talk. Because right now, all I can do is arrest you for exposing yourself to upstanding holidaymakers on a public beach.'

Adell's brow crumpled a little but he still didn't look up.

'I'm not saying you haven't had a rough go of it, what with your daughter running away, and now your wife—'

The man's eyes flashed and he looked up suddenly, making Lundström jolt in his chair and spill a little coffee on his wrist.

'She didn't run away,' Adell said sharply. 'And my wife' — his hands were on the table suddenly, fingers curling under his palms, nails scratching at the surface — 'is gone.' The word seemed to choke him.

Lundström felt the back of his neck moisten with sweat beneath his collar. 'Gone where?' he asked tentatively.

Adell began to shake a little, his hands forming fists now. He turned his head to look out of the window above the kitchen sink. It faced down over the beach. Gulls were wheeling in the sky now above the rolling waves. 'I don't know.'

Blom came forward behind Lundström and leaned in, whispering in his ear. 'When I reached him on the beach, sir, I asked what he was doing down there, because of the families, and that he was … naked, and—'

'Yes, yes,' Lundström hurried him along, 'get on with it.'

'Right, and he said, "She's gone. Marie, Marie, she's gone."'

'Into the sea?' Lundström whispered back, turning to look into Blom's eyes.

'I … I think so,' he said, rolling his lips into a sympathetic line.

'She … what, just … went in? Swimming, or?'

'No,' Adell said then, banging one of his fists on the table.

Lundström steadied his sloshing cup.

He screwed his face up in anger. 'She … she couldn't … it was Rebecca … it was just … it was just too much for her.'

'You're saying …' Lundström tried to help him get there, but he didn't want to say the words. 'You're saying she took her own life?'

Adell didn't answer.

'If you don't tell us what happened, we can't help you.'
Lundström lowered his head to try to catch Adell's gaze.

The man muttered something, hanging his head.

'What was that?' Lundström asked.

'I said ...' he started, filling his lungs and standing so
quickly he flipped his chair over backwards. 'Get out!' he
roared, throwing his hand at the door. 'Get out of my fucking
house! Right now!'

'Mr Adell,' Lundström said, hand flashing to his belt and
feeling just a flabby roll of skin where his pistol should have
been. He'd left it in the car. 'If we could just discuss this
amicably, then—'

'Get out! Get out! Right now, get out!'

Blom pulled Lundström's chair back, helping him up and
steering him towards the door. They needed to know what
happened, but neither was armed and in this frantic state they
couldn't subdue the man – he was as tall as Lundström, fit,
strongly built.

So instead, they fumbled with the door handle and then
hurried down the path towards their cars.

The door slammed behind them and when Lundström
looked back, he could see Lucas Adell's shadow turn and
collapse against the frosted glass, shoulders heaving as he
cried.

When they reached the gate, only then did Blom release
Lundström's elbow. The older man didn't know if Blom had
been trying to shield him, help him, or just ensure he wasn't
left behind. He looked pale as a sheet, whatever the reason.

'What now?' Blom asked.

Lundström stared back at Adell, still visible through the
glass. 'I don't know.'

'Do you think ...' He lowered his voice. 'Do you think he
had anything to do with her disappearance?'

'We can't rule it out,' Lundström said, looking back at Blom. He started towards his car then.

'Where are you going?'

'Stay here, make sure he doesn't leave the house,' Lundström ordered.

'What? How?'

If he'd not been so single-minded in that moment, he might have noticed that Blom asked 'how' and not 'why'. And then he might have thought twice about leaving it to his konstapel. But he didn't. He was already thinking about who he could call and what he could say to get this off his desk before it escalated into a missing persons, or worse, a murder investigation. That was the last thing he needed and, frankly, the last thing he had time for.

Whatever Lucas Adell had done with, or to, his wife, Linus Lundström wanted nothing to do with it.

3

Sonja Ehrhart

IT WAS the beginning of another long day for Sonja Ehrhart.

She pulled into the car park behind the hospital in Visby and exited her vehicle, a compact hybrid with a measly engine and an electric motor that powered it until it got past 30kph. Which it rarely did because Visby was, well, Visby. All tight streets, slow-moving traffic, and streams of tourists snapping photos of the quaint buildings and cutesy landscape. Sometimes she thought about leaving, but Gotland was her home now. She, like many others who walked the summer streets, fell in love with it. But visiting and living in a tourist town is a different thing. Before, she was happy to be swept along by the ambling crowds. Now they block the pavements while she's trying to carry her shopping home, or they choke up the zebra crossings in town, make getting to the bar at her favourite pub a mission, or getting a table at her favourite restaurant a coin toss.

But at least at work, things are quiet.

Or at least, they were.

Sonja let herself in through the back doors of the hospital with her lanyard and walked down the cool, air-conditioned corridor until she reached the stairwell. She opened the door, leaving the few people moving through the back administrative half of the building, and descended down to the basement. Where none except the dead lurked.

She followed the signs for *bårhus,* the morgue, and stopped at the next set of magnetically- locked doors to flash herself through once more.

It seemed like a lot of security just to keep the dead penned in, but she didn't mind. She rather liked the solitude of the job. Most people were creeped out by corpses, but they never bothered her much at all. She preferred dead patients to living ones, which is why she'd made the switch from general practitioner to pathologist two years out of her residency. And now she'd been doing this ... hell, nearly twenty-five years.

Sonja was closing in on the big six-O, but she still considered herself spry, and sharp as a tack-covered whip. She was tall for a woman. Not exceedingly tall, but tall enough to look most men straight in the eye, and down at the scalps of most women. Which she took a lot of interest in doing. Hair - like nails, teeth, eyes, nostrils, lips, toes, fingers, skin, bones, muscle tissue, organs, and, of course, blood - all interested her greatly. The fact that humans were meat-covered skeletons being driven by a brain protected by a natural helmet harder than concrete, run by electricity created from the ingestion of food ... well, it all stunned her, really. Still now, the wonder and function of the human body was fascinating. Truly, truly fascinating. And the only thing more fascinating than what made humans *live,* were the things that made them ... die. Some called her strange, eccentric, and worse. But she couldn't really care less, because she loved what she did, and she helped people. And that was all that mattered.

'Chef,' her assistant said, looking up from his steel desk in the corner of their shared office. It meant 'boss'. He gave her a nod and a grin. A middle-aged man with a bald head, eyebrows with hair so fine they were almost impossible to see, and a mouth wide enough to make a trout go green. Green, aha. Green around the gills. She smiled to herself.

'Fuck off, Jassen,' she said, pulling her satchel over her shoulder and dropping it onto her own desk. 'You know I don't like that shit.'

'It's why I do it.' He continued to grin, but looked back at his computer screen, tapping something into it.

She was his boss, but the last thing Sonja wanted was to be in charge of anyone. She wanted to work alone, preferably, and used to, but they'd brought on another pathologist to assist her when things started getting *busier.* Which is what they called it when teen suicide started becoming epidemic on the island.

The morgue at Visby hospital was the only one that conducted post-mortems, something that, until now were sporadic, if not downright rare.

Jassen was okay. An odd fish, like her. Because who, really, would want to be sequestered away below ground, first to be chomped up should a zombie apocalypse take hold of the world? Sonja thought she'd make quite a good zombie. She had long legs, was pretty fast. She'd infect lots of people. She looked over at Jassen. Him first. He looked slow, and clumsy. He'd never even make it out of the lab.

'What are you smiling at?' he asked, casting her a questioning glance.

She cleared her throat, pulling herself out of her tangent with a shake of the head. 'Nothing, nothing,' she said, walking around to look at the file on the surface in front of her. 'What's this?' she asked, reading the name on the cover, knowing exactly what it was.

'Juni Pedersen,' Jassen said, standing and straightening his belt. He always wore it so high up. Must be uncomfortable for his testicles, Sonja thought. 'Jumper,' he added, stepping forward and pocketing his hands. His blue shirt was rumpled and he smelled faintly of onions, though Sonja always thought that, and always felt sensitive to it.

'Jumper?' Sonja leafed open the file, seeing the intake report there, the police paperwork, the request for an autopsy, full blood panel, toxicology and drug screening. The works. Just like all the others. She turned the page to see photos of the girl in situ, and then a close up of the black heart etched on the inside of her forearm. Those damn black hearts. She saw them in her sleep. 'Where was she found?' Sonja asked, already looking for the answer on the page.

'At the university,' Jassen said.

'Another one?' Rhetorical. 'Jesus.' She sighed and put the file down on the desk. 'Tea.'

'Kettle just boiled.'

She gave him a nod before walking towards the little kitchenette they had at the back of their office. Sonja laid her knuckles against the kettle, felt it still hot, but flicked the switch anyway. When she opened the door of the fridge to find the milk, she spotted a white bread sandwich wrapped in clingfilm and picked it up. She inspected it in the cold light of the halogens and then held it close to her nose and sniffed, then pursed her lips.

It was Jassen's lunch.

Cheese and onion.

That was one mystery solved. She wished they could all be so easy.

———

Sonja sat on the lab stool next to the slab, hunched over, hands clasped, lips resting against her knuckles. She slowly stroked the underside of her chin with her thumbs, eyes fixed on the hollowed-out torso of Juni Pedersen.

The girl lay there, the wide Y-incision across her chest and stomach exposing her rib cage and now, the pale bone of her spine. Her organs had been removed, weighed, labelled, and samples had been taken for biopsy. Jassen had removed the rib separator, allowing the sharp white teeth of her skeleton to contract back down into her body like a closed Venus flytrap.

He was out of the room doing paperwork, but Sonja remained, casting her eye over the girl's body. So similar to the others, but so different. Different in that they were a mixture of boys and girls, a mixture of ages, ethnicities. They were tall, short, overweight, underweight. Some were healthy, others showed signs of illness and deficiency … there was no pattern to them. Nothing to suggest who would be next or why.

The bodies told her little, if anything. And that was what they had in common – that they were all so different, so … unremarkable. In a medical sense. The only thing that linked them – truly linked them – was the black heart.

She tipped forward onto her feet and came to the table. The girl had been cleaned thoroughly and smelled more like another piece of hospital equipment than she did a human being. Rigor mortis had come and gone, so the arm lifted easily as Sonja took it. Her skin was cold to the touch, rubbery almost now. She'd lie in a cold drawer for months following this. Like the others.

Sonja put that out of her mind and turned the girl's hand

palm to the sky so she could get a better look at the mark. They hadn't *all* been on the left arm. She remembered one or two on the right. And she surmised that was because those ones belonged to left-handed kids. Their dominant hand carved into their weak arm. And this one looked no different.

Same style, same depth, same care and precision. Just like the others, the outline was cut right into the flesh. Deep enough to scar, not so deep as to cause serious harm. But deliberate all the same, and fresh. Less than a day before time of death. And without any anaesthetic, at least none that showed up on blood panels. Done with a small blade – a craft scalpel, nail scissors, something sharp. Some were done with more enthusiasm than others, but they were all different enough that Sonja was sure there wasn't one common carver among them.

But what did it tell her?

The inside was coloured black, like the others. Marker pen, paint, even black lipstick in one case. This looked like a Sharpie to Sonja. Not surprising for a university student. And it'd be no help to the police, not that they seemed that interested anymore. No one had called or followed up on their work. At the beginning they were being hounded constantly.

Sonja lowered the arm and stepped back, retaking her place on the stool. She once again clasped her hands in front of her mouth, then grimaced and pulled away from the taste. Stupid, Sonja, get your head out of your ass.

She sighed and spun on the stool instead, looking around the lab, exhaling slowly.

Her eyes fell on the bank of drawers at the back of the room and her mind went to all the bodies lying inside them.

She couldn't believe that this could happen and that there was so little being done about it. They'd never have stood for it at her last job. They'd have been on the trail like bloodhounds with a scent in their nose. Especially the big one. She smiled at that, remembering him. He was young, sure, but he was smart, determined. And handsome. And he had big hands. She liked that, as well. And most of the time when he dropped in to see her, he could have called. She smirked to herself on the chair, and pictured him. The lithe frame, the square jaw, those cold, grey eyes that'd make your skin pop out in gooseflesh. But beyond all that, he was good at his job. But last she heard through the grapevine there was a bust up with his wife at work, messy divorce.

She bit her lip and pulled her phone from her pocket, opening it up.

She Googled his name.

Kjell Thorsen, Lulea Police.

The results flashed up immediately, news articles.

Her thumb hovered over the top one as she read the headline, though it wasn't his name that appeared in it. It was one she didn't recognise. Jamie Johansson.

Ghost story or reality? Local Polisinspektor Jamie Johansson cracks 30-year-old Krakornås Kung mystery.

She read the snippet beneath: *Jamie Johansson and her partner Kjell Thorsen, formerly of the Lulea Police investigated the murder of a teenager found dead just outside of Kurrajakk ...*

She was piqued.

Her thumbs worked.

Jamie Johansson.

More results, the top one this time: *Scandal of the highest order: Detective Jamie Johansson of Stockholm Police breaks international corruption ring.*

She read more. *A dynasty of justice: British detective Jamie Johansson catches the Angel Maker, picking up where her father left off twenty years ago.*

They kept going.

Jamie. Oil rigs. Cults. Serial killers. Trafficking rings. Jesus. Who was this woman?

She closed the app and went to her phone book instead, flicking down the names until she found the one she wanted.

Sonja clicked it and held the phone to her ear. It crackled a little, then rang oddly, an out-of-country tone. It rang. And rang. And rang.

And then he answered.

'Hjalla?' he said, a little surprised. 'Sonja?'

'Hej, Kjell,' she replied, standing and holding her elbow with her other hand. 'How are you?'

'I'm … fine. Thanks, uh, how are you? Sorry, this is just …'

'Out of the blue? Yeah, I know. I hope I'm not interrupting anything.'

'No, no,' he said. In the background she could hear music, but then there was a quiet hiss and it disappeared. She envisaged a sliding door closing behind him. 'What's going on? How's …'

'Visby?'

'That's it. Gotland's beautiful.'

'It really is,' Sonja said. 'But not so much at the moment.'

'Oh …'

'"Oh" is right,' she sighed. 'Have you heard?'

'Heard what?' He grew tentative.

'No, I suppose not. They've done all they can to keep it out of the media.'

'Keep *what* out of the media?'

'The suicides.'

'Suicides?' Surprised now.

'An epidemic. All teenagers.'

'How many is an epidemic? Five?'

'Twenty.'

'Jesus.'

'Three. Twenty-three. In twenty-three months.'

He was silent now.

'Kjell?'

'I'm here, I'm just …' He sounded cautious. 'I don't quite know why you're calling … *me.* '

'I'm calling you because no one's doing anything here. The police are stumped, and they seem not to even care anymore.' Sonja looked down at the girl in front of her. Juni Pedersen. Eighteen years old. 'They haven't got a fucking clue, and now they're just sweeping it under the rug. More will die, Kjell. I don't know how many.'

He drew a slow breath. 'I … I can make a call or two? See if I can get some more eyes on it, or—'

'No, you need to come.'

'To Gotland?'

'Yes. You never let a case go in Lulea. You were the best investigator there, and this isn't something that's going to solve itself.'

He laughed a little. 'I know you're not one to mince words, but you can't expect me to just drop everything and—'

'Where are you? Are you working?'

'I'm … that's not the point.'

'I remember you said to me on the day I left Lulea – if there's anything you ever need, just call. Well, I need, Kjell. Or was that just a line?'

'It was a figure of speech.'

'So, you didn't mean it?'

He drew another breath, then sighed, thinking. 'Twenty-three kids?'

'Between the ages of thirteen and nineteen. I've pulled

them all apart, Kjell. Down to the bones. There's nothing. I … I can't keep doing it. It needs to stop.'

He was quiet again for a while. She just let him think.

Eventually, he spoke. 'Okay,' he said quietly. 'I'll … I'll be there as soon as I can, alright? But I can't promise anything. It's not my case, and … hell … I'm not even a detective anymore.'

'You never stop being who you are.'

He chuckled a little. 'Now that *is* a line.'

She smiled through closed lips. 'And Kjell?'

'Yeah?'

'This is kind of an odd question, but … are you with Jamie Johansson?'

4

Kjell Thorsen

THORSEN HUNG up the phone and stared down at it. Waves crashed below on the rocks, the sun high overhead and blazing hot.

He was standing under a wooden pergola, shaded by a lattice of wisteria that wound around the beams above. Even through it, the shards of sunlight were hot on his skin. He could feel sweat beading at his temples, around the nape of his neck under his linen shirt. At first the warmth wasn't so bad — though when they arrived on the island, it wasn't this hot. But as spring turned to summer, the mercury seemed to climb and stay there. And now it was damn unbearable. Thorsen was a cold weather animal, bred in the far north. Sure, he had a few trips under his belt — Maja and him had travelled all over, toured Asia, the US when they were together, but Greece was something else.

Thorsen and Jamie had bounced around, but had been on Kythira for over two months now. The original plan was two

weeks, and then back to Sweden. But when they arrived …
she didn't want to leave.

Thorsen slapped the back of his phone against the
knuckles of his opposite hand, figuring out how to play this.
Jamie Johansson, if nothing else, was perceptive and hard to
navigate. She was also quick to anger, impulsive, hard-
headed, stubborn, hard-headed, and obsessive. So, if he went
back in there half-cocked, she'd tear him in two. He sighed.
There was no point trying to game the conversation, and no
point trying to hide anything from her.

Whether it was the truth she wanted to hear or not,
Thorsen was ready to go home. Their moment in the sun had
to end sometime. And this seemed like the perfect reason …
excuse … to do it.

He turned his back on their stone patio, the white wall
that separated their little lawn from the jagged rocks below,
the endless stretch of tourmaline blue sea beneath, and
opened the sliding patio door that led to their little two-
bedroom apartment.

Jamie was stretched out on the couch beneath the air
conditioner. Her usually pale skin had bronzed in the sun
despite her best efforts to avoid it, oversized straw hats and
all, and her hair had gone even whiter than normal. Her keen
blue eyes stared over the top of her book at him — A History
of Kythira. 'Did you know that Kythira was home to a
Phoenician colony that built the Temple of Aphrodite Urania,
supposedly the oldest temple to Aphrodite on record?'

'I didn't know that,' Thorsen said, feeling a little nervous.
She was looking at him in that way again, where her eyes
never moved from his, but still peeled his skin off one layer at
a time.

'Dated to the sixth century BCE. Who was on the phone?'

'Oh,' he said, resisting the natural impulse to brush it off and say 'no one'. But that would only make it worse. 'An old friend. A woman named Sonja Ehrhart, a pathologist who worked in Lulea while I was there. She moved to Gotland, and now works as head ME at Visby hospital.'

Jamie processed that. 'And what did Sonja Ehrhart, head medical examiner at Visby hospital want?' She raised an eyebrow slightly.

Thorsen's grip tightened on his phone a little. 'There's been a string of suicides on the island. Twenty-three teenagers in twenty-three months.'

Jamie was still for a moment, just looking at him. And then her eyes returned to the book in front of her and she turned the page. 'How unfortunate.'

'How unfortunate?' Thorsen felt a pang of frustration, a feeling he was very much used to with Jamie. 'Is that all you have to say?'

'What else is there to say?' Jamie replied, sighing a little, eyes moving back and forth as she read the words in front of her.

'I don't know,' he laughed a little, 'how about — that's awful, what are they doing about it? How did it get this bad? What can we do to help?'

Jamie's eyes stopped roving and flitted upwards. 'Help? I don't know if you remember, but we were fired.'

'From being decent human beings?'

'From being detectives.'

'Kids are dying.' Thorsen came forward a little.

'Kids die every day, all over the world,' she replied coldly. 'There's nothing we can do about it. This isn't our case, Thorsen.'

He scoffed, and made no effort to hide it. 'And since when has that ever stopped you?'

'Things have changed. I've changed.'

'Since when?'

'Since we almost died. Again. For, what, the third time in a year? And that's not counting the other times I willingly put my head in a noose. I'm done. With that, with police work, with all of it. I'm retired.' She picked her book up and began reading again.

Thorsen seethed, fists clenched at his side. This fucking woman. 'Jamie …' he started, trying to control his temper. 'I get it, alright? We both needed a break – from the cold, from Sweden, from the death and gunfire and *evil fucking cults*. The lot of it. But … but …' He came forward now, knelt beside the sofa and laid his hand on her arm. She seemed to stiffen at his touch, head not turning, but eyes moving to his. 'But now it's time to go home.'

'Sweden …'

'It's not your home, I know. You have no home, you're an orphan of the world.' He squeezed her arm a little. 'I've heard it fifty times from you.'

'So, why'd you say it then?'

'Because your home is your work. It's the only thing you've ever loved, the only thing you've ever wanted to do.'

'Well maybe it's not anymore.'

'You're going to become a historian instead?' He nodded to the book.

'Maybe I will. Why not?'

He laughed. 'You'd be bored out of your mind.'

'Why do you want to leave so badly?'

'Because I'm bored out of *my* mind. It ever occur to you that I'm a person too? With my own thoughts, feelings, desires?'

'So, you go back to Sweden then. To Gotland.' She kept her eyes fixed on his.

She did this. Called his bluff. Challenged him. And that

was putting it nicely. What it actually felt like was her being a pouty, sullen child. But like with a child, he had to tread lightly or risk things blowing up.

'And if I did, what would you do?'

She shrugged. 'I'd stay here.'

'Okay, then it's settled. I'll go to Gotland, and you'll stay on Kythira. On your own.' He pushed to his feet and headed towards his bedroom.

'Where are you going?' he heard from behind him.

'To pack.'

'Right now?' He heard her shuffle and get up in the other room.

'There's no time to waste, is there?' He pulled his suitcase from under his bed and dropped it onto the white duvet.

Jamie was in the doorway behind him now, arms folded, foot bouncing. 'You don't have to leave straight away.'

'I do,' he replied, going towards the wardrobe.

'I'm not coming with you.'

'I know.' He grabbed an armful of clothing and dumped it onto the bed, began stripping the hangers from the necks.

'There's no point, you know? Suicides aren't murders. What would we even do?'

We? He didn't let her see him smile. 'I don't know. Maybe nothing. But I'd like to try to help.'

'So, call someone,' Jamie said. 'Someone else should help. You must know someone on Gotland?'

'I do. She just called me and asked for *our* help.'

Jamie's foot tapped faster. 'Someone else then. Wiik, maybe.'

Thorsen stopped and stood straight, looking at her. 'Wiik is the head of violent crimes at Stockholm Police. I don't think this is really within his jurisdiction, do you?'

'Hallberg then.' Jamie shrugged, the nail of her index

finger scratching at the side of her thumb in the knot of her arms. Her grip was tight around the book.

'Hallberg is in Copenhagen last I heard,' Thorsen replied with a sigh. 'And I'm sure she's got bigger fish to fry.'

'So why does it have to be you?'

He went to her now, smiling. 'It doesn't.' He put his hands on her shoulders, felt the tension in them. She stared up at him, her eyes piercing blue against the stark white of the walls. 'But I want to go.'

'Are you coming back?' Her voice quivered a little.

'No,' he said, not willing to hide it. 'This isn't it for me. This isn't how I want to spend the rest of my life.'

She looked away, hurt.

'Not yet, at least.'

She didn't look back at him.

'But if you stay here, then at least I know where you'll be. I won't ask you to come with me, Jamie.' He squeezed her shoulders a little, and then let go.

'I've asked the same of you. More than once.'

'I know,' he said, going back to his case. 'But you're you, and I'm me.' He laughed to himself. 'Hell, I don't think the world could handle two Jamie Johanssons. I can barely handle one myself.'

She didn't share his laugh, but when he looked over she was chewing her thumbnail a little. Her eyes were on the ground, her mind working.

After a moment, she sank from the doorway and disappeared.

He followed her into the living room, hearing a door shut down the hallway. He slowed, then stooped, picking up her book off the floor. A History of Kythira. He smirked a little, tossing it onto the couch, and then headed back into his bedroom to finish packing.

The Gotland ferry sailed south from Nynäshamn into the gathering dusk.

Thorsen walked to the bow, heels clipping on the steel flooring, and pulled up at the rail, laying his hands on it, his arms forming a wide triangle. He stared into the breeze, the sun warm over his right shoulder, the sky darkening over his left.

Gotland loomed from the haze, the sea almost unnaturally still beneath.

The throb of the engine reverberated through his bones and he wondered if he'd made the right decision.

'Hey,' came a voice from behind.

He turned, seeing a coffee cup being held out to him. He took it, gave Jamie a nod.

She sipped on her own, looking past him towards the island ahead. She'd become quiet, but more than that, she'd seemed to harden.

For all her emotional immaturity, she'd seemed relaxed while away, and almost – he couldn't believe he was saying it - happy. He'd forgotten what she was like when she was working. The sullenness, the look on her face like she was just in the slightest amount of physical pain. And maybe she was. It was easy to forget she'd been shot and stabbed, beaten and starved … She was the toughest person he'd ever met, but work reminded her of all the lows. Perhaps bringing her was selfish of him. But he did give her the option to stay. Though he did know that the only thing that truly frightened Jamie Johansson was being alone.

'You okay?' he asked her.

She shrugged, then went past him to the rail, looking out

over the water. 'Well, at least it's not winter,' Jamie muttered, all but to herself.

'Yeah, there's that. I've had enough snow for a lifetime, I think,' Thorsen said, following her.

She turned away from the sea and leaned against the metal, looking at the people moving around on the boat instead. Her eyes went from one to the other, cataloguing them.

Thorsen felt the urge to apologise, though he didn't think there was anything to apologise for. And then again, he couldn't spend his entire life ensuring Jamie Johansson wasn't ever made unhappy. Hell, they weren't even together! They were just ... well, that he didn't know. But he did know that there wasn't really a name for what they were. He'd seen her looking at him in the way that women did when they felt something. In the way that his ex-wife had when they'd first met. In the way other women had before they'd slept together. And yet, she'd never acted on it, had always pulled away, broken eye contact, changed the subject, shifted positions.

They'd been in such close proximity for so long that the raw sexual attraction he'd harboured seemed to have ... not withered, but rather ... he didn't know. Become strange, taboo, forbidden. Like ... like a sibling that he didn't want to want in *that* way, but couldn't help it. Thorsen loved Jamie, as a friend, like a sister, but there was something inside him that always wanted him to reach out and just ... take her. To pull her against him, run his hands through her hair, run his lips over her neck, feel her shudder in his grasp and melt into him. He could please her if she let him. He could be what she wanted, what she needed. She was so shut down, so cloistered, not open to that side of herself. But if she just *let* him, he could show her. He could teach her. He could help her understand those parts of herself that she didn't.

His eyes focused and he saw that she was staring at him, and that he had been at her, without realising. He cleared his throat and shook his head. 'Sorry,' he said quickly, 'just jet-lagged, I think.'

'It's a two-hour time difference,' Jamie replied coolly, 'there's no jet-lag.' She sighed, sipped some more coffee, folded her arms.

'You ever been to Gotland before?'

'When I was a kid,' Jamie said. 'Not for a long time.'

'It's beautiful,' Thorsen replied. 'And there's lots of history there, museums and that sort of thing.'

She looked at him quizzically.

'So you can continue your education, become a historian after all.'

The corners of her mouth turned down and she unfolded her arms. 'We're here to work,' she said, throwing the remainder of her coffee over the side and into the water, 'not fuck around.' Jamie started walking. 'Come on, we'll be landing soon.'

———

The afternoon was wearing on by the time they docked. The sun was still high, and it wouldn't grow dark until well after 10pm.

Gotland swam out of the haze, green and sun-drenched. Gulls circled the shore, calling and wheeling in groups, hunting for scraps on the promenades of Visby, the capital of the island. Sixty thousand people lived on Gotland, and twenty-five thousand lived in Visby itself. Small by the standards of any mainland country but, despite the size, Jamie always remembered it being vibrant and full of life.

They went on foot, walking down the gang ramp and onto a concrete dock. Jamie was ahead of Thorsen, striding with purpose, her lightweight hiking boots squeaking. They'd been gathering dust in the closet in Greece for months. She only wore them when she worked. He watched her, noting the tension in her gait, her silence, the semi-scowl that seemed to have taken root on her face. Should he have brought her back? He'd emotionally blackmailed her, or as good as, to come with him. Threatened to leave her in Greece, preying on her fear of abandonment and loneliness where, in reality, he knew that it was him that didn't want to be alone. Didn't want to be without her.

They flashed their tickets at the barrier and were welcomed onto the island. There was something slightly off about not producing a badge, but they were just civilians now, and he had to keep reminding himself of that. It was still knee-jerk to pat his chest pocket for the billfold, and to be distinctly aware of the weight of the Glock at his hip. He wouldn't go as far as to say he felt naked without it, but there were definitely moments where he felt a sudden flash of panic, reached to his belt and felt nothing, and then remembered that he no longer carried a weapon.

And it almost felt like he was inviting trouble without it. Was he? By jumping back into a case like this, one he knew nothing about? He always chastised Jamie for sticking her nose where it didn't belong. Was she rubbing off on him? Or was he just bored senseless? He couldn't give her shit for doing the same thing and then be too much of a coward to admit it himself. If only in his head. Though he did feel compelled to tell Jamie, to share that information. Guilty, almost. Weird how her sullen silence could do that, could invoke a feeling so strong, so harsh in his chest. She wasn't even looking at him but he felt that if she could read his mind, she'd be disappointed.

He shook off the negative thoughts as best he could, scanning the curb-side pick-up zone for their ride.

It didn't take him long to spot Sonja – she was hard to miss.

She looked just how he remembered her, though maybe a little older, and her hair had now lost its bronze sheen and looked almost entirely grey. He did a quick mental calculation, and thought she must be sixty now, or at least on the cusp. But she still looked good. Tall, he always forgot how tall. Not many people looked him in the eye but even fewer women didn't require him to stoop or crane his head down to look at them. Sonja Ehrhart was five-ten easily, six feet in the clomping Doc Martens she always wore. Her hair was dead straight, flat, and shining silver in the afternoon sun. She had narrow, long features, and dark eyes that stood out from her pale skin. A striking woman by all accounts, and one that he'd sorely missed. He didn't realise quite how much until that moment.

She spotted Thorsen a moment later and pushed off the side of her little hatchback, jogging easily across the promenade to greet him.

Jamie was still ahead and sidestepped for her to pass, watching as the woman flung her arms around his head and all but jumped onto him like a baby koala.

She squeezed his neck hard, lifting her heels off the ground and kicking them like a schoolgirl.

Thorsen dropped his bag in surprise and took hold of her in a tight embrace to stop her from pulling him down.

'God, you even smell the same!' she said, gripping harder.

He laughed nervously, distinctly aware that Jamie was watching him with that signature look of hers. The judgemental one she wasn't trying to, but couldn't help, make.

'Sonja,' he said, the word squeezing out past her shoulder. 'It's, um … ahem …' He cleared his throat, her collarbone digging into his gullet.

She finally released and then stood back, grabbing him by the shoulders. They were on a slight slope so she was practically level with him. 'I'd say you haven't aged a day, but honestly you look like shit.' She squeezed his cheek like he was a child. 'One that's been left out in the sun to bake for a few months. What is this tan? Is it spray-on, or do you apply it with a paint roller?'

He batted her hand away, grinning to himself. 'You're a fine one to talk, what's this white hair? You auditioning to play Gandalf in a The Lord of the Rings stage adaptation?'

'I am, yes,' she replied quickly. 'And they're also looking for someone to play the orc that got kicked in the face by a horse. I think you'd be perfect!'

They stared at each other for a moment, then burst out laughing. Before he could say anything else, she hugged him again. 'It's so good to see you!'

'You too,' Thorsen said truthfully. He was filled with emotion all of a sudden. Happiness, it came spilling out of him so hard that he almost wanted to cry. Living with Jamie was … not an exercise in outward emotion. He never thought something as simple as a hug would do that. Could do that.

He swallowed it and pulled away, steeling himself, making sure not to meet Jamie's eye. 'I'm just sorry it's not under better circumstances.'

Sonja put her hands on her hips, her long legs hugged by her acid-washed jeans not giving any hint of her age. She was still so lithe, so youthful. 'Meh, fucking Visby police don't know their arseholes from their elbows. They seem to think that twenty-three teenage suicides is reason to pull the covers over their heads and wait 'til morning.' She sighed heavily. 'I'm not saying it's a cakewalk, hell, I'm the one that's been dealing with them, one after another on my slab. A damn procession.' She cycled her hand through the air to illustrate the back-to-back nature. 'And honestly, not a damn thing out of place except for the hearts.'

'Hearts?' Thorsen shook his head a little. 'You mentioned on the phone briefly, but what's it about? Is it a pattern, a calling card, or—'

'Or maybe it's a message.' Jamie appeared between them, dwarfed by the pair.

They both turned to look down at her, Sonja a little shocked. 'You're Jamie Johansson,' she said brightly.

Oh fuck, Thorsen thought. She's going to hug her.

And then she did.

Sonja stooped and threw her arms around Jamie's neck. Her arms hung limply at her side and she stiffened visibly. Jamie did not like being hugged, and she certainly didn't like being hugged by strangers.

Thorsen swallowed, waited for some sort of reaction, but Jamie just played possum until Sonja released her, straightening again.

'I'm so sorry I didn't introduce myself, I just haven't seen this string bean in an age.' She dipped her head towards Thorsen and then extended a hand. Moot, he thought, seeing as she'd already hugged her. 'Sonja Ehrhart. We used to work together in Lulea.'

'I gathered,' Jamie replied, offering her hand. 'Jamie Johansson.'

'Oh, I know,' Sonja laughed, taking it. 'Honestly,' she

began, hiding her mouth with the back of her hand, 'it's you I wanted, he just came for free.'

'What am I, the toy in a bloody Happy Meal?' Thorsen laughed.

Sonja just smiled, but kept her eyes on Jamie. 'But seriously, I'm thankful to you for coming.' She looked at Thorsen. 'Both of you. This is … this has to stop.' She let out a long breath, pressed her lips together sadly. 'Come on, you must be starved. Let's get some food.'

'I could eat,' Thorsen replied. 'Jamie, hungry?'

Jamie looked out over the town, then hitched her duffle a little higher on her shoulder and shrugged.

Sonja cast Thorsen a look and then turned towards the car. He let Jamie go first, watching her closely. But as usual, she'd clammed up and it'd take the jaws of life to get inside.

———

Visby was small, but the traffic moved slowly.

Jamie got to the car second, but elected to sit in the back anyway, letting Thorsen and Sonja talk in the front.

Every time Thorsen glanced in the rear-view, Jamie was peering out of the window, deep in thought. About the case already? About something else? About Sonja and him? Impossible to tell.

'So, String Bean,' Sonja said after a few minutes. 'What's new, why did you leave Lulea?'

Thorsen felt like he needed to provide context to Jamie. 'Sonja calls me String Bean because when we worked at Lulea, the first time my partner saw us together he said, *wow, you two are a couple of fucking string beans.*'

'Simonson,' Sonja chuckled to herself. 'What a twat he

was. Not bad looking, but a useless fucking detective. And short, too.'

Jamie offered the briefest of smiles but kept her eyes on the window.

'You never answered the question,' Sonja pressed.

'Well, Maja and I …'

'I heard.'

'So why ask?'

'I wanted to hear your side of it,' Sonja said, indicating and pulling off the main road down a side street.

'My side of it is that she was sleeping with someone else and everyone else but me knew about it. So, I got the hell out of there.'

'Hmm,' Sonja said, sticking out her bottom lip.

'Hmm what?'

'That's one way to buck gender norms, I guess.'

'Screw you.'

'In your dreams.' She punched him in the thigh. 'Love you too, String Bean. We're here.' She pulled the car to a stop on the side of the road behind a beaten-up old SUV and put it in park. Up ahead was a little sign for a restaurant. Thorsen's mouth began to salivate. Thai food. They'd caught a ferry from the island to the mainland late last night, travelled straight to the airport, flown from Athens to Stockholm, caught a bus to the other ferry, and then sailed straight for Gotland. He was going on salt and vinegar crisps, dry-roasted peanuts, some terrible plane food which included a bread roll better suited to play cricket with than eat, and a tiny carton of apple juice that would struggle to drown a fly. So yeah, he was hungry.

He exited the car along with Sonja and they stepped onto the curb together.

'You still a little bitch about spice?' she asked, barging him with her shoulder.

He stumbled a little. 'Is it a crime to want to be able to taste your food?'

She grinned at him a little, then stopped and turned, looking back onto the road.

Thorsen did too, following her gaze.

Jamie was standing there, hands in the pockets of her black bomber jacket.

'You coming, sweetheart?' Sonja asked, extending a hand.

Thorsen waited in silence, knowing she wouldn't take it.

'No, I, uh …' Jamie started, looking at the ground and shaking her head. 'I'll leave you two to catch up. I'm sure you've got lots to talk about. And I'm not really hungry anyway.' She offered a small smile.

'Where are you going?' Thorsen asked then, knowing she was about to turn tail and run.

Jamie shrugged again, allowing her shoulders to sit around her ears for a moment before slouching back down. 'Walk the city, get a feel for it,' she offered vaguely. 'You said on the phone the last victim died at the university, right?'

'I did,' Sonja said slowly. 'But we'll have plenty of time to talk about the case over some food. Come on, you *must* be hungry. And everyone loves Pad Thai.'

Jamie did love Pad Thai, Thorsen knew that. But he wasn't surprised at her reply anyway.

'No, I'm good, honestly. Don't think I could eat right now. Nauseous from the boat, I think. Just need to walk. But I'll catch up with you later at the hotel.' She gave Thorsen a nod and went to turn away.

'Hey,' he said, stepping down off the curb and taking her in his arms. 'You okay?'

She was tense at first, but then reluctantly hugged him back. Just a short squeeze before letting go.

'Yeah, I'm fine,' she said, voice low. 'Just …'

'A lot, I get it.' He looked down at her. Sonja was full on, and Thorsen guessed she'd never seen him like that. Not like he made a habit of running into old friends. And he had even fewer like Sonja … 'Call me if you need anything. And text me even if you don't. Be safe.'

She pulled away, nodding to him, then gave a brief wave to Sonja and took off, striding fast, hiking boots squeaking on the tarmac. She was suddenly a whole different person from the woman lolling on the sofa reading history books, and he couldn't help but feel responsible for that.

He watched her go for a few seconds, and then she disappeared down a side street, either knowing exactly where she was headed, or just wanting to be anywhere but there.

'So …' Sonja said, stepping down off the curb so she was shoulder to shoulder with him. 'Are you two fucking, or what?'

5

Jamie Johansson

IT WAS good to be away.

The moment she rounded the corner, it felt like she could breathe. The man she'd spent the last six months with was not the one in that car, it seemed. Whoever this Sonja person was, she had Thorsen wrapped around her little finger. He basically turned to jelly when he saw her!

And that hug? The way she threw herself at him. Hell, she might as well have grabbed his ass and stuck her tongue in his ear. And she must be twenty years his senior, too.

Jamie steamed forward, shaking her head, shaking visions from her head of those two … *string beans* entwined like a pair of fucking boa constrictors. She almost shuddered at the thought.

And where the hell was she, anyway?

Jamie stopped, realising she was on some random back street lined with quaint little houses. None of them, however, looked like Gotland University.

She sighed, brushed a few loose strands of ash blonde hair

from her face, tucking them behind her ear, and pulled out her phone. Google Maps took her in, a short enough walk, dispensed with quickly as a light jog. If there was one thing Jamie didn't let go of, it was exercising. The Greek islands had been beautiful to run, littered with footpaths along the coasts, through the mountains, and winding along the ancient streets. And for the first time in her life, she'd really come to enjoy running for the act itself, not just for the by-product – getting out of her own head.

Now, though, it was a vehicle that got her to the university well before dark, turning a thirty-minute trip into a ten-minute one.

The sea breeze signalled her arrival, the university compact and nestled just next to the port. She could even see the slip they'd pulled in at when they'd arrived. They'd been right here, and then bloody *Sonja* had driven in the opposite direction. So much for being interested in the case.

She'd outlined a few details of the latest death in an email to Thorsen and, now, Jamie let that guide her. A jumper. A student named Juni Pedersen threw herself from the roof of the administrative building.

The campus was quiet now, with brick-lined streets, glass-fronted, low-slung buildings for the most part. No students walked through it – Jamie guessed they were off enjoying their weekend. As they should be. It'd give her room to think, too. To work.

But as she approached the admin building, she realised that wasn't going to be the case.

A young woman, maybe eighteen, was sitting on the concrete wall at the edge of the curb.

Jamie slowed her approach, inspecting the girl briefly. She was petit, with mousy brown hair, shaved on the sides, and hanging longer on top in that wavy, wet-look kind of style that seemed to be so popular these days. It hung down over her face, obscuring one of her eyes completely, the pointed corners of her horn-rimmed glasses poking through.

When the girl noticed Jamie, either by the sound of her heels on the slabs or something else, she looked up.

Jamie peeled her eyes away, hands in the pockets of her bomber jacket, eyes drifting across the sky. 'Oh,' she said, looking back at the girl and lifting her chin in greeting. 'Hey.'

The girl just offered a smile, no words.

Jamie took a moment to pause and scan the ground. The blood was gone, but she knew the telltale cleanness of a pavement that once bore a crime scene. And this girl was sitting right in front of it. Coincidence? Doubtful.

Jamie lingered, nodding at the ground. 'You knew her?'

'Who?'

'Juni Pedersen.'

The girl seemed to straighten at the name, looking at the ground but not the clean spot. 'Did you?' she asked, deflecting.

Jamie shook her head, forcing the girl to look at her once more for the answer. 'Just looking into things.'

'Looking into things?' the girl parroted. 'What are you, some kind of detective?'

'Yeah, I suppose *some kind of detective* sort of sums it up these days.' She smiled a little, rocking back onto her heels. 'I guess you could say I'm here as a favour, to lend a new perspective on …'

'The string of unexplained teenage suicides plaguing the island?' she practically scoffed.

'Heard about them, have you?'

'Heard about them? Who hasn't. You been living under a fucking rock?'

Jamie shrugged. 'I'm not from around here. And basically, yeah.'

'Must be nice,' the girl said, shaking her head now. She shuffled forward, as if to get to her feet. Jamie stopped her.

'So, you knew Juni?'

The girl hovered, hands on the edge of the wall, weight braced on them. 'From around,' she answered vaguely. The girl narrowed her eyes a little at Jamie. 'You mind if I see some ID?'

Jamie shrugged again, sure. She came forward, taking her wallet from inside her jacket. She opened it and offered the girl her driver's licence.

She stared at it, then took it, inspecting the tiny writing. 'I was thinking more like a badge.' She handed it back.

'If I had one, I'd give it.'

'I thought you said you were a detective.'

'You said I was a detective,' Jamie replied.

The girl smirked. 'Fair. So, what are you?'

'Supposedly retired.'

'You're a little young?'

'To claim my pension, sure. But not to take a break. It's been a rough few years.'

'Looks it,' she said, then cleared her throat and looked away quickly. 'I'm sorry, I didn't mean …'

'It's fine,' Jamie said, though she did think that the bags under her eyes had brightened considerably since her and Thorsen had been fired. Apparently not entirely.

'So what'd you hope to find out here?' the girl asked.

'I could ask you the same question …?' Jamie rebutted, fishing for a name.

'Annika,' she said slowly. 'Annika Olsen.'

'Annika. So, what are you doing here, and on a Saturday afternoon? There's a million places to sit, and shouldn't you be out hitting a pub or drinking supermarket vodka out of a plastic cup in someone's flat?'

'You'd think …' She chuckled a little to herself. 'Weirdly, I don't want to these days. Everyone else seems to just go on with their lives, you know?'

'I do,' Jamie said firmly. 'What happened?' Jamie read the look on her face, her troubled gaze, fixed on the clean spot on the concrete. Something was drawing her back here, moth to flame. 'You saw it, didn't you?'

She picked her head up quickly, looked at Jamie in surprise. But then it faded. 'Yeah, I was standing just about where you are right now. She landed there, right next to me.' Annika looked down at the pavement again. Her hand rose to her cheek, shaking. 'I had her blood …' Her voice grew thin. 'On my face.'

Jamie just listened. Nothing she could have said would help.

'And now …' She looked at Jamie. 'They just washed her away. Forgot her. And no one seems to even care.'

'I care.'

'Who even are you?'

'Someone that can help.'

'Oh yeah, and how are you going to do that?'

'By remembering. That Juni Pedersen and all the others were real people. Real kids, with friends, families, lives. Lives that someone took from them.'

'Juni killed herself. Like the others.'

'You really believe that?' Jamie stepped closer to her. 'Of course you don't. That's why you're out here, looking for answers. Like me. If you thought she killed herself, you wouldn't be trying to understand.'

'It just doesn't make any sense.'

'So, let's make it make sense. That's what we do. That's why I'm here.'

Her knuckles whitened around the edge of the wall, her eyes twitching as she stared at Jamie. 'You really think you can find out … the truth?'

'Maybe, maybe not. But we gotta try, right? Otherwise, what's even the point?'

'The point in what?'

'Being here.' Jamie stared at Annika, waiting for the response, the decision. When she saw the flicker in her eye, she spoke. 'You want to help?'

'Help you?' She sounded a little surprised, but not taken aback. 'I already tried. To find out, I mean, more about Juni. But they wouldn't tell me. Wouldn't tell me anything, they said the police took her records, that it's a sealed case, or whatever.' She flicked her hand frustratedly.

This was defeat then, her sitting out here.

'I don't know what you expect to do if you don't even have a badge? Who are you with, anyway? Like, who called you?'

No point in, or need to lie. 'The pathologist who's been doing the autopsies on the victims. She's not satisfied the Gotland police are doing everything they can.'

'And you're going to solve the case instead?' Annika lifted an eyebrow sceptically.

Jamie shrugged. 'Not going to hurt to try, right? I've been known to figure out a tough case or two.'

'Oh, so you're some kind of savant? A genius detective, a regular Sherlock Holmes about the place?'

Jamie offered a wan smile. 'You know what, it's fine, I'll go. You just … do whatever it is you're doing, alright? Are you alone out here? Does anyone know you're out here?'

'I'm not going to kill myself too,' Annika replied bluntly.

'And jeez, lighten up. You offend easily, don't you? Just closed right up then.' Annika clapped and jumped to her feet. 'Like, instantly.'

Jamie gritted her teeth. One of her many flaws. Thorsen and her had been working on that, but not enough, it seemed. 'So, you're coming then?'

'Where to, Sherlock?'

Jamie scowled.

Annika lifted her hands innocently. 'Okay, okay, I'll stop.'

'Probably for the best.'

'You don't have much of a sense of humour, do you?'

'Not one of my strengths, no.'

'So, you really must be a good detective.' Annika laughed to herself just a little. 'Funny is totally *out*, anyway. Brooding and sullen is the new big thing, didn't you hear?' She smiled at Jamie.

Jamie continued to scowl back. She was regretting this already. And they hadn't even bloody started yet.

Annika fell into step with Jamie, her oversized hoop earrings flopping as she jogged a little to keep up with Jamie's purposeful stride.

'So where to first?' she asked, almost out of breath already.

'What are you studying?' Jamie asked.

'Journalism.'

'Mm.' Jamie thought. She'd hoped for criminology, law maybe. Journalism would have to do. She had a curious mind, Jamie just hoped she was sharp, too. 'I'm going to take a punt and say, if you've already enquired about Juni, then you've found out a few things.'

'Uh ...'

'You know where she lived?'

'Yeah, that much wasn't hard.'

Good. Maybe she'd be useful after all.

'And you know who she lived with?' Jamie asked.

'Three other girls. They're letting a house a little way off campus.'

'We going the right way?'

'Uh …' Annika paused briefly, looked around.

Jamie stopped.

'This way,' Annika said, nodding right and then heading between two buildings.

Jamie kept walking, kept thinking. 'You know these girls' names?'

'Um, Rachel, uh, Olivia, and … shit,' Annika sighed, 'I can't remember the third.'

'It's fine. What else do you know?'

'Nothing, I don't think.'

'You must know something about Juni? Or did you quit after they told you the case was sealed?'

The girl reddened a little. She seemed to take that personally. Maybe they were more than acquaintances after all. Jamie guessed that Annika knew Juni. But she didn't press, she just listened.

'I know Juni was studying English Literature. I know she was in her third year. I know she was happy, by all accounts.'

Jamie stopped in the street, the houses quiet and picturesque around them. 'She was happy? Says who?'

'Everyone who knew her.' Annika hooked a thumb over her shoulder. 'They had a vigil for her on Thursday, people came out, brought flowers, talked about her. No one heard anything about a funeral, or …'

'Yeah, they're probably holding on to her body. They won't release it until they're sure there's nothing more to learn.' Jamie bit her lip, her mind formulating a hundred questions. But she couldn't get off track yet. 'She was happy? Were her friends there?'

'Her roommates were. They said she was always happy, always went out to parties. They said they couldn't believe it. That she killed herself.'

'I don't.'

'You think she was pushed?' Annika stopped now.

Jamie paused too, looked back. 'I didn't say that. But I'm not ruling it out. Though if that's the case, then were the other twenty-two kids all pushed? From what I understand, they all ended their lives in different ways.'

'So, you think they *did* kill themselves?'

'I don't know. The thing I want to find out is what precipitated the acts. What external factor impressed the idea upon them.'

'External factor?' Annika shook her head a little. 'I don't …'

'A person, Annika. Or persons.' Jamie stepped closer to her. 'You know what a victim type is?'

Annika blinked in thought. 'I'd guess it's when a serial killer kills a specific type of person — young girls, little boys, old ladies, whatever.'

'Not just serial killers. Predators in general. Physical, sexual, psychological.' She watched Annika closely, seeing if the girl could follow. She wasn't here to hold anyone's hand and if Annika needed that, Jamie would shed her like the dead weight she was.

'Psychological,' she repeated. 'You're saying you think someone preyed on Juni and the others? Convinced them to kill themselves?'

Jamie shrugged. 'What do we know so far? The victims are all teenagers. That's a victim type, congruent with serial predatory behaviour. If there was any physical foul play involved, then there'd be some physical evidence, and with Gotland being the size it is they'd have no problem closing the whole place off and running an island-wide DNA screening. But they haven't done that, have they?'

'Not as a far as I know …'

'Right, and twenty-three physically assisted suicides … No one's that clean, or that good not to leave anything behind. Which means that whoever is doing this is doing it remotely, at least in part.'

'I don't …'

'They're choosing their victims, and then they're grooming them.'

'To commit suicide?'

'The ultimate sense of power. The power over someone's life? A lot of serial killers get off on that power.'

'You sound like you're speaking from experience.'

'I am,' Jamie said firmly.

'First hand?'

Jamie nodded.

'You've met real serial killers? Caught them?'

'More times than I'd have liked.'

'Jesus.'

Jamie went on, keen to get back on track. 'This whole thing is localised to Gotland. So, we can probably rule out someone doing this from off the island. For a few reasons.'

'Which are?'

'Well, if you wanted to make someone kill themselves just for the fun of it, why choose a specific place? Especially as a pattern of it will draw attention, as it already has. From the police, the media … And that's not the end goal here. If attention was, then it'd be like the Zodiac all over again – letters to the police and newspapers.'

'No one uses letters anymore.'

'Fine, fucking texts, emails, TikToks, whatever, the point is that this isn't for external validation. This is personal satisfaction. This person is remaining anonymous, so the pay off, the gratification, comes from convincing Gotland teenagers to take their own lives. For whatever reason makes sense to *them*. Whoever is behind this, person or persons, they're from here. This is personal. Gotland is their home. I'd bet on that.'

'Fuck.'

'Fuck is right. Whoever it is, they're moving through here' – Jamie moved her hand around to signal the city – 'looking for their victims. And finding them. In person.'

'In person?' Annika choked on that a little.

Jamie nodded. 'I think so. Everything digital leaves a trace these days. If it was someone just doing this purely online, they'd have to make first contact, and as fucked up as the internet is, you still need to reach out to someone through text, email, via a chatroom, a forum, a damn reddit thread. Something. Something traceable.'

'You know what reddit is?'

'I'm thirty-nine,' Jamie said bitterly.

'Yeah, no,' Annika said, smiling awkwardly, 'I just meant, that, um …'

'The point is,' Jamie went on, trying to ignore the slight, 'that if all the victims were contacted by the killer and a relationship was built digitally, then there'd be no way to entirely hide that. Not twenty-three times. And hell, how many would they have had to contact before they managed to get someone to take the bait? There'd be a hundred ignoring some weird text or email for every one that responded. No, this is someone that moves unseen, that no one takes notice of, that had access to all twenty-three kids at some point in time. Someone that was able to build a rapport with them, was able to talk to them, gain their trust – no, they were probably in a position of trust to begin with.' Jamie bit her lip. 'That would make more sense. They'd solidify their relationship, begin to isolate them, slowly, indoctrinate them into their way of thinking, their way of looking at the world. And then … then they'd do it. Turn them. Onto the idea of suicide. But why suicide?' Jamie shook her head, letting the train of thought lay its own tracks. 'Some sort of escape? Release? No, you said Juni was happy. Well, her friends said she was. But how much would they really know? And what would the victims get out of killing themselves? What was it that pushed them to that?'

Jamie looked up. Annika was staring at her.

'What?'

Annika shook her head, laughed a little. 'I knew it. Sherlock fucking Holmes.'

Jamie grumbled. 'Come on, we'd better get moving.'

'It's not far.'

'Good,' Jamie said. 'And let me do the talking.'

The house was a town house, three stories, with faded paint around the door, cigarette butts strewn around the front steps, and dark stains on the pavement, the faint, overly sweet smell of sugar-loaded, flavoured alcohol lingering in the air.

Annika paused in front of it and stared up at the illuminated windows. Music played faintly from inside.

'This is it,' she said, grabbing the handrail and looking back at Jamie.

Jamie stared at it. 'Rachel and Olivia, you said?'

Annika gave a firm nod.

'And you don't remember the third?'

She opened her mouth, then closed it again. 'No.'

'Let's hope she doesn't open the door then.' Jamie sighed

and stepped up, gave a decisive knock, and then stepped back down.

It took a while for signs of life to begin to show themselves. Laughs and growing voices, inside. And then the door opened.

Two girls appeared there, wearing short, form-fitting dresses. The girls were made up, a little drunk. Jamie surmised that much from the red solo cups in their hands, their surprised expressions and fading grins, and the slight wobble to their stances.

'Oh, you're not …' one of them began. They'd been expecting someone else. Or someones. For the pre-drinking, no doubt.

Jamie forced a smile. 'Hi, we're sorry to bother you. My name's Jamie, and I think you met Annika at Juni's vigil.'

Both girls looked down at Annika then, as if trying to place her.

'I'm looking into the circumstances surrounding Juni's death and I was hoping we might be able to take a quick look around her bedroom. I'm with the Stockholm Police Violent Crimes Division, formerly,' she slipped the last word in quickly, hopefully too quickly for them to notice, 'and it's really important that we get to check out Juni's belongings. I'm just following up on the Visby Police's investigation, and I'd be really grateful if I could just get in there and make sure that they didn't miss anything.'

'Um …' one of the girls said.

'What's she doing here? Who is she?' the other one said, pointing her cup towards Annika.

'I'm—'

'Annika Olsen,' Jamie cut Annika off before she could get going. 'She was in close proximity to Juni when she jumped and she's assisting me with my inquiries.'

'Uhhh …' they both said in unison.

'Thanks, girls, this won't take a minute,' Jamie said, stepping up and past them into the house.

They moved out of the way, exchanging mildly confused stares.

Jamie heard Annika slip into the hallway behind her without a word. 'Which room was hers?'

'Third on the left,' a voice echoed from behind, 'but …'

The voice trailed off behind but Jamie could still hear the girls whispering to each other, each asking the other what the fuck was going on, who was that, should they call someone.

Annika heard it too, because before Jamie got halfway to Juni's door, she grabbed her on the elbow. 'Do you think this is a good idea?' she asked, voice hushed, eyes wide.

Jamie pulled her elbow free and kept walking. 'If we're quick about it.'

'What if they call someone? The police?'

Jamie got to the door and turned the handle, glancing back. 'Like I said, we should be quick about it.'

She plunged inside, her mind firing her back to her own university days. Her room hadn't been unlike this. Small, cluttered, poorly ventilated and lit even worse. Though Jamie had always stayed on top of her laundry. Juni didn't seem so inclined.

Jamie moved old, dirty clothes out of her path with her boot and stepped into the middle of the room. 'Close the door behind you,' she said to Annika, motioning the girl inside. 'And get the light.'

Annika seemed to deliberate over it for a moment or two, then committed, stepping in and closing it behind her. The room was plunged into darkness and then burst to life once more as Annika hit the light switch.

'What are we looking for?'

'I don't know,' Jamie said truthfully. 'Visby police will already have come through here, taken everything of note — diaries, laptop, anything like that. Anything to try to figure out what made her do it.'

'So, what's the point in being here?'

Jamie stepped forward towards the bedside table, lifted the cover of the book there. Jane Eyre. Bronte. Juni was a literature student and this book was on every literature syllabus in the damn world it seemed like. Though the book looked scarcely untouched. New, almost. Only the cover and a few pages bent back. Despite its dark themes of abuse, of depression, rejection, rage, and of course the elephant in the room – arson combined with suicide as the imprisoned former Mrs Rochester burns the manor to the ground and then hurls herself from the roof – Jamie wasn't sure if this was one of the influencing factors. Though the similarity of the circumstances was striking.

Her fingers lingered on the cover for a moment and then she lifted it, looking inside. It was a new copy. Jamie picked it up, leafed through the pages. Nothing. She put it down and moved on.

'Jamie?'

Jamie looked up. Annika was still standing by the door.

'Hmm?'

'What are we doing here? What are we looking for?'

'Anything that the police might have missed.'

'Why do you think they missed something?'

'Because the case is still open.' She returned to looking, letting her hand drag through the air from the bed across the small bookshelf next to it. The spines of English literature degree staples lined the shelf. Frankenstein, Gatsby, Dorian Grey, To the Lighthouse, Portrait of the Artist, Ulysses … Euch, Jamie did not like Joyce. She let her fingers pull them out one by one, inspecting them. Most new, skim-read once and then left to wallow. She had to admit, for the average nineteen-year-old, most of these probably weren't overly appetising.

She paused then, eyes drifting from the bookshelf to the desk. It was a small enough thing, littered with some pens knocked over from a pot at the back, a reading lamp, and a few thin books. These ones looked much more thoroughly read, but it wasn't the books that caught her eye, it was the shape cut into the desk with the nib of a pen.

A black heart was etched into the wood.

Jamie homed in.

She inspected it closely. Cut into the wood with repeated strokes. Hell, it must have been outlined a hundred times.

'A black heart.' Annika was at her shoulder suddenly.

'Mm.'

'There was one carved into Juni's arm.'

Jamie looked at her.

'I saw it. It was fresh. I don't know what it was done with,' she said, voice shaking a little, 'but it looked like it'd been coloured in with a pen, or maybe a marker. I didn't get to look too closely before …'

'It's okay.' Jamie would get the photographs from Sonja, maybe even look at the mark first-hand if Thorsen could charm their way in.

'What dreams may come,' Annika said then.

'What was that?' The words sounded familiar. Jamie raised her head, trying to place it.

'Here,' Annika said, pointing to another section of the desk, the words carved into the wood just like the heart. In fact, there were little doodles all over the surface. But those seemed to be the only coherent words.

'It's a quote.'

'Shakespeare, I think,' Annika said, 'Macbeth.'

'It's Hamlet,' Jamie corrected her, eyes flying to the well-read volumes stacked at the back of the desk. They were Shakespeare plays. The Tempest, Merchant of Venice, Othello … Typical Shakespeare lit titles. But no Hamlet.

Had the police put two and two together as well? Had they seen Hamlet and taken it away for evidence?

Shit. Well, maybe not *shit.* Maybe it meant the police here *were* doing their jobs.

Jamie sighed, reaching out and taking Othello. If she remembered right – and it'd been a while – Othello committed suicide at the end of the play. And Hamlet contemplates it the entire time.

Jamie opened the play right to the back and began thumbing through the pages until she found the final monologue. She began to read, mouthing the words … 'Soft you; a word or two before you go … When you shall these unlucky deeds relate …' She sighed. Fucking Shakespeare. It made her head spin. Next part. 'I kiss'd thee ere I kill'd thee: no way but this; Killing myself, to die upon a kiss.'

'What is it?' Annika asked.

'I don't know,' Jamie said truthfully. But the last part was underlined. 'Killing myself, to die upon a kiss.'

'What does it mean?'

'I don't know,' Jamie repeated, the frustration apparent in her voice.

There was a knock at the door then and they both whipped around. A voice rang through the wood. 'I don't know who you are,' one of the girls said, 'but we called the police, and we'd like you to leave.' It was attempting to be assertive, but the tremble was plain to hear.

Annika gasped.

'That's our cue.' Jamie stuffed the play into her jacket and headed for the door, pulling Annika by the arm.

She went willingly and Jamie opened the door, not looking at the girl as she led the way across the landing and down towards the waiting, open door.

They stepped out, taking the steps quickly, and then zipped down the street. Jamie pushed Annika out in front, keeping her hand on the middle of her back, hurrying her until they were at least three hundred metres and three streets away.

Jamie slowed and Annika all but doubled over, breathing hard. Jesus, the girl could do with integrating more cardio into her daily routine.

'That was … close,' she managed to squeeze out.

'Mm,' Jamie said, pulling the play out and looking over it again.

As she did, Annika took it and twisted it in her hands.

'Hey,' Jamie said, trying to pull it free.

'Wait.' Annika forced herself to stand straight, cheeks red. 'This is a library copy.'

Jamie saw the spine now, the sticker there that denoted the fact. 'And if this is a library copy, then it means Hamlet was, too.' Jamie restrained a small smile. Maybe the police didn't get Hamlet after all.

'It could be there, if Juni returned it.'

Jamie checked her watch. It was getting into the evening now. 'I'll stop in on Monday.'

'Why? It's open now.'

'At six o'clock on a Saturday?' Jamie was a little surprised.

'Twenty-four-seven, except for Christmas Day and New Year's Day.'

'Really?'

Annika nodded. 'So, you want to go?' She grinned at Jamie. She had the hunger, Jamie could see it.

She deliberated. She should call Thorsen. Loop him in. But then again … he was probably having a good old catch up with *Sonja*. No, screw it. She was here to work, even if he wasn't. 'Yes,' Jamie said then. 'Lead the way.'

They kept a slightly slower pace heading back, but Visby was small and the university campus was smaller. The library there was spread across three floors, the first, second, and basement. As they approached, Annika took the lead, opening the glass doors and heading straight through to the main floor. There was a central space with several large, round tables. Jamie didn't know what she expected, but the place was empty.

'Exams finished up two weeks ago,' Annika said, keeping her voice quiet. 'Term isn't over, but everyone's just out partying all the time now. No more assignments,' she added, giving a sarcastic fist pump. 'Wooo.'

'You like it here?' Jamie asked, following Annika as she headed for one of the terminals at the side of the room so she could look up where Hamlet was hiding.

'University?' Annika asked. 'Sure.'

'Are you from Gotland?'

'Mhm,' Annika replied, scanning her student ID and loading up the search bar on the screen. She typed quickly.

'Are you third year?'

'Second.'

'And what do you want to do?'

She just shrugged.

'Why did you choose journalism?'

'I want to be an environmental writer.'

'And what does that entail?'

Annika turned to look at her. 'Writing about the environment.'

'I'm shocked.'

She lifted an eyebrow. 'Thought you were a detective.'

'I was being facetious.'

'So was I.'

Jamie sighed. 'You find it?'

'Basement.'

'Of course.' Jamie cast around. The place really was deserted. The tables were empty and clean, the corridors between the bookshelves devoid of movement. Even the help desk was empty. Jamie figured the librarian was probably off filing books away somewhere.

'This way,' Annika said, leading Jamie towards a sign that read *'Trappa'*. Stairs. 'So, what do you think it means?'

'What do I think what means?' Jamie asked, following Annika into the depths of the building.

Annika pushed through a wooden door into darkness. The motion-sensitive lights hummed then flickered to life, clicking one at a time as they drowned each stack of books in light. 'The hearts. On their arms.'

Jamie had considered this, but she was still careful with her answer.

Annika went to the end of a shelf and checked the code there, making her way deeper into the basement.

There was a strange smell in the air. Mildew. Old sweat. Old books. This place didn't seem well ventilated.

'I don't know,' Jamie answered.

Annika sighed. 'That seems like your answer to everything.'

'Everything I don't know.'

'So, what do you *think?*'

'If you go by the literal definition of the phrase, you'd get two results. A black heart is usually a disreputable person, someone with evil intentions.'

'Makes sense. Especially if it represents the person convincing teenagers to kill themselves. Ah, this one,' Annika said, finding the right stack and heading down.

Jamie paused, pricking her ears. The buzzing of the halogens and the weight of the building above her was making her ears ring. But for a moment, she swore there was something else.

'What's the second thing?' Annika asked, pulling ahead now.

Jamie continued after her. 'The second thing is an agricultural term – a blackheart, one word, is a term used to describe a plant, fruit, vegetable, that's rotting from the inside out.'

'That makes even more sense,' Annika called back.

'Does it?'

'Sure – looking fine on the outside, preparing to kill yourself on the inside. Sounds like Juni to me.'

Jamie was a little taken aback by the plainness of her speech. She seemed to be compartmentalising this extremely well considering Juni Pedersen had landed a few feet from her just days before. Or maybe she was just repressing that trauma, funnelling the pain into something else. Into this need to understand that she was harbouring. Which maybe wasn't the best thing. Jamie knew a little bit about repressed trauma. And about transference. About channelling it into something you think is a 'good' outlet. Sometimes it does more harm than good.

'Are you seeing someone?' she asked then.

'Like a boyfriend?' Annika asked, stopping and looking back.

'Like a counsellor.'

'Oh, no. Well, yeah, but she's shit. So …' Annika turned back to the books and kept searching for the one she wanted.

Jamie could see they were in the heart of the literature section. Thousands of dusty old copies split into their sub-genres. English gothic, American gothic, feminist first wave, modernist, contemporary … 'You should keep seeing her. Or find someone else.'

'Do you go to therapy?'

'No.'

'So, you can't exactly speak from a place of experience. And you've gone toe-to-toe with serial killers, what did you say, "more times than you'd care to remember"? And you seem pretty okay.'

Jamie sighed. 'If you say so.' She wasn't this girl's mother, or friend. It wasn't her place to try to convince her, regardless of how much she probably needed convincing.

'Hamlet,' Annika announced, stopping and crouching a little to see a row at navel height. 'Okay, five copies,' she said, grabbing the spines as a group and pulling them free. 'Here.'

She tossed three to Jamie and opened the first herself to the front cover.

'There's no list of names, it's all done electronically,' Annika said. 'So, we won't know which one Juni took out.'

Jamie fanned the three copies in front of her, her eyes homing in on the most beaten up one. The one that looked like it'd been read fifty times.

She opened that one, pausing as she did, the back of her neck coming up in gooseflesh. She turned quickly, the feeling of eyes heavy on her.

Nothing moved.

Jamie looked carefully, eyes roving down the shelves, to the gap at the far end of the stack.

'What's wrong?'

'Nothing,' Jamie said slowly.

In the distance, she heard the quiet creak of a door and then a soft thunk of it hitting the frame.

Probably nothing, she told herself. The librarian heading back to her desk. Probably.

Jamie shook it off and returned to the copy of Hamlet in her hands.

As soon as she opened it, she knew it was the right book.

The pages were dog-eared down, lines and sections were highlighted, and there were notes and doodles in the margin. Little daggers, skulls, eyes and teardrops, and, of course, black hearts.

'Holy shit,' Annika muttered, dropping her books and coming over. 'You found it.'

'Seems like,' Jamie muttered.

'Don't sound too excited.'

Jamie glanced up, saw her grinning. 'This isn't a game, Annika.'

Her smile faded. 'No, I know, I just meant … It's a clue, right, or what do you call it, a lead. Something. Something the cops missed. But you didn't.'

'It doesn't mean anything right now, not until we know more.'

'Jeez, way to burst a bubble.' Annika sighed, picking up the dropped copies, and stuffed them back onto the shelf. 'So why Hamlet?'

Jamie was already looking for that answer in the pages. She scanned quickly, leafing through, looking for the words that had been carved into Juni's desk. What dreams may come. It was pretty heavily outlined and circled, so it wasn't difficult to find. It was Hamlet's big monologue. To be, or not to be, that is the question. But what was the answer?

'To be, or not to be, that is the question. Whether 'tis nobler in the mind to suffer the slings and arrows of outrageous fortune, or to take arms against a sea of troubles, and by opposing end them. To die: to sleep; no more; and by a sleep to say we end the heartache and the thousand natural shocks that flesh is heir to, 'tis consummation doubly to be wish'd. To die, to sleep; to sleep: perchance to dream: ay, there's the rub; for in that sleep of death what dreams may come when we have shuffled off this mortal coil, must give us pause: there's the respect that makes calamity of so long life. For who would bear the whips and scorns of time … To grunt and sweat under a weary life, but that the dread of something after death … Be all my sins remember'd.'

'Well, fuck,' Annika muttered.

Jamie closed the book slowly.

'Guess that's pretty cut and dry. Now we know why she did it.'

'Hamlet doesn't make people kill themselves,' Jamie said.

'So why was Juni obsessed with it then?'

Jamie opened her mouth but before she could speak, Annika answered for her.

'*I don't know.* Yeah, you don't need to say it.' She let out a long sigh. 'Shakespeare, black hearts, suicide … It's all a bit fucked, right?'

Jamie remained silent. Just thinking.

About the book in front of her, the twenty-three kids lying in drawers in the morgue. And about that feeling, that weight that pressed on her. The weight of an unseen gaze. Of someone watching.

Was it nothing? Was she just being paranoid? Angst on account of being back at work?

God, she fucking hoped so.

6

Annika Olsen

JESUS, what the fuck was wrong with this lady?

Annika stared at Jamie Johansson as she looked into space over the top of the beaten-up copy of Hamlet that Juni Pedersen had scribbled her raving notes and doodles in. Black hearts. Black hearts. Everywhere. Why was this Jamie person resisting her own theories so hard? It sounded like she had it bang on. The black heart represented the evil person who forced Juni and the others to kill themselves. That much was obvious. Hmm, maybe this lady was one of those savants. She had something wrong with her, but she was a genius or something. She wasn't a detective anymore, after all. Maybe they fired her *because* she had something wrong with her.

When her phone started ringing, Annika jumped a mile.

Jamie pulled it from her pocket quickly and put it against her ear. 'Yeah?' she said into it.

Yeah? Who answers a phone 'Yeah?'.

'Right, sure. No, no, I'll be there in ten. Okay, great.' Jamie hung up as abruptly as she answered and then was pushing the copy of Hamlet into Annika's hands. 'Take this, check it out. Hold on to it. And keep it safe.'

'What?' Annika asked, the book forced into her grip. 'Why? Isn't it evidence? Shouldn't you take it?'

Jamie sighed, and Annika got the feeling that she was asking a stupid question. The answer confirmed that.

'It is evidence,' Jamie said. 'But I'm not a detective, and nor am I a student. So, I can't take this out of here. It'd be stealing evidence. But you can.'

'So, you want *me* to steal this piece of evidence?'

Jamie's eyebrow twitched. Another stupid question.

'Realistically, the police should already have it. But until I know what's going on with this case, it needs to stay safe. So, you just check it out as though you don't know what it is. Totally innocent. I'll come for it as soon as I can. Until then, I can trust you with it, can't I?'

'And why can't we just leave it here?' Annika asked.

Another eyebrow twitch. 'No. We don't leave things to chance. And …' Jamie glanced over her shoulder again. 'Just take it, and don't tell anyone you have it. Here.'

Jamie reached into her jacket pocket and produced a card, giving it to Annika.

'Kurrajakk Polis?' she read, tilting her head to make it out. 'I thought you weren't a detective anymore?'

'I'm not, but my number's still the same.'

'So, you just carry these around with you?'

'No.' She was practically talking through gritted teeth now. 'I just … brought some with me. I had spares. Look, it doesn't matter. Now, can I trust you with this, or not?'

Annika thought for a second. This Jamie person had come into her life like a whirlwind, and she'd got further in the investigation in an hour than Annika had in two full days. If she wanted any hope of seeing this through, and helping, then she figured this Jamie woman was the horse she'd be best off betting on. 'You can trust me.'

'Good.' Jamie reached out, hand hovering at Annika's shoulder as though she were going to squeeze it. But she didn't. Her hand just curled into a fist and retracted. 'I have to go,' Jamie said. 'Text me so I have your number.'

'I will.'

'Right now,' she added, staring right at Annika.

'Jeez, okay, one second,' she said, trying to fumble her phone from her pocket.

'I'll be touch,' Jamie said, and by the time Annika got her phone free and looked up, Jamie was already disappearing around the end of the stack.

'What do I do now?' Annika called, hitting send on the text.

'Whatever you want,' the words echoed back. 'Just don't do anything stupid!'

And then she was gone. As suddenly as she'd arrived.

'What the fuck?' Annika muttered, alone in the basement.

The door opened and then closed at the far end of the room, and suddenly, Annika felt very alone, the silence around her deafening.

'Okay then,' she said, looking around. 'Let's not get murdered in the creepy library basement, shall we? No, I think not.'

And then she started running. As unfit and immediately out of breath as she was.

She got to the top of the stairs, panting hard, and stepped out into the library's main room. Jamie was already gone. Damn she was fast. What was she, on springs?

Annika clutched Hamlet tightly, looking around. The

place was still empty, but there was a young woman behind the counter now, wearing headphones and bobbing along to a song as she sorted through some books in front of her.

Annika hadn't seen her before, but the lanyard around her neck said that she worked there, and her age told Annika she was probably a student.

As if she could feel Annika staring, she looked up. She had pale skin, a round face, with black hair. She was wearing a flannel shirt hanging off one shoulder. She lifted a hand and waved a little.

Annika waved back, then turned away and headed for the door. She'd intended to just take the book. That was the smartest option, wasn't it?

But she could feel the librarian's eyes on her as she approached the security gate, so instead she slowed and swiped the spine on the machine, flashing her student card against the reader to scan it out under her account.

She let out a shaky sigh and glanced back at the librarian, offering a brief smile and then holding the book up so she could see that Annika hadn't stolen it.

The librarian just sort of smiled and lifted her chin, like *congratulations, you can work a library scanner you fucking barnacle.*

Annika quickly stuffed the book into her jacket and headed out into the slowly fading sunshine. The warmth felt good on her skin. But the fear came quickly afterwards. She'd wanted to find out what had happened to Juni, and she'd succeeded in picking up the trail. Albeit with some help, but that was neither here nor there, really. Though despite the progress, she didn't feel excited. But rather scared at the prospect. In her mind, she'd wanted to find out why Juni had taken her own life. What had driven her to it?

But this Jamie person seemed to think it was a *who,* not a

what. And what had she said …? Someone who was moving unseen, someone who was able to get at all of these kids individually. Physically. Annika had been operating under the theory of some online circle they were all involved in. If you were to plumb the depths of the internet, dodgy chatrooms and forums were a dime a dozen. She'd figured that it was some online group glorifying, fetishizing death in some way. But the reality that Jamie had pointed out was much, much darker.

And now here she was, suddenly, in the midst of it. And if she held the key to it against her ribs, was she in danger? Jamie had said this person wanted to remain anonymous. This was self-gratifying. And if that was the case, then they'd want to keep doing it, wouldn't they? And if they wanted to keep doing it, then if anyone was to get close to stopping them, well, they'd become a person that needed to be … dealt with.

And if Annika was holding the clue that could lead to this person …

She shuddered, zipped up her jacket despite the palpable heat in the air, and then started walking.

Her apartment wasn't too far off campus, though it was only a two-bedroom that she shared with one other girl. A girl who'd now gone home to Denmark for the summer already. Which meant she'd be alone … Fuck.

How hard was it to get a gun in Sweden?

Nnngh, don't be stupid, Annika. Don't give yourself anxiety. Hmph! If you don't give yourself anxiety, who does? Now's not the time to be clever. Especially not with yourself you … you … fucking barnacle. Now, go home. Go home and think.

And for fuck's sake, lock the bloody door!

She didn't sleep well, surprisingly. The apartment was small and modern, and there were two locked doors between her and the outside world. The front door to the building was equipped with a heavy-duty code lock and the door itself was some sort of weird-ass composite material that looked and felt like it'd withstand a battering ram. And her front door was solid wood, too. Still, she'd Googled how to reinforce a door, and had ended up wedging a crutch she'd found in the cupboard – likely from a previous tenant, she guessed – up under the handle. But despite that, and locking all the windows, and keeping all the lights off so that from the outside it looked like no one was even home, she still woke up to every creak, knock, rustle, or general disturbance that occurred within a mile of the place, it felt like.

By six, the sun was already up and bright and Annika was rolling from bed, the copy of Hamlet that was the root of all her problems sitting on the bedside table.

It was Sunday, and it felt like there was little to be done. She had a gnawing anxiety at the back of her head, a little tightness in her chest that made it feel like she couldn't quite fully catch her breath.

She had no intention of leaving – or of removing the crutch – so she resigned herself to a day of reading instead. Jamie was a good detective, smart, focused, capable. She wasn't the type to be afraid of anything. And she'd even taken on serial killers and come out the other side unscathed. Now that was a person to aspire to be like, Annika thought. Though aspirations didn't always equate with what was attainable. Or even realistic.

Annika hadn't lied when she'd said she wanted to be an environmental writer. Journalism seemed like the obvious course to take, though she had no intention of really being an investigative journalist, heading off to war zones, or stowing away on whaling ships and oil tankers to get the real 'scoop'. No, she envisioned her time as a writer transpiring in front of a window, looking out over a calm vista, her research done online, her job done remotely from wherever she ended up. Though she wasn't sure where that was going to be. Hell, she couldn't even decide where she wanted to go for university. She was from Gotland, from a little town in the south. Her parents had encouraged her to go to the mainland to study at least, but she'd been indecisive. Her grades had her accepted for half a dozen places, but she'd eventually settled on Gotland because it was less than an hour to home, and by fuck, did she hate doing laundry. Having mum nearby was an easy solution to that.

Though that was a paltry excuse and she knew it. The reality was that she was scared. She knew Visby well, and home was only ever a bus ride away. While her friends had gone off to explore the world, she'd confined herself here, to small, quiet, safe Gotland.

Except it wasn't safe anymore. The world frightened her, and honestly, she figured she'd have got out of university, found a job online working remotely, and either rented a place in the city, or more likely rented a place in her home town. Her parents knew everyone, and though options were limited it wouldn't be tough to find *somewhere*. And it wasn't like anywhere was far away.

Things had become strange and fast, though. When Juni had hit the ground next to her, it had filled her with something. A sort of rage. A sort of anger. A sort of … she didn't know what. But what she did know was that she needed to understand it. She needed to understand what could drive twenty-three kids to take their lives in a place like Gotland. There was something dark going on in the place she knew and loved. And it felt wrong, it felt unnatural. And she wanted to know why.

She had always been a curious person. She'd always

enjoyed learning, enjoyed knowing things. She liked puzzles, she liked games. But all of a sudden, this didn't feel like either. And she couldn't help but feel like that copy of Hamlet was going to be a lightning rod for trouble.

Fuck. What was she even doing? Camping out by Juni's … spot, just waiting. For what? For her fear and anxiety to get the better of her once again. For her mind to reckon with what had happened and put her off this stupid notion of trying to figure out what had gone through Juni's head in the days leading up to that moment.

And then this Jamie person had come out of nowhere and, more than anything, had held up a mirror for her to see herself. As this insignificant, terrified little minnow, suddenly caught up in the riptide of something much larger than she ever imagined.

Well, she knew how to get out of a riptide. You don't grow up on the water without knowing that much. You don't swim with it, and you don't swim against it. You swim sideways, and you get clear.

And that's just what she'd do.

She'd get out of this, hand over this book to Jamie and wash her hands of the whole thing. But what would Jamie think if Annika did that? She'd think she was a coward, for sure. And she was, right? It was cowardly to just shy away from this when kids were being targeted. When peers were being approached, groomed, convinced to kill themselves. Her father was a Christian, her house a church-going household. And her father would say, all that it takes for evil to succeed is for good people to stand by and do nothing. Was this her standing by and doing nothing?

So, she'd at least need to give Jamie … something. Maybe she could be her guy in the chair. Every hero had a guy in the chair, right? Someone who stayed back at the headquarters, where it was safe, and did the Googling. And she was a ferocious Googler, she'd give herself that much.

It was decided then. She'd leave the crutch where it was, offload the book as quickly as she could, and provide Jamie with all the information she needed to find whoever was behind this. And Annika could share in the satisfaction of that, she could keep the promise she made to herself and Juni to find out why this was happening, and she could, most importantly, stay well out of the firing line.

She smiled to herself as she opened her laptop and sat down behind it, fingers hovering over the keys, cursor blinking in the search bar.

The only question was, where the fuck was she supposed to start?

Her aforementioned curiosity got the better of her, and with nothing else coming to mind, she searched for Jamie Johansson, the mystery woman who had stormed into her life and got her all caught up in this thing. The results reminded her that this wasn't someone to be underestimated. There was an actually surprising amount about her online, despite there being no social media profiles — no Facebook, Instagram, nothing. And Annika didn't trust anyone who didn't have social media. What was she trying to hide? Or hide from?

Despite that, the articles covering her cases did outline who she was. And that was someone who would stop at nothing to solve this case.

And if Annika did expect to be of help in this case, which she figured would prevent her from feeling like a *total* piece of shit, then she needed to do some real digging and figure out something that'd give her an edge.

She began leafing through Hamlet, noticing all the lines

and passages underlined and circled. Nothing happy, she discovered. Some looking around online revealed the major themes of the play – mortality, revenge, madness, religion. All pretty miserable shit, honestly.

She doubted reading the thing was going to give her any insights into what had driven Juni to jump either.

But … something struck her. There was a lot of Shakespeare in her room.

It didn't take Annika long to find the reading list for her course. A few more clicks revealed the assignment schedules. One caught her eye immediately. *Explore the intrinsic relationship between life and death in Hamlet, Othello, or Romeo and Juliet.*

The assignment was turned in a month ago.

Annika's heart beat a little harder.

She found the name of the lecturer, licking her lips. If Juni had written about Hamlet, then maybe her essay would give them some insight into her mind, perhaps reveal another clue, or at least something to reframe their investigation!

Yes. This was good. She pulled out her phone, texted Jamie immediately. 'Found out Juni submitted an assignment on Hamlet last month. Lecturer's name Dennis Lagerström. Office G201. Office hours tomorrow 2-4pm.'

She hit send and waited. If Jamie could get in there, see him, speak to him, find out what he knew, then that could shed some light on—

She texted back!

'Great. Let me know what you find out.'

Annika's heart sank.

Let Jamie know what she found out?

Her mouth was dry all of a sudden. Did she think Annika was going to go there and speak to him?

Her thumbs trembled above the screen. 'No, not me. I can't, I …'

Am scared? Am afraid to leave my apartment? Am too chickenshit to even sit in the living room, and right now I'm sitting in my bedroom with the door shut?

She hit the delete key until the message was empty, and then locked her phone.

'Fuck,' she muttered, leaning her head forward and putting it on the surface of the desk. 'If I get killed, I'm going to be so pissed.' She raised her head then, pushing her long fringe from her eyes. 'You won't get killed, Anni, don't worry. You'll just be fucking coerced into killing yourself!'

She almost yelled the last part, the words echoing and dying in the room.

There was a thud from beyond her door then and she jumped up so fast that she knocked her chair over.

'I've … I've got a gun!' she yelled at the wood now, frantically looking around for anything she could use as a weapon.

MacBook. Aluminium, sharp corners! Yes. She picked it up. Actually … 23,000kr … and a Christmas present from mum and dad … maybe not.

What else? Scissors? No, don't have them. Fuck. Uh … Drawer. Papers, bullshit! Stapler, yes!

She snatched it up, heart thundering, and walked towards her bedroom door.

With a shaking hand, she reached out for the handle. It was slick in her grip on account of her sweaty palm.

She listened intently, exhaled hard, then pulled it wide, exposing nothing but an empty living room, the fading sound of voices in the corridor, heels on stairs filtering back to her. Other students, heading out.

'Crap,' she mumbled, collapsing to her knees, breathing hard.

She popped a few staples out of the stapler and onto the floor.

'Pap. Pap. Pap,' she muttered. 'Maybe I shouldn't have a gun after all. I might actually be liable to shoot someone.' She looked around the empty apartment. 'Or, more likely. No one. Because you're alone, Annika … you … you fucking barnacle.'

Annika's Monday classes dragged. There was a lecture on best ethics practices when citing and referencing sources, and then a seminar on unbiased reporting. But eventually, they were dispensed with – though Annika made zero notes and didn't participate at all in the group discussion. Instead, she just chewed her fingers and bounced her knee under the table, her heart beating at least one and a half times its normal rate.

But despite that, two o'clock finally arrived, and Annika wasted no time heading for Lagerström's office. She knew where it was and how to get there. It was the only thing she'd done for the last four hours. That, and practise what she was going to say in her head. Though, despite all that, when she reached his office at 1:57pm, she forgot it all.

Before she'd even caught her breath, she knocked on the frame.

Lagerström was maybe sixty, with wavy grey hair and a lined face. He had square glasses on that magnified his green eyes slightly. He looked up from the papers he was reading, and though Annika wasn't in any of his classes and hadn't ever seen him before, he smiled and greeted her.

'Oh, hello again,' he said, a little hurriedly. His smile wavered. Though office hours were specifically for drop-ins, she thought every teacher probably hated them and secretly hoped no one would in fact 'drop-in'.

'Hi,' Annika said, suddenly drawing a blank. She just stood in the doorway. 'Uh …' she managed, after three full seconds of silence.

'Do you want to come in …?' Lagerström asked, sitting back a little and looking around. 'I'm rather busy, so …'

'Yes, yes,' Annika said quickly, entering and closing the door. She took the seat in front of the desk, a big, old wooden thing. He had a window behind him, and to the sides of it, on a pair of shelves were old books, first editions and other prized possessions that framed him as a man and an educator.

'So, what can I do for you?' he asked, not even thinking for a moment that Annika wasn't in any of his classes.

'I, um …' She stalled. She had her satchel on her lap and squeezed it nervously, felt the spine of the book there. 'Hamlet!' she almost yelled.

His eyes widened a little in surprise. 'What about him?'

'The play, I meant.'

'Named for the titular character. Did you just want to yell it at me, or did you have a question?' He tapped the pen in his hand against the desk. It clicked impatiently.

'I'm reading it,' Annika said.

'I should hope that's re-reading. It was on the autumn reading list.' He narrowed his eyes a little.

'Of course,' she laughed, not even convinced of its authenticity herself. 'I just meant that I'm reading it now, but I noticed some notes in the margins of my copy. I think I know who made them, and I wanted to ask you about it …'

He just waited for her to continue, obviously disinterested by this particular conversation.

'It was Juni Pedersen.'

He just continued to sit there, staring at her.

'The girl who … died. Last week?'

His eyebrows raised suddenly. 'Oh, gosh, yes, yes, of course. Julie—'

'Juni.'

'—right, right, terrible, terrible thing. Just awful. Wonderful girl. Fantastic student.'

'Yeah …' Annika said, squirming a little. This guy didn't have a fucking clue who she was, or who Juni was. 'Well, anyway, I just wanted to know whether or not she wrote an assignment on Hamlet? We were supposed to write an essay and—'

'Let me stop you there,' Lagerström said. 'I can't discuss the work of another student with you …' He sort of trailed off as though waiting for Annika to drop her name.

She declined to do so.

He went on. 'But even if I could, I wouldn't be able to say much about it. My PhD students handle the reading and marking of most of the assignments, while I supervise. It gives them a real opportunity to understand what it means to take on the role of a professor at a university, to really get to grips with the position and all the responsibility it entails.'

Annika's eyes went from his to the papers in front of him. They weren't assignments at all, as she'd expected. She didn't know what they were, but they didn't look academic, or anything to do with literature. She stared at the words for a few seconds, trying to make sense of them. She managed to make out '… he ran his hands up her stomach and then he roughly inserted his engorged …' before Lagerström adjusted his position to cover the paper with his arm.

'Is that all?' he asked then, a little sterner.

Whether he was working on an erotic novel or just enjoying one in his free time, Annika didn't know. But either way, something occurred to her suddenly.

'Who would have read and marked Juni's assignment?'

'I can't really …'

'Is that an assignment there?' She nodded at the paper under his arm.

He cleared his throat loudly, reddening a little. 'Yes, it is.'

'You're marking that one yourself?'

'Yes, I am,' he said confidently.

'Is it good?' she asked, 'or is it a little *rough?*'

'I'm sorry?'

'Do you get forward notice before work lands on your desk, or is it just sort of *thrust* upon you?'

His mouth opened a little, unsure what to make of her statement.

'I just want to know who would have marked her essay? And then I'm gone. Just tell me their name and—'

'Öberg. Alex Öberg,' he interrupted, almost hunched over the desk covering the paper.

'And where would I find—'

'Room 302. He's taking a second-year seminar. Now please, I have lots to do.'

Annika got up, gave him a brief nod, and headed out. 'I'll just close the door, shall I?'

'Please.'

'Thank you.'

He just grumbled, then the door clapped shut and Annika was in the hallway. There was another girl waiting out there, a notebook in her arms.

'I'd, uh, maybe give him a few minutes,' Annika warned the girl. 'And then knock before you go in. He's sort of in the middle of something. Seems like his work is really *getting on top of him.*'

The girl looked at Annika quizzically. 'Why is that funny?'

Annika's grin faded. 'It's not, it's just … never mind. Just, you know … knock, alright?'

Room 302 was on the top floor of the next building over. It was one of eight seminar rooms on the floor, large and low-ceilinged, with desks arranged in long rows in front of a stained whiteboard.

An older man was standing at the front. He had wispy white hair and was writing on the board in a great big scrawl. From her position peeking through the window in the door she could see that he was walking the PhD students through the process for defending their thesis – something they'd all have to do once it'd been marked. Get up there and talk about it, answer questions for the panel of professors who'd then decide if they'd done enough to be called doctor.

The online booking software for the university told Annika that the room was booked up until 3pm, which is the time she figured this class got out. It was two-fifty now, so she expected that they'd wrap up any time.

She pulled out her phone and started typing a text to Jamie. 'Found the PhD student who marked Juni's assignment – Alex Öberg. Keep you posted.' She hit send and pocketed her phone, going back to the window.

Seven students sat at the tables, but which one was Alex Öberg?

It didn't take her long to Facebook the shit out of him, find out that he was a tall, lanky guy with thick brown curls and doe eyes. She didn't really have a type, but he was kind of cute, she figured.

Though she still hadn't quite worked out how exactly to broach this subject. On the cusp of getting their marks back and prepping to defend their work, she doubted that Alex would be prepared to do anything to jeopardise his position, and she figured divulging information about the assignment of a recently deceased student to another student would probably violate some rule or other.

Which meant she'd either need to extract the information by *force*, or more likely, considering her small stature and weak constitution, by deception. Though she didn't know how deceiving she could really be.

But before she could even really make a decision one way or the other, the door in front of her was opening and students were pouring out.

She panicked.

Alex was among them.

Shit!

She wasn't prepared for this.

Annika turned quickly, running towards the end of the corridor as quickly as she could. There was a door, she just needed to get past it and hopefully Alex wouldn't see her. Her hands stretched out, touched wood, pushed, then stopped.

Before she could even realise it was a pull not a push, her forehead was rebounding off the surface.

There was a loud crack, she didn't know what from – her skull, the door? She hoped the latter.

Annika bounced backwards, yelled 'Fuck!' way more loudly than was appropriate, and then hit the ground, letting out another sound that wasn't a word, but more like what you'd get if you stood on a frog, she guessed.

She blinked, tried to get clear, but the lights were swimming in figure eights over her head.

'Fuck balls,' she groaned, screwing her eyes shut and touching her hand to her head. It wasn't cut but she could feel the welt, the sore spot. 'Dildos,' she hissed, cursing herself.

'Excuse me?'

She opened her eyes, saw dark curls above her, doe eyes.

Alex Öberg.

Dildos, indeed. Big ones.

She tried to sit up but his hands were on her shoulders keeping her down.

'Are you alright?' he asked.

She nodded, suddenly at a loss for words.

'You know you screamed the word 'fuck' and then 'dildos', right?' He grinned down at her. 'Might be a sign of a concussion.'

'I'm pretty sure there was a *fuck balls* in there, too,' she muttered, now allowed to sit up.

He helped her, and when she looked around she saw two other students were standing over her, looking down at the girl who'd just run headlong into a pull door.

'I'm fine, seriously,' Annika said, waving them off. She could see her shame reflected in their eyes.

'It's okay, guys,' Alex said, one hand still on Annika's back. 'I'll catch up.'

The other two students dispersed, leaving Annika with Alex. She tried to get up, but he stopped her. 'Woah, take your time.'

'I'd like to get up, please,' she said. 'It's bad enough I wanged my head, I'd rather not sit on a dirty floor too.'

He smiled a little, helping her. 'You, uh, have a way with words, you know that?'

She offered a brief smile back, trying to organise her thoughts. This wasn't exactly the plan she had in mind.

Alex let go of her arm then, stooping down.

Annika's satchel was on the carpet, the flap open, the contents spilled out. Her laptop, a few pens, a notepad, and Hamlet.

He seemed to forget all about Annika as he picked the book up, completely overlooking the rest.

Annika watched him carefully as he cradled it in his hands as though it were about to shatter into a million pieces. He looked up at her slowly, breathing harder. She could see his pulse had quickened in his neck, his eyes wide, mad even, his lips slightly parted, wet with saliva, shining in the harsh white light above.

'Where did you get this?' he asked, voice strained, barely above a whisper.

There was no doubt in her mind that he recognised not only the book, but that exact copy.

Her blood ran cold, her mouth opening as she tried to form words.

But try as she did, none came.

7

Lucas Adell

THE MORNING SUN was beating down on Fårösund. Despite it being no later than nine, it was already hot, and Lucas Adell knew that it was going to be one of those fierce, unrelenting days. It was doing nothing to help his mood.

After a 24-hour hold, he was finally free. The polisintendent, Linus Lundström, and his konstapel, the ever-idiotic Blom, had put him in cuffs and dragged him down to the station following what they termed his 'unsettling outburst' at the house. If they thought that was unsettling, they had another thing coming.

He was exhausted, fuelled by nothing but rage at this point. Though it was a long walk home. When they'd come back to his front door, they'd been in force. As much force as the Fårösund police could muster, at least. All three cars. All six officers. They'd knocked on his door, come inside without warning, dragged him to his feet, shoved his face against the table and cuffed him. All while Lundström watched, hands on hips like the old saggy prick that he was. With his tufty white hair, long nose, small mouth beset with lines. Once they had Adell in the station, Lundström had him put straight into an interrogation room and started asking questions he didn't have the answers to.

Where is your wife?

Where is Marie?

Did you do something to her?

Do you know where she is?

Why would she leave?

Did you kill her?

Did he fucking kill her?

Who the fuck did Lundström think he was? His wife had … she had …

He slowed, wavering, feeling ill. He looked right, catching his reflection in the window of a shop that sold knitting supplies. The large glass panel revealed a dark interior. Closed. It was Sunday.

He saw himself, gaunt, skin pale, dressed in an oversized hoodie splattered with paint, and jeans that he'd not worn in years. They'd just grabbed whatever from his wardrobe and forced him to dress at the station. When they brought him in, he was still just in a towel.

Lucas Adell didn't recognise himself in that moment. He was alone, frightened, angry. No, that didn't even begin to cover it. He was furious. At Lundström, at his wife. Marie! How could she do this? How could she just …

His knees shook, a little at first, then violently. And then they buckled altogether and Lucas Adell sank to the floor, shuddering, convulsing, retching, sobbing. His fingernails scraped at the pavement as his hands curled into fists, tears streaming down his cheeks.

Marie.

Marie. How could you do this? How could you just leave me like this?

Had she really just slipped from bed, walked through the door and out into the ocean? God damn it! He missed Rebecca too! He was just as distraught as her, but how could she abandon him, and abandon her, too! They promised they wouldn't give up hope, that they'd find her. But … but now …

Lucas flattened his hands on the ground and forced himself to his knees, the concrete splattered with his tears.

And, what, the police suspected him? Thought that he'd … killed her? Those pricks. Those absolute fucking pricks! Lundström the worst of them. He always hated Lucas, he knew that much. But to accuse him of killing his own wife? He was an idiot. Worse. He was a reckless, feckless, self-assured idiot. And they were the most dangerous of all.

No, they couldn't be trusted, or relied upon. They weren't interested in finding Rebecca or Marie, just in targeting him with some sort of vendetta.

If he was going to find the truth, he'd do it himself. Fuck Lundström. He'd find out what happened to Rebecca himself. Yes. Yes, he would. He was smart. Smarter than Lundström. And if that idiot could keep himself as the head of the Sudersand police for so many years, then it could hardly be a big ask.

And hell, Fårösund was so small, there was no way Rebecca could escape the island without someone seeing her. The ferry was the only way across to the mainland. And sure, Lundström had checked the security footage, but that only showed the cars and people going across. And none of them were searched. What if Rebecca was in the back seat, or … or the boot. Jesus. The thought made his mouth salivate like he was about to throw up. He exhaled the nausea away and pushed forward, forcing his feet to move. He needed to get home. He'd start with the ferry. He doubted that the system would be hard to crack. He could pull the security footage directly from there, then scour it for anything out of the ordinary, and then make a move from there.

It was a short walk to the ferry. When he arrived, three other people were waiting for it to return from the far side, along with a single car. There was no security shack or anything, just the boat itself.

The back of Lucas' neck began to prickle with the heat of the sun, so despite the rising temperature, he pulled the hood of his hoodie up over his head. The three others, a family, looked back at him, angry, sweat beading on his forehead. The mother cupped her hand around the boy's head. He was probably eleven. She steered his gaze towards the water and looked away herself. The husband looked on for a moment more, then turned out his bottom lip and faced front.

Who knew what they thought.

Who cared?

Not Lucas Adell.

When the ferry arrived, the family boarded quickly, and then Lucas did too.

The captain was standing in a little raised cockpit in the middle of the ferry – big enough for maybe 30 cars – looking forward. There were windows facing front and back, and the ferry would drive in both directions. All he needed to do was swivel his chair. Right now, he had his back to Lucas. Perfect.

There was a small office on his end of the boat that had the word '*Säkerhet*' on the door. Security.

Lucas hovered near it until the engines flared and the ferry pulled away, and then he knocked. He'd only have a few minutes until it docked on the other side and the captain turned back around. He'd need to act quickly.

A thin man with a thick moustache answered. He looked at Lucas in mild shock. He did look like shit after all.

'Someone shit in the toilet,' Lucas said flatly. 'All over the floor and walls. Thought you'd want to know. It's disgusting.'

The guy hung his head, sighing loudly. *'Helvete!'* he hissed. 'Thank you for letting me know.'

Lucas stepped back and he left the room at speed, striding across the steel and concrete deck towards the sign for the bathrooms. The door began to swing shut but just before it did, he shoved his foot in the gap. The heavy, sprung metal slab banged against it, sending a bolt of pain through his ankle.

He ignored it and dived in.

The room was basically a closet with a hinged window. It was stuffy in there, but the window was wide open and a sea breeze was drifting in, along with the cawing of the gulls that plagued the island. A small metal desk held an old computer — twenty years old. Lucas sighed, identifying the OS immediately. He'd not worked on XP since he didn't know when. But he still remembered and his fingers moved lightning fast.

He minimised the windows onscreen with a few keys — a program that was showing the security feeds from the front and back, as well as one monitoring the engine and hydraulic pressures as the ferry ran.

He held down the button combination to launch the console window and then typed the command to fetch the IP address. It appeared instantly and he dug further, pulling up the address for the router admin screen.

He launched the browser, distinctly aware of time ticking away, and hit the login portal. It required a password. Lucas knew the brand. Knew the age of this equipment. It all came with standard passwords until changed — and back then, they weren't complicated, randomly generated strings. They were either … 1234. Nope. Shit. Or … ADMIN.

The screen went white, then loaded the router administration page. Easy. Okay. Local network settings. Sharing settings. His eyes flitted, fingers moving quickly. Where is it. Where is it … There. Remote access. Enable. Okay, last thing. Wi-Fi password. Jesus this thing is slow. Where is it … his eyes scanned the information on screen. There. Modify. He hit the zero key four times, then enter. Saved. Yes!

Noise outside. Footsteps. Keys jangling.

The guard.

Damn it. No time to get out. He was trapped.

Without looking, his fingers splayed across the keyboard. 'Alt' and 'F4' closed the console and browser window, leaving the desktop blank.

Now what?

The waves sloshed against the side of the ferry and Lucas' head turned, just as the key scratched its way into the lock.

Only option.

He got to his feet quickly, turned, foot on the chair, and dived out of the window.

The metal frame scraped his stomach, knocked his knees, clipped his toes and sent him tumbling through the air.

He hit the water upside down, feeling the pull and churn of the ferry's engines, the propellor noise deafening.

Where he was, he didn't know.

He swam. Down, he thought. Gotta get clear.

It wailed above him, spinning and dragging him through the water. Visions of the propellors mincing him like ground beef flashed in his mind.

His arms pumped, legs thrashing, lungs burning.

And then the noise was receding.

He forced his eyes open, seeing the glimmer of the surface under his left arm. Lucas reoriented himself, clothes heavy, and began to swim towards the surface. The ferry thundered away ahead and would be heading back soon. He needed to get clear, out of sight. Swim to shore. Once he got home, he could get his laptop, come back once the ferry closed for the night, and get into the security system via the remote access he just enabled. It would be child's play. So long as he didn't get run over first.

He was a strong swimmer, though. You didn't live on the beach without being a strong swimmer.

Once he broke the surface, he caught his breath and then fell into a steady breaststroke, his hoodie heavy and wet. Though he had nothing underneath, so couldn't ditch it because it was a long way back to Sudersand and he had little hope of getting a taxi from the ferry landing without a shirt on.

Lucas swam sideways until he thought he was far enough from the crossing not to draw attention, and then headed for the northern shore. The coastline was quiet, so it wasn't hard to slip out over the rocky beach and up into the trees. Even over the course of the 500m walk from the water's edge back to the crossing, he dried out a reasonable amount, though by the time he arrived, his hoodie was more than damp and his boots were still squelching.

It seemed his phone got the worst of it, though. They'd given it back to him at the station, but after that swim he doubted that it'd be something a bag of rice could fix. It was truly dead. IP68 my arse. Though he'd see what he could do once he was back at home. Stranger things had happened.

The first driver he encountered wasn't interested in a soaking wet, moneyless paint-splattered stranger. But the second driver was convinced by the promise of a 500kr tip. Lucas' address probably helped, too. Sudersand didn't have many houses, but the ones it did have weren't hovels by any stretch.

Lucas seemed to zone out as they drove, because the ride was over almost in a blink. The driver waited while he went inside, letting himself in with the spare key hidden by the door. He returned promptly with the money and sent the grinning driver on his way.

He was tired, but his anger hadn't faded. Lundström's face burned brightly in his mind, sitting just behind his eyes. It focused him, filled him.

Time to get to work.

He showered first. Then he shaved, cleaned himself slowly and meticulously, rolling over the last 24 hours in his mind. From the moment he'd woken to discover Marie gone, right up until now. The ferry wouldn't close until the evening, and he couldn't risk going back there in the daylight to do it. At least at night he could park up near enough to the boat to get the Wi-Fi signal and then hack in from there. For now, there were other things that demanded his attention.

The police had launched a cursory investigation in to Rebecca's disappearance, but it seemed like they'd given up so quickly. And Lucas wasn't blind. He knew that Gotland was being plagued by a spate of other teenage suicides and disappearances. That someone out there was targeting teens. And, sure, Rebecca's disappearance pre-dated the first body, but … he couldn't help but feel there was some sort of connection. That the two things couldn't *not* be related.

Lucas dried himself off and exited the bathroom, walking towards the wardrobe. He opened it and let his eyes move slowly across the clothing there. His wife's clothing. All her summer clothes. Her beautiful summer dresses and camisoles, the silk scarves and sarongs she used to wear as they walked along the beach. He ran his hands over them, felt a strange longing for her, for her body. To be next to her, to smell her skin and feel her hair against his face. Anger rose in him and his fingers clenched into the fabric, the hangers straining at the rails. But then it faded, as quickly as it came, exiting his body through his flesh as a great shudder rose through him. Cold. He felt cold, suddenly.

The hair on the back of his neck prickled, a voice whispering to him from over his shoulder. 'Lucas' it said.

He whirled around, leaving his wife's clothes swinging on the rail, rumpled from his grip.

There was no one there. But his wife's voice seemed to linger in his ears. The echo of his name dying in the empty room around him.

He breathed slowly, flexing his hands. They hurt from being balled so hard.

Marie was … gone. He swallowed. He knew what had happened to her. She'd left him. She'd taken the easy way out. But he wouldn't do that. He wouldn't give in. He'd keep his promise. He'd find Rebecca.

Before he could finish the thought, he was in her room.

Pink.

She was fifteen, but she still liked pink. He'd painted it for her. The bed was covered in flowers, the handmade wooden headboard decorated with stickers of the things she loved. My Little Pony and other stuff that girls liked. She was fifteen, sure, but she still had her innocence. That was something Lucas always loved about her. The walls were decorated with posters of boy bands and other teenage heartthrobs. There was a Sean something and a Harry someone he thought, but beyond that, he couldn't be sure.

His eyes drifted around the time capsule, untouched for

over a year, and came to settle on the laptop on her desk. A MacBook Air. He'd bought it for her to show that he trusted her. It went both ways. She could have social media and unfettered access to the internet so long as she agreed to a no passwords policy. Lucas was in tech, he knew full well the dangers facing teens online these days and how social media was toxic. But he wasn't unreasonable, or cruel. He let his daughter use Facebook, Instagram, Twitter ... but he had access. He didn't think that was unfair? And neither did Rebecca. In fact, he never actually even checked her online activity. He trusted her — implicitly. They had a good relationship like that, one of mutual respect.

But now ... he had no choice. He'd always been a little afraid of what he'd find. That his daughter's innocence would be stripped from his mind if he dived into her online life. But that was a better alternative than not having her home safely.

He approached slowly at first, and then sat decisively and peeled open the screen. It lit up with a small animated picture of a bird. A robin. He smiled. He'd always called her his little robin because as a child she had a big red puffer jacket that made her look like a robin red breast. His smile faded as quickly as it came, the hole in his heart aching.

He steadied his shaking jaw and clicked the picture, taking him to her desktop screen. No password, as agreed.

It wasn't hard to get to her social pages. They were all bookmarked on her search bar. Facebook. Twitter. Instagram. He opened them all and began scrolling down her feeds. Untouched for a year. Photos of friends grinned back at him. Nothing of any significance. All people he knew. Katie. Inger. Sara. He knew these girls. There were no boys, thank goodness. He didn't think he could have taken that. Though he knew it was coming eventually. Or at least ... would have been. He swallowed the sadness and kept going. Messages.

Only a few. Friends, a few school friends that weren't regular friends. Sharing random posts, or tagging her in things. He moved quickly, looking at everything, but seeing nothing that gave him any inkling as to where to go next.

But just before he closed the tabs and logged out, he slowed, remembering something. The night Rebecca disappeared, she was going to meet one of her girlfriends. That's what she said at least. Which one … Katie? No, Sara, he thought. Yes, he was sure.

He navigated to Rebecca's iCloud, synched to her phone, and began digging through her messages. Nothing. Barely any messages at all. Just innocuous stuff with the girls. Sara more than the others. But not enough to give him anything to go on. Not even confirmation that they were meeting that night. Damn. And the police said that, too. That they questioned Sara, but she said she hadn't heard from Rebecca. He'd wanted to speak to her himself, but they'd prevented him from doing so. Lundström had prevented him from doing so, that white-haired fuck!

Lucas' fist rebounded off the desk next to him and Rebecca's laptop screen waved a little.

He exhaled the anger away and swallowed, shaking his head to regain focus.

He was heading out this evening anyway.

He'd go to Sara's house.

That way he could be sure.

Lucas glanced up at the wall, the clock there. It was the afternoon. He should eat before tonight. He'd not eaten in more than twenty-four hours.

But strangely, he wasn't even hungry.

Night fell quickly. The sun hung in the sky forever, then painted it pink from beyond the horizon for what seemed like an age. And then the sky sank to black all at once.

Lucas Adell watched from the rail outside his bedroom, eyes fixed on the ocean, just in case.

In the whisper of the wind, he thought he could still hear her voice. Mouthing his name into his ear. Lucas ... Lucas. He shook himself from what felt like a fugue state, realising it was now dark. He must have watched the sunset but couldn't remember it. He'd not eaten in a while, hadn't slept barely at all. But how could he at a time like this?

He steadied himself on the rail and gazed at the brightening stars. An unsteadiness overcame him, the sound of a sharp inhale reverberating from behind him.

Lucas turned quickly, his mind stuttering, as though he turned and an instant later turned again, outside himself for just a moment.

There was no one there, but the feeling of someone at his shoulder was unmistakable.

He steeled himself.

'Don't lose your mind now, Lucas,' he said, clearing his throat and shaking his head. Once, sharply, to cast out those thoughts.

'Keys.' He strode through the open bedroom door, not bothering to close it. He didn't really care anymore. The car keys were on the hook, where they should be, and he snatched them up, along with his work satchel, heading out the front towards his car.

He unplugged it from the charger and climbed in, the blindly bright headlamps coming to life and throwing a shadowless brilliance across what was once a family home, now just a monument to the shattered pieces of his life.

The car jetted backwards into the road, the gravel of the driveway crunching under the wheels, and then Lucas accelerated down the road with a squeal of the tyres. Sara's house was across the water, so it would be two birds with one stone.

He had his laptop with him, so he'd be able to get into the ferry system during the crossing and download the security recordings on the ride. He'd review them tonight after speaking to Sara.

The drive to the ferry was dispensed with far quicker than the taxi driver had done earlier that day and, luckily, it was there and waiting by the time he arrived.

He rolled on behind a big SUV and put the car in park. Before the barriers had even been closed behind him, his laptop was out and he was scanning for the Wi-Fi. He found the network he'd reprogrammed earlier and accessed it quickly, then went straight to the network administration page and into the devices list. Before the ferry had even left the shore, he was inside the security computer and hunting for the recordings. They were automatically stored and sorted by day and month and he had the date of Rebecca's disappearance seared into his mind. To be safe, he grabbed the files a few days either side and began copying them across to his own hard drive.

It took a few minutes, but by the time the ferry docked the other side, he'd already disabled remote access and removed his laptop from the network. They'd have no way to know that someone accessed it without having a digital forensics expert inspect the machine. And they'd have no reason to do that.

As such, when Lucas disembarked, the security guard he'd duped earlier waved at him like nothing was wrong.

He waved back, his car thudding down onto dry land with a clank of the steel ramp, and then pulled away towards Fårösund and Sara's house.

· · ·

He arrived quickly. He had made the drive a lot, dropping Rebecca off and picking her up too. Fårösund was as safe as places could be, but that didn't mean he wasn't going to be careful. And plus, with Rebecca quickly becoming a young woman, it seemed like she wanted to spend less and less time with dad. Those drives were some of the only quality time they got to spend together. The only time they really talked. He'd let her choose the music and they'd sing along together at times. She didn't seem keen to talk about her life much. Not about boys or her friends. School was fine, a breathable topic. Lucas had always been good at school, had enjoyed it. He was smart, and Rebecca followed in his footsteps. She was going to do great things.

Sara's house loomed quickly and Lucas eased to a stop outside it.

She lived just south of the village on a small street off the main road. It was a pretty house, white with brown panelling and a red tiled roof.

Sara's parents were nice enough people, though Lucas never particularly liked her father. He'd always seemed abrupt, sort of short. Especially with Sara on the occasions that Lucas had brought her home after she'd been over for dinner or something like that. He couldn't imagine speaking to his daughter as this guy had. But he hoped that Bill would have an understanding of why Lucas was doing what he was, and that he'd allow Lucas to speak to Sara.

There was only one way to find out.

Lucas exited his car and walked quickly across the street, climbing the front steps and knocking on the door.

It was early evening and the air was warm, the sinking sun warm on his shoulders.

There was a shuffling inside, and then the door opened. Sara's mother, Ebba, opened it.

She was smiling when she did, but her face dropped a little when she saw Lucas. 'Oh,' she said, surprised to see him, clearly.

'Ebba,' Lucas said, thinking that she looked older since the last time he saw her. Her face was lined, her long brown hair drawn back into a low ponytail. 'I'm sorry to drop in on you like this.'

'I …' she began, shaking her head. 'What's wrong?' she asked then.

'Nothing,' he said quickly. 'Well, actually,' he continued, catching himself, 'uh, it's Maria, she … she …'

'I heard,' Ebba seemed to interject quickly. 'I'm very sorry, but …' She looked into the house behind her. 'Bill?' she called. 'Bill? It's Lucas Adell.'

There was a groaning noise from within, as though an armchair had been thrown back suddenly.

Bill appeared in the hallway, walking quickly. He was shorter than Lucas, but stout, with a bristling moustache and a red face. His polo shirt was too small for him, tight everywhere.

'What is it now?' he harrumphed. 'Haven't you bothered us enough?'

Lucas' mouth opened in shock. He'd been here after Rebecca disappeared, asking questions, asking for help. But he didn't think he'd been so bothersome. Perhaps Bill had just got even more cantankerous in the last year. 'It's Rebecca,' he said. 'I just wanted to … to speak to Sara. It won't take long—'

Bill's eyebrows shot up, folding his forehead into a set of deeply carved lines. 'Absolutely not.' His hand reached out and took his wife's shoulder. 'It's time for you to leave.'

'Please, Bill, if I could just have—'

'I'm not telling you again! And if you keep showing up

like this, I'm going to call the police. I don't want to see you again, Adell. Stay away from my family.'

He looked dumbfounded at Ebba. She stared at the floor, and was then pulled back into the house before Bill slammed the door in his face.

Lucas wavered, confused and angry, and stepped sideways, sagging into the post supporting their porch. He tried to catch his breath, his whole body fizzing, vibrating, it felt like. There was a ringing in the back of his mind. In the distance, another noise. A bird crowing, a dog barking, maybe. He couldn't tell. It sounded almost like someone laughing, cackling. At him. At his misfortune.

He crushed the thought, forcing himself to focus. He'd not come this far just to fall at this hurdle. He had nothing to do and nowhere to be. He'd wait. Sara would have to leave some time, or maybe she wasn't even home. Whichever was the case, he'd be here.

Darkness was falling before a car even trundled into the street. There were just a few houses here. A quiet little oasis, secluded and safe. The perfect place to raise a daughter. Especially one that looked like Sara. A girl who had grown into a beautiful young woman. There was no denying that. It was surprising though, considering Bill was hardly a prize bull.

She was two years older than Rebecca. Not ideal, as far as Lucas was concerned. A seventeen-year-old was likely to be nothing but a bad influence, but it had been so difficult for Rebecca to make friends, and she'd so hated leaving the city and her old life. Maria had been stern with him. And she was usually timid, tender, loving even. But when it came to Rebecca, she could be fierce. Though it was rare. When she was, he knew she was serious. She'd told him he needed to let Rebecca explore new relationships, allow her to make friends. When they'd arrived, Rebecca was just thirteen, and Sara was fifteen. Though she'd seemed nice enough. A gregarious, charming girl. She'd helped bring Rebecca out of her shell, that much he was sure of. Though she'd always wanted Rebecca to grow up faster than she'd seemingly wanted to. Why children couldn't just be children, he didn't know. The world was filled with so much pain, so much difficulty. And as you got older, your eyes only seemed to open to that fact. The innocence of childhood was lost all too quickly.

The car approached and slowed in front of Sara's house.

Lucas couldn't miss Sara, he had to act before she went inside. Had to catch her before Bill knew he was still there.

He opened the door a crack, peering through the gap, seeing if it was her.

The courtesy light inside the car came on, illuminating the cabin. Two girls. Sara and another girl. Did he know her? Maybe, he didn't think she was one of Rebecca's friends. And if she was driving, she was older than Sara, too. Eighteen at least. Probably, judging by the fact that she was driving a Citröen that was at least twenty years old. A rite of passage for every first-time driver.

Sara leaned over, hugged the driver.

A good sign she was about to disembark.

Lucas acted, leaving his car and rushing across the road, sweeping through the gathering darkness to intercept Sara before she walked up her pathway.

Her door opened. But her feet barely touched the ground before Lucas was there, hands raised, trying to calm her before anything escalated.

'I just need a second,' he said, almost frantic.

She froze, like a deer, eyes wide 'Mr Adell,' was all she managed. Her stare went to her front door, then back.

'The night Sara disappeared,' he started, before she could do anything else, 'she was supposed to meet you.'

'What?' Sara said. 'You …' She shook her head in seeming disbelief.

'She was supposed to meet you. That night.'

'Yeah, you already … Earlier …' She pointed to the house, still shaking her head.

'I know, I know. I spoke to your father. I just … I just need to know what she said.'

'Rebecca?'

'Yes, yes! Rebecca. What did she say. That night. She was supposed to meet you. Please, I need to know. No one else will help me.' He reached out, took her arms by the elbows.

She stiffened at his touch. 'Let go of me. Now,' she said, voice like ice.

'Please.'

'I'll scream.'

His grip loosened. He realised it had been tight.

'Sorry, sorry, I just … I need to know.'

'There's something wrong with you,' Sara said coldly. 'You need help.' She exhaled, keeping her eyes locked on his. 'Go home. And don't come here again.'

She strode past him without another word, didn't look back, simply opened the door and went inside. And locked it.

Lucas swayed, ready to fall down. No one would help him. He'd never find Rebecca.

'Mr Adell?' A voice came from behind him and he turned, seeing the girl in the Citröen still sitting at the curb, engine running. She had the window open, leaning out. Her hair was dark and curly. She was probably just eighteen, face dotted with tiny pimples. 'You're Rebecca's father, right?' she asked.

He nodded slowly, walking towards the car.

She leaned back, a little cautious. 'I didn't know Rebecca very well, but ... but when she disappeared ... Sara took it hard. We all did ... And ...' The girl seemed to get choked up at it. 'What I mean is ... I think ... I think I might know something. And if I was you ... I'd want to know. She said to keep it a secret, but I think someone should tell you. If Sara won't, then ... then I will.'

'What is it?' Lucas asked, voice quiet and strained. Jesus he was tired. Exhausted suddenly. He felt like he hadn't slept in days.

'I was with Sara that night,' she answered. 'And Rebecca wasn't coming to meet us. But I do know who she was going to meet.'

'Who?' he asked, almost tentatively. His heart began to beat a little harder.

'I don't know his name — or his *real* name, at least. But Rebecca and Sara called him EZ.'

'Easy?'

'E-Z,' the girl reiterated, separating the letters. 'Some guy, he lives somewhere near Lärbro. Not far.'

Lucas' brow crumpled. 'Some guy? What guy? Rebecca didn't know any *guys* ... she was fifteen.'

The girl sighed. 'Look, I'm just telling you what I heard. I know that Rebecca kept it a secret. She wanted to keep it one ... from you.' The girl looked down, suddenly.

'From me, why?' Lucas tried to restrain his voice, but he felt his fists curl at his sides.

'I don't know. He was older, I guess. Maybe she thought that you'd ...'

'Not approve?' he said through gritted teeth now.

The girl looked out of the windscreen now. 'I shouldn't have said anything, it's not my place. I should go.'

'No, wait,' Lucas urged her, risking a step closer. 'How did she know him? Who is this guy?'

She let out a slow breath, weighing her options. 'I don't know. But I know some people who … who get things from him.'

'Things?' Realisation dawned. 'Drugs?'

She didn't answer, but her silence was confirmation enough.

'Rebecca didn't do drugs,' he said quickly. 'She knew better.'

'I don't know,' was all the girl said, not looking at him. 'I just remember Sara saying something about it, okay?'

Lucas shook his head, dismissing it. 'No, you're wrong. It's not possible. They checked her phone, the police. Her computer, everything. There was no record of any calls or texts with anyone that day. You're wrong. It must be someone else.'

The girl's jaw flexed. She seemed to be wrestling with what she said next. 'Rebecca … she … she had another phone.' She looked at Lucas now. 'Sara told me. I'm not wrong. I promise.'

His fists curled once more. A second phone?

'I'm sorry, Mr Adell. I have to go. Don't … don't tell anyone I told you, okay? But you're her father. I thought you should know.'

His jaw quivered, breathing coming in rattling lungfuls.

'I really hope you find out what happened to her,' the girl added. 'Rebecca seemed nice. I'm … I'm really sorry this happened.' She swallowed, clearing her throat. 'Good luck.'

And then she pulled away from the curb, circled, and drove out of the street.

Behind Lucas, the door to Sara's house opened and Bill

appeared on the step. Lucas stared up at him over his shoulder.

Bill looked stern and he was holding his phone in the air. 'I'm counting to three, and then I'm calling the police,' he yelled.

Lucas couldn't manage words. So instead, he just ran away.

8

Sonja Ehrhart

'So,' Sonja said, pushing her green curry around the bowl, 'you're quieter than normal.'

'Hmm?' Thorsen looked up from his Pad Thai and blinked a few times. 'Sorry, did you say something?'

'I said that your hair looks like a bird's nest. Do you have someone else hold the lawnmower or do you just kneel down and sort of …' She leaned forward and wiggled her head to illustrate how someone might attempt such an act.

He smiled for a moment, then it dropped off his face in the way the pieces of shrimp were dropping off his fork. He'd always had a voracious appetite, for food and justice. And now, he seemed to not want to eat at all.

'It's her, isn't it?' Sonja said. 'It's Jamie.'

'What is?' His eyes flashed to hers, then back down at the table.

'Oh fuck,' Sonja said, laughing a little. 'You don't have to be ashamed of it. Sure, it's clear as day she's not exactly … normal. But I don't know, she's pretty in a sort of … uncon-

ventional way. A far cry from Maja. Now, she was gorgeous.
You know I don't go that way, but hey, feed me five shots of
tequila and then ask me.'

Thorsen grinned and cringed at the same time. 'Can you
please just stop?'

'All I'm saying is that I get it. We don't choose who we
fall for—'

'Fall for?' Thorsen looked right at her now.

'Touched a nerve? I'm happy that you've found someone
to—'

'I've not found anyone to anything, alright?'

'So, you're not sleeping with her then?'

'No, we're just friends. Partners. Strictly platonic.' He cut
the air with his hand.

'But this platonic friend. You want to have sex with her,
don't you.' It wasn't even a question, and she didn't need to
be a detective to figure that one out.

His mouth just opened a little.

'So, what's stopping you?' Sonja took a bite of her
quickly cooling food. 'Her, I guess? You never had trouble
getting women in the sack from what I remember. So, unless
it's …' She held her hand aloft, fork between her finger and
thumb, and extended her pinkie finger. Then she let it droop,
making a sad noise to illustrate she was referring to erectile
disfunction.

'My …' He shook his head. 'Is fine. It's just not as simple
as that.'

She laughed. 'It's always as simple as that. Two people.
Proximity. Friction. Heat. Fucking. It's basic science, String
Bean.'

'Can we talk about something else, please?'

'What's wrong? You never used to spare *any* detail when
telling me about you and Maja, especially when you first got

together.'

'A decision I'm deeply regretting,' Thorsen growled through gritted teeth. 'Can we just talk about the case instead?'

'It's not anywhere near as much fun,' Sonja sighed, 'but if you really want to. But don't think for a second I'm going to let this thing go. And if you're struggling, I could speak to Jamie and—'

'No!' Thorsen jumped so hard he almost knocked over his chair. 'No, no,' he said, lowering his voice. 'It's alright. There's a precarious balance to our … relationship. I don't want to upset things.'

'Ah, the classic friends-to-lovers conundrum. Do you lay your soul bare and risk it all? Or stay friends and resign yourself to a metal cock cage forever?'

'Jesus Christ,' Thorsen laughed, shaking his head incredulously. 'You've got worse, you know that?'

'Impossible.'

'I thought so.'

'You just forgot what I was like is all. Nice to be reminded, eh?'

'The case. The kids. The black hearts, what's going on?'

'What's the rush?' Sonja genuinely wanted to know. As soon as they sat, Thorsen had ordered food, just a glass of water, no starters. And despite the initial lull in conversation, he seemed to be keen to push on now.

He drew a slow breath. 'I …'

'Don't lie to me, Kjell.'

'I'm worried about Jamie.'

'From what I read, she's a big girl and she can take care of herself.'

He smiled a little. 'I'm not worried she'll get hurt. I'm worried … she'll do something … I don't know.'

Sonja looked at her watch. 'We've been in this restaurant for all of thirty minutes. Seriously, how much trouble could she get into?'

'You really don't know Jamie. Now, come on, the case. Don't make me beg.'

'I like it when you beg.' She fired him a coy look and he blushed a little. 'Too easy.'

'Sonja …'

'Kjell …' She said, sultry and low.

He laughed again. 'Oh, Jeez. I see you've not lost your touch.'

'So say the men of Visby.'

'So, you're still cutting them down to size?'

'In droves, like the over-indulged men-children they are. But enough about *my* rich and vibrant sex life, I thought you wanted to talk about work?'

'I don't mind when it's not about me.' Thorsen took another mouthful of Pad Thai, relaxing a little.

'Well, you know me, I'm an open book. Though not as spry as I used to be. Still, I'll preach now what I was five years ago. Yoga and cardio. Jamie will thank you, trust me!' She laughed at her own joke, but saw Thorsen wasn't doing the same. Shit, he was hung up on this girl, wasn't he? They used to laugh endlessly, rib-splittingly, talking shit about their sex lives. It was their thing! But every time Jamie Johansson came within a hundred miles of the conversation he clammed up and went all moody like a teenager. She supposed it had been a few years since they'd spent time together, and things had changed since then. A messy divorce, and God knows what else. Eh, if he was this torn up about Jamie, though, it could only mean one thing. Love.

She'd observe, make her judgement, probably some

notes. But it was clear that he didn't *want* help. But by fuck could he use some.

'Twenty-three kids,' Sonja said then, a little more sombrely. 'Twenty-three kids are dead.'

He ate silently, waiting for her to go on.

'The first wasn't actually the first. He was a fifteen-year-old boy. After his parents went to bed, he swallowed sixteen sleeping pills. They found him in the bathroom in the morning. He had carved a heart into his left arm with nail scissors, and used his mother's eyeliner pencil to fill it in. Fifteen, Kjell. No history of mental illness, no signs of depression or suicidal ideation. He played soccer for his school, was doing well in his classes. There was no indication of anything, and then …'

Thorsen narrowed his eyes a little. 'What do you mean he wasn't the first?'

'He was the fifth.' Sonja sighed, pushing the remainder of her food away. 'It took them until him to notice the pattern. It was because they were spread all over. Four tragic suicides, all unlinked, until one officer connected some dots, and then, suddenly, five kids in a row. All within months of each other. By the time the police managed to scramble a task force, put together all the evidence they already had, there was another body. I didn't get to examine the first four before their funerals. But number five … when he hit my table.' Sonja's lip quivered a little. She'd always been able to separate herself from things, compartmentalise. But this whole thing was fucked. It was just … *fucked.* 'Someone out there is targeting kids. Forcing them to kill themselves somehow. I don't know who they are, or why they're doing it, but someone is, and it feels like no one is doing anything. I conduct my exams, I send off the results, and then … nothing. I just wait. I just wait for the next one.' She looked at him. 'Someone has to do something. You have to do something.'

He thought on it for what seemed like a long time.

'What's going through your head?'

'Killers like this … they have some sort of deep-seated motivation. Something they get from it. You said before that there were no signs of sexual assault?'

'Nothing that suggested non-consensual, no. Though a number of the bodies showed signs of recent sexual activity.'

'Not wholly surprising for teenagers. No residual DNA?'

She shook her head. 'None of them had intercourse within the last few days before their deaths as far as I could tell.'

'So, it's likely not sexual motivation. And there were no abductions. From what you put in your emails, the victims were all discovered by family or friends?'

'That's right. Usually at home, school, somewhere familiar. Nothing to suggest they'd been coerced into anything physically by someone else.'

'And I'm guessing there was nothing on their phones to suggest they were being talked into it.'

Sonja shrugged. 'I don't know – they don't tell me anything.'

Thorsen nodded. 'Okay. So, we have … someone … finding, targeting these kids. But we don't know how, or where. Then, they are groomed, indoctrinated, brainwashed, whatever, into killing themselves without a single person noticing any change in their behaviour or demeanour in the lead up to their deaths?'

'I suspect that's why the police are having a tough time solving it.'

Thorsen did look stumped. 'Well, if we've got any chance at spotting some sort of pattern or means or motive here, we'll need to see what the police have already. Do you have any contacts at Visby police? Do you know who's running the case? Can you put us in touch with him?'

'I do know who's running things. But I doubt he'll speak to you. He won't enjoy two other detectives sticking their nose in things. From what I understand, they're trying to keep the case under wraps. The media aren't allowed to report on it. They're doing everything they can to make sure that the island doesn't implode. Parents are pulling their kids from school, sending them away from the island. Tensions are running high, crime is on the up. Assaults and other altercations. People are scared, they're tense, they're angry. The city has changed, Kjell. This used to be such a happy place. But now … look around.'

Thorsen did. A few other tables were populated, but people were subdued, quiet, eating without talking.

'This place is usually packed out every night of the week.'

'It is good Pad Thai …' Thorsen muttered, taking another glance around.

'I don't know why the person who's doing this is, but … but if we don't do something to stop them, the whole island is going to go up in flames. Trust me on that.'

Thorsen processed the information, nodding slowly. 'Alright then. Let's get the bill.' He sighed, reaching for his wallet. 'Is there someone else you can connect us with? Otherwise, our hands are tied here.'

'I know a few people. I'll reach out, see if I can't get you looped in. But you'll have to be discreet.'

He chuckled a little. 'I have no problem with that,' he said, pulling a credit card from his wallet. 'But Jamie on the other hand …'

Sonja already had her own purse out. 'Yeah, I read the articles. She does like to burn things down, doesn't she?'

'She does, yes. Literally and metaphorically.'

Sonja waved the waiter over and laid her hand over Thorsen's wrist. 'It's on me.'

'I don't mind,' Thorsen said politely. 'I'll get it.'

She smiled at him. 'Please, you're my guests. And anyway, last time I checked, you're unemployed.'

He sucked air in through his teeth. 'You're right there.' He put his card away. 'Maybe I will let you get this one.'

———

They stepped out into the warm summer air and Sonja went a little ahead, turning back to face him as she reached the car.

Thorsen slowed, pocketed his hands, and rocked back and forth on his heels.

She watched him as he scanned the road and the surrounding streets, eyes lingering on the one Jamie went down.

'Kjell,' Sonja said then.

He looked at her.

'Are you happy? Be honest.'

He didn't answer right away. 'I don't know. I think so.'

'You think so?'

'After Maja, my life was a train wreck. Hell, when I was with her my life was a train wreck. We weren't happy for a while.'

'And now?'

'I'm less *un*-happy.'

'And what would make you happy?'

'Can we not do this right now? It's been a long day.'

She nodded. 'Sure. I'll get those numbers in the morning and text them to you. You want a ride to the hotel?'

'Yeah, sure. Lemme just call Jamie. God knows where she is.'

'She didn't text you back?'

He lifted his eyebrows, a little surprised.

'What, you thought I didn't notice you thumb-bashing the shit out of your phone under the table?'

He smiled sheepishly.

'Oh, go on, call her. I'll be in the car.'

He dialled as she circled the car and got in. He didn't think she'd answer, but she did.

'Yeah?' came her voice through the receiver.

'Jamie? We're all done with dinner, heading back to the hotel,' Thorsen said, reluctant to ask the next part. 'You coming?'

'Right,' she said back, 'sure.'

'Do you need a ride? We can pick you up—'

'No, no, I'll be there in ten.'

'We'll wait here then …'

'Okay, great.'

'See you soon—' But before he could finish, she hung up.

Thorsen sighed, then climbed into the car.

'She's not coming?' Sonja asked.

'Oh no, she's coming,' Thorsen said, knocking his phone on his knee.

'Then why so glum, String Bean? Isn't that what you wanted?'

'I don't know what I want. Especially when it comes to Jamie.'

'Humph, that's how you know it's—'

'Don't say it.'

She ran her thumb and forefinger across her lips, zipping them.

'Thank you.'

'Any time, lover boy.'

Thorsen grumbled and laid his head back against the headrest. It was going to be a long ten minutes.

————

When Jamie appeared from the side street she'd gone down initially Thorsen thought his anxiety would dispel, but it only seemed to intensify.

She spotted the car and picked up the pace from what seemed like a light jog to a slightly faster one.

She opened the door and slid into the back seat, not even out of breath.

Without a word, Sonja pulled away, heading for their hotel. It was a big chain, inexpensive with clean beds and copy-paste rooms. Charmless but adequate.

'Where were you?' Thorsen asked once they were moving, though he didn't turn his head or even move his eyes from the road.

Sonja watched him curiously, observing the tension in him. The trepidation, almost. A far cry from the man she knew in Lulea, oozing confidence and charisma. Now he was stiff and awkward, like he was in pain. She guessed he was, one way or another.

'I was at the university,' Jamie answered.

He considered it for a moment, then asked, 'What did you find?'

Assuming she found something? Sonja kept her eyes on the road. Not, 'What happened?' or 'Why did you go there?' Just right in there – 'What did you find?' Because the infallible Jamie Johansson must have found something.

'I met a friend of the latest victim, Juni Pedersen,' Jamie said. 'She saw Juni die. We went to Juni's house and looked around her room. There was a carving of a black heart in the surface of her desk, along with a quote from Hamlet: "What dreams may come". She had lots of other Shakespeare plays in her bookcase, but no Hamlet. So, we headed over to the library on a hunch, and found the copy that Juni checked out. It was filled with notes and drawings, sections and lines underlined and circled. Lots of black hearts. There's definitely a link between her death and that book.'

Thorsen pursed his lips, seeming unsurprised.

Sonja didn't have that much poise. 'Jesus Christ on a bike,' she said, basically scoffing. 'You were gone an hour. How the hell did you find all that out?'

Jamie met her eye in the rear-view, then shrugged.

Thorsen cleared his throat a little. 'So, you think Hamlet had something to do with her death?'

'Have you read it?'

'Jog my memory.'

'Hamlet is visited by the ghost of his father, the former King of Denmark, who tells Hamlet that he was murdered by his brother, the now current King of Denmark, and Hamlet's uncle. Hamlet pretends to go mad, while plotting to murder his uncle. The uncle, fearing Hamlet, plots to murder him instead. The play ends with the death of the King, Queen, Hamlet, the guy Hamlet is fighting, and Ophelia. Along with a bunch of other people – Polonius, Rosen-something, and Guil … uh …'

'Guildenstern,' Sonja added. 'Rosencrantz and Guildenstern.'

Jamie gave her a nod of thanks.

'So, it's a play about revenge, madness, and death,' Thorsen surmised.

'In broad strokes, yeah,' Jamie confirmed.

Sonja spoke now. 'And you think it played a part in Juni

Pedersen's death? Some of the victims were younger – I don't even know if they would have been exposed to Shakespeare before they died.'

'Only one way to find out,' Jamie said, giving another shrug. 'The police missed the connection it seems like, otherwise they'd have the book now. So, I wouldn't be surprised if they never even enquired about it.'

'So, you have the book?' Thorsen asked, holding his hand over his shoulder.

'No, I don't,' Jamie answered. 'If it's evidence, I didn't want to be the one removing it from the library. The girl I met – Annika – she has it.'

'You gave a student what could be a critical piece of evidence?'

'I didn't give her anything. A student checked a book out of the library.'

'It's plausible deniability,' Sonja interjected, punching Thorsen in the arm. 'You've got rusty. Jamie would have had to have stolen it, but the girl could check it out no problem. And presumably keep it safe?' Sonja fished for Jamie's eyes in the rear-view mirror.

'Exactly,' Jamie said, meeting them briefly.

Thorsen let out a long breath as Sonja pulled up at a red light, drumming on the steering wheel.

'So, we go forward,' Thorsen began then, 'on the assumption that there's some link to Hamlet in all the deaths?'

'Just literature in general, maybe. And maybe not even that,' Jamie said. 'There's nothing to say that whatever – or whoever – drove Juni Pedersen to jump from the roof of a building is the same thing that drove the others to hurt themselves. All we know is that Juni seemed to have an unhealthy interest in Hamlet, and then she killed herself.'

The car was quiet.

'Though if we're talking about literature, Edgar Allen Poe does come to mind.'

'The telltale heart,' Thorsen answered quickly. He seemed pleased to know that one.

'Right. The main character kills someone and puts them under the floor, riddled with guilt, they eventually kill themselves.'

'In terms of motivating someone to off themselves,' Sonja said, 'preying on their guilt is probably a good way to go about it.'

'Anyway,' Jamie cut in, tempering the conversation, 'so far, we know nothing. And until we speak to someone involved in the investigation, we could be wasting our time re-treading ground the local police already have.'

'I still think it's a solid lead,' Thorsen added. 'And your feelings about things usually lead us into some sort of trouble.' He flashed her a smile in the mirror. Sonja noticed Jamie held his gaze longer than Jamie held hers.

'At eighteen, to be so fiercely turned on to Hamlet … You'd have to be pretty inspired by something.'

'Or someone.'

'The idea of death as a release, or escape, or absolution … It's a big theme in literature.'

'And the hearts?'

'Solidarity? A rite of passage? Who knows. Annika said Juni's looked fresh. How long before they died did the others draw theirs?'

Sonja fielded that one. 'A day, two, three at the most. Most pretty much right before.'

'And Juni's?'

'No more than a day.'

Jamie thought on that as though it was important, but she didn't elaborate. Sonja could see why there was so much fuss over her in a professional sense, at least. She was whip smart, that much was clear. On the personal side of things … Sonja's eyes drifted to Thorsen … she wasn't so sure.

'We're here,' Sonja said then, pulling up outside the hotel.

'That was fast,' Thorsen remarked.

'Visby's small.'

Jamie was out of the car before Sonja could even say goodbye.

Thorsen leaned across, hugged her, and then got out, circling around to meet Jamie as she pulled their bags from the boot and walked back round to the driver's window.

It was already wound down. 'I'll find those numbers and text them to you,' Sonja said.

'Thanks,' Thorsen replied.

'Of course. I brought you into this, the least I could do.' Her eyes moved from Thorsen and lingered on Jamie, standing there awkwardly, duffle over her shoulder, Thorsen's in her hand. She resisted the urge for a moment, but then gave in. Whether she was just trying to help things, or she was just plain curious to see what would happen, she couldn't have said, but either way, she asked the question she knew would have consequences, either good or bad.

'So, did you two get one room, or two?'

9

Kjell Thorsen

THORSEN'S CHEEKS burned as he watched Sonja drive away, smirking to herself.

He could feel the cold rating from Jamie to his right and knew the second he turned his head she'd say something about it. Why the fuck did Sonja have to butt in?

Let's go inside. We should check in. I have to make a phone call. Say something, anything! He turned his head to look at her, mouth opening, but no words coming.

'What the hell was that supposed to mean?' Jamie asked, looking right at him. It wasn't even close to rhetorical.

He could only shrug. 'Who knows. Sonja is …'

'Sonja is what?' She cocked her head slightly.

Thorsen felt his palms get a little sweaty. Why would Jamie never say what she thought? Why always the interrogation? The mind games? It was like water drip torture trying to speak to her. 'Sonja is … a very sexual woman.'

Jamie's eyebrows rose.

'She's just … obsessed. No, not obsessed. Interested. Morbidly curious. About sex.'

'About your sex?'

'I suppose.'

'And about mine?'

'No, I mean. She just …'

'What?'

'She asked if we were …'

'And what did you tell her?'

He laughed nervously. 'Nothing! There's nothing to tell, is there?' He met her eye. 'Is there?'

Her eyebrows lowered and she cleared her throat, looking at the ground. 'I think we should just check in. I'm hungry.' She turned and walked towards the door, leaving Thorsen at the curb.

No wonder you're hungry, he thought. You skipped dinner. Anger flooded through him suddenly, but as he watched her walk through the door of the hotel, it dissipated, and then he was just left feeling angry at himself. Another chance, another moment where he could have just said *something* slipped through his fingers.

He sighed heavily, picked up his bag – which Jamie had left at his feet – and headed after her.

One room or two. He harrumphed to himself. He was going to strangle Sonja when he saw her.

———

It was after eleven when there was a knock on his door.

Thorsen was sitting on his bed, laptop on his lap, looking through photos of black hearts. Well, that was putting it lightly. He was tumbling down a rabbit hole of iconography with zero direction. Honestly, he was just trying to occupy his mind.

When the knock came, his first thought was wondering who it could be, but before he'd even finished that, he was out of bed and loping towards the door with his long legs, hairy and well-defined. Exposed too on account of him only wearing boxer shorts. He paused two steps from the door and looked around, snatching up his travel hoodie. An oversized grey thing from his alma mater.

He threw it on and turned the handle, worried he'd miss her.

When he opened it, Jamie was standing there. She was still in jeans, but she was barefoot, just a t-shirt with a scooped neck on top, the straps of her sports bra visible on her shoulders.

'I can't sleep,' she said, not looking at him, but walking straight in anyway.

His heart beat a little harder.

He closed the door and turned, watching her move into the middle of his room. He noticed the gnarled flesh of the scar on the back of her shoulder. She'd got it during her last case in London, had been attacked by a girl with a knife. He felt like he knew so much about her, every part of her. Except the one part he really wanted to.

She spun to face him. 'How are you feeling about it?'

'About what?' he answered quickly, guiltily almost, for some reason.

'About being here. About being back.'

He leaned uncomfortably on the wall next to the bathroom and folded his arms. 'Uh,' he hedged, shaking his head. 'It's … different,' he said truthfully. 'We've been away for a while, so coming back is a little strange. But familiar, too.' He shrugged. 'I mean, we've been doing this a while now. But I'll admit, I do miss my gun. And my badge.'

'You want to be a detective again?' She looked a little pained by the idea.

'Of course,' he said. 'It's my life. You can't just leave a part of yourself behind like that without any regret.'

'You regret leaving with me?'

'That's not what I said.' He had to tread carefully. 'Don't twist my words.' Sometimes he had to be stern with her.

'I … sorry,' Jamie said, looking away.

'I don't regret going with you. And I also don't regret coming back. The thing with life, Jamie, is that it's all just decisions. One after another, big, small. And they all affect other people. This one affected you, and it did it in a way you don't particularly like. Whether it's being back at the job, or being back in Sweden, or something else, it's clear you're unhappy. But … I don't know what I can do about that right now.' He pushed off the wall and stood in front of her.

'What else would I be unhappy about?' she asked lightly, folding her arms.

He drew a breath, so tired. So tired of this. 'Sonja,' he said flatly. 'You're obviously upset that her and I are close. I understand, it's jealousy. It's nothing to be embarrassed about.'

'I'm not jealous,' she scoffed. 'And I'm certainly not embarrassed. You're the one that should be embarrassed if anything.'

Thorsen took a breath, steadied himself, measured his response. 'I was jealous, you know? Of Wiik. When we were at The Farm, after all that shit with the church on the island, and Michael … We almost died, and then Wiik shows up, throwing his weight around. And I could see that you and him had history, that you cared about each other. I was jealous. It came out in a way that I'm not proud of right now.'

'You have nothing to be jealous of. My relationship with Wiik is nothing like what we have—' She cut herself off abruptly, swallowed, cleared her throat. 'I just think that you and Sonja have a strange relationship that, honestly, is a far cry from professional. Especially considering the circumstances.'

Thorsen raised his eyebrows. 'Excuse me for having a fucking friend with a sense of humour.'

Jamie's nostrils flared a little. Oh, shit. Here it comes, Thorsen thought. 'And, what? I'm just some cold fucking bitch, I suppose? That what she said? It's not that I don't like her because you and her have this weird Oedipal thing going on. I don't like her because she's nosy, and she talks when she has no fucking clue what she's talking about.'

'Sonja is excellent at her job,' Thorsen said defensively.

'I'm not disputing otherwise. But she doesn't know me, and I don't appreciate her talking about me behind my back. Especially when …'

'Especially when what?' Thorsen replied, almost fiercely now. 'When she's saying things that hit a little close to home? When she says the things out loud that you're too afraid to? Yeah, it is uncomfortable, isn't it? You don't think I feel uncomfortable with this shit, too? You think I know what the fuck is going on? What's going on right here?' He gestured animatedly to the small space between the two of them. 'Sonja is weird, yes, loud, yes, talkative, yes, and probably a little inquisitive, sure.'

Jamie snorted a little, shook her head.

'And yes, yes, she is … sexual. Weirdly so. She's interested in sex, and we've always talked openly about it, because that's what *friends* do.'

'We don't,' Jamie said quickly, still not meeting his eye.

'No, we don't. And I think that's part of the problem, don't you?'

Jamie's mouth opened a little, but she said nothing.

'I don't particularly like her digging around in our relationship, but she's not trying to drive us apart, or fuck things up, she's ... she's just ...' He let out a long sigh, out of breath, heart beating hard. He ran his fingers through his hair. 'Jesus Christ, Jamie,' he muttered. 'I just ... I don't even know what to say to you. I never do. I never know what to say to you.'

'Have you had sex with her?' Jamie asked then, grimacing a little like she had a sour taste in her mouth.

'What? No,' Thorsen said, sideswiped by the question.

'But you would? You've thought about it?'

'No, I—'

'That's a lie,' Jamie said, cutting him off.

'Yeah, whatever, fine, I've thought about it. But she's ...'

'Twenty years older than you?'

'I was going to say a friend.'

'So that's the line? You don't want to *fuck* your friends?'

The word sounded so alien coming from her in this context. She used the word liberally, but never when talking about ... that.

'Yeah, I guess?'

'Are we friends?'

'You and me? Of course we are.'

'So, you wouldn't fuck me, then?'

The breath left his body all at once, his hands tingling with a sudden rush of blood. 'I ...' he squeaked out, unable to muster the air for anything else.

But before he could, she looked up at him, for just a moment, a look of rage, of frustration, and of pure dejection in her eyes. And then she left, rushing past him, her shoulder just glancing his as she flew towards the door. The force was nothing, but it was enough to bowl him over.

He turned, staggering around until he was staring at the closing hotel door.

Before it even reached the jamb, he heard her door snap shut next door.

And then his closed, slowly reaching the wood, the dead-bolt clicking into place.

Locking it.

————

Thorsen slept like shit. He tossed and turned all night, and then eventually dropped off some time before dawn. A thud somewhere down the corridor roused him at six and he sat upright in bed, his neck slick with sweat, the sheets damp around him.

'Fuck,' he muttered, letting out a long breath.

He rolled from bed and went to the bathroom showering in cold water to wake himself, enjoying the unpleasantness of it. What a fucking idiot. Why didn't he just say something? Anything? You goddamn pussy. Grow a pair of fucking balls.

He launched his fist against the wall of the shower cubicle, the pain reverberating through his knuckles and wrist. It's not too late, he told himself. It's not.

He dried and dressed and slipped out of his room by twenty past, and found himself in front of Jamie's door a second later. He leaned his head against it and knocked. 'Jamie?' he called through the wood. 'Can we talk?'

No response.

He knocked again, a little louder. She'd be awake. She slept even worse than he did. At least, when they'd first got to Greece, she did. She'd rolled around all night, mattress squeaking terribly, and then she'd get up, make coffee, go out onto the patio to watch the sea. And then eventually, she'd grab her running shoes and …

'Shit,' he said, peeling himself off the door. She's gone running. She always did when she had a lot on her mind.

Over the few months they were away, she'd actually stopped doing that. Her early morning runs to escape whatever the night brought her.

She'd begun sleeping in. The mattress had stopped squeaking. She'd grown contented with that life, had come to peace with whatever lived in her head. And he'd taken her away from that, brought her here. And now, she was out there, again, trying to outrun it all.

He felt like a piece of shit all of a sudden.

But it didn't change the fact that there was a long day ahead, and — he checked his watch — breakfast started at seven.

He turned, began walking.

It was quarter to eight when Jamie appeared in the dining room. Thorsen had finished his food five minutes after the buffet opened.

She looked tired, but he could see she was at ease after her run. He just wondered if it was the case or their exchange which had kept her awake. He knew which one had precluded his sleep.

He lifted his chin, then his coffee cup to her, and she adjusted her head, walking over. She seemed to make a point of not looking at him as she approached, pulled out a chair, and sat. All in silence.

Thorsen cleared his throat. 'I, uh …' he began, not sure where to go with it. 'I texted the police officer that Sonja wanted to connect us with. She's going to meet us here for coffee at ten. I wasn't sure what time you'd be back, so I thought—'

'Ten is fine,' Jamie said, quiet, looking at the table.

'Do you … do you want to talk about last night, or—'

'I'm going to get some food,' Jamie said, exhaling, forcing her voice to brighten. She smiled at him, but Thorsen shuddered, unable to help but feel like she was all but dead behind the eyes in that moment. 'I'm starving. Do you want anything?'

'Uh … no, no,' he said, unsettled by the calmness of her demeanour.

She pushed back from the table and got up, walking towards the buffet table.

As he watched her go, he couldn't help but wonder what would have happened if he'd taken his chance. Said yes. If this morning, they'd woken up together.

Whether everything would have been infinitely better.

Or if it would have been a whole lot worse.

Honestly, he didn't know.

10

Jamie Johansson

BREAKFAST WAS PAINFUL. The run did little — actually,
nothing — to clear her head. After she'd left Thorsen's room
the previous night, embarrassed, ashamed, practically, she'd
not slept. Jamie was no stranger to insomnia. She'd seen more
sunrises than any one person had any right to. But that still
didn't make the nights she lay awake easier.

What the hell was she thinking? That, what, Thorsen was
just going to scoop her up in his arms? Tell her that he loved
her? Yeah, right. Fairy tale bullshit. She'd never subscribed to
it before, and she wasn't about to start now. The fact that the
closest thing to a relationship she'd had in the last three years
was being stalked by a deranged serial killer told her everything she needed to know. Jamie Johansson was better off
alone.

She just needed reminding.

When she got back to the table, Thorsen was silent, not
meeting her eye. He'd come to terms with it, she supposed.
He was embarrassed for her, no doubt. She was sure he'd just

want to move on, forget it — she certainly did — so she ate her eggs, choked down the cold toast, and then loaded up on coffee to stave off the grogginess.

She'd got twelve kilometres in that morning, but it wasn't the run that was making her tired, it was this case. They'd only been back a day, but it already felt like an eternity, like they'd picked up right where they'd left off, exhausted and, in Jamie's case, miserable.

The quicker they could get this thing resolved, the better. She didn't know where she'd go, but, frankly, anywhere was better than here. Which was a shame, because Gotland was actually quite beautiful.

'So, who is this person?' Jamie asked, unable to bear the silence any longer. She'd lasted almost an hour since she sat down.

'I'm not sure,' Thorsen answered quickly, as though he'd been waiting for her to speak. 'Sonja said she'd met her a few times — she's a police officer working on the case — and she seemed … unhappy with the progress they were making. Sonja let her know we'd be getting in touch, and she seemed amenable to some extra hands.'

Jamie just nodded. 'But whoever is running the case …?'

'I don't know if they know we're here. I doubt it.'

'Right, because Sonja went behind their backs.' She didn't intend for it to come out with that much bite.

Thorsen shifted uncomfortably on his chair. 'She wanted to help catch the person murdering kids,' he said, equally as snappy. 'I don't think that really makes her a bad person or anything.'

'No, no, of course not.' Did she mean for that to sound facetious? Because she thought it sort of did.

'Look, I know you've got a problem with her, but that's

not really the issue at hand, is it? Or certainly not the biggest one.'

'And what is?' Jamie asked lightly.

'The fact that someone is killing kids.'

She swallowed. 'Right, that's what I thought you meant.'

He narrowed his eyes at her a little, trying to figure her out. But before he seemed to be able to, someone was standing at their table. Jamie and Thorsen both looked up at her. She was probably forty, stout and strong. She had short, curly hair, and was wearing a blue button-up shirt, rolled to the elbows, showing off tattooed forearms.

'You Detective Thorsen?' she asked, looking at Thorsen.

'I am,' he said tentatively.

'Detective Larsson,' the woman said, extending him a hand. He shook it firmly and then it was offered to Jamie.

She shook it too, and Larsson squeezed hard enough that her knuckles hurt.

'Do you mind?' she asked, pulling out the chair in front of her.

'Please,' Thorsen said, smiling, then glancing at Jamie.

She didn't need to look at her watch to know that this woman was almost an hour early. A while back she'd noticed Thorsen texting under the table. She didn't know what about, but now she guessed it was to ask Larsson to come sooner.

She couldn't say she was displeased there was something to take the attention from whatever was happening between the two of them.

Larsson took stock of the situation, laying her thick arms on the table and interlacing her fingers. They were nail bitten and red. Now that she was sitting, Jamie could see she looked tired, stressed.

'Doctor Elmhart,' Larsson began, 'she said you two could

help. I don't know how, but I hope she's fucking right.' Larsson chuckled a little to herself, though it seemed abject.

'Can you tell us what you have so far?' Thorsen asked.

Jamie just listened.

'Other than a whole lot of dead teens?' Larsson scoffed. 'Not much.'

Thorsen let out a long breath. 'Okay, well, it's been a year. You must have something?'

'We know everything there is to know about the victims. We've traced their movements as far back as we could, scoured their phones, their laptops, everything we could to try and figure out a link or root cause. We've been through their lives over and over and over again. And …'

'Nothing,' Thorsen finished, sighing.

'We've done everything. Looked at everything. Turned over every stone. There's nothing we've missed.'

'Well, that's not true,' Jamie said, not meaning to be so cutting.

Larsson adjusted in her seat. 'Well, obviously we missed *something*. But we don't know what.'

'That's the thing with tough cases,' Jamie said tiredly. 'You don't know what you're looking for until you've found it.'

'That's really helpful, thanks,' Larsson said, all but sneering. 'So glad you came all this way.'

'You want our help, or not?' Jamie replied coldly.

Thorsen cleared his throat. 'Everyone's stressed, that much is clear. So why don't we all just take a breath, hmm.'

'Right,' Larsson said, turning back to him and softening a little. 'My apologies. It's just this whole case … and now, everyone's scared. The brass is trying desperately to keep it out of the media … but I don't know how long they can. And once they start asking questions … well, we don't have the answers. So right now, any help we can get, I'm ready to take.'

'And what about your bosses?' Jamie asked. 'Are they ready to take our help?'

'If you solve the fucking case, I'm sure they're not likely to look a gift horse in the mouth.'

'So, we're doing this fully under the table, got it,' Jamie said, nodding. 'Just wanted to clarify that.'

'She always like this?' Larsson asked Thorsen.

'Yes,' he answered flatly.

Jamie stiffened a little. She thought he might defend her there. Had expected it, at least. Now, he wouldn't even meet her eye.

'I don't like the sound of doing this without the blessing of the Visby police,' he added.

'It's bigger than that. The NOD is in on it, handling the case.'

'Jesus Christ,' Jamie muttered. 'You want us to stamp on the toes of the National Operations Department?'

'I don't want you to stamp on anyone's toes,' Larsson said flatly. 'I want you to help solve this case. That's all that matters. Who cares who cracks it?'

'I doubt the NOD will see it that way,' Jamie all but scoffed. 'Who's in charge? What's their name?'

'You're familiar with all the NOD senior investigators, I suppose?' Larsson replied coolly.

'Try me.'

'Dahlvig.'

Jamie's eyebrows raised. 'Polisöverintendent Ivar Dahlvig?'

'You know him?' Larsson seemed surprised.

'Yeah, he stamped on *my* toes back in Stockholm two years ago.' Jamie shook her head. 'If he's how I remember him, he won't appreciate our interference,' she said, glancing at Thorsen.

He cleared his throat, grabbing Larsson's attention. 'What do you have for us? You can't expect us to be of any help if we have nothing to go on,' he said, keen to move the conversation on. He didn't even acknowledge Jamie.

'Of course not. Here,' Larsson said, producing a folder from under the table and handing it to Thorsen. 'It's everything we have – files on all the victims, crime scene photographs, autopsy reports, interviews with families, suspect list, the whole thing.'

'And you're just … giving it to us?' Thorsen asked, a little surprised, opening it and looking over what was inside.

'Ehrhart vouched for you, and that's good enough for me. That, and the fact that I'm too fucking tired to do a full background check on you both. The doc said you're here to help, and like I said …'

'You need all the help you can get.' Thorsen sighed. 'Problem is, this is only one page.' He looked over the top of the folder, expression pensive to say the least.

Larsson cleared her throat nervously. 'It's the broad strokes.'

'Broad strokes? It's a list of bullet points. This can't be all you have after a year-long investigation?'

'We have lots of information but …'

Jamie interjected now. 'No clue what any of it means.'

Larsson shot her a cold look. 'All cards on the table – we're at a dead end, but no one's willing to admit it. Especially not those dicks running things. Their pride is costing people their lives. I'm from here, Visby born and raised. These are my people and this is my island. I don't care what we need to do to solve this, even if it means bringing in you two.'

Jamie and Thorsen looked at each other now. "You two"? What was that supposed to mean?

'So yeah, if it means catching the fucker who's doing this, I'm willing to risk a rap on the knuckles from the NOD.'

Jamie took it in, thinking.

Thorsen spoke again, laying down the file. 'You've been on this investigation since day one, what do you think is causing it? Was there anything going on before the first death? Anything you think might have precipitated the crimes?'

'We've been searching for just that. But no, nothing. Crime was at an all-time low for the island. It was a haven – for visitors and residents. That's the worst thing of all. No one was prepared – hell, they're still not. The whole island is going mad. We're inundated with calls and emails constantly, asking what we're doing, what's going on. People are suspecting their neighbours, their friends. Our tip lines are lit up like a fucking Christmas tree with bogus shit – everyone's losing their minds, and we're flailing here. I don't know how long it's going to be before the shit truly hits the fan, but it's coming. Trouble is brewing on the island and when it blows up … the whole fucking place is going to be in flames. I promise you that.'

Thorsen looked at her, trying to figure out how much was hyperbole and how much was genuinely what she thought. Her stoicism said it all. The island was on the verge of exploding.

Thorsen sighed. 'Just so we're not re-treading ground here – online histories? You've looked at them?'

'Our digital forensics team scoured every single victim's entire history. Phones, laptops, tablets, hell, even their games consoles. Everything. We thought chatrooms, forums, messenger services, the lot. There's nothing to link them together, no common threads. And unless they're all using bomb-proof VPN services, encrypted browsing, or had burner devices specifically for the purpose of communicating, then the online angle is a bust, too.'

'And is there a chance they could be using those services and devices like that?'

'They're all paid things, right? So even if they were, there'd be subscriptions to them, receipts from purchases, that kind of thing. But nothing. We even went outside the kids, to the sellers directly, pulled records directly from the best services, from the vendors of those devices, hell, we even got Amazon to send us a list of shit that'd been sold across the island!'

'And?'

'And eight months and a bajillion hours of chasing our tail later, we've got absolutely fuck all.' Larsson sighed.

'What about their physical movements?' Jamie said. 'Any way they could be crossing paths? Any commonalities? Sports teams, community groups, school trips? Anything?'

Larsson shook her head. 'No, nothing. Apart from the kids at the university, none of the other deaths were close. And even at the university, none of them shared classes, friend groups … no links at all.'

'I'll still need that information,' Jamie added.

'Of course you will.'

'I'll also need photographs of the victims' bedrooms. I suspect we won't be able to just turn up at their houses.'

'No, I'd rather you didn't,' Larsson said. 'There's a USB stick taped in the back of the folder with everything on it – crime scene photographs, photographs of their homes, interviews with the families, online histories, forensics records, statements from teachers and friends, lists of personal effects, movement histories, bank account histories, phone histories, autopsy reports, medical histories, everything.' Larsson put her hand on the table and leaned in. 'Everything.' She said it as though to emphasise how much work they'd done despite the lack of results. Her eyes lingered on Jamie. 'But why the photographs of the bedrooms?' she asked, inspecting the woman in front of her.

Jamie shrugged. 'Just in case.'

'In case what?'

Thorsen spoke now, carefully. 'We have … a theory.'

'A theory?' Larsson's eyebrows shot up. 'You've been here all of five fucking minutes. We've been working this for a year.' She looked at Jamie incredulously.

'And if you were capable of solving it, it'd be solved already,' Jamie said, letting her dislike of Larsson run free now.

Thorsen drew in a slow breath. 'It's nothing concrete, just a theory.'

'Well, what is it?' Larsson huffed, keeping her attention on Thorsen.

'We're really not ready to share anything,' he hedged. 'It's a long shot.'

'Right now, we've got no shot. So, anything is going to help.'

'I really don't think it's worth sharing at the current moment.'

'I'm asking you to,' Larsson said, a little more firmly.

'It would just muddy the waters.'

'I'm willing to take that risk.'

Thorsen smiled at her, sat back in the chair easily. 'You'll be the first to know once we know. For now, there's nothing to share. Really.' His easy tone was assertive enough for her to get the picture.

She huffed, slouching backwards. 'Fine, just … keep me

posted, alright?' She checked her watch then. 'I have to go. Thanks for this.'

Jamie couldn't tell if she was being sincere or not.

Larsson stood, offered Thorsen her hand and shook hard. She gave it to Jamie then, but the shake felt more like gripping a dead tentacle than a hand.

She left without another word, and Jamie and Thorsen sat slowly.

'File?' Jamie asked, reaching across the table.

Thorsen handed it to her. 'Nothing much in there.'

Jamie decided for herself, opening it to read the page. It was indeed just some bullet points that outlined the case – and Thorsen was right, it wasn't anything much to go on.

Number of victims, a timeline of the cases. It noted which ones were clustered geographically, but generally focused on the victims from the university. It seemed to be the only link they'd discovered. That and …

'Chlamydia,' Jamie said, surprised.

'What about it?' Thorsen asked, sipping some of his coffee.

'Four of the victims had it.'

'Teenagers with chlamydia,' he replied. 'Shock.'

'Well, two consecutive victims had it, then it skipped one, and then the next two had it.' Jamie thought on that. 'Did Sonja do a sexual assault assessment on the victims?'

Thorsen stopped sipping his coffee now. 'I'll find out.'

Jamie nodded, pursing her lips. 'It could be nothing, but, you know, better check.'

'The victims that had it – all female?'

'Two and two,' Jamie replied, scanning the scant information available.

'Guys and girls,' Thorsen parroted. 'Interesting.'

'Mm.' Jamie tried to meet his eye. 'Thanks for the backup, there. About the bedroom photographs.'

He smiled briefly. 'It's what partners are for.' He didn't look at her though. 'You expecting to see Hamlet on all of their shelves?'

Jamie followed his gaze to the window in front of them, to the brightly lit street already bustling with the morning crowds. 'I guess we'll find out.'

11

Annika Olsen

'WHERE DID YOU GET THIS?' Alex Öberg asked, gripping Hamlet in his hands so tightly Annika thought he was going to rip the thing in two.

'I …' she began, words failing her. Or at least lies. As she stared up at him, she realised that it wasn't anger in his face, it was … sadness. The kind of intense sadness that came with rage, with self-hate, with all those bad things. But it wasn't any of them. Alex Öberg, as he clutched the book, looked as though he was about to burst into tears. His eyes glistened, cheeks reddening, jaw quivering.

'I … I got it from the library,' Annika said, getting up onto her knees.

Alex's knuckles whitened. 'Do you know what this is?'

'I know it belonged to Juni Pedersen …'

'Why …' he croaked. 'Why do you have it?'

She swallowed. How much should she tell him? How much could she? 'I'm … looking into what happened.'

His eyes moved from the book to Annika.

'I knew Juni,' she said carefully. 'She was my friend, and …' The words began to come faster, her throat tightening. 'She was my friend, and she landed … next to me.' Her hand went to her cheek, where Juni's blood had spattered on her skin. 'And … and the police … don't seem to be doing anything. And I want to know why.'

'Why the police …?'

'Why she did it,' Annika said firmly, getting to her feet now. She looked down at the book held between them. 'And I think this is the key. This book is holding some secret, and … I was hoping you may know more about it.'

His hands shook, his breathing shaky too. 'I don't …'

'Alex,' Annika said, swallowing, lowering her voice. 'I know that she wrote an essay about it. And I know you graded it. That you read it. Was there anything that—'

'I can't … I can't …' he muttered, the words barely audible. He shook his head, a tear rolling down his cheek now.

'What do you know?' Annika pressed. 'Please, help me. Help me understand. Help me find out why she did it … or … who did it to her.'

Alex looked up, eyes wide, pulse racing in his neck. 'What did you say? Who did it … *to* her?'

'I don't know,' Annika said truthfully. 'I don't know if she … or if someone else … but I need to find out. And I know you know *something*.'

Alex Öberg licked his lips, then broke eye contact.

'Tell me, Alex.'

'I did grade Juni's paper,' he said. 'She also came to see me the week before she submitted it.' He let out a long, rattling exhale as though just saying that aloud had lifted a weight from his shoulders. 'Jesus,' he muttered, shaking his head. 'I should have known, then. That something was wrong, you know? She was asking all about Hamlet, about death and life after death. About the words 'What dreams may come', what they meant, what did Hamlet mean when he said them? What was the meaning of death? What did I think about it?' He held the book up. 'And this, she had this with her, kept flipping back and forth through the pages, manic, almost. I remember, I was scared by it. But I thought, I don't know – that she was just really excited about Hamlet.' He laughed at his own stupidity. 'I should have said something. Especially when I read her assignment – they're anonymised, but I knew right away it was hers – she dug into the ideas more, of death and what it meant, of it absolving sins, of Hamlet wanting to live forever in a dream state, that kind of thing. The essay was reasonably good, interesting, if not scatterbrained. But it was unstructured, unfounded, uncited, there was no effort to adhere to the brief, let alone to best practices.' He realised he was going off course and took a beat. 'What I mean is, I knew something was off, but I focused on the rubric, scored it badly in the hopes it would, I don't know, pull her out of whatever rabbit hole she had gone down. I could tell it was passionately written, but … my job was to grade them, you know? I couldn't show favouritism, or special interest—' He cut himself off again. 'I should have said something to someone then and there. But I didn't. The marks went out, I didn't hear from her. And then … a few weeks after, I heard that she'd …'

Annika looked at her feet, her own eyes filling now.

'I thought it was my fault,' Alex said, voice barely a whisper. 'I thought that she jumped because of what I wrote.' He sobbed once. 'I thought that she killed herself because of me.'

Annika's eyes flooded and tears spilled down her cheeks. Alex too. His grasp loosened around the book and it fell to his side in one hand, hanging there, twisted and creased from his grip.

'You can't blame yourself,' Annika said. 'Trust me. Juni and I … we used to be friends. We used to be close. A few months ago, she began pulling away. I didn't do anything about it. We started losing touch before that, last year or something … and I just thought … I don't know. I thought I had a lot going on, that I had my own friends, that it was … that it was her loss, or whatever. If I'd have known … if I'd have said something, or made more of an effort …'

'That's not your fault,' Alex said. 'None of it is …' He thought on it for a moment, wiping off his cheeks. 'Is that why you're doing this? Because you feel … guilty?'

She swallowed hard, steeled herself as best she could. 'I do feel guilty. But it's not why I'm doing this. I'm doing this because there's someone out there convincing, forcing, brainwashing people into killing themselves. And I don't feel like anyone's doing anything about it. So, I'm going to. Or at least I'm going to try.' When she looked up, Alex was staring at her.

'Okay,' he said, taking another breath, finding some strength in his voice. 'I'll help.' He looked around. 'But there'll be students here in a minute, maybe we should go somewhere else and talk about it?'

She nodded quickly. 'Yes. I mean, yeah, of course. That would be good.'

He smiled at her and she felt herself blush a little, suddenly aware of how she must look, puffy-eyed and snot-nosed. She looked away, bashful almost.

'I know a coffee shop.'

'Alright,' she said, gathering up her things from the floor.

As they began walking, Alex spoke again. 'How did you find out about me, anyway? How did you know I graded Juni's assignment?'

'It was Lagerström. He told me.'

'Lagerström?' Alex was surprised. 'He shouldn't have – how did you … I mean, it's all supposed to be private information. Confidential, you know?'

'You could say I, uh, had to play *hard ball.* In a way, I guess I had him *over a barrel.*'

She felt a hand on her arm then and stopped. Alex was looking right at her. 'Wait, you know about his erotic novella?'

Annika struggled to hide her surprise. 'You already knew?'

'We're his PhD students,' Alex said, scoffing a little. 'Who do you think he forces to proofread that shit for him?'

They laughed as they walked out of the building and into the afternoon sun.

The coffee shop was close to campus. Alex was inside getting Annika a latte. She could see him waiting in line. She figured she had a few minutes, and probably needed to update Jamie. She called, but Jamie didn't pick up. Answering machine. Shit.

She cleared her throat, turning away from the window. 'Hey, Jamie,' she said quickly. 'It's, um, it's Annika. I just wanted to let you know that I tracked down Alex Öberg who marked Juni's assignment on Hamlet – he spoke to her about Hamlet before she died, too, met with her. I'm going to find out more information, and I'll let you know. But so far, I know Juni was into the meaning of death, of it absolving sins, or something. That, and of death being like an endless dream state, or something? I don't know, I'll try and get hold of the essay if I can. 'Kay, uh, talk soon, I guess."

She hung up the phone, but she'd barely managed to touch the screen when she heard a chair move behind her.

Annika turned quickly, seeing Alex there, standing awkwardly, a thumb hooked over his shoulder. 'I, uh – sorry, I didn't mean to eavesdrop. It's just, long like, kind of, and I, uh …' he stammered, trying to find his words. He closed his eyes then, shook his head a little. 'I actually don't want coffee.'

'Oh,' Annika said, taken aback. 'Sorry, I just thought … it's okay, we can talk another time if you're busy, or—'

'No, no! It's not that,' Alex interrupted quickly. 'What I mean is … I'm hungry. Are you hungry?'

'I guess …?'

'Great. Can I, uh …' He cleared his throat, dropped to a more manly key and stood more confidently. 'Can I take you to dinner?'

Now she was really taken aback. 'Oh, uh … yeah, yeah, of course,' she replied, holding back a grin, feeling her cheeks flush. 'I'd like that.'

He breathed a big sigh of relief. 'Shit, great. No! I mean, not shit. Just great.' He laughed. 'That's great.'

She nodded, brushing her fringe around the rim of her glasses. 'Now?'

'Yeah, now.' He extended his hand to her and she took it, feeling his palm a little sweaty.

She didn't mind at all.

They began walking.

Alex made no effort to hide his own grin. So, Annika let hers out, too.

'So, Annika,' he began, swinging her hand a little. 'What kind of books do you like to read?'

12

Lucas Adell

'EZ,' Lucas muttered to himself as he drove, heading straight to Lärbro.

It was a small village a little way south. Not far. Not so far you couldn't ride a bike there, Lucas thought.

But who the hell was this EZ? And what the hell was his daughter messing around with him for? Drugs? A second phone? No, not his Rebecca, surely. He shook his head, fastening his grip on the steering wheel. The speedometer climbed as he accelerated, whipping through the countryside. Lärbro, 5km, a sign said. Faster now.

How was he going to find this scumbag? This fucking drug dealer who'd been involved with his fifteen-year-old daughter? It made him sick. Sick. And if he'd done anything to her, killed her, or given her something that she'd overdosed on … if he'd spiked her, or drugged her and …

Bile reared up in Lucas' throat. That piece of shit. He'd tear him apart.

No, no, focus, Lucas. You don't even know who this guy is yet. How are you going to find him? Lärbro is small, but not that small. What are you going to do, go door to door? No, you're better than that, you have more tools at your disposal.

Välkommen till Lärbro. The sign came up fast, buildings looming out of the gathering darkness. Dusk had fallen quickly now. Perfect, Lucas thought.

He stamped on the brakes and wrestled the car into a lay-by, already reaching for his laptop in the passenger seat. He pulled it onto his thighs and opened a browser page. Think, Lucas. How to find someone? Facebook, duh. He logged into his, searched for 'EZ'. Random people popped up, none with their locations set to Lärbro. Not visibly anyway. There were dozens of them, mostly men, a lot of fake accounts or defunct ones. He exhaled. Far short of trying to hack each account, he didn't think he'd get anywhere, and then it'd be working one by one. But that was stupid anyway – if this EZ character was a drug dealer, then he wouldn't be on Facebook, especially not with his drug dealing moniker.

Okay, regroup. What do you know? EZ. Probably stands for a name. Maybe, anyway. Alright, and Lärbro isn't exactly big. If he lives here, his information is probably on some register somewhere. When was the last census done? He Googled it quickly. Two years ago. Island-wide census for estimation of population and calculation of taxes and … blah blah, government bullshit.

Okay, Gotland official website, site search, census, results … take census. This page is no longer available. Alright. No problem, open the console … here we go. Yep, html code shows it's just a form with an expiration date baked in – probably logging data on an AWS server. Hmm, not likely to be very hackable. AWS is pretty bomb proof. Lucas had used it plenty of times. 2-factor auth, IP detection. Maybe he didn't need to hack the server directly though …

Hmm, what hosting are they using? He scanned the console, scrolling down. WordPress. Typical. He basically scoffed to himself. Alright, a WP site with an embedded form, probably a standard form-builder app. He doubted the government would spring for bespoke. And the beauty of WordPress sites was that they all had a public-facing login page and if you knew the prefix … 'wp-admin' followed by the URL … bingo. The login portal appeared.

Okay … now what. Username … could be tricky. Maybe not. Back to the government site, then to the contacts page … here we go. Email directory. Local page to the area, okay, administrator … there's only one. And he doubted anyone else would have the login. Grab her email, okay. Open Sublime Text, write a quick Python script to brute the login portal. Here we go, easy peasy. Now, common standard passwords for WP sites – he hoped she wouldn't be smart enough to change them … especially not for a temporary census data collection form. Usual suspects: 1234, admin, guest … his fingers danced over the keyboard like lightning. Alright, here we go. Execute.

The script did its work, the login page fluttering in the background as the script hammered through the passwords.

Then the words 'password invalid' came up. Shit. Reset password? Hack her email address? He'd have more trouble doing that than he would hacking this. Hmm. Alright, think, think.

Okay, Facebook, right. It was usually the best place to start when you wanted to hack someone. He used her full name, found her right away.

Her profile said she was 53, single, lived alone. No children that he could see. Jesus, the privacy settings were wide open. It was a chum bucket of information. A smorgasbord. Alright, alright, where do we start? Dog pictures. Hundreds of them.

Chihuahua cross something fluffy … alright … dog's name? Peanut.

Try Peanut.

Password invalid. Shit.

Don't stress. Keep looking.

Dog's birthday? Dog … dog … dog. Dog-a-versary? Lucas raised an eyebrow. A post from a few months ago … celebrating two years with my amazing Peanut … and a date. Lucas checked the defunct form. Three weeks before the form opened.

No. Surely not. Too easy?

Peanut12052017.

Password invalid.

He ground his teeth.

Wait, did WordPress force special characters now?

Pe@nut12052017.

Login successful!

He let himself smile a little. That was almost too easy. Okay, here we go.

He navigated quickly to the directory where the form entries were stored. Sort by last name, reverse A-Z ordering. Can't be many people with a surname starting with 'Z' in Gotland, let alone Lärbro.

He was right, there wasn't.

It took just a second to locate the only one with a local address.

Zagorski. First name … Emil.

Emil Zagorski. EZ. Living here in Lärbro. Twenty-four

years old. Twenty-four? Jesus Christ. Nine years older than Rebecca. That piece of shit.

Lucas jabbed the address into the satnav with force, then took off again.

Minutes later, he was there, parked outside.

The street was quiet, just a house every fifty metres. Modest, old. The garden overgrown. The place inconspicuous. Anyone would think it was abandoned. It looked like. Was EZ even here? Maybe he'd fled after he killed Rebecca.

Jesus, that was a grim thought.

Lucas flexed his hands. They were shaking. What was he going to do? Knock on the door, and when EZ opened it, shove him inside, beat him until he told Lucas where Rebecca was?

It was as good a plan as any.

As he opened the door, the courtesy light flashed on and he caught a glimpse of himself in the rear-view mirror. Gaunt and drawn, his face lined, the circles beneath his eyes carved into his cheeks, charcoal-dark, his eyes bloodshot and wide.

He needed sleep.

But first, he needed answers.

Lucas swept from the car across the road, reaching the front gate quickly. It was rusted but the fresh scratches on the latch told him it was still in regular use.

That was something, he supposed.

He was nervous as he lifted the small bar, checking over his shoulders for any signs of anyone watching. The street, however, seemed quiet. This was a quiet town. Not even that, really. A few houses dotted along three streets. Barely a hamlet.

The perfect place to stay off the radar while you did heinous things to teenagers.

His anger grew, his eyes widening, focus sharpening. Fist

balled, he walked up the front step and banged on the door. Stern but not frenzied. He'd have to keep his cool if he was going to stop himself from ripping EZ's face right off his body.

After thirty seconds of silence, he rapped again, glancing at the windows. All the blinds drawn, curtains too. No way he'd see inside.

Then it dawned on him. Shit, if he was a drug dealer, a bang on the door like that might mean the police were here. How could he have been so stupid?

He jumped down off the front step and walked across the garden, dried out and unkempt. He picked his way through the near-dead, knee-high grass and went around the side of the house, following the cracked and uneven paving stones until he found himself in the back garden. It opened onto the fields that populated northern Gotland. No fence, just wild flora stretching away. But no fresh tracks through it. EZ hadn't slipped out the back and made a run for it then. That was something, at least.

Lucas eased up the back staircase towards the door, a worn out old wooden storm door that hung lopsided on its hinges. He reached out and pulled it open carefully, willing it not to squeak, and held it there with his heel.

The back door itself was wood, with a single glass insert in the middle. Inside was dark, and Lucas cupped his hands to the glass to get a better look. A kitchen, he could tell. But not much else.

Before he could even try the handle, the thing swung inwards of its own accord. The light pressure he applied to the glass was enough. It wasn't locked, not even closed.

He froze as the door opened slowly, listening as it sighed into the darkness.

His heart hammered.

He waited.

Nothing. No sound. No movement. Was EZ out? Was he asleep? He could leave, right now, turn and run away, back to his car, go home.

No, no! This was Rebecca. He'd found this guy. *The* guy. The one who knew something. He was here. He couldn't chicken out now.

He nodded to himself, took a deep breath, and then stepped inside.

If EZ was here, he'd get the drop on him, pin him down, force him to answer his questions. And if he wasn't … then Lucas would look around. For answers. If he could find a laptop or computer, he'd take it, and figure it out from there.

As he crossed the threshold, he paused, noticing the marks on the door frame. Gouges, like someone had put a pry bar into the jamb and levered it open. Where the deadbolt catch should have been there was just a hole in the wood, splintered and raw.

Had someone broken in here?

If so, when? Who? Someone chasing EZ for money? The police?

Fuck, he didn't know. Couldn't know.

But there was no going back. Ignore it, press on, do what you came here to do.

The interior was cool despite the heat of the day and the kitchen smelled like old food and unwashed dishes. A glance at the sink told him he was right in his assessment. In the dying light, he could see ants scurrying across the countertop, feeding on the remnants of food strewn there.

Jesus, Rebecca, he thought. This place is a fucking dump. Why the hell would you want to come here? He could only imagine the sort of person who called a hovel like this home.

He traced his way inwards, careful not to make any sound

or turn on any lights. He wanted to be on EZ before the guy even knew he was there.

Ahead, there was a doorway. Living room, Lucas thought, as he approached.

Inside was total darkness. Like walking into the deep night.

He'd have to move slowly, cautiously. He'd have to take his time, and—

His foot hit something metal and it went skittering into the room ahead.

Fuck.

A fork or spoon. Why was it on the floor?

He looked about again, saw that the table was sitting oddly, off-centre in the room. The chairs, too, were kicked away, and one of them was leaned back against the wall like it'd tried to fall but couldn't.

He looked down then, saw a broken plate on the tiles, a splatter of food, and the knife that went with the fork he'd just kicked.

Jesus, what happened here?

Lucas' mouth was dry now. 'Hello?' he called. He didn't know who this guy was. He could be in there with a gun for all Lucas knew. 'Hello, EZ?' he risked.

No answer.

Maybe he wasn't home.

Lucas remained still, straining his ears. No sound.

Okay, forward. Same plan. Find a computer, then get out.

He stepped into the living room, eyes struggling to pick anything out. There were heavy curtains covering the windows. He might as well have been walking into a goddamn cave.

Instinctively, he put his hands out in front of him, forcing himself to breathe slowly, evenly.

Small steps, shuffle forward. Get to the window, pull back the curtain. Don't draw attention to the fact that you just broke in here. No lights, no flashlight. Just a little fading sun to light the way.

His fingers cut through the air, then hit something suddenly. Right in the middle of the room.

He stopped, groping the thing. It felt cold, wet. Lumpy. He'd thought it was the back of a sofa or something, but now … what the fuck was this? He moved his hands across it, unable to picture what it was. And then he felt it. An ear.

He recoiled, stumbling backwards, his hands sticky, and backed into the wall next to the kitchen door.

His shoulder hit the light switch and the whole room burst to life.

Lucas' eyes stung and he shielded them from the glare, squinting through his reddened fingers.

That's what he noticed first, his hands. Covered in blood.

And then the thing he'd walked into.

The person.

In the middle of the room, a man was tied to a chair. His hands were pinned behind his back, his mouth filled with what looked like an old sock. His head was hanging backwards, dead eyes turned skywards, face bloodied from a fierce beating, left eye swollen shut. The guy looked young, his hair long and shaggy, greasy looking.

Lucas didn't need to check for signs of life, the kitchen knife buried in his chest up to the hilt was enough of a giveaway. Blood had spilled down his stomach, soaking his shirt and jeans, and had pooled around him on the floor.

And now Lucas had left footprints in it.

He gagged, pressing the back of his hand to his mouth, tasting the blood on them.

He didn't waste any more time before he turned, scrambling away, mouth filling with vomit as he ran across the kitchen.

He shouldered his way through the door, hurdled down the stairs and fell forward into the long grass, onto his hands and knees, sick and bile spilling between his teeth and onto the earth.

He wretched, his empty stomach folding on itself as it tried to expel the little that was in there.

His fingers curled into the dry grass, the dust congealing onto his bloodied knuckles. Was that … EZ? Someone had broken in and … tortured him. Beaten him. Stabbed him! Killed him … He was dead. And so were Lucas' chances of finding Rebecca! But why? Why had someone killed him? Was it a coincidence? Could it be? Or was someone else looking for EZ too? Or maybe … someone was trying to stop Lucas finding him … Had EZ known something about Rebecca? Had he killed Rebecca?

Lucas punched the ground in frustration, his hand rebounding off the dry dirt.

Whatever was going on, whatever reason someone had for killing that piece of shit … Lucas may never know. So, what now?

There was a roaring in his ears, an urge to scream in frustration. But he resisted it. Breathed. Shook off the rage as best he could.

Do nothing, a voice seemed to say. His voice of reason? Do nothing, just leave. Get out of here, before someone sees you. Before you're caught here.

Sanity found him in a flash and he got to his feet, turning a full three-sixty to check his surroundings. Quiet. Dark.

Night had almost a full hold on the island now.

Lucas steadied himself, turned, and made it back to the path.

Then he was at the front of the house, through the creaky gate, onto the street, loping like a wounded animal.

He made it to the car, smeared red on to the white handle as he pulled the door open and climbed in.

And then, with EZ's blood on his hands and vomit on his chin, he tore away from the curb and just drove.

13

Sonja Ehrhart

SHE'D PERHAPS BEEN TOO cruel.

Sonja was thinking about that all weekend. After dropping Kjell and Jamie at their hotel, she'd thought stirring the pot would make things better, or at least force some sort of change. But ... she'd not seen Kjell in a while, and he was obviously torn up about the whole thing. So, was sticking her nose in really the best option? Were they that close anymore?

She shook it off, glad to get back to work, and scanned herself into the hospital. She descended the stairs as normal and walked along the coolly-lit corridor. The white walls and pale 'daylight' lighting made it feel very clinical, very ... dead, almost. She thought that was apt though, considering she worked at the morgue.

If she wasn't so weird, the thought might have induced a grimace or something. But she just kept bobbing along to the song playing in her headphones – Hungry Like the Wolf. Duran Duran. Her long legs carried her forward, totally alone

She paused briefly at the magnetic door and flashed her

card again, turning and using her shoulder to open the door to save the files she had under one arm, and the coffee she had in the other. But as soon as she entered, she froze.

The office stretched out in front of her, her and Jassen's desks in place, but their contents strewn across the floor. Papers and folders littered the ground. Torn from drawers and from surfaces and hurled about.

Her breathing quickened, her eyes darting around. No movement. What the hell? A break-in? Or Jassen just having a laugh?

She glanced over her shoulder. Magnetic door. You'd need a key card …

'Jassen?' she called, timidly, even. Her voice shook a little.

There was no response.

'Jassen? You in here?' she asked again, moving forward slowly.

She made to drop the files she was carrying – files on the latest victims that she'd been poring over at home. But then didn't. Firstly, there was nowhere to put them. No empty space. And secondly … she was preoccupied by the blood.

Her eyes homed in on it, oozing under the door to the break room in a dark puddle. She couldn't tell if it was still spreading, but it was dark, shining in the glow of the halogens.

Her heart hammered and she started forward, not perturbed by the sight or smell, but rather by what she expected to find on the other side of that door.

'Jassen?' she repeated, quieter this time.

No response.

Her hand reached out, coffee still in it, and she hooked two fingers around the handle, pulling gently.

It swung towards her, smearing the blood and sweeping it deeper into the office.

It lapped at the toes of her boots, but she didn't notice.

There, on the floor just beyond the door, was Jassen. He lay with his head towards her, on his back, legs splayed under him, shirt soaked with blood, rumpled around the nape of his neck like he'd run away, but been grabbed, yanked backwards and down to the ground.

Her eyes flitted across his body, the damage there. Single stab wound to the gut, it looked like. She could see it. The assailant chased him into the break room, grabbed him by the back of the collar and pulled him down. From his position, standing right where Sonja was now, he knelt, plunging a knife into Jassen's gut to subdue him. Then, he … pulled it out, drew it upwards … her breath caught in her throat as her eyes came to rest on Jassen's throat. The wound there was self-explanatory. One hard rip across the skin with a large, sharp blade, serrated in part, clear from the jagged cuts at the corners of the slice. The attack had been deliberate enough to puncture the trachea, to sever one of the carotid arteries.

So that explains all the blood, Sonja thought.

Jassen was dead. She would know, it was kind of her job to. But it didn't look like he'd been dead long. Hell, he was usually here no more than an hour before her. Which meant …

Sonja whipped around, staring through the window into the lab.

At first, she didn't notice him.

Her eyes went to the slab – empty, gleaming, as she'd left it on Friday. Then, her eyes flitted to the drawers. The bodies. They were open, several of them, the sheets pulled back, exposing the victims. A boy, two girls. She didn't recognise them at first. There had been so many.

Their pale corpses lay still, white against the silver steel beneath them.

She only noticed him when he moved.

He was standing behind the furthest drawer. The one that contained Juni Pedersen. Sonja recognised her now, gasping as her eyes made out the visage of a figure, dressed all in black. A black coat, black gloves, black trousers. His head was entirely covered by a black mask, with just the tiniest holes for eyes. They glimmered black through the fabric and Sonja shuddered beneath their gaze.

He was holding Juni's arm, the palm and forearm pointed to the ceiling, the black heart there, trapped between his fingers, stark on her flesh. It was as though he was inspecting it, admiring it even.

Sonja's jaw was clamped shut, darkness pulsing around the edges of her vision as her heart beat so hard she thought it might burst.

She was rooted to the spot, unable to move, to do anything.

There was only one thing in her mind, one thing she was sure of. This was the Black Heart Killer. Here, in her lab. Why, she didn't know. Who, she couldn't tell. But she'd never been more certain in her life.

And then he moved.

Lightning quick, with purpose.

He dropped Juni's arm and skirted the drawer, gliding across the empty lab like a wraith.

Sonja filled her lungs with a rattling breath. One thought seized her.

Run.

She did.

The files spilled from her grip, the coffee too. They hit the ground simultaneously, the first bursting outwards like petals of a flower, the second hitting the ground base first, the liquid shooting into the air like a fountain.

It splattered on the tiles where Sonja had been a moment before.

She galloped towards the door, scrabbling at her neck for the lanyard.

Her hand clattered into the concrete, her body hitting the wall as she tried to grab and shove her card against the reader.

She heard the door to the lab open on her right, but didn't have time to look back.

The light turned from red to green on the reader and she gripped the handle, pulling hard.

It opened towards her as a heavy hand closed about her shoulder, pulling viciously.

She sailed backwards, her shoulder straining, pain lancing through her hand as she tried desperately to hold on to the door handle.

Sonja screamed, her arm twisting awkwardly as he dragged her backwards.

Her voice echoed down the empty corridor outside, her long, bony fingers locked around the worn metal handle.

She felt her jacket pull across her shoulder, down her upper arm a little as the killer tried to drag her free.

An idea formed in her mind, her body responding as quickly as it did.

Sonja drove her left shoulder forward, pulling the arm free of her jacket sleeve.

There was a grunt behind her as the killer stumbled.

She released the door handle then, twisting fully so she faced him, her right hand following the first, her leather jacket leaving her hand behind.

The killer staggered, holding on to it, and slipped on one of the files strewn on the floor.

She needed no more encouragement, and slipped through the security door before it closed, dragging it shut behind her.

No sooner had it clicked into the jamb than he was there at the glass, face hovering an inch from it, beady, black eyes fixed on hers.

Sonja stood there, fists balled, breathing hard, watching him, waiting. There was no way he could get to her. This door was two inches of steel, and if he went for the main doors in the lab and somehow got through those, she'd be long gone by the time he made it to the corridor.

And he seemed to know this. There was no haste to him. He made no effort to escape through the fire exit at the back of the main lab. The one that led to the emergency staircase.

He just hovered there, watching her, inspecting her.

She shivered a little.

The killer's shoulders rose as he drew in a deep breath, and then exhaled slowly onto the glass, fogging it.

Sonja watched as he lifted his gloved hand, index finger extended, and pushed it against the surface.

Slowly, he moved it upwards, cutting a sharp line into the mist. His line curved to a stop, and then moved again, drawing a valley.

She knew right away what it was he was drawing, but it still filled her with a sickening sense of dread.

When his finger reached the lower point, he began filling in the outline, squeaking back and forth as he cut out the centre, leaving behind his message.

A black heart.

14

Kjell Thorsen

THORSEN ROSE QUICKLY, the words not really registering. 'What did you say?'

He could see Jamie watching him from across the desk. They'd managed to talk their way into one of the conference suites that the hotel offered. A big table with plenty of space between them. Jamie and he had set up on opposite sides, each doing their own research based on the file that Larsson had given them. Though Thorsen felt like he was feigning his. He couldn't even think straight, let alone conjure leads out of thin air to solve this case. That was always Jamie's party trick.

Sonja sighed heavily in his ear, her breathing shaky. 'I said that our lab was broken into. And I was ... attacked. By the killer. The Black Heart Killer.'

Thorsen blinked, leaning on the table with his other hand. 'Jesus Christ,' he muttered. 'Are you okay? Where are you now?'

'I'm still here,' Sonja said, 'at the lab. The police are here, the NOD, it's … I just … I wanted to let you know.'

'I'll be right there,' Thorsen replied. 'Don't move.'

'You really don't have to,' Sonja said. 'I'm fine, honestly, I just wanted to let you know. The NOD, they're on scene, it's all being handled.'

'I'll be there in a few minutes,' Thorsen said decisively, hanging up.

He grabbed his coat off the back of the chair and threw it around his shoulders.

Jamie carried on working.

'You coming?' Thorsen asked, pausing momentarily.

'For what?' Jamie said, looking up now.

'There was a break-in at the hospital, Sonja was attacked, by the killer.'

'Oh,' she said, fingers hovering over the keys of her laptop. 'Is she alright?'

Oh? Is she alright? Thorsen kept a lid on the sudden anger in him. Why was Jamie like this? What the hell was wrong with her? Why the fuck couldn't she just be normal for once?

'Yeah,' he forced out through gritted teeth. 'She's fine. But that's not the point.'

'So, what is? You don't need me to help check if she's okay.' Jamie went on typing, eyes returning to her screen. 'I don't even know the woman.'

Thorsen's fists curled at his sides. He tried to breathe calmly. 'Fine, for the case then. You know, the one we're here to work. Leads, evidence … this is the first time the killer has surfaced in two years. Don't you think that's worth looking into?'

Jamie sighed, leaning back from her computer as though the interruption was wholly unwelcomed. 'I do, and I'm sure Dahlvig does as well. Which is why I'm sure there's a fleet of detectives and forensic techs there right now, going over that place with magnifying glasses and forceps. What exactly is it you think I would be able to add to that?'

'What if they miss something?'

'Then he should get better detectives.'

'I'm pretty sure that's *us.*'

'I'm not that arrogant.'

Thorsen didn't try to hide a scoff.

'And plus,' Jamie said, 'in eighteen months and twenty-three victims, he's not left a single shred of physical evidence anywhere. Not a thing,' she said evenly, looking right at Thorsen. Her gaze seemed to make it worse, make his anger worse. 'And this will be no different. There won't be anything to find. The place will be clean. I guarantee it.' She readjusted her position and found her place on screen again. 'I'll be of more use here, doing research, going over everything Larsson gave us. But I understand why you need to go.' She glanced up again then. 'Though I was going to go and speak to some of the victims' families this afternoon if you wanted to come with me?'

He just shook his head in disbelief, then laughed. The only thing he could do. And then he moved towards the door. 'No, Jamie,' he said, reaching it. 'I'm going to check if Sonja is okay. She's my friend, and that's what friends do. They look out for each other.'

'You never mentioned her in the two years we've been working together.'

'That doesn't mean she's not my friend. Not that I'd expect you to understand.'

Jamie raised her chin defiantly and nodded. 'Gotcha.'

He narrowed his eyes, mouth opening to speak, to ask what the fuck that was supposed to mean. But then he thought better. He was tired. Too tired now. Too tired to deal with it anymore.

Without another word, he left, storming towards reception and the front door.

He slowed, came to a halt, and then sagged forward, crouching and holding his head in his hands. He wanted to scream. But that would do nothing except be more proof of how much she was fucking with his head.

No, no. Sonja was what mattered. Jamie always did this. Skewed focus towards herself. He needed clarity, he needed space. He needed to focus on what mattered. Sonja was attacked. The killer showed himself. Leaving Jamie was the right thing to do.

'Sir?'

Thorsen looked up from his position on the ground.

A young receptionist smiled at him, her eyes bright, her teeth brighter. 'Are you alright?'

He forced a smile. 'Yeah, I am ... would you mind calling me a cab?'

'Yes ... right away.' She cleared her throat. 'Are you ... sure everything's okay?'

'Yeah,' Thorsen sighed, staying right where he was and once more burying his head in his hands. 'Just fucking peachy.'

Thorsen had some trouble getting past the police cordon – the hospital was entirely shut down. And without a badge to flash, it was a tall order to explain. But another phone call to Sonja managed to get him inside. Though it took some persuading. He thought he'd have to name drop Dahlvig to make it happen, but luckily, that wasn't the case. Still, he knew he'd end up coming face to face with the guy soon enough.

And though he didn't seem to have Jamie's knack for psychic-level intuition, he was dead right.

It wasn't hard to find his way to the morgue – he just followed the trail of techs, all dressed in white suits, laying little evidence cards on the ground and snapping photographs. They were like little insects, crawling all about, doing their work, oblivious to everything going on around them.

Thorsen had to step between them not to kick over their little signs or mess up their cordons.

'Kjell!'

He looked up to see Sonja waving to him, standing outside the door to the morgue, leaning against the wall. Her long white hair looked almost ghostly in the pale lighting, and her usually youthful face looked drawn and lined. He seemed to notice, for the first time then, that she was a lot older than him.

But she still hugged him all the same, strongly, despite her thin arms.

'Sonja,' he whispered, hugging her back. 'Are you alright? Tell me what happened.' He held her by the shoulders, searching her face.

She sighed and shook her head. 'Jesus, I don't know where to begin. I came in, everything normal, then, uh, I noticed the offices were a wreck.' She nodded sideways through the open door, and he saw that they were indeed a wreck. Files and papers everywhere, and at the far end, a sheet laid over what Thorsen knew had to be a body. There were little platforms set up – stepping stones on pointed legs that allow techs and detectives to move through pools of blood without disturbing them.

'That motherfucker opened Jassen's throat,' Sonja said. 'Fucking ruthless.'

'You saw him?' Thorsen asked, grabbing her attention again.

She just nodded. 'He was in the lab, pawing at the kids. He had the drawers open, admiring his fucking handiwork, I bet,' she growled, letting out a long breath. 'I barely got out of there, managed to slam the door in his face. If I hadn't …'

'But you did, and that's all that matters.'

'Right, yeah. I called it in, and the second I started dialling the police, he ran, slipped out through the lab and up the fire escape.'

Thorsen took another glance around the room, catching the eye of a man standing past Jassen's body, in the break room. He had a white shirt on with a black tie tucked in between the button holes. His sleeves were rolled to the elbow, showing off veined forearms. He had sandy-coloured hair, brushed back, and a thick moustache. His roughly stubbled face gave the impression that he was older than his years, but his sharp blue eyes told Thorsen he still had the drive of a younger, hungrier man. He guessed this was Dahlvig. And as he left the man he was speaking to and strode across the little platforms towards Thorsen, Thorsen knew he'd guessed right.

Dahlvig stepped into the corridor, and though he was shorter than Thorsen, he could tell that Dahlvig feared no man.

'Ivar Dahlvig,' he said, offering his hand. 'Polisöverinten-dent, National Operations Department.'

Thorsen shook it, finding the grip firm. 'Kjell Thorsen. Formerly of the Lulea Police.'

'Thorsen?' Dahlvig repeated the name, pursing his lips under his bristling moustache.

'You know me?'

'I've heard of you.'

'From Lulea?'

'From the trafficking ring case. And that shit up north where that woman was hunting people. And that case with the guy dressed as a bird.'

'You heard about that, huh?'

'Hard not to,' Dahlvig chuckled. 'Not every day someone dresses up like a giant bird and starts mutilating people.'

'No, it's not,' Thorsen said, offering a brief smile.

'But despite your mild notoriety, I still have to ask: what the fuck are you doing at my crime scene?'

'Oh …'

Sonja came to his rescue. 'He's here as a personal favour. To me.'

'To you?' Dahlvig looked at her now. 'And why are you personally asking detectives to come to my crime scene?'

'I thought you could use the help,' Sonja answered flatly. A certain chain of respect was in place for those in law enforcement. Sonja, however, didn't seem to subscribe to it. 'It's been almost two years, and twenty-three bodies have hit my table. I hazarded a guess that fresh eyes would be welcomed.'

'Fresh eyes.' Dahlvig nodded. 'And that's what you are?' he asked Thorsen. 'Fresh eyes, here to help crack this case?' He made a point of looking around Thorsen's flanks down the corridor. 'Just tell me you didn't bring Jamie Johansson with you?'

Thorsen laughed. 'No,' he said.

'That's something at least.'

'No, I meant, she's back at the hotel. I didn't bring her *here,* right now.'

'Jesus Christ,' Dahlvig said. 'No. Out, now,' he ordered,

pointing back down the corridor. 'It was good to put a name to the face, but this is a closed investigation, and I won't have you and Johansson—'

'Sir, please,' Thorsen interrupted. 'Just hear me out.'

'Hear you out? Hear out the detective trying to ram his dick in my case?'

'I'm not trying to *ram* anything … look,' he went on, keen to navigate away from whatever metaphor Dahlvig was trying to get at. 'I'm not even a detective anymore, and neither is Johansson. We left the Kurrajakk police force months ago. I'm simply here to see if there's anything I could do to help. Sonja and I are former colleagues, and she just wanted to see this madness come to an end. That's all. I'm not here to interfere with your case. The opposite. You have my word on that.' He extended his hand to Dahlvig.

'Your word?' Dahlvig replied, staring down at it. 'And what is that worth, hmm? Kjell Thorsen?'

'My word is worth everything.'

Dahlvig measured him. 'And what about Johansson's word? Because if there's one thing I know about her from my own experience, as well as what I've heard, she doesn't give a damn about anything — especially not chain of command, orders, or protocol. And that is one thing I cannot afford to have within a hundred miles of this case. So, I'll ask again — politely, but for the last time.' He gestured towards the corridor once more.

'What if I told you Johansson didn't even want to be involved in the case?'

'Then I'd say you're full of shit. If she's here, then she's already involved.'

'She isn't. She's here because we're …' He risked a glance at Sonja. 'Because we're travelling together. That's all. Johansson is strictly retired.'

'You're screwing her?' Dahlvig seemed surprised.

Thorsen cleared his throat and looked away.

'Apologies if I caused offence. I just don't know why anyone would want to. From all accounts, I hear she's about as much fun as a bee sting on the ball sack.'

Thorsen noticed Sonja hiding a smirk out of the corner of his eye.

He just found himself angry once more. 'I'd appreciate it if you kept your opinions to yourself, sir.'

Dahlvig narrowed his eyes at Thorsen, noting the hunching posture, the tension in his shoulders. He shrugged briefly, but didn't apologise. 'So, you just want me to let you poke around, is that it?'

'The opposite,' Thorsen said. 'Before bird men and psycho people-hunters, I was actually a normal detective. And a good one at that.'

'I'm sure.' Dahlvig checked his watch. 'So, tell me what you want, I'm busy.'

'I'd like to assist with the case. Officially.'

'Officially? Oh.' Dahlvig smiled. 'We're clearly short-handed, as you can see.' He raised his chin at the dozen techs in the corridor, then nodded into the office, where another half dozen were working, alongside three, no four detectives that Thorsen could see. And this was just one scene.

'You can never have too many brains working at once.'

'Right, so we should set things aside to bring you up to speed? Tell me, where'd you park your white horse?'

'I'm already up to speed. And all your detectives don't mean dick if they're missing things.'

'Oh, so you want to *insult* my investigation before you save it. Good strategy. I can't wait to work with you.'

'And I bet that they found nothing, am I right?' Thorsen pointed into the office. 'Clean. This guy's dropped twenty-three bodies in as many months without leaving a single piece of evidence. And I guarantee that he didn't start now. He broke cover, sure. But that doesn't mean anything unless you find something to help close the net. And I'd be willing to bet that he slipped out of here without anyone noticing, too, right? Gone. Just like that.' He snapped his fingers.

'Oh, so we're looking for Keyser Söze. I'll put the word out.' Dahlvig sighed, looking bored.

Thorsen set his jaw. He'd totally stolen Jamie's assumption that the morgue was clean and passed it off as his own, but he'd also just axed her out of the investigation altogether. So why stop now? If he had any chance of Dahlvig not kicking him off the island that morning, he had to lay it all out there.

'I know you missed something,' Thorsen said. 'You, all your techs, all your guys.'

'Oh yeah, and what's that?'

Thorsen licked his lips. This was it. Sorry, Jamie. You had your chance. 'Hamlet.'

'I missed Hamlet,' Dahlvig said, nodding slowly. 'Stellar observation, Thorsen. Care to elaborate at all?'

He cleared his throat. 'I want to work this investigation.'

'And you're going to withhold evidence until I give in? Blackmailing an NOD officer. Strong play there, former detective.'

'Just a polite request. I'd never dream of hampering an investigation.'

'Which is why you're telling me about this now, only when you can leverage something out of this situation? Rather than the moment you discovered it?'

'The first night we arrived,' Thorsen said, standing a little taller, 'we went to check out the university, where Juni Pedersen jumped from the roof.'

'You and Johansson?'

'Me and Sonja,' Thorsen said quickly, looking at Sonja.

Her eye twitched, but she said nothing for or against Thorsen's lie.

Thorsen went on before Dahlvig could question her. 'There, we ran into a student, a friend of Juni's. After speaking, we went to Juni Pedersen's house, and managed to look around her bedroom.'

'Woah, woah,' Dahlvig said, 'you went to Juni Pedersen's residence?'

Thorsen ploughed forward, trying to recall the beats of Jamie's story. 'Inside, we noticed some things. There were lots of Shakespeare plays on her shelf, a black heart carved on her desk—'

'We already found that.'

'And the words, 'What dreams may come', which is from—'

'Hamlet, yes,' Dahlvig said. 'But there was no copy of Hamlet in her room. We catalogued every inch of that place.'

'That's because the copy of Hamlet she'd been reading wasn't *in* her room.'

Dahlvig moved his mouth, a little frustrated. His moustache danced.

'It was in the library.'

Dahlvig closed his eyes. 'And you found this copy?'

'I did.'

Sonja raised her eyebrows now, but luckily Dahlvig didn't see.

'Okay,' he said, holding his hand out to Thorsen. 'Give it to me.'

'I don't have it here.'

'But you do have it?'

He chuckled a little. 'Well …'

'Jesus Christ, Thorsen,' Dahlvig muttered. 'So, where the hell is it?'

'It's safe, I promise. We didn't want to remove it from the university, but it's safe.'

'Still there? In the library?'

'It's with the student that helped us – Annika Olsen. But that's not all.'

'Oh fuck.'

'We found out that Juni submitted an assignment on Hamlet shortly before she died. We're currently looking into that, to see whether it's a lead worth pursuing.'

'Do you have the assignment?'

'No, but we found the lecturer who set it. Our contact is meeting with him today.'

'And his name is …?'

'Uh …' Thorsen hedged. Fuck. He didn't actually know. Jamie hadn't told him. Shit. 'Uh …'

'Uh … uh …? You don't remember? Or you're full of shit?'

'No, I wrote it down. It's in my notes,' Thorsen said quickly. 'Back at the hotel.'

Dahlvig looked unhappy. 'I want that book. And I want that name.'

'Of course. I'll get them for you. Does this mean that I can …'

'Assist with the investigation? It doesn't really seem like you're giving me much choice here. Though I don't like the way you operate, Thorsen. Johansson's rubbing off on you, and you'll do well to cut her loose before she costs you your career.' He paused, then smiled. 'Though I guess she already has, *former* detective.'

Thorsen looked at his feet, hiding his grinding teeth.

'I don't appreciate anyone going behind my back, but this

is a lead worth pursuing, and you're right about one thing … twenty-three bodies and zero leads is not a good look. But let's get one thing straight.' He stepped closer to Thorsen. 'If you're working for me, you're working for me. Not with me, not alone, not around me. For me. Which means if you have a thought, an idea, an inkling, or just a bloody itch, you tell me first. And then you move. If I find out you lifted a finger without prior approval, I'll not only cut you loose, I'll chop your fucking balls off. Metaphorically, and literally. I'll have you arrested, and then charged with impeding an investigation, and believe me when I say things, Thorsen, I don't make idle threats and I don't do any paperwork unless I mean it. So, if I slap you with something, you better believe it'll stick. Got it?'

'Got it.' Thorsen nodded firmly.

'Now, get out of here, grab my details from the officer at the end of the hallway. And one more thing.'

'Yes, sir?'

'Keep Johansson out of my shit. If I even think for a *second* she's working this case, it's on your head.' He locked eyes with Thorsen for a few seconds to let it sink in, and then he turned back to the office and walked inside.

Sonja already had her hand on Thorsen's arm, pushing him towards the exit. 'I'll walk you out,' she said firmly.

He let himself be walked.

They paused briefly at the officer, who gave Thorsen Dahlvig's details, then they carried on. Sonja was silent, and glaring at Thorsen.

And even when they reached daylight and he was steered further into the car park and out of earshot of the cordon near the door, she didn't seem to soften.

'What the fuck was that?' she asked, folding her arms sternly.

'What was what?'

'Don't play dumb, it's not cute, and it's not you,' Sonja said sharply. 'You just about threw Jamie under the bus there. And yesterday, you were willing to leap in front of one for her.'

'Why do you think the killer showed himself now?' Thorsen mused, not really trying to change the subject, just not interested in the other line of conversation.

Sonja scoffed. 'You hearing me, Kjell? You passed Jamie's work off as your own, lied to Dahlvig, and dragged me into it, too. You see how fucked up that is?'

'What do you want me to say?' Thorsen asked. 'You heard Dahlvig. He doesn't want Jamie anywhere near this thing. She doesn't want to be here, either, so what does it matter? This way, everyone gets what they want.'

'Except you,' Sonja answered coldly. 'You want her.'

'I want my life back,' Thorsen replied, just as coldly. 'He's right, Jamie cost me my career. And now, who knows, maybe I've got another shot at getting it back.'

'What happened, Kjell? Talk to me? What happened between you and Jamie?'

'Could we not? I'm so tired of it.'

'Hey, talk to me,' she insisted, grabbing his arm.

He pulled in a long breath. 'What do you want me to say, huh? I'm in love with her? Well, it doesn't seem to be any kind of fucking secret. But we could never be … she's not … she's not normal. And a relationship would be a fucking shit show. If you could even call it a relationship. Whenever I'm around her I'm walking on eggshells, second-guessing every-thing I say, trying to navigate our conversations like a mine-field. Hell, it's fucking torture! I'm pretty sure I've got Stockholm Syndrome at this point. Some space would do us good.'

'You really believe that?'

'I thought you'd be jumping for joy. I thought you hated her.'

'I don't hate her. I just want you to be happy.'

'I am happy. Or I will be, I think. Once I get back to work. We're not … together. We're not sleeping with each other. We're not anything. We can't even have a simple fucking conversation. So … yeah. I just want to get back to work. And this is my chance.'

'And you're willing to kneecap Jamie to get there.'

'She'll understand.'

'Somehow, I doubt it.'

Thorsen sighed. 'Can we … can you just … can you just be a friend right now? Can we just get back to working together, and forget about Jamie, for once?'

She watched him carefully, then nodded. 'Okay. Whatever you say, Kjell.'

He felt a weight lifted, though the hot and sickening ball of lead in the pit of his stomach – guilt, he thought – didn't shift. 'Why did the killer show himself now?'

'I don't know.'

'It seems strange, right?'

'Does it?'

'Yeah. All this time without any hint of his presence. And now he shows up here, kills … that guy.'

'Jassen. My colleague. My friend,' she said.

'Right, right. I'm sorry, I spoke without thinking.'

'You seem to be doing a lot of that right now.'

He ignored it. 'I wonder if it's because Jamie and I arrived.'

'You're thinking highly of yourself.'

'It's the only thing that's changed, right? Why come here now, otherwise?'

'I don't know. He was looking at Juni Pedersen's body. Maybe she was special. How the fuck should I know?'

Thorsen bit his lip. 'I don't know. I'll think on it.'

'Why not ask Jamie? I'm sure she'd have some thoughts.'

He did his best to ignore that comment, too. 'I'm going to go. I need to find that book, and that name for Dahlvig. Are you all good? Can I check in with you later?'

Sonja sighed. 'Sure, whatever you want. I'll be heading home soon enough.'

'Okay, great.' He hugged her briefly, but it was like putting his arms around a mannequin. She was cold and stiff.

He released her, stepping back, distinctly aware of her judgemental stare.

This was what he wanted, right? He was going to get his badge back. His life back? He was about to gain it all.

So why the hell did he feel like he'd just thrown it all away instead?

15

Jamie Johansson

JAMIE WAS HEADING out of the door when Thorsen walked into the lobby of the hotel.

He was scowling. Not really surprising considering she'd been dodging his calls and it was now up to six missed ones.

'You're not answering your phone,' he said, barring her way, hands on hips, looking stern.

'I was working,' Jamie replied coolly. 'Everything alright?'

His eye twitched a little. 'What's the name of the student you're speaking to, the one with the book: Annika, right? Annika Olsen?'

'Yeah,' Jamie replied, keeping a poker face. 'Why?' What was going on, she didn't know. But Thorsen seemed anxious. And that wasn't his usual state.

'I just need to know. What about the PhD student she was looking for. I don't think you ever told me his name.'

'Didn't I?' Jamie asked, playing a little dumb. She knew Thorsen well enough to know when he was massaging her.

He seemed to do it a lot. Or at least try. She knew she was difficult. But it did give her a very good sense of when Thorsen was being himself and when he was trying to get something.

'You didn't. Want to bring me up to speed?'

'What for?'

'We're partners. Don't you think we should share information?' He played at being hurt.

'Of course. So, what happened with Sonja? She okay? Did you run into any trouble at the scene?'

'Trouble? Like what?'

Jamie shrugged. 'I don't know. The first sign of the killer in person in almost two years. I guessed the place would be a zoo. Awash with techs and detectives. I thought Dahlvig himself might be there.'

'Is that why you didn't want to come?'

'So, he was? Did you speak to him?' Jamie watched him like a hawk. She could practically see his cogs turning. She just wondered whether he was about to lie to her. She never let on, but he had a tell. Raised eyebrows. Well, sort of. They kind of crumpled in the middle like he was trying to be sincere.

'No, no,' Thorsen responded. 'I just spoke to Sonja.'

Lie.

Alright, then. If that's what you want to do.

'I'm glad she's okay.'

'I didn't say …'

'If she wasn't, I suspect you'd still be there. Her being such a close friend, and all.'

He blinked, seemingly shocked by the barbed nature of the comment. Rich, Jamie thought, but kept her countenance even.

'I'm headed out,' Jamie said. 'I'm going to drop in on the family of the first victim.'

'No!' Thorsen said, too quickly. He regained composure. 'I just mean, before we jump into anything, we should sit down, get each other up to speed. I'm sure you've got some thoughts after a morning of research. Did you hear from Annika? Did she find out more about Juni's assignment?'

'Mhm,' Jamie said. 'She texted me a few minutes ago actually, said she found out who graded it.'

'Oh?' Thorsen tried to play it cool. 'Want to loop me in?'

'Sure, I'll tell you in the car. Come on, I called a cab.' She made a move to leave.

He stopped her, hand on her arm, grip tighter than she would have liked.

Thorsen looked nervous, skin flushed.

Her first thought: He's screwing me over.

It was violent and insipid, invading her mind. She didn't like it, didn't like jumping to distrust. But she didn't know the man standing in front of her. He had guilty written all over him, and it looked like it was taking everything he had just to look at her.

She tried to fight the idea. Tried to have faith. But she couldn't. Something was off, and she didn't like it. She trusted her gut more than Thorsen right now.

'What did you do?' she asked.

'What do you mean?' he replied.

'Let go of my arm, Thorsen.'

His grip loosened.

She pulled her arm free and walked past him. There was no urge to look back.

. . .

Jamie stepped into the afternoon sun, feeling it warm on her face.

She didn't expect Thorsen to follow her, so she wasn't surprised when he didn't. But she was a little disappointed. She wasn't so broken she couldn't admit that to herself.

But it didn't matter. It was just a matter of time until this happened. Until they split. Until he grew bored, unhappy. Until she was alone again.

But that's how she functioned best. It was exhausting being with someone else, and she wasn't even with him.

What had happened in his room last night – that was proof enough. He didn't really want her. He'd seen her baggage, had lived with her, had experienced enough that the hesitation was clear. He'd alluded to wanting her, but he didn't, not really. Whether he thought he did, had convinced himself he did, that he was the one for her, the one to *save her* ... when it came down to it. He wasn't. In truth, no one was. Jamie didn't need saving, or changing. She was who she was. And she knew, deep down, no one would ever want to be with her. Not truly.

Except, maybe Elliot. But he was even more fucked up than she was.

Jesus, were those her only options? Grow old alone or shack up with a serial killer? What a life.

Her cab pulled up to the curb and she climbed in.

'Vart vill du gå?' Where do you want to go?

Jamie hesitated, shaking off the last dregs of uncertainty.

She gave the address of the first victim and the driver explained it was a long drive. Her face seemed to give him the answer he needed, and with a sigh, he set off.

Jamie resigned herself to thinking, to focusing on the case. She had her satchel with her, and she'd used the printer in the hotel's business centre to print off a few choice things.

Photographs of the room of the first victim – bookshelf in particular, desk, too.

Unfortunately, no copy of Hamlet. The desk, as well, was clear. No carvings or etchings.

The victim was male, too. Sixteen years old. Matteo Franssen. He was in secondary school, his final year. Popular enough by all accounts. A good sportsman, smart. He wanted to go to the mainland to study for university. A normal kid. With no real interest in books or literature. None that would fit the pattern Juni exhibited. Though Jamie wasn't even sure if that was *the* pattern that linked them.

It was one of the major holes in the investigation so far: what linked the victims? They seemed to pop up so randomly, and even within the university, they'd seemingly been chosen with no mind to *who* the victims were. There was no clear victim-type emerging other than the age range. Nothing to help the police predict the next move.

Nothing that they noticed, at least.

Juni Pedersen's obsession with Hamlet didn't seem coincidental. It just didn't. There was something at work there, some theme at play. Was her interest in that just the vehicle that the killer used to deliver his ideology? To convince her? He didn't put Hamlet in her hands, but it appears to be the way he conveyed his message.

What did Jamie hope to find when she arrived at Matteo Franssen's house? She really didn't know.

The drive was long, by Gotland standards at least. Around 35 minutes.

Jamie got out of the cab, but before she could ask the driver to stick around, he drove off, stranding her on the outskirts of a small town she doubted had a cab service of its own. Fuck. Looks like she'd be taking a bus back.

But right now, it didn't matter.

She hiked her satchel up her shoulder and went to the front door.

The house was modest enough, with a painted wooden exterior and a neatly mown front garden.

She knocked without thinking about what to say.

A woman in her late forties opened the door. She had short, flat hair that looked unwashed. It was black and her skin was pale. She didn't look unwell, but nor did she seem full of life, either. She looked like a woman who'd lost her son and never quite recovered.

'Mrs Franssen?' Jamie asked, smiling as warmly as she could.

'Yes?'

'My name is Jamie Johansson. I'm …. a former detective helping the case that involved your son. I was wondering if I might ask you some questions, and—'

'Why? The police already asked my husband and I questions. Lots of them. Too many.' Her face began to contort, the anger clear there. 'What more could you want to know? How could it help?'

'I'm sorry to dredge it all up again, but it would really be helpful—'

'The police don't have anything, do they?' She scoffed a little, tears forming in her eyes. 'Two years and twenty-three children, and you people know *nothing.*' She shook her head. 'Disgusting.' She made to close the door, but Jamie stopped her.

'I know,' she said, hand slapping against the wood. 'It's terrible. It's beyond terrible. But look,' she went on, straining against the door. 'I've just arrived, and I'm trying to help. All

I want to do is know who Matteo really was, look around his room a little.'

'Oh, that's all, is it?'

Fuck, this was harder without a badge. And the fact that she was on her own, and out of bounds, too. She'd specifically disobeyed Larsson's request to not just turn up at the houses of the victims. But she had to hear this first hand. Had to ask what she thought the police may not have. Even if she didn't know what that was.

'Please, Mrs Franssen. I've lost people, too. I know how hard this is, but it could really help, if you'd just …'

'Fine,' she said, releasing the door. It flew inwards and banged against the wall. 'If you're insistent on being so … incessant. Then fine. Come in. Ask your questions. Look in his room. Then, kindly, piss off and leave us alone. We've been through enough.'

She walked back into the house and Jamie followed tentatively.

The woman walked into her living room and sat on the sofa.

Jamie took a place on the matching, floral-patterned chair. 'I know this is hard,' she began. 'But I'd like to start with Matteo's hobbies and interests.'

She snorted. 'Not only do you push your way in here, you also want to ask questions I've already been asked?'

'Specifically, his reading habits. Was he a fan of Shakespeare at all?'

'Shakespeare?' She practically laughed at it. 'No, what the hell are you talking about?'

Okay. That was a dead end then. There was also no Shakespeare on his bookshelf. Right, regroup, rethink. The killer had physical access to the victims. They were all in education, too.

'Did Matteo talk about any new teachers or friends at school in the months leading up to his death?'

'New teachers? What, no? What are these questions? You think the school had something to do with this?'

'I'm not saying that. I'm simply trying to uncover new avenues of questioning—'

'Jesus, how long have you been working on this? You don't think that the police already went to his school? That they already looked into this? I think I'd like you to leave now. This has gone on long enough.'

'Please, Mrs Franssen, I apologise. I'm just trying to look for something new here.'

'Well, there is nothing new. Now, if you wouldn't mind.'

'Do you think I could look at Matteo's room quickly before—'

'Get out.'

'Mrs Franssen—'

'I said get out. Or I will call the police.'

Jamie closed her mouth, nodding slowly. 'My apologies. I'm sorry to have taken up so much of your time.'

She rose, then headed for the door. Mrs Franssen didn't follow. But Jamie thought she could make out the sound of quiet sobbing as she let herself out of the door. Shit, she was out of practice. That was worse than she remembered.

Jamie closed the door behind her, stepped down onto the path and looked up.

Thorsen was just closing the door of what looked like Sonja's car and walking towards her.

She almost did a double take. 'What are you—'

'Jamie, I'm sorry,' he said, cutting her off.

She reached the curb and stopped, standing right in front of him. 'Sorry for what?'

'For lying to you.' He let out a long breath. 'I did see Dahlvig at the scene.'

'And?'

'And I asked him if I could work the case.'

'I? Not *we?*'

'Shockingly, you seem to have made an impression on him, and it's not a positive one. He doesn't have a particularly high opinion of your methods.'

'Mm,' was all that Jamie replied with.

'And he also doesn't want you working the case.'

'Hmm. But he just loved you, I bet?'

He pursed his lips, tempering himself. 'No, he didn't. He actually thought that I'd be just as much of a liability as you.'

It occurred to her then. 'Oh, so that's why you wanted to know Alex Öberg's name,' Jamie said, smirking a little. 'You gave him my theory about Hamlet and told him about Annika.'

Thorsen's jaw flexed. He didn't need to say it to let her know she was right on the money. She could tell as soon as he heard the name that he was desperate to reach for his phone to tell Dahlvig. Was that why he came?

'You've got your name now,' she said. 'Alex Öberg. The PhD student that graded Juni Pedersen's Hamlet essay. Now what?'

'That's not why I'm here,' he said. 'I came for you.'

'For me? Why?'

'Because we're partners. Whether things are weird between us, I do care about you. And you can't just go running off alone. It's *never* worked out well for you.'

'Oh, right. So, nothing to do with Dahlvig not wanting me working the case, and you needing to babysit me?'

'Don't do that, Jamie. Don't twist something complicated

into something simple. The world's not always black and white.'

'That's the thing, Thorsen. It pretty much always is. You're just in shit because you lied, and because you want it all. You want to fuck me over to impress Dahlvig, but you also don't want to fuck me over. So, choose.'

'Between you and my career?' He seemed shocked by the black-and-whiteness of it.

'You put yourself in this position, not me.'

'Jesus, I don't know why you have to be so goddamn difficult all the time.' He lifted his hands and made a choking motion in the air. 'Honestly, it's like wrestling with a wolverine. Except more painful.'

'Sounds like a good thing that you're jumping ship then.'

'Jumping ship? What are you talking about?'

'You're clearly trying to throw in with Dahlvig and the NOD, and that's fine. You've gotta do what you want to do. But that's not somewhere I can go, and you've got to know that. So yeah, it sounds like you're moving on to me.'

He just stared at her. Seemingly in disbelief. 'You think I'd just leave? First sign of a job offer?'

'You tell me, Thorsen,' Jamie said, sighing. 'I don't know what's going on anymore. I thought we were good, we were happy. I don't even know why we're back.'

'Now who's lying? Whether you wanted to admit it or not, you were bored too. And now you've got a whiff of a case again, you can't help yourself. Look – you came here on your own. When Larsson told you not to, when you told me you didn't want to. So, don't play high and mighty with me, alright? You live for this shit. More than me. More than I ever have.' He was pointing now, but at what, Jamie didn't know. Symbolic, she thought. 'So why don't you …' He trailed off, searching for the words, maybe. Though when they came,

Jamie didn't expect them. Some sort of line seemed to have been crossed. Thorsen was … unleashed.

'So why don't you just shut the fuck up for once.' He sighed. 'Spare the psycho mind games, the reverse-reverse-psychology, the gaslighting, all the bullshit that comes second nature to you. Just fucking stop, alright, for once. It's tiring, and I'm tired of it.' He pulled his phone from his pocket. 'Just stand there for a damn minute, and let me fill Dahlvig in, because this is his investigation, and he's going to arrest you if you stick your nose in. And me. And I'm not going to jail for you, Jamie. Not when it could easily be avoided if someone just stood up to you for once.'

She opened her mouth to reply, shocked, going on autopi-lot, but he shushed her with a finger to his lips, the phone already at his ear.

'Sir,' he said as Dahlvig answered. 'Sorry for the delay. I have that name for you … Uh-huh. Mm. Right. Yeah. It's Alex Öberg, PhD student at Gotland University. Of course. Yep. I'll let you know as soon as I have anything else. Okay, thank you—' But before he could finish, Dahlvig seemingly cut him off.

Thorsen lowered the phone and looked at Jamie again.

'Right, what did you find out?' He lifted his chin at the house behind Jamie now.

She was still reeling from Thorsen's outburst. A little intimidated, she had to admit. And a little of something else. Angry, sure, but not … angry. She felt charged, she supposed. Her skin was alight, her cheeks flushing.

'I didn't find anything out,' Jamie said, her voice thin, a little strange. 'But I read over all the information on Matteo Franssen's death.'

'And what? What did you think?'

'I thought that there was nothing out of place.'

'Okay? And what does that mean? Explain what you're thinking here.'

'It's too clean. Too good.'

'Too good?'

'For a first kill. Where's the shit? Where's the sloppiness? The training-wheels kill.'

Thorsen nodded slowly. 'Right. A serial killer's first kill is rarely all neat and tidy. They take a while to develop a style, an MO.'

'Exactly. And this guy is prolific, right? Twenty-three bodies? More than one a month. He's gotta be grooming multiple kids at the same time. So, we're supposed to believe, out of nowhere, with no preamble, he just starts murdering this perfectly? I don't buy it. He's killed before. I'd bet on it.'

'Hopefully you won't have to.' Thorsen sighed.

'If that's a new thought to anyone, then I'll be surprised. But just in case, take it to Dahlvig. If it helps … great.' Jamie lifted her hands. 'I'm not supposed to be anywhere near this. So …'

'So what?'

'So, I'm walking away. You've got this. You can handle it. And if you need me, you have my number.'

'Yeah, no, I don't buy it. You're not going to leave this alone. You can't. It's physically impossible for you.'

'You're being a little more direct than usual.'

'Well, obviously, whatever I was doing before wasn't working. You were miserable, and so was I.'

'I wasn't miserable.'

'Well, I was.' He sighed. 'So, let's cut the rhetoric completely, shall we? Do you give a fuck what Dahlvig thinks of you?'

'No.'

'Do you want to work for the NOD?'

'No.'

'Do you want to be a detective again?'

She hesitated for a moment. 'Not right now.'

'Great. So then it's settled. We work this case and I don't tell Dahlvig you're involved. Win-win. I get to keep an eye on you, and we catch the bad guy. Sound good?'

'Uh …'

'Well, you don't really have another choice unless you want to fuck off back to Greece on your own?'

She just sort of blinked, then gave a brief nod. 'Fine. But after?'

'We'll deal with that once we're done. You might change your mind. And maybe I will too. I haven't decided yet. But right now, I have to make a call. If you want to wait in the car, feel free. Sonja took off work for the week so she said I could borrow it.'

'Who are you calling?'

'Larsson. I'm going to ask for a record of all teenage deaths and suicides in the last … five years?'

Jamie nodded. 'Make it ten. The killer's likely to be mature – very careful. Measured. He might have been active for years.'

'Good.'

'Oh, and include disappearances, too. Unsolved, preferably. The exhibitionism of the suicides might be an evolution of his methods. It may not have started that way.'

'Good call.' He turned his back on her.

Jamie just stared at it, not really knowing what to do now.

So, she just stood there, and watched him make the phone call.

Unable to look away.

. . .

It took all of twenty minutes for Larsson to respond to Thorsen's request.

Apparently, there were not a lot of teenage suicides, deaths, or disappearances on Gotland. Thankfully.

And there was only one that stuck out to Jamie. A teenage girl called Rebecca Adell. She was fifteen when she disappeared. Unexplained, sudden. No body. The case pre-dated this one. And by a good amount. Could this be their training-wheels kill? The one that got their killer hooked?

The police report was filed by a Linus Lundström. They'd see him after they went to see Lucas Adell, the father.

As Thorsen drove north across the island, Jamie scanned the reports. Plural. First, Rebecca Adell disappeared off the face of the earth. And then, within a year, Marie Adell, Rebecca's mother, also disappeared. She walked into the ocean one morning and was never seen again. Leaving Lucas Adell alone.

'Jesus,' Jamie said.

'What is it?'

'Adell lost his daughter and his wife.' She let out a long exhale. 'Poor guy.'

Thorsen was stoic. Though he looked like he had something to say. He was massaging his chin the way he did when he had thoughts he needed to get out.

'What are you thinking?'

'Hmm?'

'I thought we were cutting the bullshit? Or does that only apply to you calling me out on *my* bullshit?'

He cracked a brief smile. 'Alright.' A sigh. Or an exhale. She couldn't tell which. 'I was thinking about last night.'

'Last night?' Jamie asked. 'When last night?'

'When you came to my room,' he said, his voice

quavering just a little bit. He kept his eyes on the road, the pace steady.

Jamie's phone began vibrating then. She had it in her hands, looking at the police reports about Lucas Adell on her screen. But now, it was ringing. Annika Olsen was calling her.

'Need to get that?' Thorsen asked, glancing down.

'No,' Jamie answered firmly, cutting the call off and sending Annika to voicemail. 'What were you saying?'

'Last night,' he went on, albeit slowly. 'When you came to my room. It … surprised me. In a good way.' He looked at her now.

She shivered a little, realised she was gripping her phone so tightly that her knuckles were white.

'I was just surprised,' he said. 'I'd been waiting for you to ask me something like that for so long … I froze.'

'Mhm.' She couldn't speak.

'I wanted to say yes, so badly. But I froze.'

Jamie's palms began to sweat, her heart beating faster.

'I wanted you to know that.'

She couldn't speak.

'Jamie?'

'Uh-huh,' was all she managed.

He let out another lengthy breath, then laughed nervously. 'If you could say something, that would be good.'

She cleared her throat. 'Good to know,' she said, barely able to control her voice. 'That's … good.'

'Good? Good how?' He looked over at her again, the car drifting to the edge of the road, the tyres juddering on the painted line.

He pulled it straight.

'I don't know,' she said. It was the truth. After last night, she'd shut that part of herself down so hard that she wasn't sure how easy it would be to open it up again. She'd put herself out there, something she'd never done. And she'd been humiliated. So, yeah. She didn't fucking know. 'Let's just concentrate on Adell for now. We can talk later. At the hotel.' Each word was hard to squeeze out.

'Alright,' he said.

But he didn't sound alright.

Pretty far from it.

Though both seemed to want to talk, for the rest of the drive, they couldn't. Luckily, Gotland was small, and when they arrived at the ferry crossing, it was there waiting for them.

Soon, they were across and ploughing onwards.

Jamie watched the countryside roll by. Idyllic and quiet. She couldn't believe it was the scene of such terror. She had the window down, the warm air rolling through her fingers.

She could hear gulls cawing, could smell the sea.

Jamie didn't know where she would have liked to 'end up', but to her, this seemed as good a place as any.

And then, suddenly, they were back in reality.

'We're here,' Thorsen announced, slowing down in front of an imposing, modern home. Through the trees to its flanks, Jamie could see the white of the sand and the distant glitter of the ocean.

'Ready?' Thorsen asked.

Jamie just nodded, mustered herself, and then got out.

Thorsen parked in front of the house's open gateway. Through it, gravel stones led to the front door – all frosted glass. Ivy crawled across the outside, but Jamie barely noticed, her mind full and whirling with her and Thorsen's conversation.

He stepped ahead and knocked on Lucas Adell's front door, then stood back and waited.

A few seconds later a dark shape swam behind the glass and then the door opened, revealing an average height, middle-aged man with a bald head.

'*Ja?*' he asked. Yes?

'Good afternoon,' Thorsen replied, giving a nod and a smile. 'My name is Kjell Thorsen, and this is my colleague, Jamie Johansson. We're here on behalf of the National Operations Department, and we were wondering if we could ask you a few questions in relation to your daughter's disappearance?'

Adell's hand tightened on the edge of the door, his lips quivering a little. He cleared his throat, blinking a few times. 'Rebecca? She is, uh … I'm sorry, what is this about?'

'We're looking into the string of suicides that have been happening on the island, and—'

'And you think Rebecca's disappearance has something to do with them?' Adell asked, eyebrows raising.

'We don't know. We understand that Rebecca's case predates the first confirmed suicide, but we're simply trying to cover all possibilities to help us find out why this is happening.'

Adell considered this, looking from Thorsen to Jamie and back. 'You'll excuse me if I ask to see some identification.'

'Of course,' Thorsen said. 'I don't have anything official with me, but I'd be happy to put you in touch with the lead investigator.' He pulled his phone out. 'I can call him if you'd like, his name is Ivar Dahlvig, he's a *polisöverintendent*, and would be glad to—'

'That's alright,' Adell said, stepping back. 'It's fine.' He sighed a little and opened the door. 'I'll be glad to help however I can. Losing Rebecca …' He choked up a little.

'Something no parent should have to suffer through. Anything I can do to stop this, I will.'

'We appreciate that,' Thorsen said, stepping inside.

Jamie followed.

Adell closed the door behind Jamie, who was looking around – not out of professional obligation, but simply out of admiration. The space was beautiful. They entered into an open plan kitchen, which led into a living area with a vaulted, twenty-foot ceiling. A gallery landing wrapped around the wall to a set of stairs at the back of the house, which was almost entirely glass, leading out onto a house-width deck, straight onto the Sudersand beach and down to the sea.

The house was filled with natural light, the smell of open wood and the ocean running through the entire place.

'Tea?' Adell asked, heading for the stove. He pulled an old-fashioned steel kettle from it and held it up.

'I'm fine, thank you,' Thorsen asked.

'Do you mind if I make one?'

'Go ahead.'

Adell nodded and busied himself filling the kettle. 'Sit, please,' he called over his shoulder.

Jamie and Thorsen did, at the stools on the kitchen island-cum-breakfast bar.

Thorsen cleared his throat and then spoke. 'I'm sorry to bring it up, but can you tell us what happened when Rebecca disappeared?'

Adell paused, standing over the stove as the blue flames bit at the bottom of the kettle. 'There's not much to tell. One night, Rebecca went out to meet some friends. And she never came back.'

Thorsen looked at Jamie, but spoke to Adell. 'Friends? Which friends?'

'Uh …' Adell said, shaking his head. 'It's been a long

time now. But she never met them, and they said she'd not arranged to meet them at all. It was as though she dropped off the face of the earth.' His voice shook a little.

'The investigation at the time, did it come to anything?'

Adell shook his head once more as the kettle began to whistle. 'No, it didn't. And the details … they were never given to me, fully. The person in charge, Linus Lundström, the local intendent here … fucking *prick*,' Adell spat. 'He never had a chance of finding Rebecca.' Adell turned now, anger in his eyes. 'He doesn't know his arse from his elbow,' he said. 'And that bastard was in charge of the whole thing.' He shook his head once more, in disgust. 'He abandoned the case as quickly as it was handed to him. He never liked our family.'

'Why not?' Thorsen leaned forward a little.

Adell scoffed. 'Small town police chief thinks his little slice of back-woods heaven is getting spoiled when anyone with a modicum of education or success moves here.' Adell looked around. 'I didn't build this place, but I suppose because I bought it – or could afford to – that made us the scourge of the earth.'

Jamie spoke for the first time now. 'You have some pretty strong feelings about him.'

'Wouldn't you if he bungled the search for *your* missing daughter?'

'You think he did it intentionally?'

'Is anyone intentionally a fucking idiot?' Adell turned back to the whistling kettle and poured water into his waiting cup.

They let that sit for a moment. Then Thorsen spoke. 'Can you tell us what happened to your wife?'

Adell's shoulder sagged a little. 'She's gone. Dead. Killed herself,' he said bitterly.

Another suicide? Jamie thought. If Rebecca was the first victim, was her mother a victim too, or simply just a horrible coincidence? 'I'm sorry for your loss,' Jamie said instead.

'Yeah,' Adell muttered, stirring his tea. His shoulders began to shake. 'Marie was … She was everything.' His voice cracked again. 'I just … I don't know what to do.' He turned back to them. 'We moved here to escape the city, the hustle and bustle, to be somewhere quiet, and peaceful.' He grimaced, but not at the heat of the tea. 'Now, the silence just reminds me that I'm alone here. This place is more of a mausoleum than a house. I'd burn the fucking thing down if I had anywhere else to go.'

Jamie swallowed, steeling herself. Usually she could compartmentalise, but she knew what Adell was going through, and right now, she felt like she was cracking. She understood the loss he was feeling, the anger, the shadow that death cast over your life.

'Mr Adell …' she began, but before she could continue, Thorsen's phone began buzzing in his pocket.

He reached into his jeans and pulled it out, glancing at Jamie. 'It's Dahlvig,' he said, getting up. 'Excuse me a moment.' He smiled at Adell and walked into the living area, answering it. He spoke quickly and quietly, hanging up just a few seconds after he answered.

Thorsen swept back to the kitchen island, putting a hand on Jamie's shoulder. Adell watched, tea in hand.

'Öberg missed an afternoon class as well as a one-on-one with his PhD supervisor,' Thorsen whispered into Jamie's ear. 'He's not answering his phone, and no one's seen him. Very out of character, apparently.' Thorsen relayed the information quickly, and despite his professional nature, the skin on the back of her neck still came up in gooseflesh. 'Annika was supposed to be meeting him this afternoon, wasn't she?'

Jamie looked up at Thorsen now.

'Call her,' he said to Jamie, the words firm.

Shit, she'd screened Annika's call in the car. What if she was in trouble?

Jamie rose from her seat, too.

'Thank you for your time, Mr Adell,' Thorsen said. 'If we have any more questions, we may be back in touch.'

'Of course,' Adell said, putting his tea down. 'I'm not going anywhere.' He sort of shrugged sadly. 'Here if you need me.'

'We appreciate that.' Thorsen was already pulling on Jamie's arm, leading her out of the house.

The front door opened and then closed behind them.

Thorsen crunched across the gravel and circled Sonja's car, climbing in and starting the engine.

Jamie was dialling her voicemail before they even pulled off. One new message. *"Hey, Jamie, it's, um, it's Annika. I just wanted to let you know that I tracked down Alex Öberg, who marked Juni's assignment on Hamlet – he spoke to her about Hamlet before she died, too, met with her. I'm going to find out more information, and I'll let you know. But so far, I know Juni was into the meaning of death, of it absolving sins, or something. That, and of death being like an endless dream state, or something? I don't know, I'll try and get hold of the essay if I can. 'Kay, uh, talk soon, I guess.'*

Jamie hung up. 'Annika,' she said out loud. 'She found Öberg.'

'Is she with him?'

'I don't know,' Jamie said, dialling Annika's number. Straight to the answering machine. She tried again. Same thing. 'Fuck, she's not picking up.' Jamie's grip tightened on her phone.

'You think something's wrong?'

'I don't know,' Jamie said, her mind reeling. Alex Öberg, PhD student at Visby University, where three victims had died already. Studying English Literature. Had direct contact with Juni Pedersen. 'But Öberg met with Juni before her death, Annika said. Apparently, she was talking about death absolving sins – about it being an endless dream state.'

'What the fuck does that mean?'

Jamie just shook her head. 'I don't know. But why wouldn't Öberg come forward once Juni died? Why wouldn't he talk to the police about the essay, or about that meeting?'

Thorsen looked over, graven. And then his phone buzzed again.

He answered it and put it on speaker, not slowing the car down. 'Thorsen.'

Dahlvig's voice echoed from the speaker, tinny against the roar of the tyres on the road. 'Where are you, Thorsen?'

'On the road,' he answered.

'No fucking shit. How far out of Visby?'

'An hour, maybe?'

Dahlvig sighed. 'Why the fuck are you an hour outside the city? Where are you?'

'Just following up on another lead—'

'I don't care. Your contact. Olsen, was it? Did she meet with Alex Öberg?'

'Yes,' Thorsen answered.

'Where is she now?'

'I don't know.'

'Can you call her?' he asked, the air of condescension clear in his voice.

'We tried – straight to voicemail. Her phone is off.'

'Shit, that's … wait, did you say *we?*'

Thorsen looked at Jamie. 'Uh, no, I didn't.'

There was silence on the line.

'I called her twice. Her phone was off,' Thorsen reiterated. 'What's going on?'

He sighed heavily, angered, clearly. 'After you gave us Öberg's name, we looked into him. His PhD is in Shakespearean Studies, and his academic records show he regularly volunteers at libraries. We can place him at three libraries right now around the time of deaths of other victims. And we've barely started looking. I got unis out to Juni Pedersen's house with Öberg's photos. They confirmed that they'd seen him. He'd been hanging around with Juni, had come over to the house several times. They had a relationship, right up to her death.'

'Jesus Christ,' Thorsen muttered. 'It's him?'

'We don't know, but we need to find him, right now. Keep trying Olsen, we're sweeping the places he frequents. But if it is Öberg behind this, then he may have gone to ground if he thinks we're closing in. Send me Olsen's details, we need this net as wide as possible.'

'Yes, sir, of course.'

'And Thorsen?'

'Yes, sir?'

'Don't lie to me. And Johansson?' he asked into the ether.

Jamie looked at Thorsen. 'Yeah?'

'Stay the fuck out of my investigation. Or I will arrest you. And Thorsen.'

He hung up before either of them could say anything else.

'What are you thinking?' Thorsen asked after a minute of silence.

'I don't know,' Jamie said, biting her lip. 'It just … I don't know. It doesn't make sense to me.'

'What doesn't make sense? Öberg had the means, the opportunity. Hell, he was sexually involved with the latest victim, and you yourself pointed to the chlamydia being a potential lead. Olsen found him, and now they've both just disappeared? You don't think that makes sense?'

Jamie just thought on it.

'Just because you didn't figure it out, doesn't mean they're wrong.' He looked over at her again. 'You found Olsen, you found Hamlet, that led to Öberg. You should be happy. You might have solved this.'

But Jamie wasn't happy.

And they rode the rest of the way in silence.

16

Annika Olsen

ANNIKA STARED out of the car window, watching as the trees jostled by in the twilight. Their branches scratched across the paint, squeaking and squealing as they bounced along the track.

They'd left the tarmac behind what seemed like a long time ago, passing by a 'Road Closed' sign and entering into the trees.

Her heart was beating hard, palms sweaty. 'Where did you say we were going?' She looked over at Alex, whose eyes were fixed on the pathway ahead.

He guided the car around huge potholes and troughs, plunging them deeper into the woods. 'You'll see,' he said cryptically. He licked his lips, his once bright eyes now seemingly dark and bloodshot.

She nodded slowly. 'And why did we have to leave our phones back at your house?'

'Because they can track them.'

'Who can track them?' Annika asked, unsure if she wanted to hear the answer.

'The police, most likely.'

'And why would the police be tracking our phones?'

'They won't be,' he said, glancing at her, smiling for just a brief moment. 'At least not yet.'

She shuddered. 'I think I want to go home now,' Annika whispered.

'Not yet,' he replied. 'You've got to see this, first. You need to.'

She swallowed, then went back to looking out of the window. Everything had been fine. They'd gone from the café to dinner – a casual little restaurant that served Italian food. She'd had the carbonara. Alex had been charming, awkward, sweet. Cute, too. He had a great laugh, a disarming smile. He seemed so nice, so genuine. And then he'd told her he had a surprise for her, wanted to show her something. He seemed so innocent, so trustworthy. Like she could tell him anything, like she'd known him for a long time.

He had driven her to his house, invited her inside. It was a modest studio apartment. He lived alone. He'd got a bag, a coat, told her they were going out somewhere, it would get chilly. He gave her a jacket – she was wearing it now. His jacket. It smelled like him. Good. She'd liked it at first. But now it was turning her stomach sick.

He'd said he was leaving his phone behind, she should, too. Why? Trust him. Okay.

He held his hand out. She gave it to him.

He turned it off, put it on the table next to his, offered his hand to her. 'It's alright,' he said. 'Come with me.'

And she had, without thinking. Annika, you stupid fucking barnacle. What have you got yourself into?

'We're here,' Alex announced then, slowing the car.

They broke from the thicket of trees into a wide open space, what once would have been a car park. They wound past two stone pillars, the steel gates opened, but fallen from the hinges, now grown over with brambles and brush.

She tried to read the sign on one of the columns, but she couldn't before they passed it.

Her eyes turned forward as Alex brought them to a stop, staring at the structure in front of her.

The building was sprawling, hemmed in on all sides by thick trees. It was stone, with a wide frontage, steps leading to huge wooden doors. The exterior was covered in ivy and other crawling plants, totally overgrown. The place looked abandoned, the windows and doors boarded over, the evidence of fire damage clear. Half the roof was missing, the entire right side of the building collapsed in. The stone was charred all around the windows, too, blackened above where the flames had licked upwards from each room.

'What is this place?' Annika asked, voice thin and small.

'This,' Alex said, leaning forward on the wheel and staring up at the building, 'is where it all started.' He let out a long breath, eyes fixed on the darkening sky. 'I haven't been completely honest with you.'

Annika stiffened a little.

'I knew Juni better than I let on. We were actually … we were seeing each other.' He said it quickly, like a guilty admission. 'I didn't say anything because … I felt guilty. I still do. I should have seen it, should have noticed a change in her. I just, I just … ignored it, I think. I was selfish, focused on my own work. But it was my fault. I'm the one … I'm the one who gave her Hamlet. Who turned her onto it.'

Annika's jaw shook a little. 'Where are we, Alex?'

'When Juni … died … I was messed up. But I couldn't talk to anyone about it, you know? I'd heard about the black hearts, thought I could maybe do something to help. Help the investigation, you know?'

He looked over at her and she jumped a little.

'So, I started looking into the black heart thing, searching for something, anything. I thought maybe I could help the police find out what was causing this, I could help them solve it. I could … do something right for Juni. And … I found something. It took a lot of searching, but I found something pretty … crazy. I don't know if anyone knows about it yet, but … I wanted to show you. I thought you'd understand. Maybe the only one who would.'

'And …' Annika began, trying to find her voice. 'It's … in there?' She pointed timidly to the ruin in front of them, the sky the colour of blood behind the jagged roof.

'It is,' Alex said. 'The place is abandoned, has been for years, since it burnt down.'

'What is it?'

'A hospital,' Alex said. 'Or it used to be. Will you come inside?'

She swallowed.

'You trust me, don't you?'

She stared at him, throat covered in cold sweat, heart hammering.

His strange, doe eyes stared back at her in the fading light and slowly he offered his hand to her.

Annika looked down at it, unsure whether she even had a choice.

17

Lucas Adell

MORNING CAME QUICKLY, the cool summer light piercing the sky like a needle bursting the night. Lucas stirred, cold and tired, and opened his eyes.

For a moment, he didn't know what he was looking at, but then he recognised the inside of his car and forced himself to sit up.

He was parked a few miles from EZ's house, in a lay-by by the sea.

The first gulls wheeled in the sky overhead, calling and hunting for their breakfast.

There was still vomit on his shirt from the night before. The last thing he'd wanted to do was go home to his empty house, though he knew that was the only option he had.

EZ was dead now, and he had no other leads. Who had killed EZ, and why? They couldn't have been there much in front of Lucas. But he had no idea what was going on. Jesus, he wasn't the police, not a detective. He was just a father, a husband. He was no one.

Lucas doubled forward and put his head in his hands, sobbing. Rebecca was gone. Marie was gone, and now he was all alone.

A car rumbled past on the road and he picked his head up quickly to watch it go, afraid suddenly it would be a police car that had skid to a halt next to him, that officers would pull him from the car, wrestle him to the ground and cuff him for the murder of EZ. Jesus, what was he even doing out there? What did he hope to achieve?

His heart thundered, chest tight. He felt sick, dizzy. When did he eat last? Drink something? God, he needed air.

His fingers fumbled for the door release, and then he froze, unable to decipher what he was seeing. Words, letters, smeared on to the outside driver's side window.

He blinked, trying to read it.

It seemed to come into focus suddenly, painted on to the glass in crusted red, in … blood.

The words said:

YOU KNOW WHAT THEY DID

And beneath it, a heart had been carved.

His blood ran cold.

The killer. They wrote this in EZ's blood. It was the only thing that made sense. Fuck! They must have been there when Lucas arrived, slipped out while he slipped in.

They must have come to his car, and left him this message.

But what did it mean?

Before he could think about it anymore, bile rose in his throat.

He scrabbled for the handle, pulled on it, and flopped from the car onto the dusty ground, retching and crying, cheek pressed to the cool earth. A thick, yellow liquid ripped itself from the depths of his guts and spilled from his lips.

Dark spots formed where his tears fell and Lucas Adell dragged his legs from the footwell and curled his knees to his chest.

He held them tightly, sobbing.

And overhead, the gulls continued to circle, searching for their next meal.

18

Sonja Ehrhart

THE BUZZER SOUNDED and Sonja rose from her desk. She ran her hands through her hair, brushing the long, silver strands behind her ears. She rarely got nervous, but there was a lot riding on this, and it could well blow up in her face.

Though she felt compelled to intervene. Whether he knew what was best for him, Sonja knew that this was the right call. Didn't she?

Sonja crossed to the door and opened it. 'Thanks for coming.'

Jamie was standing on her front step. 'Sure,' she said, stepping into the bright and cosy interior.

Sonja lived in a townhouse in the city, a narrow building with three floors. Downstairs, an open living room led back into the kitchen, all wood and white tile and leafy plants. At the back, a set of French doors led to an enclosed patio with some comfy-looking chairs and a glass-topped table.

'Can I get you something to drink?' Sonja asked, closing the door behind Jamie.

'Depends why I'm here,' Jamie replied, looking around and then turning to face Sonja. She put her hands in the pockets of her black jacket, shaking her long blonde plait from its position over her shoulder so it hung down her back. 'I assume it's not a social call.'

'Did Kjell ask where you were going?' Sonja enquired, pushing her hands into the back pockets of her jeans nervously.

'No. He dropped me at the hotel and then went to join Dahlvig's manhunt. I suppose he thinks I'm still there. I was a little surprised to get your text, though.'

'Manhunt? What manhunt?'

Jamie shrugged. 'They think they found the Black Heart Killer.'

'You don't sound convinced.'

'I'm not.'

'Why?'

Jamie shrugged again, sighed boredly. 'I don't think they vetted the kid enough.'

'Kid?'

'Yeah, they think it's a PhD student from Visby University.'

'And you don't?'

'I've been wrong before.'

Sonja smiled. 'I bet that doesn't happen often?'

'Often enough to have a decent collection of scars.' Jamie glanced around. 'Was that what you wanted me to come here for?'

'No, there is something I wanted to talk to you about. Sit?' She proffered Jamie the sofa.

'I'll stand,' Jamie replied. 'I have a feeling this won't be a long conversation.'

Sonja's eyebrows lifted in surprise. 'You're rather abrupt,

you know that?'

'Only when I feel that pleasantries won't serve any purpose. I suppose you want to talk about Thorsen?'

'Perceptive as always.'

'Humph. Let's just get to it, shall we?' she sighed. 'What do you want?'

Sonja shifted uneasily. Jamie was as still as a statue, and despite her small stature, was pretty imposing. A coolness radiated from her that Sonja had to admit had a strange magnetism. A sort of feeling that you were being both repelled and attracted at the same time. She was on edge just being in Jamie's presence. A strange quality, she thought. One she'd liked to have delved into. One she'd like to have exca-vated. Sat with Jamie, peeled back her layers, one by one, seen under her skin, figured out what made her tick, what drove her. She recalled sharks and the fact that they needed to keep swimming to move water through their gills. That there was this deep, biological compulsion to move forward at all times. That they couldn't turn it off, couldn't stop it, couldn't ignore it or do anything about it. That they were slaves to their base programming. Was Jamie Johansson a shark? Was she swimming because she could never stop?

'Sonja?' Jamie asked. 'You okay?'

Sonja snapped out of the tangential runaway thought. 'Yes, sorry. I wanted to talk to you about Kjell. Would you like something to drink?'

Jamie sighed again, taking her hands from her pockets. 'Sure,' she said, tiredly, as though she knew she'd be here a while. 'Tea.'

'Herbal?'

'Black if you have it. Skimmed milk, no sugar.'

'I have semi-skimmed?'

'Yeah, fine, whatever.'

Sonja busied herself in the kitchen, trying to find the right words. She was starting to see what Thorsen meant about having to carefully navigate a conversation with Jamie. 'So …'

'So,' Jamie replied.

'I've known Kjell a lot of years.'

Jamie stayed quiet.

'All I want is to see him happy.'

Jamie opened her mouth as though to speak. Sonja suspected to say 'he is happy'. But she stopped herself before a word came out, and instead just coughed lightly into her fist before lowering it.

'I know you're someone who appreciates candour, so I suppose I'll just come right out and say it.' Sonja didn't bother with the tea now. She figured this would be over soon. 'Kjell loves you.'

Jamie remained still, her face unmoving.

'Wow, no reaction at all?' Sonja remarked, leaning on the counter and looking over at Jamie, still standing there, hands in pockets in the middle of her living room. 'Not surprising, I suppose.'

Jamie smiled a little, then sort of blinked a few times in disbelief, as though she were insulted. Perhaps she was, and Jamie was more normal than anyone knew under that skin suit of chainmail.

'Do you have a problem with me, specifically, that you'd like to redress,' Jamie said, looking at the wall, 'or do you just want to sling backhanded insults from your moral high ground?'

That's a reaction of some kind, Sonja thought. 'My problem is that you're messing with Kjell's head, twisting his emotions. And it's not fair. You're dangling something in front of him with no intention of—'

'I'm not dangling anything,' Jamie said, with as much bite as Sonja had ever heard. So much so she stumbled over her words.

'You— you are, though.'

'Weird,' Jamie said, fiercely, 'considering he's the one who turned me down just last night.' She narrowed her eyes and Sonja couldn't help but feel like she was staring down a pit viper.

'He …' Sonja started, shaking her head. 'No, look, I can only go off what I heard, and today, when I spoke to Kjell, what I saw him do, what I heard him say—'

'Where he sold me out to Dahlvig for another shot at wearing a badge?'

'He told you?' Sonja was surprised.

'Didn't take a genius to figure it out. Thorsen's a terrible liar.'

'But did he tell you why?'

Jamie shrugged now. 'I didn't ask.'

'You didn't think the reason was important?'

'I think the action said it all. He turned me down, then threw in with Dahlvig. He wants out of whatever this is. And that's fine by me.'

'Forgive me if I don't believe you. And I think that's the issue.'

'Oh, that's the issue, is it?'

Sonja let out a long breath, laughed a little to herself. Kjell was dead on, this was exhausting. 'Kjell is a man. A simple man. He wants what he wants, and he's upset he can't have it. What he wants is for you to feel the same as he does, to want what he does, and you and I both know that's not something you're able to give him.'

'So, we *are* sticking with the insults. Got it.'

'You're not wired the same way as him. Maybe not as

anyone. And I'm not saying that to be rude, I promise.' She lifted her hands to show she meant peace. 'Hell, I'm out there on my own too, it's probably why I can see it so clearly in you. But Kjell? He's straightforward, he wears his heart on his sleeve. When he was married to Maja … what they had … that was love. Truly, it was.'

'That why she fucked someone else?'

'I didn't say it wasn't complicated.'

'Everything is complicated. That, this. Whatever the fuck we're doing right here, right now.' Jamie looked around. 'Life is complicated. But what happens, happens. You can't change it.'

'But that's where you're wrong, Jamie. Because you *can* change it. You can choose, one way or the other. And that's what Kjell's doing. He tried to choose you, but it didn't work. So now he's making another choice. He's choosing him. He's choosing his own happiness now. That's what pushed him to make those decisions today. He's hurt, he's afraid, and he's running away.'

'So, what, you're saying that I should chase after him? That I should go to him, profess my love, fall to my knees, tell him I want to be with him, get married, buy a house, pop out a few kids, live happily ever after? Just because that's his vision of the perfect life?'

Sonja measured Jamie carefully. 'I'm saying you should do the opposite. I'm saying you should let him go.'

Jamie's teeth ground, her jaw flexing. Her hands returned to the pockets of her jacket, the fabric bulging around her clenched fists.

'If you keep going like this — if you keep up this … this … relationship you have. You'll lose him forever. It will explode. Maybe not today, maybe not in a week, or a month, but eventually, it will all come crashing down, and that will be it.' She continued to watch Jamie. 'You know what I mean, don't you? You've pushed people away before, lost them? Friends that were once big parts of your life are now just … adrift, somewhere? How many, Jamie? Do you want Thorsen to be another one?'

'So, I cut the cord now to preserve our friendship?'

The comment was barbed, condescending, but Sonja could tell Jamie was really asking.

'You just have to decide. Really decide. Those things you talked about – the things that you think Kjell wants. Do you want them, too, with him? Do you really want to be with him, in all the ways he wants to be with you? Because if you don't, then anything you do that isn't ending it right now is cruel. And for all the things I think you are Jamie, cruel isn't one of them.'

Silence fell between them.

It was so heavy that when Jamie's phone rang, both she and Sonja physically jolted.

Without breaking eye contact with her, Jamie fished her phone from her pocket and answered. 'Yes?' she said. 'Oh, Thorsen, hi.'

Sonja stood up from the counter and folded her arms.

'Öberg wasn't at home? You found both his and Annika's phones there? Mm, yeah. That doesn't sound good,' Jamie said evenly, not seemingly phased by the conversation. 'Brainwaves about where they could be? No, I don't know. Sorry. What?' She paused, listening to Thorsen talk. 'I'm sure you'll find him,' she said then. 'Gotland's not that big. No, yeah, I'm still at the hotel.'

Sonja breathed a silent sigh of relief.

'Okay, I'll see you soon. Bye.' Jamie hung the phone up and stored it, turning towards the door.

She reached for the handle and opened it, staring into the street, drenched in the warmth of the summer evening.

'I'm not cruel,' Jamie said, not looking back at Sonja.

And then she stepped out and closed the door behind her.

19

Kjell Thorsen

THE CALL CLICKED off and Thorsen put his phone away, letting out a long breath.

'Why the long face, Seabiscuit?' Dahlvig said, stepping down out of the open door that led up to Alex Öberg's apartment.

'Find anything?' Thorsen asked, ignoring the comment.

A single shake of the head. 'Nope. Guy is clean. Fastidiously so. Place barely looks lived in. I guess stalking and murdering teenagers keeps you out of the house. We got their phones, already passed over to forensics, but it'll be a little while before we crack them. Goddamn Apple iPhones are the worst to brute-force.'

'So, what now?'

'We wait, we search, we hope. I have a team going to Olsen's place to see if there's any sign of them there. But I'm not holding my breath.'

Thorsen nodded slowly.

Dahlvig watched him, licked his lips a little like he

wanted to ask something. Then he did. He gestured to Thorsen's phone. 'Was that Johansson you were speaking to?'

He paused for a brief second. 'Yeah,' he said then. 'Just personal stuff, though. Nothing about the case.'

Dahlvig smiled, amused. 'Sure. So, what's it like, working with her?'

'What do you mean?'

He rolled his head side to side. 'Despite everything they say, I don't think we've exchanged more than twenty words.'

'And that was enough to form an opinion?' Thorsen asked, trying not to sound defensive.

Dahlvig shrugged. 'Stockholm was a gigantic fucking waste of my time. You know how much time and paperwork it is to do a handover on a case as big as the Angel Maker? We took the reins, had three dozen people working twenty-four hours a day to get up to speed. City-wide manhunt. Hundred-plus personnel. Tactical, dogs, the works. Then I meet Johansson – not even working for Stockholm Police, mind you. She's cold, bristly. Insubordinate. I could see it in her the second we got introduced. I tell her that she's done, her time as a consultant has come to an end. Direct order. And, look, that wasn't me swinging my dick around, alright? She'd just shot someone.'

Thorsen was a little taken aback by that.

'Didn't know? Yeah, a guy called Robert Nyström. Former detective himself. Previous partner of Johansson's father, Jörgen Johansson. Heard of him?'

Thorsen shook his head.

'Eh, he's an old name now. Legend in some circles, I suppose. Big bastard. Mean as hell. Violent. Stubborn. Your girl takes after him, it seems.'

'She's not my girl.'

Dahlvig shrugged. 'Anyway, Robert Nyström was suspect

number one in the Angel Maker case, you must have heard of that.'

Just a nod from Thorsen.

'Right, so Johansson is supposed to be just assisting with the investigation, under the supervision of one Anders Wiik.' Dahlvig saw Thorsen's reaction, laughed a little. 'So, you know him, then.'

'We've met.'

'I'm not a fan either. Weird fucking guy. But him and Johansson were two peas in a socially awkward pod.'

'I noticed.'

Dahlvig smiled a little wider. 'But despite being under his supervision, she finds herself a hundred miles north of the city in the middle of fucking nowhere, with an unlicensed hunting rifle. And not only does she seemingly *find* the illusive Robert Nyström, missing up until that point. But she shoots him.'

Thorsen tried to keep his reaction to a minimum. It seemed like Dahlvig was trying to elicit one.

'But anyway – after that shit show, we finally get the case dropped on us. I mean, a civilian gunning down a former police officer isn't exactly a boon for PR. And that's not even mentioning that the guy – who survives Johansson, barely – then has his fucking throat opened in the hospital the same night. Jesus, that was a fucking mess. When it landed on my desk, I couldn't say I was excited about it.' Dahlvig shook his head, put his hands on his hips. 'So yeah, anyway, once we get to Stockholm, the last thing I want is Johansson anywhere near the case. I made that *abundantly* clear. I could not have put it in more certain terms. I said: get on a plane. Go home. I don't want to see you again. You're done. And can you guess what she did? After we'd brought in that hundred-odd personnel and geared up for the biggest manhunt in the city's history and spent days prepping and reading?'

'I assume she didn't leave.'

'Ha! Maybe you *are* a detective.'

'If I remember rightly, didn't she solve that case? Wasn't the guy you were looking for just a diversion in the end, a patsy hung out by the real killer?'

Dahlvig's moustache bristled. 'And when Johansson discovered that, you don't think it was something she should have shared with us? Instead of going off alone, despite my orders?'

'I believe that Anders Wiik actually made the arrest.'

Dahlvig chuckled a little. 'Yeah, he did. While we wasted hundreds of thousands of kronas in resources and manpower chasing our tails. So, tell me, was Johansson right?'

'She was correct.'

'But was she *right*? Or should she have gone to Ingrid Falk, the head of the department, put forward her theory in certain terms, and then followed orders and stayed out of it?'

Thorsen couldn't really come to her defence on that one.

'See, that's my issue with Johansson. She can't see past her own ambition, and rarely past the end of her own fucking nose.'

'She sees a lot. It's why she's so good,' Thorsen said coldly.

'And everyone else is supposed to just sit around with their thumbs up their asses while she goes it alone?'

Thorsen shrugged. 'What do you want me to say here?'

'I want you to tell me what she's like. What she's really like. Because she comes off like a total fucking bitch.'

'She's not.'

'But she is arrogant.'

'I don't think so. I mean, she's not. It's not arrogance, it's …'

'What? Because I don't see anything else. She's not a team player, that's for damn sure.'

'She's different.'

'Different?' Dahlvig smirked now. 'That's one way to put it I suppose. So, what's your play here? You screwing her? You guys a thing?'

'No.'

'That's pretty definitive. So, it's purely in a professional interest then? She's got a nose for big cases. You plan to ride her coattails from one newsworthy case to the next until you can jump ship into a cushty desk job somewhere?'

'Is there a point to this, or are you just trying to piss me off for your own amusement?'

'I'm just trying to ascertain why *anyone* would want to partner with her.'

'I don't think anything I could say would do a good enough job of explaining it.'

'Try me.'

'I'd rather not. Doubt I could, honestly.'

Dahlvig pursed his lips, his moustache bristling like a walrus. 'I gotta give it to her. Despite her obvious failings, she knows how to make friends in high places. SPA, Europol, The Met, hell, I even heard she made a friend or two at the FBI. She's written a golden ticket to walk into a senior investigator's role anywhere she pleases. The NOD included. If she promised to behave, at least.'

'You'd hire her?'

'On paper. In reality is a different story. Though I don't really make those calls. You know what the NOD likes better than yes men?'

'People who solve cases.'

'Bingo.'

'Is that all you want me here for, then? To give you the truth about Jamie?' Thorsen was very tired suddenly. Tired of this conversation, and of talking about Jamie.

'I want to know where your allegiances lie. Johansson will be fine, so long as she gets her head out of her ass.'

'I don't know if that's ever going to happen.'

'Let me be frank, then, Thorsen – some advice, both professional and personal. From someone who's clawed their way to where they are without a golden ticket. And from someone who's twice divorced. Love isn't all it's cracked up to be. It's not worth it. Especially not when you're shitting where you eat. You should know that. You already married one co-worker, and look how that ended. Nearly blew up your fucking career, didn't it? And now, you want to jump back into a relationship with another one? I get it, alright. Johansson is … she's attractive, sure, if you like that cold, miserable thing. Not my type, but no judgement here.' He lifted his hands innocently. 'You can't have it all, right? So, take a step back here. Let Johansson do her tragic hero thing. And you come work for a real detective. Focus on your career. Work with a real agency, on big cases. As part of a good team. Steady income, pension, full benefits. Structure. Rules. Procedure. No flying bullets or galloping off towards the sound of gunfire. I've looked into your history. And despite working trafficking and serious crime in Lulea, you've seen more "action" in the last year than you did in the previous ten. And why do you think that is? You stick with Johansson, you're going to be the one getting hurt. Or worse. And I'm not being dramatic, I'll tell you that much. Her last three partners before you: stabbed, shot, got his hand crushed. In that order.'

Thorsen clamped his teeth together, eyes locked with

Dahlvig's. His phone began ringing then. Dahlvig fished it from his pocket without looking and glanced down at the screen.

'Shit, I gotta take this. Think about what I said.' He pointed at Thorsen, pulling the phone to his ear as he backed away. 'The offer has a clock, and it's already running. Yeah, Dahlvig,' he said into the mouthpiece, turning and striding away towards a bank of waiting police cars.

Thorsen just stood there. Thinking. Six months ago, he wouldn't have spent a second deliberating over it.

But now?

Now, everything had changed.

Jamie Johansson

THE SECOND THE door to Sonja's house closed, Jamie broke into a run.

Her throat was tight, chest burning. She raked in shallow breaths, willing herself into a sprint. She kept gaining speed, elongating her strides. Faster. Faster. Doing all she could to outrun Sonja's words and her own thoughts.

As she neared the centre of the city, she slowed, breathing hard.

A crowd had gathered outside a café, spilling onto the street. Cars were backing up, honking their horns, trying to squeeze past on the opposite side. The crowd didn't even seem to notice.

What the hell was going on?

Jamie tried to catch her breath, her heart refusing to slow down.

As she got closer, she could hear the din of a TV, the crowd silent as they watched. The front of the café was open, tri-folding doors exposing the interior to the street. A large flat-screen hung above the bar, turned towards the people crammed both inside and out. The news was playing, and the last time Jamie thought she'd seen a crowd like this so trans-fixed on a newscast was after the 7/7 bombing.

Her blood ran cold as she realised this wasn't far off.

A 'BREAKING NEWS' header scrolled across the screen as a female newscaster read from the prompter. Jamie didn't need to hear to know what was going on. 'THE BLACK HEART KILLER TERRORISES GOTLAND'. The words rode across the screen in huge white letters. Jesus Christ, the story was finally breaking. Two years of absolute media silence, and now the news was out. And this wasn't just a local station, this was national.

The words kept coming, the reporter drowned out by the growing murmurs and unease in the crowd. 'TWENTY-THREE TEENAGERS DEAD.'

The bartender turned it as loud as it would go, the news-caster's voice blaring into the street '... this comes from an anonymous source on the island, someone close to the latest victim. The police are failing, says the source, and are doing little to find the cause. So far, they have no leads. We have reached out to the Visby police for comment, but so far, have had no reply. We will bring you more updates as they come in …'

Jamie pulled out her phone and started dialling.

He answered quickly.

'Thorsen?' Jamie asked, the panic clear in her own voice. 'Have you seen?'

'How can you not?' Thorsen asked, the rumble of a car in the background. 'It's everywhere. Dahlvig is blowing his top.'

'Where are you now?'

'I got out of the blast radius before he went nuclear,'

Thorsen said. 'I'm en route back to the hotel. Where are you?'

'I, uh,' Jamie started, realising she'd just spoken to him and told him she was there. 'I just stepped out for some air. I'm headed there now—'

The crowd grew in volume in front of her, the agitation apparent. People began jostling, shoving. Someone pushed someone else and they stumbled back into Jamie, knocking her into the person behind. They shoved back, her phone spilling from her grip and disappearing into the throng of bodies.

'Shit!' she called, diving after it, feeling knees and thighs squeeze at her shoulders as she fought her way down.

A heel pressed onto the screen, then lifted, leaving a crack running across it.

'Fuck!' Jamie yelled, catching a shin to the ear as she picked it up, fighting her way towards the sky above.

Grunting and sweating, she swam through the crowd. It seethed like the chest of some great beast, in and out, in and out and people pushed and pulled at each other. Flecks of saliva hit her skin, screams erupting, fists beginning to fly as rage laced its way through the hive.

Sirens began to bark and howl in the distance. All around, people began surging into the crowd, as though drawn to it, looking for an excuse. Some tried to help, others seemed to just want blood.

Jamie had seen this before, and it only ended one way.

She had to get free.

And then she was.

The crowd thinned ahead of her and she broke into open space, still fighting the current of bodies as they all converged on the growing melee.

Jamie dodged and weaved between the bodies, all wide eyed and sweaty as night closed in about the city.

And then she ran faster, ran harder than she had in a long time.

She was slick with sweat by the time she reached the hotel.

What had begun as a few isolated incidents of violence had quickly escalated. As she wound deeper into the heart of the city, smoke began to billow above the rooftops. Ambulances, fire engines, police cars. They screamed by in droves. Screams of rage and pain echoed through the streets and people with bloodied faces, clutching injured body parts, dragging and carrying others, came stumbling from all sides, seeking safe haven and help.

Jamie knew that tensions had been high, that trouble had been brewing … but now, the floodgates seemed to have opened all at once. No one knew the extent of the deaths until this moment. And now, the whole city seemed intent on adding to the numbers, not stopping them.

The hotel doors opened to greet Jamie, and despite the interior being cool and calm, the silence and emptiness of it told Jamie that even here things had changed. The reception desk was abandoned, and though soft music played in the background, there wasn't a soul in sight.

Except Thorsen.

'Jamie!' he called, running forward from his position near the lifts. 'Jesus, are you okay? It's crazy out there.'

He pulled up short, arms held from his sides as though he were about to hug her, but stopped himself.

'Where were you?'

'I went for a walk,' Jamie lied between raking breaths. 'Bad timing, I guess.'

'The worst,' Thorsen said, wide eyed. 'No leads on Öberg, yet. You think Annika Olsen is okay?'

'I hope so,' was all Jamie could say.

Thorsen nodded slowly. 'We should go up,' he said. 'There's nothing we can do out there.' He gestured to the windows, the muted sounds of sirens.

Jamie swallowed. He was right. Despite being at the heart of this thing, they had no authority here.

But when she looked up at him to agree, she found he was staring over her shoulder.

The bar was located just through the lobby. There wasn't a soul in there – Jamie suspected they'd ordered all guests to their rooms and told the staff to go home – but the TV above the bar was playing the news.

Thorsen walked towards it and Jamie followed.

The newsreader had gone, replaced now by footage showing the inside of an abandoned building. There was still a frame around it, the words 'Breaking News', the headline about twenty-three dead teens scrolling on repeat, but the video was new.

Jamie and Thorsen slowed at the polished brass bar top and watched. There was no sound except for their quickened breaths.

The video was shot on a phone. It meandered through a darkened corridor, dim phone flashlight illuminating blackened walls, piles of rubble, streaks of mould and moss growing across the floor and what remained of the ceiling.

The camera lurched forward as the filmer navigated the treacherous ground, and then paused, swinging right into a room. It panned slowly, showing the charred metal frame of a single bed, a broken window, and then across to the main event.

A huge drawing filling the wall. It was damaged by fire and weathered by time, but there was no denying what it was.

A black heart, etched onto the paint. It was fiercely dark, stark and unmistakable.

And on the wall beneath, scrawled, the words 'What dreams may come'.

'Jesus,' Thorsen muttered. 'Where the hell is that?'

Jamie could only shake her head. 'I have no idea.'

'Fuck,' he said. Then followed it up with a much louder one.

Jamie jumped a little.

'Okay, okay,' he said, turning to her, lifting his hands. 'What does this mean? We need something, here, Jamie – we've gotta do *something*. Anything …'

She knew he was right. This would only add fuel to the fire. And now, seeing this on TV … was this the work of the killer themselves? Trying to incite riots, more death, destruction? Is this what they wanted?

Jamie took a breath. 'What do we know about Öberg and the victims?'

Thorsen reeled them off on his fingers. 'He's studying literature, he was Juni Pedersen's academic mentor, he was placed at several libraries that gave him access to several victims …'

'So, this place?' Jamie asked, looking up at the screen again. It had switched back to a corridor view now as the camera delved further. She caught sight of a gurney, made a guess. 'This … hospital? What does it have to do with anything? *How* could it have anything to do with anything? It looks old. Abandoned. Decades ago. Hell, it looks like it burned down before Öberg would even have been born.'

'What are you saying?'

'I'm saying that maybe the reason that Dahlvig hasn't

been making progress is because he's not been looking far enough back. It can't be hard to find a record of hospitals that burned down on Gotland. Then he needs to dig – older cases. Deaths of teens, suspicious deaths, anything surrounding this place … twenty, thirty, hell, forty years back. I don't know.'

Thorsen was nodding faster, more assertively. 'Yeah, good, I'll make a call.' He drew his phone from his pocket and stepped away. 'Dahlvig,' he said a moment later, connected with the head of the entire operation.

Jamie watched, Sonja's words rattling around in her head. Thorsen would be going, she thought. To rejoin Dahlvig. She could go with him. But Dahlvig had already made it clear he didn't want Jamie involved in this. So that made it simple, didn't it?

When Thorsen went, Jamie could just … slip away? Let Thorsen go. Let him do what he wanted to do. Let him be happy?

He was back then, stowing his phone. 'Dahlvig is scrambling. Damage control. PR statement, press releases. He has every officer on the island trying to hold this place together. Hell, they're bringing in the Home Guard. It's getting dangerous out there. They need all the help they can get.'

'You're going?'

He paused, looking at her. 'Going where?'

'To Dahlvig, to help?'

'I … no,' he said. 'I'm staying, here. With you.'

Jamie wanted to speak, but found she couldn't.

'But …'

'But what?' Jamie asked.

'Dahlvig did offer me a job. Working for the NOD.'

She forced a smile. 'That's … that's great. I'm … happy for you.'

'Would you want to come with me? Work for the NOD,

too? Dahlvig said … well, I mean, he sort of said that there'd be room. You know? That he'd consider taking you on. We could keep working together. Big cases. We could make a real difference.'

His eyes were almost pleading with her.

Jamie swallowed, then nodded. 'Yeah, sure, Thorsen,' she said, 'whatever you want.'

A grin began to form on his face.

He seemed to believe her.

That's good, she thought. It's easier this way.

'Okay,' he said. 'So, what now?'

'Now?' Jamie asked, looking back at the TV, the footage playing on loop. 'I guess we wait.'

Thorsen stirred with the sun.

The sound of sirens had died sometime during the night, but how much sleep he'd got, he really couldn't say.

The bedclothes enveloped him.

As he came around, he rolled onto his side, sliding his hand across the bed to find an empty space.

One eye opened, then the other, and he sat up slowly, rubbing his cheek, willing his vision to focus.

Jamie came into view in front of him, her back turned. She was sitting at the desk, long untied blonde hair trailing down her spine, bare shoulders jutting from the ashen strands.

She nodded her head slowly, in time with the music playing in her headphones.

He smiled, getting up from the bed, sleep still half about him, and padded forward, slowing as he neared.

Her legs were folded under her, crossed on the chair. Her running shorts reached just a few inches down her muscled thighs. His eyes traced her skin, her stomach below the band of her sports bra, her pointed collar bones. He could smell her, the faintness of her sweat, the sweetness of her hair.

She was unaware of him, eyes fixed on her laptop screen.

He reached down, his hands closing around her shoulders, his fingers sliding down her naked arms.

She jolted at first, shuddered, but then softened at his touch, turning her head to look up at him, her pale blue eyes electric in the glow of her computer screen.

Thorsen seemed to be awake then, the last remnants of sleep cast off like a pall.

He retracted his hands quickly, abandoning the momentary delirium that seemed to have seized him.

Jamie rose quickly, turning and standing in front of him. She tugged the headphones from her ears, looking up into his eyes.

She was once again reminded just how tall Thorsen was, just how imposing.

He'd fallen asleep in her bed while she'd worked at the desk. Many times during the night she'd thought about crawling in next to him. Had wondered what that would have been like, what might have happened.

But she had resisted. Had promised herself that she wouldn't, couldn't, go down that path. Couldn't open that door knowing she was intent on closing it forever.

And yet, now, with him standing there, in front of her … the way he looked, the way he smelled. There was a flash, just a glimpse of an alternate universe where she'd not only got into bed with him last night, but she did so every night. Without fear. Without trepidation. Without a second thought.

He seemed to read this in her.

Jamie's heart quickened.

His hands began to rise, once more, touching her ribs, moving across her back. Enveloping her.

As she looked at him, she couldn't help but see the confliction on his face. How he somehow looked … in pain.

She felt his fingers trace her spine, upwards, until his hand reached the nape of her neck, pushing into her hair.

It tugged on the strands, and Jamie sucked in a sharp breath, the pain surprising, momentary. Replaced by something else all at once.

He brought her face towards his.

Jamie trembled.

His eyes closed.

But before he could kiss her, she spoke.

'I think I found something,' she whispered, her voice quivering.

Thorsen stopped, his eyes opening.

'About the case,' Jamie said.

His hands left her body and he dropped her back onto her heels. She hadn't been aware until that moment that he'd practically been holding her clear of the ground.

Thorsen stepped backwards, lips twisting into a grimace. One of disgust almost.

'I found the hospital,' Jamie said, feeling shame, though she didn't know why. She wrapped herself in her arms, covering as much bare skin as she could. 'I know where the heart is.'

But Thorsen said nothing.

He just turned away and walked out of the room.

Jamie wasn't sure what would happen next. But twenty minutes later, Thorsen was knocking at her door.

She opened it, dressed, and found him there. He didn't even look at her, was instead staring at his phone.

'I texted Dahlvig,' he said abruptly. 'He's going to meet

us at the hospital, he just needs to know where it is.' Thorsen handed Jamie his phone, looking left and right down the corridor. It was open to the messages with Dahlvig, awaiting Jamie's input. She didn't think it was coincidence that the last message he sent, right above the one he expected her to type, sent just ten minutes earlier, read: I'll take the job.

Jamie swallowed the heavy, painful lump that had formed in her throat and began typing in the hospital address. She blinked, the screen blurring in front of her eyes. She felt the familiar sting in the back of her throat, the heat of tears in her ears.

She hammered the address in, hit send, and then handed the phone back, afraid Thorsen would see. But he didn't want to look at her.

Instead, he nodded and walked off down the corridor. 'Let's go,' he called, walking at a speed he knew Jamie's legs couldn't keep up with unless she jogged.

But her own seemed heavy and unwilling to move.

Thorsen glanced back. 'I'll leave without you,' he announced.

She shook her head. Hard. Threw some tears onto the hotel carpet, then took off, throwing herself forward, forcing her legs to move or let herself hit the floor face first.

Luckily, she remembered how to walk, and closed ground on Thorsen fast.

Though not fast enough. By the time she reached the elevator, it was already closing, and he made no attempt to hold it for her.

Jamie got there a second too late, her hand hitting the cold steel, the rumble of cables behind kicking in a second later.

She growled in frustration, but couldn't say she really blamed him. At the very least she understood.

Jamie hit the call button and waited for the next one, but

by the time it came and she reached the lobby, there was no sign of Thorsen.

There was someone manning the desk, but the lobby was empty once more. It was early, though. Not even seven yet. Jamie had been up most of the night, had caught a few hours on the armchair in the corner of the room, but she was already exhausted. And she knew it was going to be a long day.

By the time she reached the front door, Thorsen pulled up outside in Sonja's little hatchback. Jamie went to it, opened the door, and got in, all without a word from either of them. She barely managed to get into the seat before he pulled off at speed, the hospital address already plugged into the satnav.

The city streets themselves were empty of people, but the evidence of the previous night's destruction was wholly visible. Rubbish bins had been knocked over and the contents lined the streets. Some shop windows had been smashed, others spray-painted and defaced, the word 'LIARS' was the first Jamie spotted, written in huge red letters. The rest seemed to be profanity, but the anger was clear and clearly directed at the police.

It wasn't long before they saw the first smoke. A car was overturned, its windscreen strewn across the street. What looked like a bar had a blackened maw where its doorway had been and smoke was still drifting out.

The city seemed to be asleep now, but sirens still called in the distance. Jamie wondered how much longer this would go on, how much further it would go.

A military truck rolled by in the opposite direction, driving fast. Camo-clad soldiers sat stoically in it, rifles between their legs, pointed at the ceiling.

They looked at Jamie and Thorsen as they drove past, but didn't slow down.

Jamie glanced across the centre console, but Thorsen

seemed to take no notice, his hands fastened on the wheel, foot flat to the floor.

The city thinned around them quickly enough and they were plunged into the countryside. Idyllic and tranquil, as always.

Dew clung to the grassy fields they passed, animals grazing quietly. As if nothing was wrong at all.

Thorsen followed the route, heading further from civilisation, and then turned off the road completely, heading down a narrow, tree-lined track, overgrown and rutted with time.

They bounced and jostled forward endlessly until the trees broke and they found themselves in a wide, forgotten car park. Ahead, the hospital rose up, damaged by fire and time.

Thorsen hadn't even asked how Jamie had found it. She'd spent hours looking online, but couldn't find any record of any hospitals having burned down.

At least, not medical hospitals.

But this wasn't one of those.

This was a mental hospital.

For children.

An institution, a secure facility. Small and privately owned, it burned down in 1990. Classed as an electrical fire. It was covered by local press. Several people died, including a few patients. Children. That's how she'd found it. Public records of the deaths of children on Gotland. It was only when she discovered three on the same day that she zeroed in on it. Some sort of incident that claimed the lives of three teens all at the same time.

After that, Jamie had sifted through archived copies of the paper, stored as PDFs. She'd downloaded dozens of them, sifting through one by one until she found the right copy, the right page, the right article.

And now, here they were, the photograph Jamie had in her mind a stark difference from what was in front of them. The picture in the paper had shown the hospital in its heydey, the fire fighters spraying water in through the open windows, the flames licking at the air through the broken frames.

Now, the fire had gone, and in its place, plants and trees grew, jutting from the stonework, climbing the walls, dragging the whole place slowly into the earth. Reclaiming it.

Dahlvig was already there, along with a trio of cars and half a dozen investigators and forensic techs.

He waved Thorsen in next to a marked Volvo estate, looking stern.

Thorsen parked and got out, circling the bonnet and shaking Dahlvig's hand.

They both turned towards the hospital and started walking, already deep in conversation.

Jamie was tempted to stay right there. She'd done her part, she thought. Helped them find the place. Did they really need her now?

Her palms were slick with sweat and she wiped them on her thighs.

She'd come this far, she supposed. And she'd be lying if she said she wasn't curious.

So, with a long exhale that did little to calm her, she pushed the door open and went after them.

By the time Jamie caught up, Dahlvig was already briefing the other investigators, Thorsen included.

As she approached, Dahlvig looked at her but didn't stop speaking. She stood next to Thorsen, who also didn't look at her. Dahlvig proceeded to explain the situation to the investigators and techs, but wasted no time. And a moment later, they were dispersing towards the building in pairs.

'Sir?' Thorsen asked, at a loss for direction.

Dahlvig just motioned him towards the building. 'Get to it.' He glanced at Jamie now. 'And take Johansson with you. Maybe that sixth sense of hers will come in handy.'

'But ...' Thorsen started before trailing off.

Dahlvig was already on the phone and making a call.

'Shall we ...' Jamie offered, but she didn't get to finish before Thorsen started walking.

Jamie went after him. 'I must have watched the video a hundred times,' she said, keen to get both of their focus back on the task at hand and off what happened – or didn't happen – that morning. 'I think, based on what I could see out of the window in the Black Heart room, that it's on the second floor.'

Thorsen just grunted, mounting the front steps and heading inside after the others. They were sweeping the ground floor first, and had spread out down the three corridors ahead. One in front, and one to each side.

Jamie pointed to a sign overgrown with moss hanging off the wall in front of them. 'Stairs,' she said.

Another grunt from Thorsen.

He aimed for it. Pissed off or not, he knew better than to disregard Jamie's suggestions when it came to a case. Though it didn't seem to be buying her any favour.

The door creaked horribly as Thorsen forced it open, shoving a layer of grime out of the way. He let it close behind him, so that Jamie had to shoulder her way into the stairwell.

Thorsen was already halfway up the flight by the time Jamie got in there. The roof, three stories up, had been burned away and had collapsed, allowing a dim light to filter down.

The air in the stairwell was thick and damp, the walls black with mould.

They walked upwards, doubling back on themselves until they reached the next landing. Thorsen was waiting at the door. 'This one?' he asked.

Jamie shook her head. 'Up one more.'

He walked again, mounting the stairs two at a time.

The door to the second floor was already closing by the time Jamie got there.

She stepped into the corridor, the floor feeling a little too spongy for her liking, the wooden planks soft, half rotted.

Thorsen had his legs slightly apart, testing the strength by rocking side to side.

'A little sketchy,' Jamie said.

He shrugged. 'Let's get this over with.'

She watched as he headed for the front of the building, the 'T' junction at the end of the corridor.

The windows in each room let sunlight stream in. It was quiet here, except for the twittering of a bird somewhere in the broken roof above. Moss and ferns had begun to sprout in the patient rooms, loving the rotting wood and mulched leaves that had blown in and decomposed over the last three decades.

Jamie always found it interesting how nature began to take root against the manmade. How time seemed to wipe all things clean. How equilibrium would always be found in some way. A symbiosis could always be formed, between even the most different things.

She thought this as Thorsen paused at the junction, then went left.

'Other way,' Jamie called.

He stopped, then doubled back and headed right.

Balance, she thought. Would she find it?

Jamie followed Thorsen down the corridor. He paused at each room and glanced inside. Once he was sure that it was the wrong one, he moved on.

She hung back, thinking, wondering how they could go forward from here. If they could. Was there any way to repair the damage she'd done? Was there any going back? She knew that if they went forward, if they started something, then it would only end badly. She didn't want the things he did. She wanted everything to stay as it was. The risk was not worth it, and she knew if she let him in, really let him in, she'd end up blowing the whole thing up. She'd push him away so hard that they'd never be more than strangers. And their friendship, their relationship, meant too much to her to risk.

But how could she say that to him? She could barely admit it to herself in her own head. She was weak. Frightened. All the things that she hated. Scared. Scared of what? Of change? No. Of being alone. It was the only thing she hated more than being with someone else.

There was a flash ahead and Jamie stopped in her tracks, her mind still rolling over the events of that morning. What might have happened if she'd kept her mouth shut for a second more.

So much so that what had just happened in front of her didn't even register.

Thorsen stumbled sideways, slumping into the wall, and then collapsed forward onto his knees. The dull thunk of the impact echoed in Jamie's mind, but she didn't connect the dots until the man in the black mask stepped out of one of the rooms and into the corridor.

He stood there with a length of wood in his hand, jagged and snapped at one end, the other firmly in his grasp.

His eyes, black as jet, stared out from the eyeholes cut in the fabric, the whites catching the sunlight on his shoulder.

He advanced quickly, stepping over Thorsen's prostrate body.

Jamie's hand flew to her hip but found her gun missing.

'Shit,' she hissed, looking down and realising she hadn't been carrying it for six months now.

Her hands came up instead, warding the guy off. 'Hey, hey, stop, alright? Stop! Hey!' she screamed, backing up as quickly as she could.

The guy lunged, wood coming up and swinging hard. Hard enough to take her head off.

She ducked under it, listening to it whistle above her skull.

It impacted the wall with a loud crack and snapped in two, showering Jamie in splinters of half-rotten wood.

'Shit!' she yelled, twisting and springing forward into a run, trying to get away.

But before she even made two steps, she felt something yank her backwards by her head.

Her legs rose in front of her, pain lancing through her scalp.

She saw the ceiling for a moment, her long plait in the grip of a black leather glove, and then she hit the ground, hard enough to make the weakened floor shake.

The wind was knocked out of her and she gasped, vision swimming. And if it wasn't for the sunlight coming through the windows glinting off the blade, Jamie wouldn't have seen it at all.

It flashed overhead, fierce and sharp, locked in the killer's grip, and then plunged downwards towards Jamie's heart.

She threw her arms up, blocking the strike with her elbows, the killer's forearms rebounding off them.

Jamie's legs kicked and she tried to get up, but the killer was on her, forcing the knife downwards again.

Their arms connected and the killer knelt, trying to force the knife into Jamie's chest.

She called out, sweat beading on her throat and forehead as she fought it. But he was bigger, stronger, had the better position.

The knife inched lower, lower, closer to her body.

Jamie screamed through gritted teeth, flecks of saliva flying from her lips, blood roaring in her ears.

The tip of the knife reached her shirt, then her skin below. Pain blinded her, sending flashes of colour and darkness through her vision. She felt an intense heat as the knife broke skin, the blood welling up around it and trickling down her ribs. This was it. She was about to die.

A deafening bang rang out. Jamie wasn't sure if it was her eardrums bursting or something else.

She forced her eyes open to see blood spray the wall overhead.

The knife pulled itself free of her skin and the killer reeled backwards, standing up, clutching his shoulder with his opposite hand.

The blade hit the ground and Jamie watched, panting, as the killer turned and ran.

More shots rang out, shouts from the other end of the corridor.

Ancient plaster exploded around the masked man as the bullets missed, impacting the walls and ceiling.

He hurdled Thorsen's body, making for the far end of the corridor.

He skidded on the moss-covered floorboards, then disappeared around the corner.

Footsteps thundered around Jamie's head as two of Dahlvig's men gave chase.

One of them stopped at Thorsen, kneeling at his side, the

other carrying on, disappearing around the corner too. But there were no yells to 'stop', no more shots.

Jamie groaned, rolling onto her side, putting her hand to her sternum, to the nick there that felt like it extended down into the fascia. It throbbed horribly, still bleeding, soaking her stomach. 'Fuck,' she panted, propping herself up on her elbow and inspecting it.

'Woah, woah,' Dahlvig said, next to her all of a sudden. 'Take it easy, let me see,' he said, trying to move her hand and reaching for her shirt.

'Not a chance,' Jamie scoffed, shoving him off. 'I'm fine, check on Thorsen,' she said, nodding to her downed partner.

He seemed to be coming round. He was sitting up, groaning, rubbing the side of his head while Dahlvig's man tended to him.

Thorsen looked up at Jamie, face contorted. She didn't know into what kind of expression, but it wasn't a good one.

'You're a lightning rod for shit, you know that, Johansson?' Dahlvig sighed, offering her a hand up.

She gave him the non-bloodied one and he pulled her to her feet. She wobbled for a moment, then got steady, the adrenaline still coursing in her.

'Tell me about it,' she grumbled, walking towards Thorsen. 'You okay?' she asked as she got near.

Thorsen ignored the investigator trying to help him and got slowly to his feet. 'Why is it always me that gets hit?'

'Because you need to be more aware of your surroundings?' Jamie asked, offering a smile.

He glared at her.

'Thorsen,' Dahlvig interjected, pulling up beside Jamie. 'Get yourself to the hospital, now. We can handle things here.'

'I'm fine, seriously—'

'Seriously, it's not a request. You got smacked in the side of the head, and you're bleeding.'

Thorsen touched his scalp and his fingers came away red. 'Jesus,' he muttered, hissing at the pain.

'Sven, drive him,' Dahlvig said to the investigator next to Thorsen, an average height guy with short black hair and a wide neck.

Sven nodded, and tried to guide Thorsen by the arm.

He pulled it free, heading for the exit. 'I can walk.'

'I'm right behind you,' Jamie said, clutching at her chest, still. The wound was clean, and she was keeping pressure on it. The bleeding seemed to have stopped for the most part, but she thought she might need a stitch. And she'd likely have another scar to add to the collection.

'Hold on a second,' Dahlvig said to Jamie, turning his attention to the room that the killer had come out of.

Jamie paused, following his eye. 'What is it?'

'I want you to take a look at this,' Dahlvig replied, heading in there.

'I'm sure that you don't need me to …' Jamie began, but trailed off as Dahlvig fired her a stern look.

She watched Thorsen disappear around the corner towards the stairs and exhaled, going into the room.

'Tell me what you think,' Dahlvig said, folding his arms and looking around.

There was no doubt this was the room from the video. Black Heart and everything. She felt like she'd already walked around the place it was so clear in her mind, but being here still sent a shiver down her spine.

She let her eyes take it all in. The blackened bedframe, the charred walls, the gigantic black heart drawn right onto the peeling paint.

'Any time,' Dahlvig said from the doorway.

Jamie took a breath and started walking around. She went to the floor at the foot of the wall opposite the heart. A shelf had collapsed, taking the plaster with it, and on the floor was a charred mound of old books.

Jamie crouched and sifted through. 'Classics,' she muttered, trying to decipher the burnt covers. 'Some Shakespeare, naturally,' she sighed. 'Few others.'

Dahlvig stayed quiet.

Jamie stood and went to the metal bedside table. 'No photo frames or anything like that.' She tried the drawer, found it empty. 'No letters from home.'

She looked at the heart now, inspecting it.

'What dreams may come,' she read, then let out a long breath.

'You can read, great,' Dahlvig said. 'But what do you think it means?'

Jamie shrugged a little. 'Don't know. Escape, maybe? Annika Olsen said in a voicemail that Juni Pedersen was obsessed with this idea of death absolving sins, of it being an endless dream state.'

'An escape from reality,' Dahlvig offered.

'Maybe, yeah,' Jamie said. 'I think this is where it all started.' She gestured around. 'You know what happened here, at the hospital?'

He nodded once. 'We looked up the incident report on the way over. This was a mental institution. Secure facility. The fire was arson. In the children's ward. A patient started the fire in their room – this room – then laid down in their bed,' Dahlvig said flatly, nodding to the charred frame in front of him, 'and burned to death.'

'Suicide,' Jamie stated.

'That's what the report said.' He watched her. 'But you don't agree?'

'Considering that the killer just tried to add Thorsen and I to his body count …'

Dahlvig stayed quiet, waiting for her to expound on it.

Jamie sighed. She didn't like conjecturing. 'Did you find anything out about the person in this room?'

'Just his name, so far. Viktor Hellström. The report named him and said that he was admitted for schizophrenia. But we haven't had much time to dig up anything else. I have my people working on it. We'll know more soon. But records from back then are in paper format. They were moved from here after the fire, but it's taking some time to track them down.'

Jamie just nodded, walking towards the black heart, running her fingers over it.

'You think someone found this place, found some weird inspiration here?'

'I don't think Alex Öberg is our killer, no.'

Jamie caught Dahlvig smirk a little out of the corner of her eye. 'No?' he asked.

She shook her head. 'I don't think so. But I've been wrong before.'

'Less often than you're right, I hear.' Dahlvig folded his arms, watching Jamie.

She inspected the room again, the broken window and smashed frame, the chunks of plaster and concrete fallen off the walls. A big chunk was missing under the heart itself, the wall sagging awkwardly where the bottom plate had been burnt away, leaving a sizeable hole.

Jamie knelt there and looked across the char marks. She let her fingers trail over the surface. They came away black with the soot. 'This is where the fire started,' she said, then looked at the bed. 'Quickly spread to the mattress.'

Jamie stooped lower, looking through the hole, then

sighed and got to her feet and walked into the corridor, dusting off her jeans. Her chest had started bleeding again.

She paused for a moment at the next room over. It was in nearly as dire condition as the one where the fire had started.

She looked at the bare walls no more than eight feet apart, the tiny bed and the remnants of a mattress that would have been three inches thick. The barred windows. The steel doors that locked from the outside. Jesus, this place was as much a prison as a hospital. Enough to drive anyone to madness, she thought, let alone save them from it.

'What is it?' Dahlvig asked, at her side.

'Nothing,' Jamie said, holding her fingers to the cut on her chest. The pain was intense and doing nothing for her mood. 'Can I go to the hospital now?'

Dahlvig took a second, then nodded. 'Sure,' he said. 'I'll have someone give you a ride.'

Jamie walked off towards the stairs.

She didn't need to look back to know Dahlvig was watching her the whole way.

21

Annika Olsen

SIRENS HAD BEEN HOWLING all day.

Thankfully, night was falling fast, and with it came the cover of darkness. Though that meant that the streets would be quieter. Easier to get spotted.

Jesus bleeding-hell Christ on a cracker. How did you get yourself into this one? Annika thought as she stepped out of the small corner shop, a carrier bag full of microwaveable noodles and chocolate swinging at her side.

She put her hood up, glanced up and down the side street, and then took off.

It wasn't far to the hotel, but it was far enough that she still shit herself the entire way there.

Gotland didn't have 'motels', but if it did, they would have been like this. It was a low-slung single-storey building on the outskirts of the city. About twenty rooms nestled along a single semi-exposed corridor replete with stuttering lights and wheeling moths. Not exactly her choice of lodging, but they needed to keep a low profile. This whole thing had *not* gone to plan.

Annika twisted the key in the old lock and let herself back into the room.

The blinds were drawn, the TV playing but on mute.

She glanced around. 'Alex?' she asked into the darkness, closing the door behind her.

A tousled brown head popped up from behind the bed.

'Annika,' he said, the relief in his voice apparent. 'Thank God you're safe.' He got up off the questionably clean carpet and climbed back onto the bed.

Annika dumped their dinner next to him and climbed onto the quilted bedspread, inspecting Alex Öberg's face in the darkness. He looked like he hadn't slept in two days. And that was because he hadn't. His eyes, so bright when Annika had met him, were now sunken and bloodshot. His skin was breaking out, and his hair was flat and greasy. He'd bitten his nails down to the quick, and the continuous nervous sweat was making him smell like he'd not showered in weeks.

Though Annika didn't think she was doing much better. What had begun as a noble crusade had now turned ugly, and she couldn't help but feel like they were in serious trouble.

As Alex guided Annika through that old mental hospital, to the room with the black heart, when he'd filmed it all, and told her to put together an email to a news station, including the video, explaining what had happened, what was going on … it had all seemed so well intentioned. The right thing to do. To tell the world what was going on.

But then … the violence began. The rioting, the fighting, the burning, the looting.

Alex had said they could go public, that their status as whistleblowers would protect them. But it was clear now that there was a reason this had been kept from the press. And that reason was billowing over the streets of Visby in a thick black cloud. It was the blood flowing in the gutters and the broken glass lining the pavements.

And now they were hiding. From the police. From everyone.

'Tell me we did the right thing?' Alex asked, eyes fixed on the TV. It was replaying footage from earlier that day of a huge melee happening outside the police HQ in the city. Officers in riot gear tried to push people back as they launched bricks and bottles at them. People were getting beaten with batons. Tear gas was pluming from the ranks of furious citizens. They wanted justice, and they wanted safety. And they seemed to be willing to kill and die for those two things.

Annika turned away, grimacing. She couldn't watch. Couldn't stomach the idea that they'd been the ones who'd caused it.

'Annika?' Alex repeated. 'We did the right thing, didn't we?'

She just shook her head, tears forming in the corners of her eyes as footage of the ER at Visby hospital showed dozens of injured people wrapped in bandages, cut, burnt, and screaming.

'People needed to know,' Alex said, nodding to himself. 'They needed to. We did the right thing. It's not right what the police did, and now, everyone knows the truth. Maybe we even stopped the whole thing. Now that people know, maybe the killer will stop. We exposed him, right? Annika? Annika? What do you think?'

She swallowed, sniffing back tears. 'I don't know. What if you're wrong? What if this is what he wanted all along?' She met Alex's eyes and he paled. 'What if we just made things worse?'

22

Kjell Thorsen

'I SAID I'M FINE.' Thorsen batted the doctor's hand away, moving the pen light from his eyes. 'I'm not concussed,' he protested.

'Well, I think you are,' the doctor answered firmly. He stood straight, an older man with wispy white hair and a long nose. 'Your pupils are dilated more than normal, and there's also the fact that you got beaten over the head with a metal pipe.'

'It was a piece of wood,' Thorsen replied sourly. 'And it wasn't even that hard. I just lost my footing is all.'

'Mm,' the doctor said, not buying it. 'The person who brought you in said you lost consciousness.'

'Then he's a fucking liar,' Thorsen growled. 'Seriously?' he asked, batting the doctor's hand away again. 'Enough with the light. Don't you have other patients to see?'

'I do,' the doctor huffed, standing straight. 'But I'm just trying to make sure you're not about to collapse of a brain bleed.'

'If I do, I absolve you of all liability. I won't sue.'

'No, you won't. Because you'll be dead.' The doctor stowed the light and strode out of the room, passing Jamie at the door.

Her shirt was red with blood, but a dressing pad was visible through her open collar. She leaned awkwardly on the frame. 'And I thought I was the stubborn one,' she said, smiling.

Thorsen turned out his bottom lip. He wasn't really that happy to see her. Maybe it was the pounding headache, or just the emotional turmoil she'd put him through the last six months. Either way, he could do with a Jamie-free day. Or ten. 'You are the stubborn one,' Thorsen said, getting off the bed and wobbling a little. Shit, maybe he was concussed. 'They want to keep me for observation,' he said, parroting what the nurse told him when they brought him up there. 'The doctor's been in three times already. Tells me I might need an MRI if things get worse.'

'Might not be a bad idea.'

'With everything going on out there?' He hooked a thumb towards the window, the smoke rising over the city. 'I'm fine. I've had worse knocks to the head while skiing.'

Jamie sighed. 'Maybe you should listen to them.'

Thorsen steadied himself on the bed, resisting the urge to close an eye so he was only seeing one of her. 'Would you?'

'Probably not, but we both know I'm not the most receptive person to good advice.'

Thorsen just grunted in agreement. 'Did they catch him?'

'The killer?' Jamie came into the room now. 'Don't think so. The detective lost him pretty quickly it seemed like and Dahlvig didn't have nearly enough boots on the ground to form a search.'

'So, he let him go?'

Jamie shrugged. 'I don't know. I got out of there pretty fast. Wanted to check up on you.'

'Sure,' Thorsen said, easing back down onto the bed.

Jamie seemed to ignore the comment. 'Dahlvig is looking into the history there. Hopefully that will shine some light on things. But so far, it doesn't seem like they uncovered much. Though the fire was set in 1992, so I don't see how Öberg could be the one who lit it. Especially as the person who did was killed in that fire.'

'So maybe he read about it,' Thorsen answered, taking deep breaths and closing his eyes, the nausea coming in waves. 'Got obsessed. Do we even know what the kid was in for? The one whose room the fire started in?'

Jamie said nothing, but Thorsen guessed she was shaking her head. He thought if he opened his eyes, though, he might throw up.

'Something isn't sitting right, though,' Jamie said.

'Once they find Öberg, and he talks, they'll have a better idea of how it all fits together.' Thorsen pressed his knuckles to his lips, fighting the vomit. 'I mean, where could he be hiding?'

'Dahlvig isn't totally incompetent. I'm sure they'll find him soon.'

Jamie was at his bedside then.

He opened his left eye and looked up at her.

She craned her neck so she could get a look at the cut on his scalp. It had been stitched in the ER when he arrived, but was still hurting like all hell and they'd not given him any drugs on account of the concussion.

Jamie's hand was on his shoulder then, pushing him onto the bed. 'Lie back,' she ordered.

He resisted at first, then obliged.

'I've had enough concussions to know that sitting up makes things worse.'

'Is that why you're so hard headed?' Thorsen asked, shimmying upwards. 'Repeated blows to the skull?'

She smiled a little. 'Could well be. Though I hear it's more likely to be hereditary.'

'You don't talk about your father much.'

Jamie just shrugged. 'I wouldn't know where to start.'

Thorsen was reminded then that he barely knew a thing about Jamie. He wondered if anyone in the world did. Father: dead. Mother: he didn't even know. No siblings. No old friends checking up on her. Extended family? She never mentioned it. No uncles, aunties, cousins, nothing. Other than him, she didn't seem to have anyone else in the world.

'Are you okay?' Thorsen asked, nodding at her bloodied shirt. 'What happened?'

'Just a nick,' Jamie said. 'You don't remember?'

Thorsen squinted, then shook his head. Jeez, maybe he had been knocked out.

Jamie shrugged again and smiled. 'I tripped, must have caught myself on a nail or something. Dahlvig's men showed up, fired at the killer. Some of this blood is probably his,' she said, brushing it off.

Thorsen was fairly sure she was lying. But he said nothing about it.

'They hit him?'

'Winged him, I think.'

Thorsen nodded slowly. 'And you're sure it wasn't Öberg?'

'I'm not sure of anything.'

'You don't seem anxious. You're not worried about Annika?'

Jamie stepped back, turned, and walked towards the window. She stood there, arms folded, looking out over the city. From five stories up, it almost looked peaceful. 'No. I don't think Öberg is hiding because he's guilty. At least not of murder. I think he's hiding – with Annika – because they're the ones who went to the press about the murders.' She glanced over at Thorsen. 'Annika is a journalism student, Juni was a close friend. Öberg was in a relationship with her. They felt the police weren't doing their jobs, so they'd have every reason to want to go public. Öberg likely had the desire, and Annika the know-how of who to approach and how, thanks to her degree.' Jamie sighed. 'When Juni died, maybe he felt responsible. Guilty. It can cloud the judgement. Love is like that. It fucks everything up.'

She kept her eyes on the city this time.

Thorsen continued to watch her.

'There's more evidence that points to that than there is of him being a killer of this magnitude.'

'So where do we go from here?'

Jamie considered that. 'I guess we just pick up where we left off.'

'Lucas Adell,' Thorsen said.

Jamie nodded slowly.

He groaned, trying to get up.

'No,' Jamie said, coming back to the bedside, hands rising to push him back down. 'You need to rest. Stay for observation.'

'Observation?' Thorsen repeated, breathing through the nausea. 'You watch me. I'll be fine.'

She paused, slowly lowering her arms. Jamie took a few beats before speaking. 'Okay. But there's no way you're driving.'

Thorsen chuckled softly, getting to his feet. 'I agree with you there.'

'Can you walk?'

'We're about to find out.'

23

Jamie Johansson

THORSEN DIDN'T REALLY TALK on the drive, though Jamie wasn't sure if this was down to his unwillingness or simply because if he opened his mouth, sick would come pouring out.

When he opened the window and rested his chin on the sill like a labrador, she figured the latter.

She even risked laying a hand on his shoulder and rubbing it a little.

Though she promptly felt strange doing that and pulled away.

The city rolled by quickly. There didn't seem to be many people on the streets now, but the evidence of their presence was still clear.

Jamie just kept her foot down, and soon it was back to idyllic countryside and wall-to-wall blue skies.

They wound north, and though she wasn't sure, she thought Thorsen may have fallen asleep. The old wives' tale said that it was bad to sleep when you were concussed, but that was just a myth. It was actually important *to* sleep. You just needed to be monitored for anything unusual.

And she knew from experience that sleep helped with the nausea and the headaches.

She didn't really mind driving in silence, it gave her time to think. She rested her elbow on the door and cradled her cheek, driving slowly but steadily, taking in the scenery.

It sure was beautiful. Hateful to think that somewhere so lovely could be the site of something so brutal.

As they jostled onto the ferry, Thorsen roused and wiped the drool from his cheek. 'Where are we?' he asked.

'Close,' Jamie answered, her voice strangely quiet. It wasn't that she'd had some grand epiphany while she drove. Quite the opposite. She didn't know what the hell she was doing, or even what she wanted to do after this. But for right now, ironically, the only thing she could think of to keep her mind off what came after this case was to focus on solving it.

As they disembarked on the other side, Thorsen sat a little more upright, but still kept quiet. She knew that feeling too, the one where your mouth felt disconnected from your brain. At least she hoped it was the concussion that was keeping him quiet. This whole case – just the five days they'd been here – shit, was that all it had been? – had been an emotional rollercoaster to say the least.

They'd slingshotted from friendship to hatred and back more times than she could count.

And the next blow up always seemed just moments away.

Thankfully, Lucas Adell's house came up fast.

Jamie slowed in front of it and then pulled onto the stone-chipped drive, killing the engine.

'Jesus,' she muttered, looking up at the place.

'What is it?' Thorsen asked.

'I didn't realise this place was so …'

'Run down?' Thorsen offered.

He was right. The imposing modern design, all glass and metal, accented with bare wood was streaked with moss and water marks. Weeds grew out of the driveway, and the bushes and hedges, once cleanly trimmed and kept, were spilling onto the property.

The door was peeling, the flagstones leading to it cracked and uneven.

Jamie hadn't even noticed the first time they'd been there. How could she not have? Was she so wrapped up in her own bullshit that she'd overlooked something so glaring? It looked like no one had done a lick of upkeep here in years.

She let out a long breath and stepped onto the gravel. Two troughs had been cut into the stone where a car had been parked – a Tesla, Jamie thought. But she could barely remember that, either. God, she was out of practice. She cursed herself for not paying more attention.

She approached the front door and knocked with the heel of her hand.

Though she betted there was no one there. The house was dark, no lights, and there was no car on the drive. Lucas Adell lived alone. No daughter, no wife.

Which meant the house was empty.

Thorsen hovered by the car, leaning on the roof. 'Anything?'

Jamie shook her head. 'I'm going to go around the back, see if I can see anything,' she called, then headed for the narrow path leading around the side of the house.

She heard the car door close behind her and Thorsen's laboured, uneven steps as he followed.

Jamie ran her hand down the wooden siding, the surface slick with lichen and algae. She suspected it needed to be pressure washed, treated yearly to keep its appearance. Why had Adell stopped?

Ducking under the branches of an overgrown tree, she emerged onto the sandy bank above Sudersand beach, the sun hot on her face.

She shielded her eyes from it, squinting up and down the shore, looking for any sign of Adell. Maybe he was out here, enjoying the afternoon?

No such luck. The stretch of white in front of her was empty.

Thorsen emerged, squinting in the brightness, swearing under his breath.

'Come on,' she said, wanting to get this over with. Once she confirmed Adell wasn't here, they could go back.

The deck was expansive, and let right down onto the sand.

Jamie climbed the steps, pausing and offering a hand to Thorsen, which, at first, he rejected, then reluctantly accepted.

He squeezed tightly, pulling himself up, and held on for a moment or two until he regained himself.

The back of the house was almost entirely glass. Two sets of double doors let onto the terrace – one from the living room, and the other from what Jamie guessed was a bedroom, though the curtain was drawn.

She went forward, looking in the windows. No sign that anyone was home.

She knocked again.

Nothing.

Jamie sighed, laying her hand on the handle of the sliding door. No way it was going to be … open? The door slid easily to the side, letting a blast of cool, air-conditioned air out.

She revelled in it for a second or two, then glanced back at Thorsen. 'We don't have a warrant,' she said.

He shrugged. 'We're not police officers anymore.'

'So, it's just breaking and entering then.' Jamie turned her eyes back to the house and scanned around. Tired, she thought. Nothing looked clean. Not the natural wooden floor, or the cream sofas. Not the dusty lampshades, the random laundry strewn around, or the bloodied rags on the coffee table.

Thorsen seemed to notice them too, his breathing quickening a little as he appeared at the door next to her. 'You seeing that, or is this concussion getting the better of me?'

'I see it,' Jamie said, stepping cautiously inside. She pricked her ears, looking around, but there was no one here. Not right now at least. Though this was fresh. Very fresh.

Jamie inspected the rags – hand towels, soaked crimson. Antiseptic wash next to it. Packets from adhesive dressings and a little box that had contained gauze, another that had contained medical tape.

'Field dressing,' Thorsen muttered, looking at it all with one eye closed.

Jamie swallowed. 'Someone fixed themselves up here in a hurry.'

Thorsen didn't respond, but Jamie knew that they were both thinking the same thing.

'Let's look around,' Jamie said, heading towards the master bedroom.

Thorsen stayed looking down at the table for a few seconds.

She glanced inside, saw the bed unmade, the stench of unwashed, sweat-soaked sheets pungent in the air.

Jamie mounted the stairs then, heading up to the upper rooms. The other bedroom. Rebecca – Lucas Adell's missing daughter's room. A thin sheen of sweat began to form under her jaw, her heart beating harder.

She pushed open the first door, revealing a bathroom, the white tiles discoloured with mould.

There was more to see there, and she would come back. But now, she needed to press on.

Next room.

Jamie laid her hand on the wood and pushed inwards.

The door creaked, revealing a bright pink room. Posters of boy bands on the wall. Dolls on shelves. Teddies on the single bed. A few knocked on the floor, the covers pulled back as though someone had been sleeping there.

Jamie swallowed, walking forward, and looked down at the sheets. Stained. The kind of stains that girls don't make. She grimaced. What the fuck was going on here?

Thorsen came in after her, breathing hard, and held on to the door frame.

Jamie's eyes were fixed on something else, though.

She reached up and took down a metal-framed photograph from the shelf above the headboard.

Her heart beat harder.

Thorsen spoke from behind her, catching sight of the bed. 'I thought Adell's daughter disappeared.'

'Me too,' Jamie replied, walking over to Thorsen and handing him the photograph.

'Happy family,' Thorsen said, looking over the photo. Adell, his wife, their daughter.

'See anything out of place?'

Thorsen narrowed his eyes. 'I'll be honest, I can hardly see at all. What am I looking at?'

'Adell's arm. Here,' Jamie said, pointing. 'Around his daughter.'

Thorsen lifted it to his eyes.

'Phone, now,' she said, holding out her hand.

Thorsen fished it out of his pocket and handed it over.

Jamie held it up to his face to unlock it, then went into his call list and dialled, putting it on speaker.

'*Hallå.*'

'Dahlvig,' Jamie said.

'Johansson?'

'What was the name of Hellström's neighbour at the hospital?'

'I'm sorry?'

'Hellström's neighbour. The kid in the room next to his. What was his name?'

'Uh …' Dahlvig said. 'I suppose you'll tell me why you want to know in a minute. Hang on.' He cupped his hand to the receiver and asked something of the person with him. Jamie guessed one of his detectives.

'Tell me it was Lucas Adell.'

'Hmm?' Dahlvig came back to the phone. 'What was that?'

'Was it Lucas Adell?'

There was a voice in the background then. Dahlvig sighed. 'Why call and ask if you already know the answer? And more importantly, *how* do you know that?'

Jamie took back the photo from Thorsen, staring down at the black heart tattooed on Lucas Adell's forearm. Exactly where it was marked on each of the victims. 'Viktor Hellström didn't die in that fire.'

'What are you saying?'

'We need everything you can find on both Hellström and Adell. I think Hellström got into Adell's room through the hole in the wall, killed Adell, and brought him into his room, then lit the fire to destroy Adell's body, assumed his identity, and then escaped.'

Dahlvig let out a long breath. 'That's one hell of a theory.' He clicked his tongue a few times. 'Alright, Jesus Christ. Get here now. We're closing in on Öberg. He checked in to a hotel in the city here, paid cash. We're prepping a team to pick him up as we speak. You can brief me before we interrogate him.'

'We're at Lucas Adell's house in Sudersand. You'll want to send a team here too, techs as well. Viktor Hellström is still alive, and I think he's the Black Heart Killer.'

'Okay,' Dahlvig said, utterly calm. 'I'll see it done. Get here as soon as you can.'

He hung up then and Jamie handed the phone back to Thorsen.

'Let's get going,' he said.

'We need to do something, first,' Jamie said.

'What?'

'We need to see Linus Lundström.'

'Who's that?'

'He's the *intendent* who handled Rebecca Adell's disappearance.'

'The one who never solved it?' Thorsen asked, raising an eyebrow.

Jamie bit her lip. 'I just don't think he was looking in the right place.'

Fårösund was just across the ferry, which, when they arrived, was on the other side.

And with no badge to flash, getting it back any quicker than normal wasn't happening.

Jamie pulled into the line of cars, two back from the front, and sighed, drumming on the top of the steering wheel.

The sun beat relentlessly on the car and Jamie could see

the heat haze hovering above the road. Sweat was beading on her temples and her heart was beating harder. She had the intense urge to chew her nails, something she hadn't done in a long time.

'Jesus, how long is this thing going to fucking take?' she muttered, mostly to herself.

Thorsen was back to snoozing, though his laboured breath and semi-pained expression didn't fill her with much hope.

She wondered what light Linus Lundström, polisintendent at Fårösund, and the guy in charge of Rebecca Adell's disappearance, could shed on Lucas Adell as a person, as a potential serial killer of the highest order. But she held out a little hope that he might provide *something* of use. To help them find him, or at least nail him to the wall and confirm their suspicions.

Jamie sighed, watching the ferry begin its slow return journey.

But what then? Speak to Lundström, catch Adell, or Viktor Hellström, then … she didn't know. The NOD would close up shop here in Gotland and move on to the next big case. Dahlvig would pack up his travelling circus, and then leave. And it sounded like Thorsen had every intention of going with him. He'd even asked Jamie to tag along for the ride. And she'd said yes. Though she hadn't meant it, she didn't think.

Seeing Thorsen go would be hard. Harder than hard. Letting him go just made her feel like screaming. And keeping him here was within her grasp. It would be easy. All she would have to do was give herself to him. And it wasn't that she didn't want to. She just didn't know if she … could. If she was even able to. He was only ever angry at her, frustrated with her. He'd said so himself, speaking to her was torture. Why would that be different if they were sleeping together? That was the only thing that would change, right? That they'd have a physical side to their relationship. She couldn't imagine that it would make a blind bit of difference to the other parts. Which meant that he'd still be angry and frustrated, and eventually, their relationship would just fucking implode. The same way all her others had.

No, it was better for them both if they went their separate ways. Her closest friends were the ones she didn't see very often. Wiik. Hallberg … others … Not really others. But three friends was enough. It would have to be.

As the ferry pulled in and Jamie started the car, Thorsen roused a little, champed, and then looked across at Jamie. 'Fuck, it's hot,' he groaned. 'All good?'

'Mhm,' Jamie answered, pulling onto the boat. 'Not far now. I'll wake you when we get there.'

He just nodded, and then closed his eyes again, not seeming to notice the catch in Jamie's throat as she spoke.

24

Jamie Johansson

WHEN THEY PULLED into the station, Thorsen came around.

They exited the car and went to the front of the small building, glad to be escaping the sun. Though there was no letup in heat inside.

Two uniformed officers were working in the large central room, one at the front desk, and the other at a desk at the back. Neither looked particularly busy considering what was happening in the city right now. Jamie guessed that the carnage hadn't reached this far out.

She approached the desk and waited for the officer to look up. His nametag said 'Blom'. The man was short, with a balding head and round nose that made him look like a wrinkled child.

'How can I help you?' he asked, smiling.

'My name is Jamie Johansson, this is my partner Kjell Thorsen,' Jamie said, gesturing to the man next to her, hoping Blom wouldn't notice that he was swaying on his feet. 'We're working with the NOD, assisting with the Black Heart Killer case.'

Blom's brow furrowed as though he didn't know what that meant.

'The Black Heart Killer?' Jamie repeated.

Blom shook his head.

'Have you not been watching the news?' she asked, shocked, frankly.

He shook his head again, chuckling. 'I don't much like the news. All doom and gloom really, isn't it?'

Jamie blinked in disbelief.

The other officer looked up from the back of the room, a tall man in his thirties, and shook his head at Blom disapprovingly.

Jamie tried to shake it off. 'Uh, okay. We're looking for the intendent here.'

'You've found him,' Blom replied, pointing to the second arrow on his epaulettes.

'Intendents usually have three arrows …' Jamie said, looking at them.

'Oh?' Blom said, turning his head to look at his own shoulder. He made an odd expression, the corner of his mouth stretching out as he tried to inspect the epaulettes on his white shirt. 'Silly me, guess I must have picked out an old shirt this morning. No matter.' He beamed at Jamie once more. 'What can I do for you?'

She blinked, trying to make sense of this. 'What …? I mean … How …? Uh … I'm sorry. Linus Lundström. That's who we're looking for. I thought Linus Lundström was the intendent here.'

'Oh, no, Linus retired.'

'Lundström is retired? Shit. When? Does he still live here on the island?'

'Oh yes,' Blom said. 'He's still here.'

'Where can we find him?'

'At home, I'd suspect. He doesn't get out much these days.'

'You know his address?'

'Of course,' Blom said, reaching for a pen. 'Here.' He scribbled it down on a sticky note and handed it to Jamie.

'Thanks,' she said, trying not to think about the fact that Blom didn't ask for any ID, or question anything about their visit. That, and that he handed over the address to a police officer's house without a second thought. If this was the way the Fårösund police operated, it was no wonder that Rebecca Adell's case was bungled.

She dragged the paper from the desk, nodded a thanks, and walked out.

Thorsen followed in silence, but by the look on his face, despite the way he was feeling, he was also pretty shocked and appalled by what they'd just seen.

'Onto Lundström's house then,' he said as they got into the car.

'Guess so,' Jamie sighed.

'Is it really necessary? You think we should get back?'

Jamie bit her lip. 'I don't know. But if Lundström handled Rebecca Adell's disappearance, then he'll know Adell better than anyone else. And if Adell's running, then maybe he can shed some light on where he might go.'

'It's a long shot,' Thorsen said as Jamie started the car and pulled off.

'Sure.' She flashed him a quick smirk. 'But I sort of make my living on long shots.'

'Don't I know it.'

Considering Fårösund was able to fit on a pinhead, they were at Lundström's front door in two minutes.

The house was a pretty brick affair with ivy climbing up the front.

Jamie approached the front door with Thorsen in tow, who seemed more than happy to let her do the talking. She'd been concussed, she knew that the tongue didn't feel all that well connected to the brain. So, she didn't badger him. Plus, she knew that only two topics of conversation were on the table. The case, and 'them'. And she didn't want to talk about the latter.

Jamie knocked on Lundström's door and waited.

It opened a minute later, and a woman in her fifties with dark hair and bright eyes stood on the threshold.

'Yes?' she asked, smiling.

'My name's Jamie Johansson,' she said. 'This is my partner, Kjell Thorsen. We're with the NOD. We'd like to speak to Linus Lundström. Is he here?'

'Linus?' she asked, seeming confused by the request. 'Is everything alright? What is this about?'

Jamie sighed. 'It's about Lucas Adell. We'd like to—'

'Lucas Adell?' she asked, eyes widening. 'You'd better come in.' She stepped back immediately and beckoned them inside.

Jamie and Thorsen exchanged a quick look and then followed her into the hallway.

'Linus is resting,' his wife said, walking into the living room. 'He's in the sun room now. He likes it in there. It's very peaceful for him.'

Jamie began to get a bad feeling as his wife continued towards the back of the house, into a room with wide, floor-to-ceiling windows, double doors opening onto a manicured garden filled with flowers, and tall, leafy green plants filling the floor in front of the glass.

And in front of the doors was Linus Lundström, wheelchair bound, his head supported by a neck rest, his eyes wide and vacant.

'Linus?' his wife asked, walking around in front of him and kneeling. 'There are some people here to see you.' She laid her hand on his, immobile on his lap. 'They want to ask about Lucas Adell.'

Lundström made a guttural moan but his face remained still, his eyelids twitching as he looked up at Jamie and Thorsen.

His wife squeezed his hand. 'As you can see, Linus isn't the conversationalist he once was,' she said, smiling at him. 'Though he still communicates as best he can. We still talk,' she added, squeezing his hand again, looking at her husband with love.

'What … what happened?' Jamie asked, trying to shift the lump in her throat.

His wife let out a long breath. 'Two years ago,' she began, 'someone broke into our house and attacked Linus.'

'A burglary?'

She seemed to consider her answer before speaking. 'They didn't take anything. It was late, I don't know, I was sleeping. There was a noise downstairs, and Linus got up, went to check.' She looked at him, chuckled a little. 'This is Fårösund. People don't even lock their doors here. He went downstairs, and then … when he didn't come back, I went down to check on him. And that's when I found him, on the floor. And the blood … there was so much blood.' Her eyes began to fill.

Linus' breathing quickened, his lips vibrating, but unable to form words. His eyes started to shine too.

'Whoever attacked him … they … they hit him over the head, and then …' She leaned her head forward, sweeping her dark hair from around the nape of her neck, touching herself there. 'They stabbed him, here. In the spine. The doctors said it was a miracle that the cut didn't kill him. But … I don't think it was supposed to.'

Jamie swallowed. 'And Lucas Adell?'

Lundström's wife looked up.

'You think he's responsible?'

Mrs Lundström steeled herself. 'Linus was recovering for a long time. But eventually, once we began communicating, he told me. He didn't see his face. But he knew.'

'He attacked Linus as revenge for not finding his daughter?'

She nodded slowly. 'I think so. Lucas Adell had just lost his wife, too. She disappeared, without a trace. Walked into the ocean, and never came back. But even before the attack, Linus never liked the man. Never trusted him. Always said that to move to Sudersand … you'd have to be running from something.'

'Was your husband working on Marie Adell's disappearance when the attack happened? I'm just trying to piece together a timeline here, understand it. Understand why Adell would attack your husband if he was looking for Adell's wife?'

'Linus' first thought was that Adell was responsible for her disappearance. He even suspected Adell had something to do with Rebecca's disappearance. Adell's daughter, I mean.'

Jamie nodded, allowing her to go on.

'When his wife suddenly vanished, Linus thought he'd … perhaps …'

'Killed her?'

'There was no evidence. Lucas Adell was very smart.'

'So that was his motive? That Linus was looking at him for the murder of his wife?'

'It was just a theory, but there was nothing to suggest that was the case. Linus questioned Adell but released him the next day. There was no evidence to support it, so he couldn't hold him. It was ruled a suicide in the end.'

'After Linus was attacked?'

'Before.'

'So … why would Adell attack your husband?'

'He's psychotic?' she offered, scoffing a little.

Jamie swallowed. That was likely the case.

Thorsen interjected then. 'What was your husband working on at the time of the attack?'

His wife looked up, thinking. 'It was a murder, I believe.'

'In Fårösund?' Jamie asked, surprised.

'No, a nearby village. Lärbro.'

'Still, a murder is out of the ordinary here to say the least, right?'

'Yes, it was rather a shock when Linus told me. But, not wholly surprising. At least not to Linus. He was aware of the boy for some time before that. He'd been arrested for possession of … drugs.' She whispered the last word as though it were taboo. 'Not the nicest person, from what Linus told me.'

'Boy? How old?'

'Oh, I don't know. Twenty or something, I think. I didn't really enquire. But I know Linus had dealt with him before.'

Linus Lundström watched his wife carefully, but made no further sounds.

'Anyway, the boy was found in his home. Linus said he'd been beaten up or … tortured, was the word he'd used.' His wife shuddered visibly. 'Anyway, it was something to do with drugs, Linus thought.'

'And what about suspects for that murder?'

She shrugged. 'I don't know, Linus didn't tell me much. Just that they'd collected evidence, were testing it, you know.'

'And did he think there was any link to Lucas Adell there?'

Linus made a loud noise. Or as loud as Jamie thought he could make.

'Yes?' Jamie asked.

Another noise.

'You think Lucas Adell committed that murder?'

More noises. Excited noises.

'Shh, shh,' Mrs Lundström said, hushing her husband gently. Drool began to run from the corner of his mouth. 'It's alright, Linus. It's all behind us, now.'

But Linus Lundström wouldn't quit. He kept making noise, eyes going left and right wildly.

'I'm sorry,' his wife said then, choking up. She stood, beckoning Jamie and Thorsen to their feet. 'I don't think there's anything else we can do to help. Linus needs to rest now, before he becomes even more agitated.'

They were shooed quickly from the room as Linus did his best to scream, trapped in his own body.

Jamie and Thorsen let themselves be guided to the door, where Mrs Lundström half-closed it the second they were on the step. 'I'm sorry,' she said. 'But this is all too much, I shouldn't have let it go on that long. We've done all we can to put it behind us, and … and we've heard nothing from Lucas Adell since the attack. We don't want to be mixed up in this again.'

The fear was clear on her face.

'I hope you find what you need,' she added, 'but please don't come back here again.'

She promptly shut – and locked – the door.

Guess times had changed in Fårösund.

Jamie sighed heavily and turned to Thorsen. 'Jesus,' she muttered. 'That was …'

'Yeah.' Thorsen shook his head gently. 'Adell broke in specifically to paralyse Lundström?' He said the words with incredulity. 'What the fuck?'

'It's cruelty, is what it is,' Jamie replied, heading for the car. 'Adell had an axe to grind with Lundström and this was his way of making sure he suffered as much as possible. A quick death would have been a mercy for him.'

Thorsen just absorbed that. His eyes seemed sharper now, but Jamie could tell he still wasn't firing on all cylinders. 'So, Lundström doesn't solve the disappearance of either Rebecca or Marie Adell. Which is enough motive to make Adell hate him.'

'Lundström thought that maybe Adell was the one who killed them. Or at least Hellström, did. Adell was obviously living two lives to build a family. One as Adell, and one as Hellström.'

Thorsen considered that. 'So, he murders his wife and daughter? Then he goes after this other guy, the drug dealer? Why?'

Jamie could only shrug. 'I don't know. But it sounds like Lundström had some evidence to suggest that Adell was involved in that. Maybe he got wind of it and came after Lundström to derail the investigation.'

'Well, I assume it fell flat on its fucking face if that idiot Blom took over.'

'Mhm, I'd agree with that. And an attack that leaves someone paralysed is one thing. But it's not murder. Likely the attack on Lundström fell through the cracks as a burglary gone wrong. Blom steps up as intendent, fails to solve both.'

'And Adell walks away from it all scot free.'

'Ready to wreak havoc on the island as the Black Heart Killer.'

'Right. So, Rebecca Adell disappears, then Marie Adell

disappears. This drug dealer gets killed. Lundström is attacked. And then the first suicide takes place, what, six months later?'

Jamie did the maths in her head. 'Yeah, it's thirty-six months since Rebecca Adell's disappearance, predating the first suicide by almost a year.'

Thorsen let out a long sigh and checked his watch. 'Shit. We should get back to the station, Dahlvig is waiting on us. I'm sure they've brought Öberg in by now.'

'Yeah, okay,' Jamie said. 'We should probably update Dahlvig on what we found out, too.'

Thorsen grinned as he circled the car and climbed in.

'What's so funny?' Jamie asked, getting into the driver's seat.

'Just you, wanting to keep your senior officer in the loop. It makes a change.'

'You think that little of me?' Jamie asked, pulling away from the curb and heading south.

'I don't think little of you. I think a lot of you, actually. It's just nice to know you can play by the rules is all.' He looked over at her. 'You'll need to when we go work for Dahlvig full time.'

He kept grinning at her, and she tried to hold on to hers.

Pretty quickly, though, she had to look away. Because hers was slipping.

And she'd promised herself she wouldn't lie to Thorsen.

She just couldn't tell him the truth.

Not yet.

25

Kjell Thorsen

As they drove, Thorsen was feeling good. Even despite being clobbered over the head with a piece of wood and seeing two of everything.

He really felt like they were making headway, and now that they'd cleared the air, he felt like he and Jamie could really press on, and focus on what mattered. When they were working, they were fine. A great team. Six months off had really fucked with their dynamic. Hell, it was natural to have feelings for your partner. You spent so much time together that proximity was bound to cause friction. And with friction came heat.

So, yeah. Normal. Totally normal. They just had so much built up that when they left Kurrajakk and struck out for some down time, they didn't know what to do. So, putting cases and investigations back into the mix would fix it. They could fall back into their old pattern. Being friends, being colleagues. And, hell, down the line, if anything happened, great. If not … well, Thorsen wasn't banking on *not*. Jamie just needed time. To digest, to readjust to the idea of it. It needed to sink in, really, before she came to understand it. The last few days had been a shock to her system. But the fact that she wasn't pulling away told him everything. The fact that she wasn't trying to blow up their partnership and run away, the fact that she was on board with the idea of coming to work for the NOD, of working for Dahlvig, of playing by the rules. That was a really, *really* good sign. She was showing maturity, and she was showing that she was committed to *this*. Whatever it was. That she wanted to try. And wanting to loop Dahlvig in? That showed growth.

He was proud of her. And he was hopeful for the future.

He loved his job, but he loved Jamie too. And he was prepared to admit that to himself at least.

Thorsen let out a long breath, closing one eye to take in the scenery in semi-clarity.

The island may be going to shit, and there may be a serial killer on the loose, but Thorsen was feeling … happy.

So much so that he kept his grin all the way back to Visby.

26

Jamie Johansson

BY THE TIME they arrived at the station, Dahlvig's team had already captured Alex Öberg and Annika Olsen. Four officers armed with sub-machine guns had knocked down the door to their shitty hotel room and then burst inside.

Öberg and Olsen had been lying on the bed when they had. And with guns shoved in their faces, they'd both promptly flopped to the floor, hands on heads, screaming that they were sorry.

No weapons or materials suggesting that they were dangerous in any way were recovered from their hotel room.

But they were still being questioned fiercely about the whole thing.

When Jamie and Thorsen got inside, they saw Öberg and Olsen had already been separated and were being questioned in two separate rooms by Dahlvig's senior detectives. He was in neither room, but instead in the viewing room, a compact studio of a sort with four huge monitors filling one wall and a series of chairs laid out in front of the desk below them. Each would display a feed from one of the four interrogation rooms. Here, two were active, with cameras set up over the shoulder of the interviewers, pointed right at Öberg and Olsen, showing their terror in 4K resolution.

When Jamie opened the door and stepped in, Dahlvig and the other detective next to him, a woman in her late forties with a severe expression, both turned to look at them.

'Close the door,' Dahlvig said, waving his hand and looking back at the screens.

Thorsen did so and they stood at the back of the room.

'Did you send a team to Adell's house?' Jamie asked.

'As soon as they're done with Öberg's hotel room, they're headed there.' Dahlvig didn't turn around to speak.

'You don't think Adell's house is a bigger priority?'

'No.'

'Why not?'

'Because we don't abandon lines of inquiry midway through on a hunch.'

'It's not a hunch,' Jamie started. 'There's evidence to suggest—' But she stopped speaking when Thorsen squeezed her arm hard enough that it hurt.

He flashed her a hard look and she cleared her throat.

Play along, Jamie. She cleared her throat and stayed quiet.

Dahlvig didn't say anything else, just kept his eyes fixed on the screens, and then used a dial in front of him to turn up the volume from Öberg's interview.

His voice filled the little room, strained and shaking. 'Please, please,' he said. 'I'm sorry! I didn't mean to do anything wrong. I just wanted to help, to do something for Juni.' He almost choked on her name.

'Juni Pedersen. The latest victim,' the interviewer clarified, though Jamie could only see the side of his face. 'Can you describe the nature of your relationship with her?'

'My relationship? We were, uh … I liked her. I really did.' His eyes began to well up. 'Please, please—'

'The relationship was sexual in nature?'

'What?'

'You had intercourse with Miss Pedersen before she died?'

'I …' Öberg began, shaking his head. 'Yes, I did. But—'

'Have you ever had an STI, Mr Öberg?'

'An STI?'

'A sexually transmitted infection. Like gonorrhoea, or *chlamydia*?'

'No, no! Never. Why?'

'Would you be prepared to take a blood test to confirm that?'

'Why the hell are you asking me about chlamydia? I didn't do anything wrong!'

'We need to know where you were on the day that Juni Pedersen died.'

'I was … I don't know. In class? Like everyone else?'

The interviewer was peppering him with questions, trying to make him slip up, contradict himself, put a foot wrong. A classic, albeit basic, technique.

Jamie resisted the urge to interject, and had finally given in to the urge to chew her fingernails.

'How did you get the footage of the hospital? We know it was you who leaked it to the press.'

'I took it, on my phone,' Alex Öberg said, trying to keep up.

'How did you know about the hospital in the first place?'

'I follow a YouTuber who lives on Gotland. He's an urban explorer, who goes to abandoned buildings and that sort of thing. He climbs them and goes inside and—'

'And one of his videos showed the hospital with the black heart?'

'Yeah, he—'

'And what is this person called? The name of the channel?'

'Uh, Jacob, I think. It's like 'ClimbWithJacob' or 'ClimbingJacob' or something like that, but—'

Dahlvig nudged the arm of the detective next to him and snapped his fingers twice in quick succession.

She seemed to know exactly what he meant and got up quickly, leaving the room, pushing Thorsen aside to get to the door.

Before it even closed, Dahlvig pulled the chair out a little and pointed to it, eyes still fixed on the screen.

Jamie and Thorsen glanced at each other, and then Jamie proffered it to him.

He waited to see if she would change her mind, but then slowly went forward and sat.

Dahlvig looked at him briefly, but Jamie couldn't make out his expression.

The interview went on, interrupting Öberg at every turn.

'You saw the heart in the video. When was this?'

'Uh, I don't know. Last year? Maybe longer.'

'So why go there now, release the footage only recently?'

'I didn't … I didn't think anything of it. I didn't know anything about the black hearts until I met Annika, and she said that Juni had a heart drawn on her arm.' He held his out, and pointed to his pale skin. 'After she said that, I sort of remembered seeing the video, and then I looked it up again—'

Dahlvig leaned forward, pressed a button, and then spoke into a microphone sticking out of the desk. 'Ask Olsen whether she was the one who told Öberg about the black heart.' He released the intercom button and the person on the screen which was showing Annika's interview – on mute – adjusted their position and began speaking in response to Dahlvig's prompt.

Alex Öberg's interviewer went on. 'So, you heard about the heart from Annika Olsen, made the connection to the video, and then went to the hospital yourself, with Miss Olsen, shot the video, and then released it to the press. Is that about right for the order of events here?'

'Yes. Yes. That's it. But I swear I never did *anything* to Juni. I … I liked her. I really liked her. And I should have done more to help her, but I never thought that she would … That she'd …'

The interviewer took a moment to wait for Alex Öberg to really begin to crack, and Dahlvig stepped in.

'Tell him that sounds like bullshit,' he said, grabbing the microphone and opening the intercom link with Öberg's interviewer. 'Tell him we can put him in at least three of the libraries that victims visited before their deaths.'

The interviewer collected their thoughts as Öberg began to snivel.

'Tell me about the libraries.'

'The what?'

'The libraries.'

Jamie always found it so infuriating how interviewees had the incessant need to repeat everything you said as though you were speaking a foreign language. It was hard to keep your cool sometimes, but the interviewer seemed deft, composed, experienced.

She had to admit the whole set up was impressive. And for all of Dahlvig's faults, he ran a tight ship. And people seemed to respect him. The job wasn't always so easy, and there was lots of red tape. You had to be meticulous, leave no stone unturned. So as much as Jamie thought Öberg was innocent, she saw why they had to waste time interviewing him.

'We can place you at three libraries that victims visited prior to their deaths. You volunteered, right? All over the island?'

'I … Yeah, yeah, I did,' Öberg said. 'But … I never knew anything about …' He began to look around. 'No, no. That's not … I never … I did it for the experience. For my CV, and for … it's a bloody university-sponsored programme, part of my PhD! They assign us! Send us on these placements, a few weeks at a time! All over the place!' He began to get worked up. 'I never met any of them! I mean, I don't think … we deal with lots of kids, you know? School trips and after-school clubs, and, and, and …' He began to get flustered, ears reddening, sweat glistening on his forehead.

Dahlvig leaned in again. 'Press him,' he said into the mic. 'Press him hard.'

'Don't lie to me,' the interviewer said. 'You tell the truth now, and things will go a lot smoother. You're using the libraries to target the victims, right? You had ready access to them. You said so yourself. After-school clubs and trips?'

Something struck Jamie then. Something Öberg said. A word he used.

She came forward without thinking, mouth opening, hand reaching for the mic over Dahlvig's shoulder.

But she stopped herself just behind him, freezing.

Thorsen saw, looked up at her. 'What is it?'

She swallowed. Don't get sucked into this. Temper yourself. For once.

'Maybe we're looking in the right place …' she said.

Dahlvig turned to look at her too.

'But at the wrong person.'

Dahlvig's eyes narrowed a little. 'Talk.'

'I still don't think Öberg is the killer. And Adell can't be ignored. But Adell wouldn't be able to approach teenagers without anyone noticing, not be able to coerce them into killing themselves without a single person batting an eyelid. He's a forty-year-old man — cruising parks and playgrounds for kids? Not a chance he wouldn't be seen, not even on Gotland.'

'Get to the point, Johansson,' Dahlvig urged her.

'If Adell is killing them, but he's not the one who makes first contact …'

'Then someone else is doing the grooming,' Dahlvig said. 'Two killers.'

'Right. And the obvious choice is …'

'Öberg,' Dahlvig said.

'He said 'we' and 'us'.'

'We?'

'*We deal with lots of kids.* That's what he said. It's a university programme. Öberg's not the only student doing a PhD at Visby University.'

Dahlvig turned to the mic quickly. 'Ask Öberg what other students.'

The interviewer put his finger to his ear, the signal to repeat.

'Ask Öberg what other students volunteer at the libraries as part of the PhD programme.'

The interviewer began speaking again, but Dahlvig was already focused on Jamie once more. 'Who are we looking for? Who do you think? Profile.'

'Uh,' Jamie said, caught a little off guard. 'Female, I'd say.' She took a breath. 'Attractive, probably. If she's grooming teenage boys. Charming, I'd say. Someone 'cool'. It's both male and female victims, right? She'd need to be someone the boys found attractive, and someone girls looked up to, wanted to be friends with, could be influenced by.' Jamie thought then. 'There were signs of sex at Adell's house. His bed. His daughter's.'

Dahlvig nodded, quicker and quicker. 'So, the girl lines them up, brings them to Adell's house—'

'It's big, too. Remote. Beautiful. Right on the beach. Impressive.'

'She brings them to the beach house, they're in awe of the place. Introduces them to Adell …'

'He starts feeding them all the literature bullshit. Fills their minds with these ideas of death and release, absolution, redemption, whatever. And what teenage kid isn't already filled with self-doubt and angst?'

Dahlvig pursed his lips, turned back to the screen. 'Ask him if there is a female PhD student who volunteers a lot. Lots of different libraries. She'll be attractive. Now. Do it now.'

The interviewer segued awkwardly out of the question he was asking and into that one.

As he was asking it, Öberg's eyes grew wide.

'Yes, yes,' he said suddenly. 'There is, yes! She's in my seminar group. Eva. Eva Wallin.'

'Eva Wallin?' the interviewer confirmed. 'Tell me about her.'

'She's pretty, like you said. But she does loads of volunteering. Like, way more than anyone else. All over the island.'

The interviewer took his time. 'Right. Who is she? What do you know about her?'

'She's twenty-two, or twenty-three, maybe. She's pretty, like I said. Uh, pale skin, dark hair. Kind of alternative?'

'Alternative?'

'Yeah, like lots of ear piercing, a nose ring, a few tattoos. She dresses kind of weird.'

'Kind of weird?'

'Like oversized flannel shirts, skinny jeans with big boots. Band T-shirts, lots of like bangles and stuff.'

'And that's weird?'

'Not weird, then. Quirky, I guess?'

The interviewer took it in. 'Do you know her? What's she like?'

'Keeps to herself, mostly. But she's nice. Seems nice enough. Not social though. She doesn't live on campus. She's got an older boyfriend, I think. He's picked her up a few times, after classes.'

Dahlvig was on the mic instantly. 'The older boyfriend. How old? What's he look like? What car does he drive?'

The interviewer relayed it.

Öberg was talking fast, feeling like he was pulling his own head off the chopping block with every word. 'A Tesla. He drives a Tesla. He's probably like forty, maybe older. I only saw him once. Oh, and he's bald.'

Jamie's heart kicked up a gear. 'That's Adell,' she said. 'There's a Tesla charging port on his drive, and he's as bald as an egg.'

Dahlvig hung his head, in relief. In triumph, maybe. 'Keep him talking,' he ordered into the microphone, 'I want everything he knows about Eva Wallin.' Then he pushed back from the desk and got up, standing in front of Jamie.

He gave her a single nod.

She returned it.

And then Dahlvig headed for the door.

'Where are you going?' Jamie asked.

'To find Eva Wallin. And Lucas Adell. You did good work today,' he added, stopping at the door frame.

'What about Viktor Hellström?' Jamie asked.

'What about him? He's Adell. Catch one, catch the other.'

'I mean, have you found out any more information on him?'

'Not really my top priority right now. I'll hear his story when he's in cuffs and in an interrogation room. It's not really of consequence at the moment.'

Jamie opened her mouth to protest. But she wanted to trust Dahlvig, and he was right. And had been right. Whether Öberg was the killer or not, he was linked to the case, and Dahlvig's line of inquiry had uncovered a link to Eva Wallin. The missing piece to their puzzle. Sure, it was Jamie's doing that brought Annika Olsen into the case to begin with, and she found Öberg, who then revealed Wallin. But still, Dahlvig was the one who caught Öberg. So maybe there was room for their methods to co-exist? For Jamie's intuition to work *with* Dahlvig's rigor.

'So let me,' she said instead of fighting him.

'Let you what?'

'Dig into Hellström.'

'Why?'

'You've got your hands full. Finding Wallin and Adell. You're pooling resources, right?'

He sighed. 'Don't dance around me, Johansson. I don't have the time, or the energy.'

'We've uncovered more about this case in the last three days than your team did in two years. I have a feeling there's more to Hellström. Something that could make a difference. So let me dig into him. You don't need me to help find Adell. You have your channels, your team, your processes. Let me do this. If nothing else, I won't be under your feet,'

He let out a hard sigh. 'You're always under my feet,'

Dahlvig said. 'Even when I promised Thorsen I'd arrest him – and you – if you came within a hundred miles of my case.'

'Bet you're glad you didn't though?'

Dahlvig's jaw flexed. 'Fine. Just … just don't do anything reckless.'

'Wouldn't dream of it.'

'I mean it, Johansson. Seriously. No, look at me.' He stared at her, cold enough to make her shiver a little. 'Nothing stupid. Research, and report. That's all. You're at a desk, you're on a computer. And if I hear you've gone out on your own. Then you're gone.' He cut the air with his hands. 'For-ever.' And with that, he turned and strode away.

Jamie unclenched her fists and flexed them at her side. This was good.

She heard Thorsen get to his feet behind her and come to the doorway. He smiled, put his hand on her shoulder. 'That was good. Well done.'

'Thanks,' Jamie said.

'Nice to be back?'

'Uh …' she said.

'I would have asked the same things,' Thorsen interjected. 'About Öberg, and the libraries. A different volunteer,' he said. 'It's just this damn concussion. Makes it hard to think, you know?'

She put her hands on his shoulders in the doorway. 'You're a brilliant investigator,' Jamie said, smiling at him. 'I wouldn't lie to you. You're going to be a huge asset to Dahlvig's team. You'll do great.'

He sighed, as though he needed to hear that. Then he lifted his hand and put it on top of Jamie's. 'We'll be great.'

And then he stepped into the hallway and headed for the buzz, audible from the room at the end of the corridor.

Dahlvig's team, working like bees, flying around, doing their work.

Jamie turned her head, looking the other way.

The corridor stretched out into silence.

And at the end, above the door, the word *Utgång*.

Exit.

27

Jamie Johansson

BEFORE JAMIE COULD DECIDE which way to go, someone was calling her name.

'Jamie?'

She turned to look towards the bustling office, seeing a woman there – the same detective that Dahlvig had sent out of the room to look up the YouTube channel.

'Jamie Johansson?' the woman repeated.

Jamie nodded.

The detective sighed, and then beckoned Jamie towards her. 'I'm supposed to set you up with a login.'

'Right,' Jamie said, hesitating.

'What are you waiting for? Now.' She turned her back and strode into the office once more.

Jamie exhaled, and followed. She had just asked Dahlvig if she could do this. Maybe taking off without a word wasn't the right call here.

Once she reached it, she was taken aback by the din in there. Dozens of people – the full might of Dahlvig's team –

were all talking on phones, typing wildly on their keyboards, or sliding their chairs around from one desk to another, speaking to each other, exchanging notes and papers … It was frantic. A far cry from Jamie's normal way of working.

She didn't see how a team of this size could fail. And she wondered what the fuck they'd all been doing this past eighteen months. Jesus, a year and a half. What had happened in all that time? It couldn't have been long before that that she'd seen Dahlvig in Stockholm. She wondered if this was his first case after the Angel Maker. That'd explain the sour taste in his mouth. She solved that case when he was running it, and she'd sort of done the same here. No wonder he didn't like her.

'Here,' the detective said, waving Jamie towards an open desk. It was piled high with files. A dumping zone for stuff people didn't have space for on their own desks.

She bent forward, scribbled something on the notepad next to the keyboard. 'This is a temporary login,' she said. 'We'll be able to see everything you do, and if you need to share something with us, just shout, give us your user code, and we'll be able to see your screen, alright?'

She circled the details on the pad a few times with the pen, then stood up in front of Jamie, sizing her up. She didn't look too happy. Though Jamie didn't know if she was to blame for that, too. 'Questions?'

Jamie looked around. 'Where's Thorsen?'

'How should I know? I'm not his keeper.'

'Right,' Jamie said. Though, seriously, where was Thorsen? He'd been just ahead of her. Who knew? Bathroom, speaking to Dahlvig … maybe he'd just gone for a lie down. Either way, she figured leaving this desk to go find him wasn't the right call

The detective walked off, and Jamie pulled the chair out,

ready to sit. She didn't know how she felt about resigning herself to a role like this. Either in the short, or the long term. But for now, she just needed to play along, follow through on this. Make sure Thorsen came out of it looking good. And then … then she'd see how she felt about the whole thing.

She sat, interlaced her fingers, cracked them out in front of her, and then logged in.

'Okay, Viktor Hellström,' she said. 'Let's see who you really are.'

The rabbit hole was tough to find, but once Jamie did, she went tumbling down it.

Nearly three hours passed before she was knocking on Dahlvig's office door.

Thorsen had not reappeared, but when Jamie texted him he'd replied 'needed to lie down'. She said to call if he needed her.

He didn't.

Dahlvig beckoned her inside and asked, 'Where's Thorsen?'

'Bathroom,' she answered, without missing a beat.

He didn't seem to care. He had bigger fish to fry. Like trying to find Adell.

'Make it quick,' he said.

'Viktor Hellström,' Jamie said. 'I have something.'

'Will it help us find Adell?'

'I don't know.'

He stared at her for a second, then said, 'Go. Two minutes.'

'I checked with the team, and got what they had so far on Hellström, then went from there.'

'Faster, more concise. I don't care about who found out what. Just the facts.'

'Right,' Jamie said, focusing her thoughts. 'Viktor Hellström, born 1978, to Paulina and Nils Hellström. His father was an English professor, first in Gothenburg, then here in Visby. His wife, Paulina, was—'

Dahlvig made a cycling motion with his hand. Go faster.

'From his session notes dredged from the hospital archives, it sounds like Viktor Hellström had a twin sister, and they were both badly beaten and abused as children. Viktor shared that his father was a terror, forced them to read and learn, history, literature. When they didn't, he'd punish them.'

Dahlvig clasped his hands in front of his face, listening carefully.

'Viktor did what he could to protect his sister, but he was young. Though it wasn't the beatings that stuck with Viktor, but rather what Nils Hellström did to his sister. As she matured, it seemed to get worse. Until she couldn't take it anymore. She killed herself just after turning thirteen. Filled her pockets with stones and then waded into a lake on their property.'

'Didn't Sylvia Plath do that?' Dahlvig asked.

'Plath stuck her head in an oven. Virginia Woolf drowned herself.'

'Fuck,' Dahlvig said. 'Poetic, I suppose. One way to stick it to her father.'

'Viktor was the one who found her early the next morning, along with a note she'd pinned to her dress. Guess the final words?'

He thought for a moment. 'What dreams may come.'

Jamie nodded. 'In a fit of uncontrollable, dissociated rage, he goes back into the house, takes a knife from the kitchen, and goes to his parents' room. He climbs on top of his father, and stabs him in the chest. Thirty-nine times. Then, he cuts out his heart.'

'Fucking hell,' Dahlvig muttered. 'At thirteen?'

'Yeah.' Jamie took a deep breath and ploughed onward. 'His mother wakes during the attack, obviously, and flees the house. From the notes, it sounds like Nils Hellström didn't spare her, either. They were all his victims. Then, from a neighbour's house, she calls the police, who quickly arrive and arrest Viktor. They find him sitting on the edge of the bed, his father's heart on the floor between his feet. He's not even there,' Jamie said, waving her hand in front of her face. 'Catatonic. So, they take the bloodied knife from his hand, and then commit him to the secure mental hospital where we found the heart mural. What happens next is a little hazy,' Jamie sighed. 'But from what I could find out about the hospital and its practices, they still engaged in the kinds of therapies outlawed elsewhere. Shock therapies, ice and water therapies, and a whole smorgasbord of drugs and pharmaceuticals.'

'Barbaric,' Dahlvig said with a fair amount of disdain. But he didn't interrupt.

'He was there a year and some change when the fire started. Originally, he was thought to have died in the blaze, but we now know that he managed to get into the neighbouring room which belonged to one Lucas Adell, who was suffering with OCD and mild schizophrenia – voluntarily committed by his parents – presumably kills Adell, drags him next door, starts the fire, then goes back into Adell's room. When the smoke starts billowing, everyone's going crazy. All the rooms are opened, patients are running for the exits, along with staff, and everyone else. I'm filling in the blanks here, but I'd guess that Hellström escaped during the frenzy, and found his way to Adell's parents' house.'

'Why do you say that?'

'Shortly after, a letter arrived at the hospital – attached to Lucas Adell's file – saying that Lucas Adell had returned home safely, and told them of the fire. And that they wouldn't be bringing him back. There doesn't seem to be any record of them following up. No paperwork filed. That's the final thing in Adell's file.'

Dahlvig nodded along. 'Is that all?'

'No, I followed the trail on Adell from there, now that Hellström was 'dead'. Adell was home-schooled from that point onwards, and then left Gotland to attend college. I'm guessing that Viktor was locked away, tightly. But those doors never stay closed forever.'

'Wait, am I missing something here? Adell's parents home-schooled Hellström? What, they forget what their own son looks like?'

Jamie sucked air through her teeth. 'I think the more likely answer is that Hellström killed them, and then escaped the island.'

'Jesus, you got their address?'

'Yep, and I already filled out the report here – requisition for sniffer dogs, ground radar, and CSTs to attend.' Jamie offered Dahlvig a few sheets of paper. 'I'd start with the back garden.'

Dahlvig afforded a small smile at that. 'That all?'

'Almost. Hellström attended Stockholm University. He studied computer science and economics. He went from there to work in finance, in data analytics and stocks. He did well for himself. Worked hard, was successful, made some good investments. Got married, had a kid. Then, left the big city and moved back to Gotland.'

'He came back? Why?'

Jamie shrugged. 'Why does anyone do anything? He's from here. Maybe he wanted to come home. Maybe he wanted to build a family and prove that he wasn't his father. Who knows?'

'I'll make sure to ask him.'

'When his daughter disappeared, and then his wife killed herself – walking into the ocean—'

'Like Hellström's sister.'

'Yeah. I think it broke him. Unleashed Hellström back into the world. We called into Fårö police station, found Linus Lundström, the intendent assigned to both his wife and daughter's cases. He came up with nothing, and Lucas Adell broke into his house, stabbed him in the spine. Paralysed him on purpose as revenge.'

'Fuck.'

'Fuck is right. But it was also to prevent Lundström from linking him to the murder of a guy called Emil Zagorski. He went by EZ, known as a local drug dealer. He wasn't connected to the Rebecca Adell disappearance officially, but I think there's probably a link there somewhere. He was tied to a chair, tortured, then had his throat opened. And Lundström thought that Adell was responsible – far as we could tell – there was some evidence that was never followed up on, so it's likely this Zagorski was involved in Rebecca Adell's disappearance and Adell killed him too.'

'That's a lot of bodies.'

'Yeah, it is. And Lundström thought Adell was suspect number one in his wife's disappearance too. Walked into the ocean? Too coincidental for me.'

'You think Adell killed his wife too?'

'Adell, Hellström … depends whether they're separate in his mind, whether they're aware of each other, or simply two sides of the same coin. Does Adell know he's Hellström or are there just gaps where Hellström takes over …'

'Okay then,' Dahlvig said, letting out a long sigh. 'At least now we know who we're dealing with.' He eyed Jamie. 'And you found all this out in three hours?'

Jamie nodded, then corrected herself. 'Well, me and Thorsen.'

'And he's …'

'In the bathroom.'

Dahlvig's eyes went to the open door behind Jamie, scanning the office floor. 'Right.'

Jamie lingered for a moment.

'Was there something else?'

'Uh, no, I don't think so.'

'Alright then, get out,' he said, shooing her towards the door. 'And Johansson?'

'Yeah?' she said, pausing and looking back.

'Don't lie to me. Even if you think it's the right thing to do.'

She opened her mouth to respond, then closed it, and nodded instead.

And then she walked out and shut the door behind her.

It took her a little while to locate Thorsen. He'd managed to find an upper floor office with a couch that wasn't occupied, and had promptly got his head down for a few hours.

Jamie cracked the door, peeked inside, squinting in the half-light of dusk that was filtering in through the closed blinds, and saw Thorsen on his back on the sofa.

'Knock knock,' she said gently, rapping on the door.

He roused and groaned, putting his hand on his head. 'I'm awake,' he announced, though his snoring had said otherwise.

He pushed himself to a seated position then and rubbed his eyes. 'What time is it?'

'Getting late,' Jamie said. 'You've been out a while.'

'Needed it,' he said, putting his elbows on his knees and leaning forward.

'I can tell. How's the head?'

He grimaced. 'Feels like I've got an axe buried in it.'

'That's not surprising. What about your vision? Blurred? Seeing double?'

'Not anymore.'

'Muddled thoughts? Brain fog?'

'Better.'

'That's good. You've just gotta take it easy the next few days. Week or two if the symptoms don't clear totally.'

He nodded. 'You come to check on me?'

'And let you know I found out some stuff about Lucas Adell's past. I'll fill you in later. Think I'm about ready to head back to the hotel. You coming?'

He pushed himself to his feet. 'Yeah. Did, uh, did Dahlvig ask about me? Did he know I was sleeping?'

'No.'

'No he didn't ask, or no he didn't know I was sleeping?'

'Either? Both? I think he'll cut you some slack considering the circumstances. But either way I covered for you.'

'Oh?' Thorsen said, reaching the doorway.

'I said you helped with the research, then had to go to the bathroom when I came to tell him about it.'

'Really?'

'Explosive diarrhoea.'

'And he believed that?'

'I was very graphic in my description.'

He cracked a smile. 'Shut up.'

They headed for the stairs, the upper floor empty now. It

was mainly offices up here, and the regular Visby police staff had either finished for the day or had been scrambled to deal with the blowback from the release of the news story.

Though Jamie had not heard as many sirens today. Perhaps things were dying down.

They descended slowly, exiting into the corridor that led to the main office that Dahlvig was working out of.

There was no hustle and bustle suddenly. Just silence.

Jamie and Thorsen exchanged a look and then walked towards it, the noise of a TV echoing through the space.

Mostly everyone was huddled around a few screens, watching intently, blocking what was playing.

Jamie scanned the room quickly, saw Dahlvig at one of the screens with a few of his detectives. He snapped his fingers a few times and called them over wordlessly.

As Jamie and Thorsen neared, their apprehension growing, what was playing on the TV became apparent.

A single voice rang out, gravelly and cold.

'… I cannot be stopped. No one is safe.'

As Jamie reached the group, she looked between their shoulders, seeing a news station playing a video of a man in a black mask speaking into the camera of a phone.

'Your children are not safe. One will die every month until you fix this. You know what you did, and this will not stop until this is put right. I will burn the whole island if I have to.'

The video paused, and Dahlvig ordered the detective at the desk to rewind and play it again.

It repeated then, again and again.

Jamie listened intently, trying to discern whether that was Lucas Adell's voice or not. She thought it was, but it sounded so odd. She couldn't be sure. But who else would wear a black mask and release a message like that? Jesus Christ. Was he speaking to them? You know what you did … Going to his home? Releasing the video of the hospital? What was he talking about? Did he expect them to abandon the investigation?

Thorsen's phone began vibrating then and he pulled it from his coat pocket. 'Hey,' he said quietly, pulling it to his ear and stepping away from the crowd.

Jamie followed him a little.

'Yeah, yeah. Of course, I'll be right there.' He hung up, turning back to Jamie.

'Who was that?'

'It was Sonja,' he said.

'She okay?'

'She needs to see me, urgently.'

'What about?'

'Wouldn't say, but she wouldn't ask if it wasn't important.'

Jamie bit her lip. About the conversation they had? 'I'll come with you.'

'No, no,' Thorsen said. 'She wants to see me alone. Keys?' He held his hand out.

'What about your head?'

'I'm good to drive,' he said. 'Seriously. And I should go now, before things go fucking mental out there.'

Jamie was hesitant.

'You stay, with Dahlvig. He'll need all the help he can get. And I'm sure you already have some ideas about that.' He nodded towards the screen. 'My head's still a little foggy, I'll be of no use here.'

'Should you really be driving, then?'

'I'll be careful. Keys.' He curled his fingers, asking for them.

She handed them over. 'Be safe, alright? Call me when

you're done, let me know you didn't wrap the car around a lamp post.'

'Sure.' He stepped forward then, and hugged her. 'Thanks, Jamie,' he said.

And then he released her and left.

She watched him go for a few seconds, and then turned back to the task at hand: figuring out Adell's game, what his next move was going to be …

And how the hell they were going to stop him.

28

Kjell Thorsen

THORSEN STEPPED from the station and breathed a sigh of relief.

As much as he wanted to be there for Jamie, and to prove to Dahlvig that he was the right choice to bring into his inner circle, Jesus was he tired. The concussion had eased in the sense that he wasn't seeing double anymore, but the pain in his skull, both inside and out, reminded him that he had indeed been clobbered over the head.

A deep-seated nausea had taken root in his guts, so eating wasn't on the table. He wasn't really interested in seeing Sonja feeling the way he was, but there was a vicious throbbing at the base of his skull, and – though he wouldn't admit it to Jamie – he was a little worried he'd been pre-emptive in leaving the hospital. At least Sonja would give him a once-over, drive him back there if she deemed fit. And he could ride the night out in a hospital bed if there was a need for it. All without Jamie knowing.

He doubted she'd leave the station before dawn. He

smirked a little. He had her. On the hook. Back in the swing of the job. It was a done deal. There was no way she'd walk away from it all now.

Thorsen stopped then, realising he was right in front of Sonja's car already, her keys in his hand. He glanced back at the building, not remembering leaving it or walking the hundred-odd feet to the car.

Deep breaths, Kjell, he told himself. Take it slow now.

Inside the car, things felt weird. He was aware of the interior and the way the wheel felt. And when he reached for the ignition, he found himself jiggling the indicator instead. Yep, that works, he thought, brushing it off. Start the car now. Keys, right, ignition, twist. Nothing. Handbrake? No, that doesn't matter.

He stared at his feet and looked around, a little confused.

Then it clicked.

Right, foot on the brake. Automatic.

Ignition.

Into drive.

The car lurched forward and he stood on the brake a little hard, causing the car to judder. Fuck, maybe he shouldn't be driving.

No, no, he'd be fine. He just needed to be careful. And if he went back inside, he'd never hear the end of it.

Cautiously, he pulled onto the road and eased his way along.

Dark had fallen and the light from the car, though bright, did little to raise his awareness.

The streets were quiet now, eerily so. The army was still patrolling the streets, so the worst of the rioting and looting had been quelled. Though after the announcement that had just gone out from the killer, he doubted they'd be able to hold back the flood.

He needed to get to Sonja's fast, before all hell broke loose.

En route, he had to pull over twice to search for the right way. But eventually – in double the time his app told him it would take – he arrived, pulling to a halt at the curb with a large sigh of relief.

He climbed from the car with some difficulty and walked towards her door, pinballing from the gate post to the door pillar for support.

He knocked once and the door, pulled to but not closed, swung inwards.

'Sonja?' he called out.

'I'm in here,' she replied.

'The door was open,' Thorsen said, stepping in and closing it behind him.

'Oh, right.'

He stepped into her living room, seeing her leaning against the kitchen counter. She looked weary, with deep bags under her eyes. Her bloodshot eyes.

'Is everything okay?' he asked.

'Did you bring my car?' The question was quick, nervous.

'Yeah,' he said, holding up her keys. He held them out but she made no move to come and get them.

It all became clear then.

As clear as the cold touch of a gun barrel being pressed into the nape of your neck can be.

Thorsen turned his head slightly, seeing the dark outline of a man in black, face hidden, featureless behind the mask.

'Do I need to tell you not to move?' he asked, voice cold and gravelly.

Thorsen's left hand moved upwards to join the right. He clenched his jaw, considering his options. Sonja was a statue under the cold glare of the LED spotlights above her.

'Lucas Adell,' Thorsen said then, swallowing. 'Or is it Viktor Hellström?'

He ignored the question. 'We're leaving, now.'

'Leaving where?'

'Leaving the island. The three of us.'

Thorsen needed to buy time, to think. A lot of time. His brain was moving through tar. 'The entirety of the NOD is after you. There's no getting off the island.'

'There's a way,' he said, twisting the gun so the muzzle bit into Thorsen's skin. 'And we're leaving right now. So, turn around, slowly, and—'

'If it's me you want, let Sonja go,' Thorsen said.

'It's her I wanted, but when she told me you had her car … well, that was just good luck.'

'Luck?' Thorsen mustered, heart thundering. 'Luck how?'

He jabbed him with the gun again. 'Don't talk, just move,' Adell ordered. 'And if you try anything, I'll execute the doctor.'

'You'd kill an innocent woman in cold blood?' Thorsen asked, realising halfway through who he was speaking to.

'I'm not fond of doctors,' he growled. 'We don't have the best history.'

Thorsen felt the gun barrel leave his neck and then felt its cold presence hovering next to his ear, aimed right at Sonja, who paled.

'So,' Adell said, voice even and calm. 'What will it be?'

29

Jamie Johansson

JAMIE AWOKE AROUND DAWN.

She'd worked into the night, and then all but passed out on one of the couches in the break room. She hadn't been the first to go in there, and nor had she been the last. People had come and gone throughout the night, grabbing a nap here and there, or coming in to brew coffees.

Each time, she'd roused a little, checked her phone, then gone back to sleep.

Now, there was a hand on her shoulder and she started a little, seeing Dahlvig over her.

'Time to go,' he said.

Jamie sucked in a sharp breath and sat up painfully, her back aching. 'Go where?' she asked, pulling out her phone and checking it.

It was just after six, but the time wasn't what worried her. It was the radio silence from Thorsen.

He'd been gone all night without so much as a text.

Jamie'd sent him three messages, and then by midnight had to assume that he'd gone back to the hotel, to bed.

Though it wasn't like him not to reply. So much so that she'd even called the hospital at 3am when she'd got up to pee to see if he'd been admitted, and checked Visby police's incident reports from the night to make sure he'd not smashed Sonja's car into a wall.

Both were absent of any mention of him.

'Visby University,' Dahlvig answered.

'Hmm?' Jamie said, rubbing her eyes.

Dahlvig handed her a cup of coffee. It was steaming. She held it tightly, letting the aroma stimulate her brain.

'We're going to Visby University,' Dahlvig said.

'Why?'

'Because Eva Wallin – the other PhD student that Öberg named – just started her shift there at the library, and we're going to go and get her.'

Jamie sipped the coffee, trying to decode that. 'I'm not sure I understand. Why me?'

'Because she's working at the Visby University library, and you've been in there before. You know the layout, right?'

'No more than if you looked at a map of the place,' Jamie said, checking her phone again. Still nothing. 'And are you sure she's there? The city's going crazy, why the hell would she be at work?'

Dahlvig shrugged. 'Don't know. But I've had someone posted there, watching it for the last hour, and they said she just arrived. If I had to guess, I'd say she's keeping up appearances in the wake of the big bad man in black's reveal. Trying to play it cool. Or maybe she's waiting for him to contact her, tell her what to do next.' He shrugged again. 'It doesn't matter. Right now, she doesn't know we're coming, and I'd rather not announce it with sirens and a fleet of people.'

'But why me? Surely there's someone on your team who's—'

He sighed, a little frustrated. 'Shut up, Johansson. And then get up. You've got first-hand experience on site. And you've got a tactical history. I checked. So, wash your face, brush your teeth, drink your coffee and then get your ass outside.'

He turned and walked away. Jamie watched him go, then cupped her hand to her mouth and nose and breathed into it.

Yeah, maybe brushing her teeth was a good call. She sighed, shook the last of the grogginess from her mind, downed the rest of her coffee, and then headed for the bathroom.

When Jamie emerged from the station, Dahlvig was waiting for her right outside, parked up in an inconspicuous older model BMW saloon.

She climbed in with a slight groan on account of her back and Dahlvig immediately pulled away.

Jamie kept her eyes on the city, noting how quiet the streets were. There were now signs up, notices slapped on shop windows and doors saying that the army were patrolling the streets, that anyone caught out after dark would be stopped and questioned, and without good reason would be arrested.

She saw the remains of riots and destruction. Tear gas cannisters, now empty, lining the gutters. Spray paint across buildings, proclamations of government conspiracy, paintings of black hearts.

Dahlvig seemed to take no notice as he drove on.

'I can't get hold of Thorsen,' Jamie said then, her anxiety spilling out. She'd been thinking it on repeat, and now it just came tumbling from her mouth.

'Trouble in paradise?' Dahlvig replied, eyes fixed on the road.

'He left last night to see Sonja Ehrhart, but I haven't heard from him.'

'That where he went?' Dahlvig asked, sticking out his bottom lip. 'Thought he'd just turned in for the night.'

She detected the mild derision in his tone. 'Thorsen wouldn't just leave like that unless it was important.'

'If you say so.'

'He's the most dedicated detective I know.'

'Sure.'

'What's your problem?' Jamie said then. Whether it was the lack of sleep or the fact that he was as good as shit-talking Thorsen, she wasn't sure. But either way she didn't like it. 'Do you not like Thorsen?'

'I don't know him,' Dahlvig said calmly. 'All I know is what I see. And that's what I base opinion – and decision – on. It's called being a pragmatist.'

'And what's your opinion of Thorsen?'

'I'm still looking. But I don't see him, do you?'

Jamie noticed his eyes linger on her for a few seconds before he returned them to the road.

She stayed quiet from then on.

The university, mercifully, came up fast.

Dahlvig swung around the empty forecourt and pulled into the staff car park, slowing next to a Volvo estate car. He paused next to it and wound down the window. A guy in his fifties looked back, dark hair and bearded. His expression said he was tired, but he still looked sharp.

Jamie could see a monocular on the dashboard.

'Any change?' Dahlvig asked.

The guy shook his head. 'She's still in there, unless she's slipped out the back.'

Dahlvig nodded. 'Alright, good. Hang back. I'll call you if we need help.'

The guy nodded this time and then wound the window up, as though he knew the conversation was done.

Dahlvig pulled forward into another space and killed the engine. 'Why did you leave?' he asked then.

'Why did I leave what?'

'Police work. Being a detective. I know you were fired from your position in Kurrajakk, but that whole thing was a lapse in judgement if you ask me. A vague attempt at searching for something you didn't really want to find.'

'And that was?' Jamie asked, defensive suddenly.

Dahlvig ignored her and went on. 'It's just luck, really, that you fell ass-backwards into those cases. Fucking weirdo in a feathered bird costume starts killing people in a town that's seen no crime in decades a few months after you get there?' He tsked. 'Then it was a missing persons case that somehow got you sucked into a Europol trafficking investigation? And then all that bullshit with that, what, *cult* in the north? Jesus, you're a lightning rod for shit, aren't you?'

'Maybe I just see what other people miss. I didn't invent those crimes. I just found them, and stopped them. I don't think you can chastise me for that.'

'I'm not,' he said bluntly. 'I'm asking why you left?'

'Why I left …' Jamie repeated. 'I was tired. I needed a break. The last few years have been difficult. Traumatic.'

'I'll say. Did it work?'

'My break?'

'Do you feel rejuvenated? Ready to come back?'

She stayed silent.

'Because, pragmatically, I think you're a fierce detective with a sharp mind, sharper eyes, and a track record of success. Despite your wanton disregard for authority, procedure, and proper application of the law.'

She didn't know what to say. And if she did speak, she didn't know if that would change the outcome of this conversation. Or exactly what outcome she was hoping for.

'I don't mince words, Johansson. I want you to work for me. But I need a team player. Not the detective you have been.'

'What about Thorsen?'

'What about him? I'm asking you.'

'If I'll come work for you?'

'If you can be a team player. Because for all your positives, you're reckless, and you get people hurt. Don't try to deny that.'

She couldn't. Instead, she just looked at him, and nodded.

'If you work for me, I can help with that. I can keep you focused. And I can make sure people don't get hurt. I can support your positive attributes, and temper the bad ones. I was a detective myself, and I miss being on the front lines. But I'm a better intendent.' He glanced at Jamie. 'Don't look at me like that. I'm well aware I'm not a people person. But I do my job, and I handle cases properly. That may not sound flashy, but there's more to doing my job than just catching bad guys no matter the cost.'

'Is that why you took two years to make headway on this case?'

'It's exactly why I want you to work for me. This case highlighted some weaknesses in my team, and they're weaknesses that you could fortify.'

Jamie thought on it, watching the sun climb between the

university buildings. 'What about Thorsen? You already offered him a job.'

'I did no such thing. And I don't care about Thorsen. It's you I want. And if you two are in a relationship, then it's all the more reason to split you up.'

'We're not.'

'You sure about that? Because that kind of thing doesn't fly with me. Ever heard the saying don't shit where you eat? Thorsen obviously hasn't. He worked with his ex-wife. And now he's working with you. The guy is a romantic, I suppose you could call it. But I wouldn't. I'd just say that he lacks the ability to separate his head from his *head.*'

Jamie sighed, gritting her teeth. 'We work well together. He's my partner. He watches my back, I watch his.'

'I don't see him here right now. And that would be how it is with me. You won't have a partner. You'll have a team. Your *own* team. You'll run them. Detectives, forensic techs, digital forensics, access to resources. Local and regional police at your disposal. A budget to requisition whatever you want.'

'So long as it goes through you first?' Jamie answered dryly.

'That's exactly how it is. It's me,' he said, putting his hand in the air. 'Top of the totem pole. Then you. Then everyone else.'

'You want me to be your number two?'

'You'd be my number four. I have two senior investigators I trust implicitly. And I don't trust you at all … yet.'

'And yet you want me to work for you?'

'I don't believe you're beyond training. But think about what you'd be working on. Trafficking, terrorism, serial killers. Leave this force-hopping behind. Find a place where your unique skills are appreciated, and where you can put them to work.'

Jamie stared out of the window. 'No Thorsen?'

'If you can promise me that you and he won't start fucking – *ever* – then I'm not wholly against the idea.'

'And if we did?'

'I'd have him transferred out of the team.' Dahlvig shrugged. 'I don't give a shit who you're screwing. Just so long as you're not fucking up my investigations.'

She swallowed. 'Can I think about it?'

'I'd hoped you would. It's a big decision. In the meanwhile, you ready to do this?'

Jamie glanced around. 'Just the two of us?'

'Quick, quiet. Easy.'

'And what is this, the practical part of my interview?'

He smirked a little. 'Sure. Why not.' He opened the car door and stepped into the cool morning air.

When Jamie joined him, she could already feel the sun warm on her side.

Dahlvig walked quickly, but he wasn't as tall as Thorsen, so didn't carry quite as much speed.

As they neared the door to the library, he reached into his jacket and pulled out a Glock 17 semi-automatic pistol, slowing to face her.

He switched it in his hands, offering her the grip. 'Remember how to use one of these?'

Jamie took it, inspected it quickly, and then ejected the mag. She checked it – 17 rounds, fully loaded. Hollow points.

She snapped the mag back into the grip and then pulled back the barrel, chambering a round.

'I'll take that as a yes,' Dahlvig said.

'You don't think we'll have to use them? One girl?' Jamie

asked, finding herself calmer than she thought she would be holding a gun again. Doing this again.

'Who knows?' Dahlvig said. 'She's a killer if Öberg is right about her. If you're right about her.'

Jamie reserved judgement. It would be the first time she'd thought lightly of a young female killer. And she had the scar on her shoulder to remind her not to do it twice.

'I'll lead,' Dahlvig said. 'Remember. Quick, and quiet. Eyes open. If you see her, call out. And keep me in your peripheral. We sweep floor by floor. Got it?'

Jamie nodded.

'Got it?' he repeated, more firmly, meeting her eyes.

'I got it.'

'Good. Then let's go.' He pulled his own Glock 17 from his rib holster and chambered a round.

And then he went in.

Jamie followed smoothly, falling back into old rhythms without missing a beat.

The interior was cool and empty. She remembered Annika saying all the exams were basically done now, so the only people who were still studying were those who had classes through the summer, or Masters and PhD students working on their research projects for coming deadlines. But with everything going on in the city, Jamie wasn't surprised that the place was a ghost town.

She didn't think they'd be so lucky as to see Eva Wallin standing at the main desk. But nonetheless, when Dahlvig walked through the door and into the atrium, he had his pistol held behind his back, his gait light and casual.

He scanned the room quickly, but with the focus of a raptor, and then sighed a little, turning his head to ensure Jamie was looking at him. He subtly pointed to the upper mezzanine decks, as though they should check there.

Jamie listened carefully, eyes moving across the raised stacks. She shook her head then and nodded towards the stairs to the basement.

Dahlvig considered, did another sweep of the upper floors, then nodded in agreement, gave a little 'move' signal, and started walking.

They pushed through the double doors and descended into the basement.

When they got there, Dahlvig paused and eased open the door as quietly as he could.

The same smell as before, dust and books, stale air, pressed in on Jamie. The low ceiling conjured claustrophobia, and the stacks and stacks of books evoking that same strange sense of eyes on her. She wondered now whether the first time, when she had felt that, that there really had been eyes watching her. The eyes of Eva Wallin, curious as to who was hunting down a copy of Hamlet and why. Wondering if the net was closing.

Was this girl a cold-blooded, black-hearted killer, same as Lucas Adell? Or was she just another victim, indoctrinated and twisted by the darkness of Viktor Hellström's tortured mind?

As they moved inward, Jamie became aware of a strange sound. Humming. A disjointed tune.

Dahlvig heard it too, stopped, and gestured for Jamie to carry on down the main corridor between the stacks, while he went around to cut off any escape.

She waited for him to get to the far end and then motion her onwards.

They moved in unison, Jamie snatching glimpses of Dahlvig as they crossed off one corridor of books after another.

He walked with the calm collectedness of someone well-practised at this. Jamie thought she was prone to picking out people's faults. But she could tell Dahlvig was good at his job. Was a well-rounded investigator. A pragmatist. Capable in the field. A good manager of people. Perhaps he wasn't so bad. And perhaps this wasn't the worst opportunity in the world. Because … and she hated to admit this … she was enjoying herself.

God, that's so fucked up, she thought. But she couldn't ignore it.

The humming got louder, and then, all of a sudden, she was there.

Jamie stopped in the space between two stacks, staring down its length. Dahlvig was at the other end.

And about halfway down, on her knees, was a girl. She was early twenties, with dark hair, pulled back and messy. She had headphones in, and was humming along to whatever track was playing as she pulled books from a little box next to her and slotted them onto the shelves.

She seemed unaware of Jamie and Dahlvig's presence, but as Dahlvig began to close in on her, pistol hanging loosely at his side, she stopped fiddling with the books and looked up.

She glanced at Jamie first, who was holding her pistol in both hands, muzzle at the floor. Her eyes widened and she pulled her headphones from her ears roughly before twisting her head to look at Dahlvig, who was considerably closer.

Jamie recognised her as the girl from the library when she'd first been here. She'd noticed her behind the desk on her way out but thought nothing of it.

Dahlvig's eyes flitted to Jamie, as though looking for confirmation that this was Eva Wallin.

Jamie had no doubt that it was. She matched Öberg's

description perfectly, down to the oversized flannel and skinny jeans.

Jamie nodded firmly and Dahlvig spoke.

'Eva Wallin,' he said, lifting his empty hand to signal she stay on the ground. 'We're with the NOD – Visby police. Don't move.'

But she immediately got to her knees and then to her feet, sort of half hunched over, bracing herself on the stack. She looked over her shoulder at Jamie then, the fear in her eyes clear as day.

Jamie knew that look. Same as a rabbit facing down a fox. And a rabbit only knows how to do one thing.

'Don't run. Don't do it,' Dahlvig ordered, voice harder now.

But she did, sweeping an armful of books off a shelf and onto the ground in front of Dahlvig, and then turning and sprinting towards Jamie.

She bounced from one shelf to the other, making them shake and sway, closing the ground quickly.

Dahlvig's voice echoed in the quiet of the basement. 'Don't shoot her!' he yelled.

But despite the gun in her hands, Jamie had no such intention.

The girl slowed her pace half a step, wound up and then swung her fist wildly in Jamie's direction with the reckless, formless abandon of someone who'd never thrown a punch before.

Jamie saw it coming a mile off, stepped forward so that it was going over her shoulder, and then parried with an arm block, deflecting the strike with her left.

Before Eva Wallin even knew what was happening, Jamie's right hand was up, the pistol flashing, the bottom of the grip flying towards the girl's forehead.

The blow landed, short and sharp, with a dull crack, right between the eyes, and Eva Wallin stumbled backwards, squealing.

She threw her hands to her nose and tried to run forward again, sobbing.

But Jamie was a stone wall, and caught the girl by the shoulders. She hoped that would be it, but when Eva Wallin tried to force her way by, a quick knee thrown into her stomach corrected her.

Eva made a protracted wheezing sound and then staggered sideways before collapsing to her hip, legs folded under her, hands still on her face. Blood was dripping through her fingers now.

Dahlvig was there then, standing over Wallin. He crouched a little, hands hovering above her. 'Jesus Christ, Johansson! You broke her fucking nose.'

'No, I didn't,' Jamie said, ejecting the round from the chamber of her Glock and pushing the pistol into the back of her waistband.

'How do you know?'

'Because I've broken enough noses to know.'

He glanced up at her and smirked a little. 'Fair enough. For a second there, I thought you were going to shoot her.'

'You thought wrong.'

He stuck out his bottom lip and nodded a few times, then pulled a set of cable ties from his pocket and tossed them to Jamie. 'I'll get her up, you cuff her. We need to get her back to the station and into an interrogation room.'

He hoisted Eva Wallin to her feet, the girl still mewling, and turned her so Jamie had access to her wrists. She had her eyes clamped closed, tears running from them. She was sobbing quietly, still and pliable now. She didn't say anything as Jamie laced the ties around her wrists, interlocking them, and pulled them taut.

'Nice work,' Dahlvig commented as Jamie pushed Eva along by the shoulder.

She said nothing in reply, but instead pulled the pistol from her jeans and offered it back to Dahlvig.

'You hold on to it,' he said. 'This isn't over yet.'

30

Kjell Thorsen

SONJA DROVE while Thorsen sat in the passenger seat.

He still wasn't fully aware of why Adell wanted him there too. Or why he wanted Sonja, either.

But what he did know, was that they were headed north. That they'd been forced to leave their phones at Sonja's house. And that Lucas Adell currently had his pistol pressed into the back of Sonja's seat, and promised to put three bullets in her spine if Thorsen moved his hands from his knees, even for a second.

And the way in which he said it made Thorsen believe that he wouldn't hesitate for a second.

'Where are we going?' Thorsen risked.

Sonja yelped a little and Thorsen thought it was likely that Adell had jabbed her in the back with the pistol.

'Just keep driving,' Adell growled. 'We're nearly there. Take a right here.'

Sonja slowed and pulled off the main road onto a singlelaned track winding through the fields that separated them from the sea.

It was nearly two in the morning, and there were no other cars on the road. Where they were going, he couldn't even guess. But as they wound closer to the water, it became clear.

A sign appeared in front of them that read *'Hideviken'*.

The headlights broke through the hedgerows and illuminated a tiny hamlet by the water, just a cluster of houses facing a small dock. And tethered there were a handful of boats.

Thorsen understood then, and his supposition was confirmed when Adell ordered Sonja to pull in next to one of the jetties.

'You outside first,' he said to Thorsen. 'Go down to the white boat at the end, get in. There are cable ties in the glove compartment. Tie your hands to the wheel.'

'Both of them?' Thorsen asked. 'How am I supposed to do that?'

He jabbed the back of the seat again and Sonja squealed. 'Figure it out. You're smart enough. I don't have to tell you what happens if you don't.'

Sonja dragged in rattling breaths, tears running down her cheeks. 'Just do what he says, please,' she pleaded.

Thorsen let out a frustrated breath and opened the door, walking down the jetty, the still summer waters lapping gently at the posts. He was illuminated by the headlights, tracing his path towards the boat, and then he suspected the open water.

Adell would make them drive into the night, and then what, execute them? Toss them overboard?

He didn't know. And it didn't seem like he had much hope of trying anything. If he did, Sonja would die first, and then he'd go next. Adell had no qualms about killing children, and Thorsen was under no illusion he'd kill the both of them in a heartbeat.

It would take hours to cross the sea to any sort of major landfall in the small single-engine boat that Adell had directed him to. Which meant that he had a few hours to think of something. Or, more likely, for Jamie to catch up to them.

But how she'd find them, Thorsen had no idea.

All he could do was hope.

31

Jamie Johansson

'I'M SORRY,' Dahlvig said, rocking back on his chair. 'Is this boring for you?' He eyed Jamie, standing behind him, watching Eva Wallin in the interrogation room as her interviewer, Dahlvig's number two, prepped some papers in front of him.

Jamie looked up from her phone screen. 'No, it's just that I haven't heard from Thorsen. Not since he left last night.'

'It's seven in the morning. He's probably asleep. Now put your phone away, and—'

'This isn't like him,' Jamie said. 'Something's wrong.'

'Something's wrong,' Dahlvig repeated back, nodding. 'Something's wrong. Hmm. Sure you're not just feeling a little cold-shouldered? Thorsen was ready to throw you under the bus to get a chance at working with me. So maybe you want to rethink your priorities here a little?'

Jamie resisted the urge to snap back. She glanced up at the screen showing Eva Wallin, fidgeting nervously as the interviewer sweated her.

'I think you've got this handled,' Jamie said then.

'This interview? The one that's going to break a two-year-long investigation? You really want to miss this?'

'No, I don't,' Jamie replied curtly. 'But I also know when Thorsen is acting out of character, and when that means something's up.'

'So, you want to ride out of here to check in on your boyfriend rather than wait another thirty minutes and tie a bow on this thing?'

'You have my number,' Jamie said. 'If you get stuck, feel free to call me.'

Dahlvig curled a smile. 'You've got some balls, you know that?'

Jamie smirked a little. 'Eva Wallin ran. Then she crumpled. She sobbed the whole way to the station. The girl may be involved in some heinous shit, but she's not a killer, not like Adell. Hell, she's about to spill her guts whether your man there asks a question or not. I did my bit. I came in, I found Adell, I got us to Öberg, who served up Eva Wallin on a platter. If you need me to hold your hand to the finish line here, then just admit it. Otherwise, I'm going to go, and then come back once I've found Thorsen. Does that work with you?'

Dahlvig laced his hands behind his head, staring up at Jamie. 'People that work for me don't talk to me like that.'

'Then it's a good thing I haven't accepted your offer yet.'

'This how it's going to be? You fighting me at every turn?'

'Depends if you're going to jerk the lead just to remind me who's in charge.'

'Depends if you're out of line.' Dahlvig eyed Jamie for a few more seconds. 'I'll chalk this up to being the sort of team leader who never lets her guys down.'

'Thanks, *chef,'* Jamie said, nodding. 'I'll be back soon.'

'Here,' Dahlvig said then, rummaging in his pocket and tossing the key to his BMW to Jamie.

She caught it. 'Your car?'

'Technically it's Visby police's car. But I don't think that changes the sentiment.'

'Thanks,' Jamie said again, this time a little more sincerely.

He nodded. 'We look out for our own. Now go, make sure Thorsen isn't dead.'

Jamie didn't laugh. Instead, she just cleared her throat nervously, turned, and moved for the door. Quickly.

It was still early and the roads were mercifully quiet.

She was ringing Thorsen continually but he wasn't picking up.

Jamie considered going to the hotel, but if anyone knew where he was, it was Sonja. He went to her house last night, so she'd be able to tell Jamie where he'd gone from there.

When she pulled up outside, the house was dark, her car not parked anywhere on the street. Not surprising if Thorsen still had it and he wasn't here, but … Jamie didn't know, she expected it to be, she supposed. That Thorsen would have gone to bed here, slept off the concussion under Sonja's supervision.

Jamie exited the car and went up the path, knocking on the door without pausing.

There was no response.

She knocked again, louder this time.

Was Sonja in work? Jamie didn't think so. Her lab was probably still a crime scene, and Jamie knew she was on leave. She'd have no reason to go to work.

Jamie stepped back, thinking. There was no check-in at the hospital, at least not last night. Though it was possible that Thorsen stayed the night here and then went there early this morning.

But, no, he'd have seen her messages and called. He'd have responded, surely?

Jamie got down off the porch and went to the windows. Blinds drawn.

Fuck. It was a town house, too. No side paths to get through. Though there was likely a back entrance via an alleyway.

Jamie ran back to the car, climbed in, and then circled the street, swinging down the alleyway that split this row and the one behind.

It took her a moment to get her bearings, but when she was confident it was Sonja's house, she parked behind it and wasted no time climbing the fence.

She landed in a well-maintained back garden, mostly landscaped and low maintenance. There was a water feature, stone walkway, and a pergola with a nice little deck under it. Cute, Jamie thought. Requires no work. Private. The kind of garden she might enjoy once all this catching killers bullshit was over.

Jamie walked up the back steps to the patio doors that opened into the kitchen and reached for the handle. She jiggled it.

Locked.

Fuck.

She scanned the interior. Dark.

No lights. No movement.

She pulled her phone out then and tried Thorsen again.

It began ringing, and in the darkness, something began to glow.

She peered in, watching as Thorsen's phone lit up on the kitchen counter. Right next to another one.

Her heart sank and she cut the call immediately.

She'd been pretty sure something was wrong before. But now she was certain.

As she ran back through the garden, she was already calling Dahlvig.

'They're gone,' she said, the moment he answered.

'What?' Dahlvig replied. There were voices in the background. Jamie guessed that they were mid-interrogation with Eva Wallin by now.

'Thorsen and Sonja Ehrhart,' Jamie said, pinning her phone on her shoulder as she climbed the fence and dropped down next to the car. 'He went over there last night, and now they're both gone.'

'So maybe—'

'No, their phones are on the kitchen counter. Thorsen wouldn't leave his behind, not in the middle of an investigation.'

'Jesus, you didn't break into her house, did you?'

'Looked in the window,' Jamie said, getting into the car and starting the engine.

He sighed with relief. 'Alright, alright. How do we know for sure?'

Jamie swallowed, thinking. 'We don't. But *I* know something's wrong … and I'm going to find him. Whether you help me or not.'

There was silence for a few seconds. 'Okay,' Dahlvig said then. 'Get back here, we'll put our heads together. Alright?'

Jamie hung up, then gunned it back towards the station, leaving a cloud of dust rising through the early morning sunlight.

. . .

Back at the station, things were abuzz. Everyone was still looking for Adell, and if they weren't, they were plugged into the interrogation.

Despite that, Dahlvig still tore himself away to greet Jamie when she arrived. He came down the corridor to meet her, quelling her with his hands.

'Take a breath,' he ordered.

She hated being told what to do. But she did anyway, forcing herself to breathe.

'Okay, what do we know?' he asked.

'Last night, Thorsen went over there. Then, radio silence.'

'What did he go there for?'

'Sonja said she needed to see him. Urgently.'

'Is that strange?'

'I don't know. I don't really know her that well. But ...'

'But what?'

'Something you said about Wallin.'

'What was it?'

'That she was going about her business as normal, as though she was waiting for instruction from Adell.'

'Right?' Dahlvig folded his arms now, listening intently.

'And Adell, going public now, all of a sudden. Two years of radio silence, and then he makes an appearance at Sonja's lab, kills the technician there – out of pattern and not his victim type or kill type at all. Then, he appears at the hospital too? Or was already there when we got there.'

'What are you saying?'

'It just doesn't make sense. Does it? Why go to the morgue now? Why go back to the hospital now? After all this time?'

'Do I need to say that Adell is crazy?'

'No, no, he's definitely got severe mental issues – likely multiple personality disorder or schizophrenia at the very least. But we still know that he's hugely smart, highly effective, and charming, too. I met the guy as well. Didn't really suspect him of being a monster at the time.'

'There a point you want to get to here?'

Jamie swallowed. 'He's … emotionally driven. Hellström, Adell, whoever you want. His first kill, his father. It was revenge. For his sister, right? That was an emotional kill. And losing his wife and daughter – that fractured his mind. Emotional trauma. Coming to the morgue now? Why? Thorsen and I arrived. I spoke to Annika. We went to the library, got the copy of Hamlet. And Eva Wallin saw us there. Adell must have known about the book, right? So, Eva probably told him about it.'

'You're still talking but not saying anything.'

'What I'm saying is that since that happened, it's been a chain of events that has pushed him to make impulsive decisions. He's sentimental – his house unchanged, his daughter's room unchanged. He lamented over his wife and daughter like it was yesterday when we were there. I think …'

'You think what?'

'I think that he's smart enough to know the net was closing. From the moment that Eva Wallin saw us at the library, he knew that the clock had started counting down. And someone that smart, when they know that it's over …'

'They run.'

'They run.' Jamie exhaled. 'He sees me in the library. He goes to the morgue, to look over his kills, to reminisce, to lament, maybe? I don't know. Why else would he go there and look at the bodies? And then, the hospital. The story breaks, shows the room where he was created. He goes there, again, to remember, to see, to be reminded. Maybe to relive it all one more time before he leaves for good. And it just so happened we were there at the same time. And then, finally, he goes live on socials. A video. An announcement. An attestation that he's going to keep killing. That this will not stop. That someone will die every month. On the island of Gotland. And why would he tell us to pool all our resources here? To look at Gotland?'

'Because he's not on Gotland anymore. Fuck.'

Jamie nodded. 'The announcement was a distraction. And I think it's too coincidental that both Sonja and Thorsen go missing the same night.'

'Why Ehrhart and Thorsen, though?'

Jamie shook her head, thinking. 'I don't know? Sonja interrupted him while he was with the bodies … and Jassen did the same, right? Got his throat opened for it. Thorsen … we caught him off-guard at the hospital? We were also in his house poking around … I guess they're both people that got away? That he wanted to kill, but couldn't … Maybe they're unfinished business for him? Maybe he can't let anything go. He's an obsessive. Methodical. Hell, he's been killing teenagers for two fucking years without relenting. One after another. A process. Bang. Bang. Bang. Unwavering.'

Dahlvig nodded, then let out a long breath. 'Alright. Shit. I don't think I can argue with that, or your abilities to get inside the minds of killers. So where do we go from here?' He looked at her, waiting for an answer.

But she didn't have one to give.

It had only been two hours, but Jamie already hated being in charge of a team.

Dahlvig had rounded up a group of investigators, pulling them from their efforts to find Adell their way, and instead put them under Jamie's purview. He was an expert delegator, Jamie had to give him that.

He introduced her and ordered them to follow her instructions, and gave them a brief rundown of the situation – that it was entirely possible the video announcement that Adell gave was a distraction, and that while the frenzy began, Adell abducted Kjell Thorsen and Sonja Ehrhart, and would be attempting to escape the island in some form.

Then, he just stopped speaking, and looked at Jamie.

As did the four investigators now suddenly working for her. They had their arms folded, or they were scowling, all tired and stressed, and now suddenly being told they were working for this random stranger who'd just waltzed into the station, and Dahlvig's good graces.

'Uh …' Jamie began, sideswiped by the whole thing. She took a breath, shook her head once to kick start her brain, then just started talking. 'Means of exit – the ferry, the airport. I know they're both closed on account of the shitstorm going on out there, but I want to make sure that Adell didn't slip through the net yesterday, or earlier. We last saw him at the old hospital, so any time after that, alright? I want to make doubly sure that he didn't get off the island earlier than we think.'

'We already checked the airport and ferry,' someone said.

'So, check them again,' Dahlvig barked.

The group quietened.

Jamie clenched her fists to stop them shaking. She'd rather face down an armed killer than a chance at public speaking any day. 'The other thing,' Jamie said, trying to calm her breathing. 'Last night, Kjell Thorsen was called to Sonja Ehrhart's home. While there, I suspect they encountered Lucas Adell – AKA Viktor Hellström. With Sonja's car missing, I'm fairly sure they would have used that to leave the city at least. It's a blue hatchback – a Honda Jazz. Not sure of the year, but it's a newer model. I'll give you

Ehrhart's address – find surrounding CCTV and scour it. Thorsen left here around nine last night, so get him arriving, and then leaving Ehrhart's place – I want to find that car, and track its movements.'

'Excuse me,' a guy piped up from the group, arms tightly knotted. 'But how exactly do you know this? We've been searching non-stop for Adell, and now, all of a sudden, you know where he was, and when?' The guy all but scoffed. 'And, also, who are you even?'

Dahlvig opened his mouth to speak, but Jamie got there first. 'My name is Jamie Johansson,' she said. 'And how I know this is because Kjell Thorsen is my partner, and he left here last night to go to Sonja Ehrhart's house. He didn't respond to any of my attempts to contact him following his arrival there, and when I went to check on his whereabouts, I found Sonja Ehrhart's car missing, and both his and Sonja's phones left at her home. As such, it's my guess that they left under duress with Lucas Adell.'

'Your guess?' the guy asked, raising his eyebrows.

Jamie nodded. 'Yes. My guess, and you should heed it. Because I can guarantee you my guess is better than yours.'

The guy did scoff now. *'Chef,'* he laughed, addressing Dahlvig. 'You can't be serious about this? We've been working this case for two fucking years! And now she walks in here and—'

'Get out,' Dahlvig said then. Cold and quick.

'Sorry?' the guy said.

'Get out. Of the office. Of the building. I don't care. You're done. Out.'

The guy's eyes widened. 'You can't be serious?'

'Do I look like I'm joking?'

'You'd lose a man now, in the middle of all this?' He gestured around.

'You've been sitting around with your thumb up your ass for six months complaining about resources and manpower and how impossible this is to solve. Jamie arrived less than a week ago, with no resources, or even a badge. And she found and identified Lucas Adell in that time. Which means that what she just said is as true as any statement could be: her guess *is* better than yours. Way better. As such, you should feel pretty privileged I chose you to be on her team. But it was obviously a mistake. So, I'll say it again, once, and it's not an order that merits a response. Get your shit and get out of my building.'

The guy's mouth flapped and he looked at his colleagues for support.

They all averted their eyes.

He nodded then, smirked a little as though the whole thing was some outrageous affront to him, and walked away towards his desk.

As Dahlvig handed the brief back over to Jamie, the guy could be heard slamming drawers and making as much noise as possible at his desk.

Jamie cleared her throat. 'They left Sonja Ehrhart's home sometime after Thorsen arrived. Late model Honda Jazz, blue. If the ferry is shut and the airport, too, then they'll be looking for another way off the island.'

The group just looked at Jamie.

'That's it,' Dahlvig said then. 'Go. Find Adell.'

They dispersed back to their desks and Dahlvig turned to Jamie, giving her a slight nod. 'You did good.'

'That was horrible,' Jamie said honestly.

Dahlvig smiled a little. 'You'll get used to it.'

'Will I?'

He shrugged, clapping her on the shoulder. 'Guess that's up to you.'

. . .

They kept coming to her desk and bothering her.

Like children in an art classroom showing their works in progress to the teacher, looking for praise. None dared shy away from the assignments to look her up, that much was clear by the fact that they kept asking personal questions when they came around. Where did you work before this? How do you know Dahlvig? What brought you to Gotland? All asked casually, but with intent. The things they were bringing her were fine, but not useful – she wished they'd just get on with their jobs instead of trying to buy favour, prove their worth, or figure out who they were working under.

Stills of Sonja's car were what they showed her mostly. Three people inside.

All within city limits.

Then, nothing.

The car headed north in each of the five shots they had of it. Traffic cameras mostly.

But then, as it left the city, nothing.

And that seemed to be what they were coming to her with now.

Nothing.

Just buzzing around like bees, waiting for some sort of order.

But Jamie didn't have it to give, and she was struggling to focus.

She sent one away after they told her that they'd been looking at Bunge Airbase, a small defunct former military air base in the north of the island that still had a few private planes there. Little single-engine things.

From the research she'd done on Adell, there was nothing to suggest he could fly a plane. And even if he could, planes were picked up on radar and contacted. It was a stupid idea. But instead, she just said 'Good', and sent them away.

Others were eyeing her now. They had nothing to report, but they wanted to come over and prove they were working hard.

Jamie glanced around.

Fuck this.

She got up and jogged out of the room.

She needed space, and peace to work.

She needed to find an office where no one would bother her, and she needed to focus. To think.

Even just moving, her mind churned through what she knew. She'd looked at Adell's movements since his daughter disappeared. Everything at Fårö, the Lundström attack, even the case with EZ, the drug dealer that was tortured and killed.

The Lundström attack. It made sense, but something was niggling at her. Adell attacked Lundström out of spite, right? For fucking up Rebecca's investigation. And his wife's. But … he didn't attack Lundström right then. No, he did it out of self-preservation. To prevent himself being caught by Lundström for EZ's kill.

That's what was sticking in her throat. Why attack him and leave him paralysed if it was self-preservation?

Jamie slowed in the corridor, coming to a halt. She felt like the gears were grinding, trying to mesh and turn, but they were stuck.

If it was self-preservation, why not just kill Lundström and dump his body somewhere? Just disappear him totally. That would have been cleaner, simpler than paralysing him as he did.

No, that was emotionally driven. That was an act of retribution, a show of wrath and anger. Killing the real Lucas Adell. And Jassen, Sonja's assistant. Those were quick, heart-

less kills. Cold blooded. Kills of necessity. But the others …
EZ. To torture him before killing him? Why? And Lundström
… that was punishment.

But why punish Lundström after killing EZ? Did EZ have
a link to Rebecca? Had he killed Rebecca? And Adell was
taking revenge on EZ … got his confession, maybe. And then
Lundström's incompetence was finally revealed, the case
solved.

Jamie found herself in front of a random door at the end
of the corridor. She knocked on it.

No answer.

She pressed down on the handle and a small office was
revealed to her with a computer on a desk.

Perfect.

She went inside, locked the door behind her, and set to
work.

With solitude and a thread to follow, she made headway
quickly.

Drilling down into Adell's psyche and the Lundström
incident, she came to two conclusions – one; Lucas Adell, or
Viktor Hellström, leaves nothing to chance. He's methodical
and he's smart. Which makes him highly dangerous. And
two; there was no way he wouldn't have an escape plan in
place from the beginning.

EZ, or Emil Zagorski, was an only child, and grew up on
Gotland. His parents moved to the mainland, and he went
with them as a teenager. He returned to Gotland at eighteen,
though to care for his grandmother, who lived at the house in
Lärbro, and was ill. She died not long after, and though the
house was left to EZ's parents, he continued to live there.
Though that wasn't the interesting thing. His grandparents
also left behind a car, which EZ drove. As well as a small
fishing boat.

When Jamie read that, the hair on the back of her neck stood on end.

It all suddenly fit into place. The gears churned, smooth and clean. 'Holy fuck,' Jamie said, the truth dawning on her suddenly.

Jamie all but jumped to her feet and ran to the door.

She unlocked and pulled it wide, freezing in her tracks.

Two of her 'team' were standing there, looking nervous. 'We, uh, we have some ideas on where Adell might have gone,' a woman said, smiling at Jamie.

Jamie shook her head. 'Doesn't matter. I know where he went.'

'Oh, to Bunge Airbase?'

Jamie sighed and squeezed past, running for Dahlvig's office. 'Not even close.'

32

Kjell Thorsen

FROM THORSEN'S GUESS, making landfall in Sweden would take around four or five hours considering how slow and old this boat was.

It had two measly outboards, and a small covered cockpit. Hardly fit for a long sea journey.

And Thorsen realised pretty quickly it was going to be *long*. Firstly, because around his feet there were half a dozen full jerry cans of petrol. And secondly, because as soon as they hit open water, Adell instructed Thorsen to turn right, and head south-east.

Adell had ensured his hands were tightly tied to the wheel, and had pushed the throttle to around three-quarters of the way up. Enough to keep pace, but not so high to burn out the engines.

Thorsen racked his brain for where they were going.

South-east. Latvia. Lithuania. Kaliningrad. Poland? Fuck, that was a lot of coastline to consider. Wherever they landed, Adell could likely slip ashore and just … disappear.

And Thorsen guessed that would mean he and Sonja would be executed. If they weren't thrown overboard into the Baltic Sea before they hit landfall, at least.

He still had no idea why Adell had wanted him.

He risked a glance over his shoulder, seeing Sonja sitting in an angler's chair behind him. And at the back of the boat, with the pistol on his knee, Adell, staring right at Thorsen.

'What do you want?' Thorsen called over the rumble of the engine and the slap of the waves against the hull.

'She knows what I want,' Adell called back.

'Who?' Thorsen yelled.

'Your partner,' he answered. 'Johansson.'

33

Jamie Johansson

'YOU WANT A HELICOPTER?' Dahlvig asked, looking up from his screen.

'Yes,' Jamie answered firmly. 'We need to get to the mainland.'

'Why?'

'Because Lucas Adell has a boat. And I think he's already left the island.'

'And he's going to the mainland?'

'I don't know.'

'So why do you want to fly there in a helicopter?'

'I … have a theory.'

'You have a theory?' Dahlvig sighed. 'You want to share it?'

'I don't know if I'm right yet.'

'Well let's hear it, and we can decide together whether it holds water.'

Jamie hesitated.

'Come on, tell me.'

'I'm going to look really stupid if I'm wrong.'

'You're going to look even stupider if we fly to the mainland in a helicopter and you're wrong there. And I'm going to look even stupider than that if we go without you telling me the reason first. So talk.'

Jamie took a deep breath. 'I think … Rebecca and Marie Adell …'

'Yes?'

'Are still alive.'

Dahlvig just stared at her for a few seconds. 'I'm sorry. Did you say they're still alive?'

'I think they could be.'

He clamped his eyes closed, shook his head a little. 'How … why?'

'Emil Zagorski, EZ – the drug dealer that Adell killed. He had access to a boat. And I looked into the investigation that Lundström launched into his death. They requisitioned his phone records during that time, and among all the obviously drug-related texts, there were some, communicating with a number, discussing the price for something else. To 'get me out of here'. The person speaking to EZ asked for the price, then said they'd get the money. Then arranged to meet.'

'And you think that was … who?'

'Rebecca Adell. Those texts pre-date Rebecca Adell's disappearance by just under a week. There was no evidence that Rebecca ever left Fårö island in the north. No ferry crossing. Lundström searched the island for her, but she was never found. I think it's because she was picked up by EZ on his boat, and transported to the mainland.'

'Without her mother and father knowing?'

'No. I think her mother knew. I think that her mother helped Rebecca escape her father, and then waited six months. And then she went after her. Rebecca came back for her, or … I don't know. Found someone to help her. Adell was left thinking they were dead, and they went on with their lives. Then, searching for Rebecca, convinced that Lundström bungled the investigation, he stumbles on EZ. He tortures EZ to get him to tell him what he did with Rebecca's body, and then he reveals he actually got Rebecca off the island instead. In a rage, Adell kills EZ, and then goes and paralyses Lundström as recompense for not finding this out when Rebecca disappeared.'

'So, the killings that started after that? They were, what? Adell's way of lashing out? Psychosis?'

'A message. A threat. Blackmail. You heard his address. One will die every month until you fix this. You know what you did, and this will not stop until this is put right. You. Marie Adell. You know what you did. You took my daughter from me. And you have to make it right. You have to bring her back.'

'Jesus Christ.'

'Adell's got a black heart on his forearm. Tattoo. No one would know except his wife. He targeted teens, killing them in poetic revenge, marking them with the black heart. I'll keep killing until you bring her back. You made me think she was dead, that you'd killed yourself. It's all just his twisted way of trying to bring his family back.'

Dahlvig nodded along. 'And Eva Wallin, who's still spilling her guts right now in Interrogation-3, I might add – another good call there for you – and the other teens, the sex Adell had with them? What was that all about?'

'Just a tool, I think. Just a way to make them more invested in the relationship, in Adell as a god. Who the hell knows? He's sick. Twisted. Maybe he just fucking enjoyed it.' Jamie let out a rattling breath. 'Either way, Adell took hostages for a reason. He took Thorsen for a reason. It's out of character for him. He wants something.'

'And what's that?'

'Me.'

'You.' Dahlvig didn't seem convinced.

'He wants me to find his family.'

'Why you?'

'Because I'm the one who found him. He went unnoticed for two years, and I found him. He's not been able to find his family – and I'm sure he's looked. So, he wants me to do it. And that's why he took Thorsen. He wants me to bring them to him.'

'And do a hostage swap?' Dahlvig's tone was a little incredulous, but he wasn't laughing her out of the room. 'Jesus, if you're right …'

'I hope I'm not. But if I am wrong … then Thorsen and Sonja are as good as dead already, and Lucas Adell is gone. Probably forever.'

'So, what do you propose?'

'Divert all our resources to finding Rebecca and Marie Adell. Get to the mainland, get them into custody. Then try to contact Adell.'

'How?'

'Long range all-frequency broadcast. Adell's on a fishing boat. It'll have a radio. If I'm right, he'll be waiting for a call. The sooner we do it, the better. If he thinks we can't, then he'll kill them.'

Dahlvig watched her closely, lacing his hands together in front of his mouth and resting them against his lips. 'I want you to prepare yourself for a possibility here.'

'What possibility?'

He just stared at her.

'No, I'm right.'

'But if you're not. And Adell is just trying to escape …
Then he might have already—'

Jamie threw her hands up. 'Are you going to give me the
helicopter or not?'

He drew in a slow breath. 'If I don't, you're liable to steal
it, aren't you?'

'Yeah, and that'd be bad. Because I have no fucking clue
how to fly one.'

Dahlvig stood up and cracked his back. He looked tired.
'Well then I'd better make that phone call.'

34

Kjell Thorsen

BY THE TIME the sun began to rise, the vague and translucent outline of land was manifesting itself ahead of them.

They'd been on a south-eastern heading for four and a half hours, and by Thorsen's best estimate, they were coming up on the Latvian coast.

Adell called from the back of the boat and told Thorsen to adjust south, keeping land on their left.

He did so wordlessly, his eyes stinging from the salt water and the exhaustion.

How long had they been driving now?

Did Jamie know they were even gone yet?

Thorsen glanced down, eyeing the radio harnessed on the dash. Unfortunately, his hands were still tied to the wheel. Tightly. He couldn't slip or break the ties. If he twisted himself awkwardly, he thought he might be able to just reach the throttle, but that was about it.

What good that would do, he didn't know.

And though his mental acuity seemed to be returning little by little, no great ideas of how to get out of this came to him.

So now, all he could do was wait, and pray, that Jamie would find him.

And that she'd do that before they reached their destination, and Adell decided to finally use that revolver he'd been holding to Sonja's head all night long.

Thorsen sighed, swallowed, and then pressed on, keeping land on his left, and open water ahead.

35

Jamie Johansson

THEY SWEPT over the coast at speed.

The flight had taken just over an hour, and it'd taken Dahlvig just twenty minutes to scramble a helicopter from the airport. He'd directed his entire team to begin the hunt for Adell's family. Though Jamie could tell that he felt he was rolling the dice. His knees bobbed quickly, eyes fixed out of the window as they rode.

He'd asked her how sure she was they were alive.

And without thinking, she'd answered one hundred percent.

Thankfully, she was right.

Just as they crossed over land, Dahlvig's phone rang.

He shoved the earpiece up under the headphones they were wearing and cupped his hand over the bottom of the phone and his mouth.

Jamie couldn't hear much – except his responses, picked up through the microphone next to his face, and fed to her ears. But all she got was, 'Yeah. Yeah? Right. Mhm. Send it over.' And then he hung up and looked at her.

She waited for him to speak as he pushed the microphone closer to his mouth.

'They found them,' he said, pushing up from his seat and climbing forward towards the gap between cockpit and cabin. He reached through, put his hand on the pilot's shoulder, and told him where they were going: Lidingö. A municipality of Stockholm, a beautiful little community on an island just on the edge of the city.

Dahlvig instructed the pilot to get them there, gave him an address, told him to get them as close as possible.

When he finally sat back next to Jamie, he started talking. 'You were right, they're alive. Both of them. Holed up with some friends of Marie Adell's from when they lived in Stockholm. Apparently, the friends denied it at first, but you threaten anyone with an obstruction of justice charge, start tossing around the words 'National Operations Department' and telling people they're interfering with a national investigation, they tend to change their tune pretty quickly.'

'I bet,' Jamie said, breathing a sigh of relief.

'You didn't think we'd find them, did you?'

'I did. Or at least, I hoped we would,' Jamie said. 'I couldn't be sure it would be easy. If you fake your death to escape someone, I figured they might try a little harder to stay lost. I'm honestly surprised that Adell didn't go after them.'

'Well, he *did* think they were dead, didn't he? And what's he going to do, call up his wife's friends and ask if, by chance, she might not be dead and instead is hiding out in their guest room?'

Jamie shrugged. 'Supposed we'll find out when we get there.'

Dahlvig leaned forward and put his hand on her shoulder.

'Another good call,' he said. 'But what happens next is going to be difficult, alright? If this does turn in to a hostage negotiation, I need you to know that we aren't turning Marie and Rebecca Adell over in exchange for Thorsen and Dr Ehrhart. You know that, don't you?'

Jamie nodded slowly. 'I know,' she said, the words catching in her throat.

'If they are still alive, and this works – let's find Adell … I'm not putting anyone else in harm's way. Thorsen knew what he was signing up for, and Dr Ehrhart …'

'We try to minimise collateral damage, I get it,' Jamie said coldly. 'But what happens, happens.'

He inspected her face to try to see whether she was full of shit or not.

She wondered if she convinced him.

'We're good at this,' he reassured her. 'Once we know where they are, we can call on tactical, and if it's not Sweden, we can bring Europol in, contact local police forces. If Thorsen's alive, we'll do all we can to keep him that way. I promise you that.'

Jamie just kept her eyes forward. 'Let's just take this one step at a time. First, we need to make contact with Adell. Once we've done that, we can figure out how we're going to bring the fucker down.'

'Bring him *in* you mean,' Dahlvig corrected her, eyes narrowing.

'Yeah,' Jamie said, turning her attention to the window and the city outskirts below. 'That's what I meant.'

They landed in a field behind a church less than five hundred metres from the home where the Adells were hiding. Marie was a Stockholm native and before she'd met Lucas Adell, had a thriving social life with lots of friends. Though she and Lucas had been happy together at first, when Marie had reached out to them secretly, explaining that she and her daughter weren't safe, she found offers of safe haven without any trouble at all.

As Jamie and Dahlvig skirted the church and made the trip towards the house, Jamie wondered what that would be like. To live with someone, to be in love with someone that was dangerous. To have a child with them, raise a family with them, and slowly come to realise that this person was capable of terrible things. Had done terrible things. That no matter what happened, one truth prevailed above all else. You are not safe. Your child is not safe.

The story of a family moving to the remote north of Gotland to find peace and solitude and raise their child some-where safe, somewhere quiet, became all the more troubling with each new fact that emerged. Lucas Adell took his family from the city, away from friends and words that would poison his wife and daughter against him. He hid them somewhere remote, where they couldn't easily leave or travel. Where he could control everything – who they saw and when, what they did, who they spoke to, what they did online.

A prison with a sea view.

Jamie felt fire rile in her and quickened her pace.

They must have heard the rotors of the helicopter because when Jamie and Dahlvig reached the house, the front door was open and a middle-aged man with a round stomach and greying hair was standing on his front step, hands on hips. His name was Feldsson, and though he was speaking before they even came in the gate, Jamie didn't listen to a word he said. The angry look on his face showed he wasn't happy, but Jamie was already ten hours behind Adell, and she wasn't wasting another second.

Feldsson raised an arm to bar their entrance, but Dahlvig was there before Jamie got to the step, pushing him against his own door frame. 'National Operations Department,' he said, forearm against Feldsson's chest. 'Don't even think about it.'

There was some rhetoric about 'Do you know who I am? I'll have you fired, blah blah fucking blah,' but Jamie couldn't have cared less.

She slipped past into the hallway. 'Mrs. Adell?' she called, looking around. The house was beautiful, tall and classically Scandinavian, surrounded by trees. Jamie had been calm on the chopper. But now, now that she was moving, everything felt frenetic. She knew Thorsen was out there somewhere, and now that her suspicions about Marie and Rebecca Adell had been confirmed, she was convinced she was right. That Adell knew exactly who *she* was, and that he wanted her to bring his wife and daughter to him. Otherwise, what would be the point of taking Thorsen? Why not just execute him the moment he walked into Sonja Ehrhart's house? Or better yet just find another way north. If he didn't want to take his own car for fear of being picked up by the police, then he could have easily found another means of transportation. But no, Adell was smart, and he was informed. He looked into Sonja after he ran into her at the morgue. And he looked into Jamie and Thorsen, too, probably after they visited his house. He needed to know who was knocking on his door finally.

He went after Sonja because he thought he could leverage Thorsen into getting his wife and child back to him. But then, the chance to leverage Jamie by using Thorsen must have been even more appealing.

Perhaps he knew Jamie would find them faster. Or maybe

he knew that Jamie would do anything to get Thorsen back. Whatever it took. She'd make it happen.

Love trumped friendship.

Love? Jamie shook the thought from her head. Fuck. Focus. One step at a time.

'Mrs. Adell?' Jamie called again, louder. 'Mrs. Adell!' As she walked into the kitchen, she slowed.

No need to shout anymore, they were sitting at the kitchen table sipping cups of tea.

Marie and Rebecca nearest to Jamie with their backs to her, and who she guessed was Mrs Feldsson sitting on the other side, one hand on Marie Adell's, glaring at Jamie.

She got up slowly, squeezing Marie's hand, and then walked out of the room, still glowering.

Jamie waited for her to pass, then walked around the table and put her hands on the backs of the dining chairs.

Marie and Rebecca both looked as white as a sheet. Marie was maybe early forties, attractive, but she looked tired. Rebecca Adell looked terrified. She was eighteen now, Jamie thought, and pretty. Becoming a woman. Curly hair, big eyes.

Jamie cleared her throat, not really sure how to start this.

'We're not going back,' Marie Adell said. 'You can't make us.'

'We're not going to. We know the truth. Who Lucas Adell is.'

Marie scoffed. 'You can't know who he is. *What* he is.'

Jamie swallowed. 'I do. But that doesn't change the fact that I need your help. That we need your help. Dahlvig appeared in the doorway, arms folded, barring the way. Jamie could see the Feldsson's behind him, hovering.

'Our help? I can't help you,' Marie said. 'Just let us be. Let us be free.'

Jamie glanced around. 'This is freedom? Hiding here?'

'It's more than we had.'

'He knows you're alive.'

Marie looked up at her now. Rebecca reached out and grabbed her mother's hand.

'He knows you're alive, and he's escaped Gotland. We need to find him, and you're the key. He has two of our people, and we need to get them back. We need to catch Lucas. And we need to end this. And you're the only one that can help.'

'I can't. I won't.' She looked at Rebecca to reassure her.

'If you don't, he will come for you. Maybe not today, or this week, or even this year. But he will come for you, and you know that. This is all because of you. The killings. The black heart.'

Jamie glanced down at Marie's forearm, covered by a knitted cardigan. But despite that, Jamie knew that there was a black heart tattooed there. Matching Lucas Adell's.

She instinctively put her other hand over it. 'This isn't our fault. None of it.'

'I know. I know it's not. You did nothing wrong. And you couldn't have known … It was kept quiet to keep order. But when the truth came out, when the story broke, and the black heart appeared on that video … You knew, didn't you? You knew it was him, that he was doing it for you. But you didn't come forward, and you could have.'

Marie Adell's eyes began to fill. 'He could kill a thousand others before I let him anywhere near Rebecca again.' She clutched her daughter's hand. Rebecca's eyes glistened now, too.

'I'd do the same for my family. But these are other people's children. They can't be saved now, it can't be taken back. But we can still catch him, can still make him pay for what he's done. Only then you'll be safe. You know that.'

Jamie took a slow breath, letting it sink in. 'We can't make you help us … But if you don't, we'll have to walk out of here, and we won't be able to protect you. You'll be on your own. And you'll be running. Forever.' Jamie sighed. 'And what kind of life is that, really?'

Marie Adell looked at the table, a tear running down her cheek.

And then, it was Rebecca who spoke.

'What would we have to do?'

Jamie tempered the rush of adrenaline she felt. 'Just talk to him. Keep him talking. Long enough so we can find out where he is. That's all.'

She looked at her mother. 'I can do that.'

He mother looked back at her.

'She's right,' Rebecca Adell said. 'If he knows we're alive, he'll come for us. He won't stop. Not ever. You know that.' Rebecca's voice shook a little. 'If we can end it, we should.' She looked at Jamie now. 'Are you sure you can find him?'

Jamie held her gaze. 'I'm sure.'

'Okay then,' Rebecca said. 'Just tell me what to do.'

They boarded the helicopter together, the rotors already spooling. Marie and Rebecca climbed in first and Dahlvig grabbed Jamie's arm as she mounted the step to get into the cabin. 'Coastguards have been scouring the coast for any sign of Adell's boat. There's no sign.'

'He won't be coming to Sweden, not now,' Jamie said. 'He's too smart.' She had to raise her voice over the growing engine noise.

'He'll head east. South, maybe. He'll want to get to land,

find somewhere to regroup and figure out his next move, wait for our call.'

'So, what's your plan here? Have Rebecca jump on the radio, broadcast across all frequencies? Just whisper the word 'Daddy?' over the air and hope Adell's listening?'

Jamie pulled her arm free of his grip. 'That's exactly my plan. You just have to be ready to find him.'

'And how do you propose we do that?'

'Triangulation – directional finding. Home in on the source, fly this fucking thing right down his throat.' She slapped the side of the chopper.

Dahlvig was staring right at her. 'You gonna keep your head through this, or do I need to make you sit this out?'

'I'm good,' Jamie said.

'You sure?'

'We're wasting time,' she shouted now, the rotor noise growing to a roar. 'Let's go!'

They pulled smoothly from the ground and swung south, back out over the water and towards Gotland. Dahlvig was a man of his word, and one of means, Jamie had to give him that. He said that there would be resources at her disposal, and he was right. By the time they made landfall at Gotland, he'd already arranged for the Swedish Coastguard to run a triangulation from their northernmost and southernmost stations, which would give them the best chance at zeroing in on Adell's exact location.

He had also relayed the situation to his number two, who'd managed to scramble together a tactical team, who were already getting prepped to make a water incursion.

Jamie listened, impressed but pensive, as they swung back over the station and landed on top of it.

Two of Dahlvig's team came to meet them, beckoning Rebecca and her mother down out of the chopper and onto the landing pad, spiriting them away into the building to get them prepped.

Jamie expected Dahlvig to disembark, too, and tell Jamie to go with him, but he made no such effort. Instead, he just made a circular motion with his hand and gestured for the pilot to take off once more.

He looked across at Jamie. 'I figured you wouldn't want to sit on the sidelines.'

She smiled a little. 'You couldn't make me if you tried.'

'Yeah, I'm starting to get that picture. We'll stay high, confirm Adell's location, and call in tactical. You good with that?'

Jamie nodded but gave no verbal confirmation.

'I briefed the team, they know to keep Adell talking. They'll be broadcasting on all frequencies, so it should come through for us here, too,' Dahlvig said, tapping his headphones. 'Right?' he confirmed with the pilot.

He nodded, pulling back on the yoke and dragging them into the air once more.

'Head for open water,' Dahlvig commanded. 'The broadcast will start any minute, we're not wasting time here.'

And he was right. Before they even cleared the beach and hit the open water of the Baltic Sea, there was a crackling on the radio and then a timid voice came through.

'Dad?' it asked. 'Dad, are you there? Daddy? It's me, it's Becca … I'm … I'm sorry. Daddy? Please, answer me. Are you there?'

Then there was silence.

Dahlvig let out a long sigh, then looked at Jamie. 'And now we wait.'

36

Kjell Thorsen

THE RADIO CRACKLED SO LOUDLY it startled Thorsen.

'Dad?' it asked. 'Dad, are you there? Daddy? It's me, it's Becca … I'm … I'm sorry. Daddy? Please, answer me. Are you there?'

The words echoed through the morning air, still cool out on the water.

They cut through the engine din, and before Thorsen could even look around, Lucas Adell was at his shoulder, pistol pressed firmly to the small of Thorsen's back.

Thorsen stiffened, but didn't move.

Adell reached out and pulled the throttle back, killing the engine.

The boat rocked, the prow sinking a little as they settled into a slow drift across the still surface.

His hand shook, halfway to the receiver.

Thorsen breathed carefully, feeling the bite of the muzzle on his skin.

Adell licked his lips, eyes fixed on the radio. His breathing was fast, ragged almost as his fingers twitched.

And then he snatched it from the cradle and held it to his lips, thumb on the talk button, eyes flitting back and forth as he searched for the right words.

Then he spoke.

37

Jamie Johansson

JAMIE'S SKIN broke out in gooseflesh an instant before Adell's voice rang in her ears.

'Becca?' he asked.

Dahlvig tapped the button on the side of his headphones to mute his mic and then dialled a number on his phone. He began speaking a second later, shuffling forward so he could position himself to direct the pilot.

'Is that really you?'

'Hi, dad,' she said, her voice quaking.

'Where are you?' he asked quickly.

There was silence for a moment.

Adell knew she wouldn't say. He knew what this was.

'I'm coming for you, okay?' he said, with as much love as a psychotic killer could muster. 'I know you're scared, but I'm coming to get you. Just wait for me, okay?'

More silence.

'Becca? Tell me where you are. I'll come get you, alright?'

The silence held.

'Becca? Becca.' The tone began to change. Grow colder. 'Becca. Answer me. Answer your father.' The anger was clear in his voice now.

'I'm here, I'm here,' Rebecca said quickly.

Dahlvig listened to the person on his call – Jamie presumed someone at HQ taking directions from the coast-guard stations triangulating the frequency.

He turned his head, yelled something to the pilot, who nodded, then swung them right, heading south.

The nose of the chopper dipped and they gained speed, swooping a little lower towards the water with a sickening lurch of Jamie's stomach.

'I ... I can't talk much,' Rebecca said. 'They're listening.'

Adell paused, maybe to think.

Jamie didn't know what the hell their strategy was, but she guessed trying to bait Adell into a conversation like this was as good as any. He knew that his plan had worked, that Jamie had understood the deal here. And just then, as though he was reading her mind, Adell spoke to her.

'Detective Johansson,' he said coolly. 'Are you listening?'

Jamie said nothing.

Dahlvig just stared at her.

'I know you are,' Adell went on. 'And I don't know what game you think you're playing, but you're going to lose it. Do what I say, get me my daughter, and I won't put a bullet in his spine.'

Jamie heard Thorsen grunt in the background. A pained grunt.

Dahlvig's jaw flexed a little as he considered his options. Then he nodded, pointed to her mic, and made a cycling motion with his hand. Keep him talking.

Jamie let out a long breath, then enabled her own mic. 'How do I know he's not dead already?'

Thorsen's voice came to her then. 'Jamie,' he said, voice strained, 'I—'

But that was all he said before he was cut off and Adell interjected. 'My daughter, Jamie.'

Hearing her name sent a shiver down her spine.

'You have something I want. I have something you want. Give her to me, and you get him back.'

Jamie licked her lips. 'I can't make her do anything. But if you tell us where you are, we can pick you up, and I can take you to her.'

He laughed a little. 'And this is the part where you tell me that you can help me, hmm? That you can, what, stop the voice in my head? Give me my life back, suppress me with drugs and hollow out my brain until I'm some empty husk? Is that what you want to do to me? Lock me in a padded cell to be fed my meals through a slot in the door like some animal?'

Jamie resisted the urge to tell him he was an animal. 'There's no good ending for this. What you're doing. It's gone too far. You hurt too many people.'

'That wasn't my choice. It was theirs.'

'You can't win this.'

'Then I suppose I'll just have to kill your friends here and solve this myself.' There was an audible click – the hammer being pulled back on a revolver.

'Wait!' Jamie said. 'Give me …. Give me some time. A few minutes. Just let me work something out.'

'Time, I'm afraid, is not a luxury you, or *he* has right now.'

Jamie muted her mic and looked at Dahlvig, searching for an answer. He was a statue.

She racked her brain for how she was going to get

Thorsen out of this. How she was going to navigate this –
Dahlvig, Adell, his family, and the entirety of the NOD and
probably the coastguard listening too.

She thought of Thorsen then. Pictured him. A pang of
emotion struck her chest, and a hot pit of lead set itself in her
stomach.

They were still maybe thirty, forty minutes straight flying
from reaching the coast, and potentially finding Adell. But it
may as well have been thirty or forty days. Adell had no
patience.

And Jamie was backed into a corner.

'Can I be honest with you, Viktor? I don't want to speak
to Lucas. I want to speak to the man who murdered twenty-
three children. The man who drove his wife and daughter to
fake their deaths just to escape him. That's who I want to
speak to.'

'Then speak,' came the cold reply.

'You have one card. And you have a revolver pressed to
his spine. Play it, and you're done. You're finished. I'm never
bringing your daughter to you. Or your wife. I wouldn't
subject them to being with you for another second. So, decide
what you want to do, carefully. Let him go, and I won't come
for you. I can't say the same for my friends at the NOD, but
I'm saying *I* won't come for you. And that may not seem very
appealing, but I'm very good at what I do – I found you in a
week when they couldn't in two years. So, think about that.
But if you kill Thorsen, I will never stop hunting you. And I
will make sure you die in a padded box, being fed through a
slot, like an animal, with your arms strapped to your body,
rotting in your own filth. I will hunt you to the ends of the
earth. I promise you that. It will be my only priority, my only
thought, both waking and sleeping. If you think you're a
person of conviction, then you understand what I'm saying.

You'll never be able to stop running. Never. So, Viktor, what will it be? Kill him and scuttle away like a cockroach, find a hole to die in? Or let him go, and give yourself a head start? Or do you want to wait? I'll be there soon, and we can sort this out face to face. And then you'll see what it's like when you meet a woman who's not afraid of you. One who'll fight back. You decide.'

Viktor didn't reply. There was only static on the airwaves.

Dahlvig pulled his headphones from his ears and held them between his knees. Jamie did the same, leaning forward.

Dahlvig sighed heavily, and shook his head. 'That was a tough call, I don't envy you.'

'You think I just killed him?'

'I don't know,' Dahlvig said. 'But either way, I don't think this is going to end the way you want it to. It was a good play, but there's not much else we can do now. We have an approximate location – coastguard has looped in the Latvian authorities. If we get a confirmed sighting, we'll know how far out we are. But it's at least half an hour. And I don't think Adell is going to wait for us to come knocking …'

'He'll wait,' Jamie said, trying to keep her voice even. 'Arrogant as he is. He'll wait.'

'You're betting Thorsen's life on the assumption that his ego is as big as yours?'

Jamie looked out at the cold blue sea below them. 'I'm betting it's bigger.'

38

Kjell Thorsen

'SHE'S RIGHT,' Thorsen said, Adell still at his shoulder. He looked at the man, the receiver so tight in his grasp Thorsen thought it might shatter.

Adell looked at him, his eyes filled with cold fury.

'If you ever want to see your daughter again, you've got to turn yourself in. If you want to survive, then you've got to run. And if you want to die …'

Adell's eyes twitched for just an instant, and then there was a flash of steel in the morning sun and a blinding pain lancing from above Thorsen's right ear.

He wobbled, nausea rearing through him, and then slumped against the wheel, feeling the warmth of blood running down his cheek.

'She'll bring me my daughter,' Adell growled, standing over Thorsen. 'And if she doesn't, she'll watch you die. And then I'll kill your fucking friend back there,' he hissed, leaning in, pointing to Sonja, 'and then I'll kill her, too. I'll gut your Jamie like a fish and leave her to bleed out.'

If Thorsen could have managed to smile, he would have.

Because honestly, he thought that was funny.

But he couldn't smile, he couldn't speak, he couldn't do anything. Another blow to the head was the last thing that his brain needed.

As he stood there, only on his feet because he was propped up by the wheel, his eyes began to fog over, the world growing blurry. A deep throbbing developed in his ears, and then darkness came.

39

Jamie Johansson

'IF YOU KEEP CHEWING THOSE NAILS,' Dahlvig said, head against the divider between the cockpit and cabin, 'you'll have none left.'

'They grow back,' Jamie said bitterly, looking over at him. 'How are you so calm?'

'My doctor says I have high blood pressure,' he replied, taking a deep breath and closing his eyes. 'Pays not to get worked up about things.'

'You don't think this is worth getting worked up for?'

'This job is dangerous enough without me adding in the risk of an aneurysm or stroke. I want to grow old, weirdly. Have a life after this.' He opened one eye, watching Jamie.

She didn't respond. Though she knew what he was getting at and she could see he knew what she was thinking too.

Jamie didn't have a death wish, but she also had no plans for her future. No idea of settling down somewhere, and living out her days quietly. That had been the dream six months ago. Retire. Leave it all behind. But this? There was no substitute. She was a junkie for whatever high this was. Life dangling in the balance, playing for the highest stakes. She hated to admit it, especially to herself. But Thorsen was right. She had no chance of leaving this behind. And unless she died today, she'd be walking out of it all with the intention of wearing a badge and gun again.

The pilot cocked his head a little then, listening to something in his ears. His own voice came over the radio to Jamie and Dahlvig a second later. 'Latvian coastguard picked up a small fishing vessel off the coast, unregistered and not responding to calls. Adjusting our heading now, it could be our target.'

The chopper's engines whined as the pilot pushed forward on the yoke and increased the rotor speed, hurling them forward.

'How long?' Dahlvig called.

'Five minutes until visual, about ten before we're on top of them.'

'Okay,' he said, 'take us up. I want to keep them in view until tactical arrive.'

'No,' Jamie called. 'Stay low.'

'He'll know we're coming,' Dahlvig said.

'He already knows. I want to be right on top of him.'

'Why?'

Jamie just looked at Dahlvig. 'I don't want him having time to think. If we stay high, it could be ages before tactical arrive. And once he sees them coming, he knows he'll have no chance. He'll execute Thorsen and Sonja out of spite. The only chance we have is to get there first, goad him into an engagement. Get the drop on him.'

'You understand the words you're saying, don't you?'

'I do.'

'You want to take on a killer with two hostages in a head-on engagement.'

'I do. But you want to knowingly hold back when the same killer has promised to murder those hostages. The only thing that's keeping them alive right now is the fact that he's waiting for me to come there and meet him head-on.'

'And if you're wrong?'

'Then they're already dead, and we hope that Adell fires on us so we can fire back and kill that piece of shit.'

Dahlvig ground his teeth a little. 'If this goes south, I'm pulling us out of there, alright? Whatever happens. If Adell threatens to kill them, or I don't like how it's going, we pull back immediately. Got it? And whatever happens, it's on you. You, Johansson. You sure you're ready to live with that?'

'I'm already living with it. I don't sleep at night anyway.'

He elected not to say anything else. All they could do now was wait.

Kjell Thorsen

THE THUNDERING SOUND of rotors cut through the haze and Thorsen pushed himself from the wheel with some effort.

He had one eye screwed closed, which was tempering the double vision some, but he could still barely see. There was a horrible, metallic tang in his mouth, and his breathing felt heavy. Honestly, he wasn't even sure if he was awake or asleep.

There was a swaying motion in his inner ear, though he wasn't able to tell if it was the sea or just his brain sloshing around in a pool of blood. Either way, the chug of rotors grew, and though he couldn't see the source, or even ascertain if it was real or just a hallucination, a weak smile spread across his lips.

Jamie.

Jamie Johansson

'Thirty seconds,' the pilot announced.

Jamie had her cheek to the window, staring forward, the little white boat in the distance growing larger by the moment.

Dahlvig pointed to the seat next to the door and Jamie moved into it.

He drew his weapon and chambered a round, laying the pistol on the seat next to him.

Jamie did the same thing.

The chopper dipped one way, then swung the other, broadsiding the boat about fifty feet off the water.

They slowed to a hover and Dahlvig reached forward, grabbing the handle to the door and pulling it open. The hammer of the rotors filled the cabin immediately, so loud it made Jamie's skull vibrate.

She grabbed onto the webbed strap next to the door and looped her wrist through it, leaning out to get a better look at the situation.

Jamie saw the flash first, then heard the shot.

She pulled her head back instinctively, the bullet fired from below exploding off the headliner and firing sparks into the cabin.

The hole in the ceiling of the chopper smoked gently and the pilot wrestled them around before levelling them out again.

Dahlvig swore and Jamie caught her breath – that was close to her head. Too close.

She gingerly peeked out again, seeing Adell standing at the back of the boat, his arm around Sonja's neck, the gun pressed to her head.

He yelled something, but Jamie couldn't hear it over the thunder of the rotors.

She knew what he was saying, though. 'My daughter. Bring me my daughter.'

Jamie risked a glance at Dahlvig. He was stoic.

This was her show, her play. Her risk.

And the outcome was on her.

How, exactly, she was going to win though, she didn't know.

She stared down, and Adell stared back.

There was a stillness to it all. An eerie calm.

And then, it happened.

All at once.

42

Kjell Thorsen

THE GUNSHOT SOBERED HIM UP. Sharp enough to send a bolt of electricity through his brain.

Thorsen forced himself to his feet, spitting saliva all over the wheel and the backs of his hands.

He breathed hard, the effort nearly enough to make him pass out.

His knees quaked as he looked back at Adell, Sonja in his arms, sobbing, eyes screwed closed.

Above, through the window next to him, he could see a helicopter, sleek and black, hovering above the waves. And hanging from the door, her.

There she was.

Pale, her hair the colour of ash.

Jamie.

Thorsen swallowed, feeling his heart humming in his chest.

This was it, all he could do. Everything he had left to give. And he knew it would cost him.

Thorsen looked down at the wheel, his bound wrists, and turned it all the way to the right.

He took one last breath, flexed his shaking hands, and then grabbed the throttle, ramming it forward.

The engine flared, the boat lurched, nose rising, tail dropping into the water. The whole thing twisting and snaking.

There was a scream behind him, a splash, and then gunshots.

One. Two.

He gripped the wheel hard, holding on for dear life.

And then, as his vision pulsed between sea and sky, he felt a strange coldness spreading across his back.

And tasted blood in his mouth.

43

Jamie Johansson

THE BOAT MOVED SO SUDDENLY, Jamie didn't know what was happening.

It twisted and then spurted forward.

Adell and Sonja both stumbled.

Adell tried to stay on his feet, but Sonja didn't manage to.

He let go of her to keep his balance, but Sonja staggered to the side of the boat and went over, splashing into the water, swallowed by the churning wake.

The boat swung in a tight circle, the engines howling, and Adell went to a knee, turning to face the driver.

The revolver in his hand rose, glinting in the sun, and then two shots loosed.

Fire breathed from the muzzle.

Pop, pop!

No!

Jamie's arm flew outwards, her pistol already in her grip and levelled at Adell.

She fired fast and true, finger rebounding off the grip, bullets peppering the deck of the boat.

Adell danced left and right, shielding his head, and then dived overboard.

The chopper began to swoop around, following the boat, which now seemed to have slowed, the throttle let off.

Jamie leaned lower, trying to get a look at the driver, knowing who it was, and what had happened even before she saw Thorsen's body slumped against the wheel, a huge red stain spreading from between his shoulders, soaking his white shirt.

Her heart seized in her chest.

From the corner of her eye, she saw Dahlvig's hand shoot out, making a grab for her arm.

But he was too slow, and she was already out.

The turbulent wind beneath the rotors threatened to burst her eardrums, but then it was above her and fading, the rush of air buffeting her skin and clothes as she plunged towards the cold surface below. Dahlvig's voice rang out above her.

She raked in a breath, filling her lungs, threw her arms across her chest, and braced for the impact.

It was like hitting concrete.

The pain was sharp and fierce, moving through her ankles, knees, and into her hips. The water smacked against the backs of her arms, went up her nose, pressed into her eyeballs as she plummeted through the water and into the depths.

It was cold. Cold enough to punch the air from her chest.

And suddenly, she was scrambling, clawing towards the surface, kicking and dragging her way through the saltwater.

Sunlight above her.

She broke the surface, pulling in a breath, searching for the boat.

Jamie looked around. A flash of white.

There.

Swim.

Thorsen!

But then he was there, Adell.

In her peripheral, grabbing for her.

Hands on her throat, pushing her under.

Water was in her mouth, filling it.

She coughed hard, forced herself not to breathe it in.

A muted impact reached her ears, dulled by the liquid.

She was dragged sideways, still held under.

Her eyes opened and blurry shapes moved above.

The grip released from her neck and she swam to the surface once more, catching a glimpse of Dahlvig wrestling Adell back, his arm around Adell's neck.

They both yelled out, sinking beneath the waves and then reappearing as they wrestled.

The boat, get to the boat.

Jamie swam overarm, powering forward towards the little fishing vessel ahead.

It grew larger as the waves of the Baltic Sea, freezing and stinging, lapped at her neck and hair.

She shivered, struggling to breathe as she got there, her hands numb and awkward.

It took two, three attempts to grab the rail.

Her muscles seemed not to want to work as she tried to haul herself up, heavy and soaked.

She thought of Thorsen, bleeding out, dead already, and the rage filled her, fuelled her.

Upwards, hauled from the sea as though by invisible hands she swung her leg up, hooked it over the rail, and then pulled herself onboard.

She hit the deck hard, coughed, panting raggedly, and

crawled forward, getting to her knees, then her feet, stumbling towards Thorsen, his back now entirely crimson.

'Thorsen!' she called out, arms stretching out in front of her, her right hand still locked around her pistol. Though she couldn't feel it, her fingers ghostly white, devoid of blood and feeling.

She reached him, limp and lifeless, and sank down beside him, trying to cradle him, to turn him over.

His hands were zip-tied to the wheel.

'Jesus Christ,' she managed, the shiver in her bones making the words vibrate as she spoke them.

Instinctively she forced the muzzle of the gun between the wheel and the plastic tie and twisted hard, snapping the plastic.

As the tension released, Thorsen slithered down into her arms, lying in her lap. His eyes fluttered weakly, his breathing shallow and weak, sounding like he was breathing through a straw.

No exit wounds on his chest, but she knew he'd taken at least one shot to the back. Fuck! Heart, lungs – there was no good place to get shot.

She could feel his blood hot on her thighs as he lay there.

'Thorsen? Can you hear me?' she asked, tears running down her cheeks.

She squeezed him hard, sobbing.

'Wake up, come on! Wake up!'

His eyes opened a little, a moment of clarity in them.

He tried to speak, but no sound came out.

The tiniest hint of a smile forced its way onto his lips as he looked at her.

And then it was gone, and he fell limp in her grasp.

She just stared down at him, not breathing, not thinking. She didn't know if he was alive or dead.

A gunshot rang out, then another, and Jamie looked up. She could just see over the side of the boat, could see Adell and Dahlvig still locked together, wrestling for Dahlvig's gun, held above them, each with their hands on it.

'Jamie!' Dahlvig tried to call, the word choked by the sea. 'Jamie!'

Her pain was replaced by something darker. A black desire to see someone pay for this.

She rose to her feet, pistol still in her grip, and walked to the side of the boat.

'Jamie!' Dahlvig yelled again. 'Shoot him!'

She looked down at the weapon in her hand, a detached clarity in her mind. She could feel nothing. It was as though she was watching the world on a screen, a passenger to her own life.

Her head turned, eyes resting on Thorsen's body for a moment.

She drank it in. Let it consume her.

And then she looked up, raised her gun, and fired.

The first shot struck true, hitting Adell in the side.

His hands left Dahlvig's gun and Dahlvig kicked him away, getting free of the grapple.

And Jamie could have left it there. Adell was done.

But she didn't.

She exhaled, brought her other hand to the bottom of the grip of her pistol, and put Adell between the sights.

And then she fired.

And fired again.

And again.

Putting every bullet she had into him.

Nine, she counted. Each one puncturing him in a new and painful place.

And even when he'd floated face down, head beneath the surface, she kept firing.

Only when the hammer fell on an empty chamber did she stop, take a weak, cloying breath, and drop the gun.

By the time Dahlvig reached the boat and pulled himself onboard, half-drowned and exhausted, Jamie was already back at Thorsen's side.

Cradling him.

Head resting against his chest.

Quiet sobs escaping her.

As she listened to his fading heartbeat.

44

Jamie Johansson

'Here,' Dahlvig said, appearing at Jamie's side.

He offered her a bag of crisps. Some random Latvian brand she'd never heard of.

She declined, shaking her head, her chin on her arms, rested on Thorsen's hospital bed.

'You have to eat,' Dahlvig said.

'We have to get him out of here.' Jamie watched his heart monitor. 'He's going to die here.'

Dahlvig let out a long breath. 'He can't be moved. Not yet.'

'Look at this place,' Jamie said. 'It's a fucking shit hole. He's going to catch an infection, sepsis, something. He'll die here, not get better.'

She felt a hand on her shoulder. 'I'll arrange for him to be airlifted to Stockholm as soon as he's stable. He'll have the best care; I promise you that. I look after my people. The surgeon said he came through the surgery like a champ, though. He's strong. He'll pull through and be back on his feet in no time.'

Jamie stared at Thorsen. He was pale, unconscious. He looked half dead. The bullet had torn through his chest, punctured a lung, but it was the least of his worries. The concussion he'd sustained originally had been bad enough, but a second blow to the head had caused a bleed and swelling in the brain. They'd had to induce a coma to let it heal, but gave no indication of when that might be, or what he'd be like afterwards. They said nothing definitive, just used words like 'hope' and 'might', and 'it's not uncommon' when they talked about him making a complete recovery. Though none of it instilled confidence. Not least because of the hospital being a relic. Built in the 80s and not renovated since, the whole thing felt archaic, and the thought of Thorsen dying here turned Jamie sick to her stomach.

Dahlvig pulled up a seat next to her and eased down into it.

More than a day had passed since the boat, and Jamie hadn't eaten, barely drunk anything.

'You can't stay here forever,' he said, looking at Thorsen.

'I'll stay as long as I need to,' she answered.

Dahlvig sighed. 'We did everything we could. It's a miracle he's alive. Sonja, too. And he has you to thank.'

'I bet with his life.'

'We all bet with our lives every day. It's what we do.'

'That doesn't make me feel better.'

'It's not supposed to. But it is the reality of things. And it will keep being the reality of things forever. We deal with bad people. We hunt them. We stop them. And they don't like that. Sometimes people get hurt. We try to prevent it, but sometimes it's inevitable.'

Jamie didn't reply.

'But all we can do is carry on. Carry on working. Carry on fighting. Carry on … or quit.' Dahlvig got to his feet, looking down at Thorsen.

Slowly, his eyes turned to Jamie.

She looked up at him.

'So, Jamie Johansson. What do you want to do? Do you want to quit … or do you want to fight?'

AUTHOR'S NOTE

We're here at the end. I don't really know what to say. Other than you've just read 671,084 words to get to this point. With the prequels, too, that's at over 950,000. The next book will make it a million. A million words of Jamie Johansson. That's just wild to me. Especially considering that it was February 17th 2020 that I first wrote the words 'He didn't know how he got in the box' and all this has happened in less than three years.

Honestly, it's been a rollercoaster. In every sense.

I actually moved country while writing this series, emigrating from the UK to Canada, where I now live. My partner and I undertook that journey together, and bought a house, then renovated it from the studs! All I can say is efff you, asbestos! Heinous stuff. Truly heinous. Oh well, we did it, and we built our home by hand: hanging plasterboard, framing walls, redoing plumbing, plastering and painting, laying floor, tiling, fitting bathrooms and kitchens … the list goes on.

During this time, I also wrote another book, *Savage Ridge,* set here in the Pacific North West. I got an agent: the wonderful Viola Hayden at Curtis Brown. I also struck a deal with Canelo to publish it.

Personally, professionally, it's been a tremendous and terrifying ride, and these books have been a real outlet for my creativity (and dark thoughts!), and I thank you so much for coming on this journey with me and allowing me to continue to write.

I love connecting with you through these stories, and I hope that you'll be here for many more. The idea that people wait for my next book still truly boggles my mind. But I love it. It gets me out of bed in the morning and makes me smile to no end.

Anyway, I just wanted to say thank you. If you're here, you've probably read a whole lot of Jamie, and if you still want more, then brilliant! Because there's more coming.

As I write this, the next book is already well underway and will be touching down very soon … or it's going to be out already if you're reading this after August 2023. Spooky! Time-travel! Witchcraft! All jokes aside, these are the times when I can be my most real, and I need that after living in a fictional world for so long with each writing period.

Anyway, rambling over, let's just leave it with this: thank you. And see you after the next one.

Jamie, are you ready for more? Hear that? She says yes. So I guess … here we go again!

All the best,
Morgan

WHAT COMES NEXT?

The Last Light Of Day

After a year of stability working for the NOD, Jamie's life is once more upended. A call from her estranged mother forces her back to the UK and draws her into the heart of a violent trafficking investigation. The bodies of young women have been discovered in the Brecon Beacons, but the events leading to their deaths are unknown. Covered in injuries, their bodies tell a violent story.

When a survivor emerges, beaten but alive, a harrowing story begins to take shape ... though, if Jamie is to gain the girl's trust and extricate the truth, she's going to have to stay one step ahead of those who want to silence her for good.

With little time to pause for breath, Jamie will have to work out who to believe, who to side with, and who to trust with her life.

As the light light of day begins to fade, darkness quickly closes in ...

———

Discover a brand new Jamie Johansson adventure with The Last Light of Day, *a Welsh-set thriller by every definition, and one that will once again test Jamie's strength and resolve in the face of impossible odds. Has she finally bitten off more than she can chew?*

Order your copy here to find out! Out August 2023.

————

Find me on Facebook @morgangreeneauthor to join the discussion and talk about everything Jamie. See you there!

WHAT COMES NEXT?

The Last Light Of Day

After a year of stability working for the NOD, Jamie's life is once more upended. A call from her estranged mother forces her back to the UK and draws her into the heart of a violent trafficking investigation. The bodies of young women have been discovered in the Brecon Beacons, but the events leading to their deaths are unknown. Covered in injuries, their bodies tell a violent story.

When a survivor emerges, beaten but alive, a harrowing story begins to take shape … though, if Jamie is to gain the girl's trust and extricate the truth, she's going to have to stay one step ahead of those who want to silence her for good.

With little time to pause for breath, Jamie will have to work out who to believe, who to side with, and who to trust with her life.

As the light light of day begins to fade, darkness quickly closes in …

———

Discover a brand new Jamie Johansson adventure with The Last Light of Day, *a Welsh-set thriller by every definition, and one that will once again test Jamie's strength and resolve in the face of impossible odds. Has she finally bitten off more than she can chew?*

The Last Light Of Day *is due to release in August 2023.*

———

Find me on Facebook @morgangreeneauthor to join the discussion and talk about everything Jamie. See you there!

Printed in Great Britain
by Amazon